Bello:
hidden talent rediscovered!

Bello is a digital only imprint of Pan Macmillan,
established to breathe new life into previously published,
classic books.

At Bello we believe in the timeless power of the imagination,
of good story, narrative and entertainment and we want to use
digital technology to ensure that many more readers
can enjoy these books into the future.

We publish in ebook and Print on Demand formats
to bring these wonderful books to new audiences.

About Bello:

www.panmacmillan.com/imprints/bello

About the author:

www.panmacmillan.com/author/pamelahansfordjohnson

Pamela Hansford Johnson

Pamela Hansford Johnson was born in 1912 and gained recognition with her first novel, *This Bed Thy Centre*, published in 1935. She wrote 27 novels. Her themes centred on the moral responsibility of the individual in their personal and social relations. The fictional genres she used ranged from romantic comedy (*Night and Silence, Who Is Here*) and high comedy (*The Unspeakable Skipton*) to tragedy (*The Holiday Friend*) and the psychological study of cruelty (*An Error of Judgement*). Her last novel, *A Bonfire*, was published in the year of her death, 1981.

She was a critic as well as a novelist and wrote books on Thomas Wolfe and Ivy Compton-Burnett; *Six Proust Reconstructions* (1958) confirmed her reputation as a leading Proustian scholar. She also wrote a play, *Corinth House* (1954), a work of social criticism arising out of the Moors Trial, *On Iniquity* (1967), and a book of essays, *Important to Me* (1974). She received honorary degrees from six universities and was a Fellow of the Royal Society of Literature. She was awarded the C.B.E. in 1975.

Pamela Hansford Johnson, who had two children by her first marriage with journalist Gordan Neil Stewart, later married C. P. Snow. Their son Philip was born in 1952.

Pamela Hansford Johnson

THE
HONOURS BOARD

First published in 1970 by Macmillan UK

This edition published 2012 by Bello
an imprint of Pan Macmillan, a division of Macmillan Publishers Limited
Pan Macmillan, 20 New Wharf Road, London N1 9RR
Basingstoke and Oxford
Associated companies throughout the world

www.panmacmillan.com/imprints/bello
www.curtisbrown.co.uk

ISBN 978-1-4472-1616-2 EPUB
ISBN 978-1-4472-1615-5 POD

To
Hal and Nancy Milner-Gulland,

*whose excellent school is better than this one,
with admiring affection*

Chapter One

Annick did not really, as some persons suggested, put out his tongue at new parents: he only seemed to do so. This was because they made him so nervous that he had to lick his lips before a single formal greeting could find its way through them.

He was aware of this disadvantage, the freezing of his spine whenever floral mothers and military-looking fathers descended upon him fluting and bellowing, but he could not overcome it. He had a weakness for meek parents, which was probably the genetic reason why the academic record of Downs Park was so thin. Half-way up the stairs hung the Honours Board, listing the scholarships of dim boys to dim schools: he knew in his heart that some of them had not really been so dim as all that, and might have been entered, without too much risk of failure, for schools of greater lustre: he had always known it, but always, at the last moment, his resolution had failed him. To enter a boy for Eton, Winchester or Westminster would have seemed to him like calling without introduction at the stately home of someone unknown to him and demanding tea.

This did not stop his compulsion to read, in the *Times*, the lists of scholarship winners to these schools.

'B. Paston, Scventrees S., Winchester.

'R. Piggott, Liston House, Eton,'

but never, never did the name of Downs Park appear: he could hardly have expected that it would. On such occasions of irrational disappointment he would turn to his wife, who always attempted to hearten him – which she could not – with a roll-call of the school's recent successes in games. He did not care at all about games, though he had to pretend that he did.

Today, a burnished one of summer, he was showing a parent over the place, a pleasant meek parent, round-bodied, round-faced, with large blue eyes and a silly look, who was called Quillan. Her husband was abroad, on a legal conference, so she had come alone to make preliminary inquiries. He had walked her all round the three houses knocked into one, which comprised the main body of the school, through the scratched and scribbled classrooms, the neat, bare dormitories with their hospital corners, the changing-rooms, the gym. Now he was leading her across the playing-fields and past the little wood known as the Thicket, to where there was a sudden, huge beneficent sight of the sea. From other angles at ground level the sea was hidden by arbitrary foldings of the downs, but in fact it was only a ten minutes' walk from the school, and the senior boys bathed in it when the weather was warm enough. When it wasn't, they used the kidney-shaped swimming pool at the far end of the grounds.

He pointed to a cottage, wistaria-draped, about five hundred yards from the main building. 'My second master and his wife live there – Mr and Mrs Massinger. He teaches maths and geography, she takes a hand with the games. Both young, live wires. Yes, there they are now, on the tennis courts.'

Since the boys were on holiday, the courts were free for more energetic members of the staff, those who had returned from their own holidays in time to open up the school for the new term.

Mrs Quillan saw a tall couple, both red-haired, tall, blooming and muscular, bounding about the court, shouting cries of ringing encouragement or condolence. She turned her meek eyes on Mr Annick. 'Peter isn't too good at games.'

'Isn't he? Well, we'll see what we can do about that,' he replied without enthusiasm, 'if, of course, we can find him a place. We sometimes have one or two last minute drop-outs.'

It was the old thumping lie, and he never failed to tell it. Downs Park had room for ninety boys and was seldom quite up to strength, but it was necessary to excite the parents, to make them feel privileged.

'But he *is* bright,' Mrs Quillan murmured, looking sillier than ever.

It would have disconcerted Annick horribly had he known that she had won a distinguished First in Classics at Cambridge and the Chancellor's Medal, and that her husband had a First in Law. His momentary feeling of comfort, of easement, would have fled.

Grace Annick, small, trim, bright-eyed, with a mass of curly, dark hair, came bounding over the turf towards them. She took the younger boys for P.T. three times a week, and showed it by her cotton sweater and shorts.

'Introduce me, Cyril!'

He did.

'And how old is Peter?' she asked.

'Well,' Mrs Quillan replied apprehensively, 'he's a little old to be entered now – he's just nine. But he's had so much bronchitis.'

'He won't have bronchitis here,' said Grace. 'Not by the sea. And anyway, it's about due to clear up of its own accord, at his age. It almost always does.'

They were returning through the Thicket, a pleasant, budding, bird-haunted place, much loved by the boys and sometimes used for retreats of a dubious nature.

Mrs Quillan said, 'Peter was top of his form in everything but maths. That's his weak spot.'

'Mr Massinger is an inspired teacher,' Grace said untruly. 'He'll soon have Peter interested. He makes the subject live.'

'Hated them myself,' said Annick, and was loved for it by the new parent. He would have been startled to know how much parents instinctively liked him. The private schools for small boys were all too often headmastered by types who looked like city slickers and were as smooth as seals. Annick was long, clay-faced and not too tidy, but his light grey eyes were so kind that every nervous parent immediately felt trustful, and the boyish flap of his coal-black hair across his forehead was somehow reassuring.

Furthermore, he still retained a slight limp from poliomyelitis in his childhood.

'I have to ask,' said Mrs Quillan, as they strutted back towards the school over the beautifully-maintained and bounding turf, 'though I know it sounds idiotic, and of course there are things you can't know because boys are secretive – do you find much bullying here?' She blushed hotly.

'We set our faces firmly against *that*' said Grace, the ballerina muscles of her legs distending as she took her over-long strides, 'from the very beginning. You needn't fear for Peter at all. And anyway, I keep a very close eye on the new boys, cuddle them a little bit, see they're happy.'

'Oh, I'm not frightened of Peter being bullied,' said Mrs Quillan surprisingly, 'I just thought you might check the tendency in him. He's not a sadist, but he is so tall for his age and it makes him bossy. Do you cane?'

Annick forgot his nervousness, in the moment of shock. 'Good God, Mrs – er – do you want him caned?'

'Of course not. I'm only asking. My husband would never forgive me if I didn't.'

'The worst thing that happens to any naughty boy here – which is rarely – is a tap or two with a soft-soled slipper. Purely symbolic!' Grace gave a sort of shout on these last two words, though her normal voice was soft, beguiling. It was she who first suspected that the meekness of this parent was illusory, and she believed that her husband needed stiffening.

'Anyway,' Annick said comfortingly, though he was still put out, 'a new boy in the lowest form is very small fry, so I don't think you need fear for any development of Peter's – ah – Attila-like characteristics.'

They had reached the school house. Mrs Quillan was silent for a little while, while she received miscellaneous information about classes, bedtimes, laundry. Helen Queen, the secretary, brought in tea, brown bread and butter, cucumber sandwiches, hot scones dripping and beaded with butter at the joins, gingerbread, soft, dark as night, full of pieces of ginger, gingerly iced all over the top surface. A Fuller's cake gently crumbling, aromatic, packed with cream and walnut meats. The parent absorbed, or seemed to absorb, all she was told, until she had eaten a hearty meal. Then she said, 'But you can't put Peter in the lowest form.'

'It's customary as a beginning,' said Annick, 'just while they find their feet. Then we can get them sorted out.'

'But I don't suppose many of them there can either write or spell properly.'

'Some not quite perfectly, perhaps, but—'

'Peter has done both since he was five. And he's made a good start in Greek.' Mrs Quillan was still looking meek, but with the meekness of a cat who will not be budged from a sofa. She added, 'He would feel an awful ass in the lowest form.'

Annick said hastily, 'We shall both be in London next week. May we call upon you there and perhaps meet Peter himself? I should he better able to assess his capabilities.' Pompous, he thought, but a correct headmasterly noise.

When the parent had gone, he sat down and wrote to Peter's former headmaster (children 5 to 8½) with whom he had often had dealings in the past. 'The mother seems very confident about this boy, but you know what mothers are. Can he conceivably be anything remotely as good as he's cracked up to be?'

The reply came by return of post. 'No exaggeration. If anything, meiosis. Snaffle this one at all costs.'

As he went downstairs to his study Annick glanced at the Honours Board.

Chapter Two

Rupert Massinger walked by the path at the back of the cricket pavilion, where some boys were at their old game of writing rude words in the sand with a stick. Bailey was in tears, for he was being derided by his fellows for writing PHUCK. Since his father played polo, 'puck' was a familiar word.

He liberated Bailey, sent the rest off with ferocious warnings and scuffed the path smooth with his toe. Later, when he told of this incident to the headmaster, Annick felt a leap of hope. Surely a boy of eight who could substitute a 'ph' for the more obvious 'f' might even be potential scholarship material?

The warm weather had lasted well into September, and the sun gilded the sweat on the faces of the footballers. Blossom Massinger was refereeing the game, workmanlike in slacks and dribbling a whistle. Rupert, who had a free period, went quietly indoors to study, in typescript, some pirated letters written in Venice by a dirty old man called Fr. Rolfe. These had been lent him by the new young master, Stephen Smith, who seemed to know all about such kinds of oddity.

Rupert read happily and steadily, until the phrase 'my raging yard' put ideas into his head. Not so steadily, he rose and went out on to the playing fields to summon his wife. 'Bloss, I need you for ten minutes. Mulliner can take over.'

Mulliner, twelve, officiously accepted the whistle.

Rupert and Blossom went indoors, Rupert panting hard and his wife, who was always afraid his insatiability might spend itself upon someone other than herself, pretending to pant. She made towards the bedroom, but he pulled her back. 'Bathroom floor this time.'

Rupert Massinger was thirty-five, mentally lazy, and of private means. He wanted to buy the school the moment he could persuade Annick to retire. He had several times broached the idea of a partnership, but this had been received with no enthusiasm. After delectable sessions with Bloss, he wanted to beat – or at least, to use some instrument less symbolic than Annick's soft-soled slipper – but such desires were of short duration. He was well over six feet tall, and rather stout. The boys called him old Ruddy. They neither liked nor disliked him. The cleverest among them knew him for a poor teacher, but it was not that which made them neutral towards him. Simply, he was noisy, and the number of boys who flinch from noisy men is great.

Appeased by his brief but successful performance on the floor, charmed by the sweet-smelling stillness of the day, he strolled across to the Thicket to smoke a pipe. There he found Peter Quillan, crouched on his haunches, gloomily stripping down a leaf to its skeleton.

'Hullo, Peter! Not at work?'

'Nature study, sir. Mr Canning's somewhere around.'

Quillan was a lanky pale boy with fine straight hair like dusty silk, a long aristocratic nose which he had derived from neither of his parents, a small hard chin and round, bold eyes of a peculiarly pigmented blue, almost cobalt. He was ruthlessly determined, feared no one and worked with a kind of pleasurable, almost gluttonous intensity. His mathematics were still weak and Rupert, knowing him to be Annick's pet, chose to take him down a peg.

'Pulling leaves to bits, eh? That won't get you anywhere much, will it? Though of course, if Mr Canning thinks it will, far be it from me to suggest that an extra period of maths in lieu would profit you.'

Peter stared at him. 'But that would be hard on you, sir, wouldn't it? I mean, having to sweat indoors on such a lovely day.'

The smoke from the pipe was blue on the delicate roof of green, scarcely touched by summer's end. Birds and little creatures rustled in the undergrowth.

'I could make a sacrifice if called upon to do so, Peter. For anyone quite so dense as you are at my pet subject.'

'I'm quite good at geography.'

Rupert taught this, too.

'A *non-sequitur*. Well, don't you think you're dense?'

'I don't know, sir. Look, that's a good shape, isn't it?' He held out the leaf skeleton on his palm.

'But what's the object of the exercise?'

'Oh, we were to bring in as many of these as we could find from different trees and draw and label them.'

'And where are your little classmates?'

'We got separated somehow, sir. I think they're on the downs.'

'Then hadn't you better cut off and join them? I'm sure Mr Canning will rejoice in the stray lamb that returns to the fold, if he doesn't clip you one.'

Peter sighed wearily, as if all the sorrows of the world were on his bony shoulders. 'If you say so.'

'Sir.'

'Sir.'

He gave Rupert a long look of contempt and left the Thicket. The leaf had fallen from his hand and he did not pick it up.

As Rupert emerged from the wood, he saw a gaggle of boys running and tumbling back to tea and behind them, slow and at ease, Leo Canning. At once he felt the surge of meaningless rage which was part of his sexual pattern: sex with Blossom, then thoughts of the school and a new discipline, then a delightful and balmy half-hour with a pipe, and then a brief spell of violent irritation.

Canning was twenty-four. He was tall and looked very thin as if deprived in early youth, which perhaps he had been. He had eyes like diamonds, eyes full of ideas and of a multiplicity of interests. He had been five years at a grammar school, two at a technical college and three as assistant to a garage proprietor, when he was suddenly seized with the idea not only that he would like to teach but would enjoy something of the cosy and genteel life which such a place as Downs Park seemed to offer. He had applied in vain to a dozen prep schools before he met Annick, who disregarded his Midlands accent and lack of suavity, and realized that he could put Canning not only on to senior maths, but on to science teaching. This would be a unique score for the school, for serious science was hard to come by so far as small boys were concerned: and if it were of little use in scholarship examinations (although a relevant question might very occasionally emerge in the general paper) it looked splendid on the syllabus. So, to Rupert's fury, a good-sized classroom had been set aside as a lab for Canning's exclusive use. That, Rupert thought, was one salary to be dispensed with if ever he took over the school.

Looking back he saw Blossom, still at her refereeing, but now running up and down with a marked diminution of energy. He glanced at his watch. Nearly time for her to go and feed Pauline. He thought of their infant daughter who, by some (as he thought) genetic freak, was not a redhead but had an outcropping of black hair like a shaving brush.

Canning was almost upon him. Rupert said, 'I sent one of your truants back to you. I hope he arrived. Little tick.'

'Oh, Petey. He wasn't on the run. He was moony this afternoon so I sent him to look at leaves in the Thicket. I think he's contemplating another poem.'

'For Christ's sake, Leo! He's supposed to be doing nature study.'

'Better for him to write poetry than go about pulling a lot of grotty leaves to bits. Silly subject, except for specialists.'

This made Rupert angrier than ever. It was a constant thorn in his side that it was Canning, and not himself, who taught scholarship maths: he did not see why the man should not do his humbler jobs with a better grace.

He observed (drily, he thought, though Canning's diamond eyes flickered) that an usher was paid to teach, not to brood about what he was teaching.

'Mooky soobject, all the same,' said Canning, and fell into step with him as if they were the best of friends.

It was tea-time, and the boys were massing for the last substantial meal of the day. (Before bedtime there would be cocoa, bread and cheese and currant buns.) After the meal there would be the solemn concourse to listen to the 5.50 p.m. news bulletin, details of which Annick would explain, and a brief discussion would follow. Then came a blissful hour of fooling about for the boys, and drinks for the staff.

'Rups! Bloss!' Grace called to them as they were making their way back to the cottage. 'Sun's over the yardarm. Come and have a sherry with us.'

'I don't know that we can, Mrs Annick' said Blossom, 'no sitter.'

'Helen!' Grace hailed the secretary, a plain, wan girl with a beautiful body. 'Can you sit with Pauline for an hour while we indulge ourselves?'

Helen assented with some alacrity. For some reason, she never minded being alone at the cottage, typing Rupert's slender correspondence or keeping an eye on the baby.

The others went upstairs to the Annicks' pleasant if somewhat dusty suite of rooms: Grace was no housekeeper and could not spare the two daily women from work in the school itself. Besides, she was supposed to have her arduous job as matron, though all the donkey-work, the sewing of name-tapes, darning of socks, vests, sheets and pillow-cases, was done by Betty Cope.

'Sherry' was a generic term for drinks in general: in fact, the Massingers drank gin and the Annicks whisky. To see them sitting in their gold-moted comfort, looking out over the striped gold of the falling day to the gap where a strip of blue, blue sea was visible, nobody would have thought that the two couples cordially disliked each other. The Massingers thought Annick a premature dodderer, and the Annicks thought the Massingers raw and stupid.

'Peace, peace!' Grace cried enthusiastically. 'Isn't it wonderful?' She beamed down at the boys scurrying about their various employments, like wasps in their buttercup-yellow blazers with black braiding. It was a hard colour on the sallow ones, but at least it was always visible, and these things must be considered. The long-sighted could see a Downs Park boy scuttling along, in the lee of a hedgerow, from half a mile away.

'The end of the day,' said Rupert heavily. He pulled at his pipe. 'Headmaster, I wish you'd take your slipper to Quillan just once in a while.'

'Petey? What for?'

'Yesterday I was going along behind the gym when I saw him jump that fat child, Searle, and knock him down. They had a thorough scuffle and pummel in the dirt and then stopped it suddenly and lay gazing into each other's silly eyes for quite three minutes. Would you say that was altogether healthy?'

'Perhaps not,' said Annick, 'but altogether ordinary. Petey thinks Dicky Searle looks like Rupert Brooke.'

'And why the hell should he jump Rupert Brooke? Searle had scratches.'

'Searle's always got scratches. You can't tell whether they're new ones or old.'

'You know, Headmaster,' Blossom said earnestly, the rose of her mottled cheeks darkening a little, 'his mother did say Quillan was a bully.'

'If he is, I'm not going to cure him by patting his backside. Anyway, he's not a bully in the accepted sense, only a letter-off of steam. And for so chilly a youngster, he's quite popular with his peers. No, Rupert, there are going to be no executions. Certainly not for playing at Rupert Brooke with Searle.'

They changed the subject to the more agreeable one of the Christmas play, which was to be *Twelfth Night*. Annick was proposing to make an innovation, which was that Olivia was to be played by Betty Cope, who was a very small girl.

'Viola is all right for a chap and Maria up to a point, but a male Olivia can look damned silly. Anyway, I'm never certain whether putting these boys in female roles is really good for them. Either they're sunk in shame, or they preen.'

'You'll have noticed' said Grace, 'that Cyril never lets them get stuck in the girls' parts. A boy who plays Kate Hardcastle one year is going to get Bolingbroke the next. It stops them from getting set in their ways.' Her pleasant, rosy face beamed approval of all her husband had ever done, and was ever likely to do.

The sun was falling rapidly now, and the damp nostalgic smell of the dew was rising. Far out to sea, a light flashed on and off. The boys had been called to indoor employments, not so much because the night air was bad for them, but because it was bad for them to become invisible. 'Policemen,' Annick muttered, following his own thoughts, 'policemen, the lot of us.'

There was a ring at the doorbell, steps on the stairs and – 'Penny!'

'Hullo. Can I have a bed?'

The hairs rose on Rupert's neck, as they always did at the sight of the Annicks' widowed daughter. She was twenty-six, and her new husband had been killed in a motor accident less than a year before. A big girl of dark and sullen handsomeness, with a very slight and fascinating hint of moustache.

'Hullo, Rups, hullo, Blossom.'

Rupert felt his wife's furious tremor. She was afraid of Penelope. Well, she needn't be, not if she made herself agreeable when he needed her to be. The last thing he wanted was to participate in any scandal connected with the school which, when he took it over, was going to be as white as snow no matter how scarlet its former sins. He saw himself, the picture of health and strength, presiding over an angelic staff, of whom only about two would be the old originals. Canning would go. Mrs Murray would go. Two excellent beginnings. He would not wriggle and stutter like Annick: he would stand on the front steps with his arms open in welcome to all parents, however bloody, and he would try to step up the social tone by getting more parents with titles. Annick seemed afraid of titles.

'A bed, of course, dear,' said Grace. 'But why?'

'Car broke down. I forced it as far as the garage and walked.'

Tossing her coat on to a chair, Penelope poured herself a drink. She ran an antique shop not far distant, and had been on her way to Chester after a hinted prize, intending to drive all night. 'Mind you, I don't quite know what I want a bed for. I slept all the afternoon.'

'Do you want food?'

'I'll eat staff supper, God help me. What is it?'

Both staff and boys suffered from Mrs Terry's cooking which, though wholesome, was horrible: but nobody could be found to replace her. The chicken, boiled or roast, was inevitably pallid, surrounded by mushrooms swimming in a nameless glue which was Mrs Terry's *specialité de la maison*. The staff, certainly, were served with fruit and custard rather than the weighty puddings which she concocted for the boys – Dead Man's Leg, as they called a roll of glistening wet suet with currants inside, or Bloody Baby, which was an iron-hard baked jam tart. Boys notoriously complain about their food and would do so if this were provided by the chef from Lapérouse or the Pyrenées at Vienne: but Downs Park boys had reason for complaint. The vegetables were always sodden and Mrs Terry knew it, though she protested half-tearfully that she did not know how to amend matters. 'I *lean* on the greens,' she would say, miming the action with her considerable bulk. Yet the boys returned home healthy and with increased weight, which seemed to be an indication that good food was not necessarily nice food.

Rupert looked down the high table: it really was high, being elevated by a clear foot from the refectory tables and benches where the boys had eaten their supper an hour ago. To his right was Mrs Murray, educated at North London Collegiate School and the Sorbonne: she taught French and was known by the boys as The Blub, because tears came to her eyes when they mulishly refused to make unfamiliar and contemptible sounds. To his left was Betty Cope, matron in all but title. She was lesbian and sporadically *dévote*: this last trait was of infinite use to Downs Park, since she could be relied upon, in a community of agnostics or strict non-thinkers, to take church parade every time and certainly at all times when other people did not feel like it. Influenza would not have deterred her. A pretty, tiny girl of twenty-four and very lonely. Why on earth had she ever come to work at a boys' school?

A couple of places further down was Stephen Smith, fresh from Cambridge, aged twenty-two and like a ventriloquist's dummy: his face was cheerful and wooden, his hair like an application of bootblack to a plastic surface. He taught English, junior Latin and history. Since he was ingenious with ideas for popular amusement, he was a favourite with the boys, and a great pet of Grace's. Rupert liked him too: Stephen lent him books and had a mind 'like a cesspool', this being no great disadvantage where Rupert was concerned. There was so little fun to be had. He did not suspect that out of sheer amiability of soul, Stephen could be all things to all men.

In the half-hour before dinner, Rupert had suffered something of a disappointment: it had occurred to him that Bloss on the drawing-room hearth-rug would be pleasant; but he had only made a beginning when Pauline, who was teething, started such an uproar that frustration was inevitable. He looked down the table to where Penelope, dark as the Queen of Night, was peeling a black grape. She raised the Nile-green flesh to her full mouth. Well, would it be so reprehensible if he had, as it were, a stand-in? He did not know how well she was enduring her deprivation. One could always find out.

Chapter Three

Mrs Murray was fifty-six, stoutish and plain. Her features were so flat that she seemed to have no profile. When, widowed two years ago, she had taken up teaching, she had believed that she loved boys and now she hated them.

She was desperately lonely and in the night wept in her despair. She had never been able to accept the kindly attempts of the Annicks to draw her into the family life of the staff; asked for sherry or a chat, she would almost invariably find some excuse for not going. The beauty of the world, the paragon of animals, all were tarnished in Mrs Murray's sight, even on so beautiful, bee-haunted a day as this Friday when she was taking the Remove. As usual the boys were stealthily out of hand. Richard Searle had dipped a snail in an ink-pot and was setting it to trail across his book. David Maitland was making spit-balls and piling them up like miniature cannon balls in a heap. Morgan was humming under his breath, just quietly enough to escape rebuke, since when Mrs Murray's eye fell on him the tune fell to a mere soundless breathing. Only Peter Quillan, as usual, was paying any attention at all, and that was of a pretty flaccid order.

He had not, of course, been kept in the lowest form for more than ten days: his presence there had been an absurdity, and Annick had been compelled to put him into the Remove where most of the boys were two years his seniors, thus violating his long-held, if not strongly-held, belief that it was better for children to study with their own age-groups. He saw to it that Peter at least played with his age-group, in so far as Peter could be made to play: but there again, being a good deal taller than most of them, he did not seem to fit in.

'No, Hewison,' Mrs Murray cried, 'you must learn to get the sounds right.' She stretched her mouth with two fingers as if about to emit a piercing whistle, and there was a general snicker. '*Ah*. Say "ah".' She let her lips slacken as she ran down the French scale of vowels. 'Ah, é, ee, o, ou, ü! Try it. Ah, é, ee . . .'

'It sounds so absurd,' said Hewison, a stolid looking boy with a winemark on his cheek.

'It's you who are absurd. Why should you despise this beautiful language? None of you even tries.' Her tears began to gather.

Oh, she was so lonely! She rarely talked much to any member of the staff except Betty Cope, from whom she took a certain rather suspect comfort. When she first learned of Betty's proclivities she had been sickened and horrified: then one day, watching the Titania figure crossing to the dormitories with a pile of darned linen, she had been even more horrified to find herself thinking, 'I wish she loved me!' But Betty was young, and was lonely quite in her own way.

'Oh, sit down, Hewison! We'll do some more reading. Open your Perrault, page thirty-nine. *Riquet à la Houppe*. Maitland stop that disgusting game you're playing. Read, and then translate.'

A hopeless performance on both counts, drawled, deliberately incompetent, though Maitland was not really a fool.

'I cannot bear it!' Mrs Murray cried, causing a sudden stir of interest, since she rarely spoke with real energy, but was merely mistress of the dreary rebuke. 'Do you realize that next year I've got to get most of you through Common Entrance somehow?' She plunged for what little comfort she could find. 'Quillan! Go on from there.'

Peter read a paragraph fairly well, but not putting his full effort into speaking the language in any way that would appeal to a Frenchman: intelligent though he was, it seemed to him somehow pretentious, if not downright disloyal, to speak it as histrionically as it needed to be spoken. But then he translated rapidly and fluently and sat down sharply at the end, leaving Mrs Murray's poor heart just a little assuaged. In the Remove, only he and Richard Searle were scholarship material; Peter certainly – but he had three years yet to go – and Richard just possibly.

'Yes, that was a bit better. Thank you, Quillan.'

The bell rang and she was released to employ herself for an hour. She wondered whether she would go home and make coffee: would she have time? There was coffee to be got at the school, but this was Rupert Massinger's free period too and she could not bear the idea of him being breezy with her.

Like several other members of the staff, she lived in Chalkwood, a fair-sized village fifteen minutes away over the downs. She had two rooms, a large sitting-room and adequate-sized bedroom, both rather untidy and aching with a strewn loneliness of their own. She had not loved her husband but she missed the noise he made, missed his nagging, even missed his maddening performances on the recorder.

Today she decided that she would not go home; by the time the coffee was made she would have a bare ten minutes to drink it. So she walked to the Thicket and sat down on a fallen tree to do the *Times* crossword puzzle. No boys were free at this hour, so all was quiet. Nothing would happen. Nothing ever did. She was not sure she wanted it to.

Chapter Four

English turf, barbered, emerald, springy, diamond-chipped with dew, is difficult to maintain: but Annick had put in a good many years on his. At the end of September the weather was still dry, and all the sprinklers were playing over the grass. These were just another of the multiple reasons why the school did not pay its way but he couldn't see how they could be dispensed with.

He looked across the three conjoined houses, rosy in the evening light. How much longer could these schools exist economically, or be regarded still as social and academic necessities? Already he had detected a trend towards the day preparatory schools, such as the Hill at Hampstead. So much of his and Grace's private means went into maintaining Downs Park that both had been wondering how long the depredations could be allowed to continue. The Massingers, greedy to take over, had far more money and would at once make rigorous economies of a nature, he, Annick, could not bring himself to undertake.

But he had other things on his mind, and one was his white hope, Peter Quillan. Peter was as popular with his compeers as a boy could be who walked through games, kept his own counsel and laughed rarely, for he was equably-tempered and had recently lost his tendency to jump on other boys and bear them, not too painfully, to the dust. But for the past week or so, Peter had been seen more and more on his own, less in association: and he looked troubled.

In fact, there he was now, with hanging head, walking aimlessly between the late firing of chrysanthemums. Annick called to him. 'Petey! Come upstairs and I'll give you a Coke.'

The boy perceptibly hesitated. Then he came to join the headmaster and they fell into step.

The sitting-room was empty, for Grace was supervising the matronly duties that were now too seldom her own. The light was darkening across the fields, but over the sea lay a band of rose-pink sky and Jupiter was aloft. Annick told Peter to sit down and brought Coca-Cola for them both.

'Well, we don't have much time for talk, do we?'

'No, sir.'

'I thought you'd been looking a bit hot and bothered lately. Anything wrong?'

Again the hesitation. Then – 'No. Not much.'

'What, then?'

'I don't know, really. You get restless. What star's that, sir?'

Annick told him. 'Bright, isn't it? Well, it's early days I know, but have you any idea what you're eventually going to do?'

'Read for the bar,' Peter said without hesitation. 'My father's told me about it and I might as well.'

'Why not do classics?' Annick felt a shaft of disappointment. 'You're quite good enough.'

The boy pondered, looking down the length of his long nose so that he slightly squinted. Annick turned on a single reading-lamp, needing more light in which to see him but not wanting a sharp disturbance of the evening's mood.

'Well, sir, it seems to me you must come to the end of it before long. Wear them out. I couldn't go on with that for ever.'

'Good God, I don't suppose Porson thought he'd ever come to the end of them!'

'I don't think I'm Porson, sir.' Though Peter did not know who Porson was.

There was a silence. Peter swallowed up his Coca-Cola. Annick had a strong sense of a divided mind. The boy wanted to get up and go, equally wanted to stay. He shuffled his feet, picked up a book on the sofa at his side, then laid it down without glancing at it.

'How's the maths coming on?' Annick asked him.

'Well, sir, not brilliantly. It's something I've been wondering about.'

'What's that?'

'If only I could do maths with Mr Canning.'

Annick, surprised, suggested that this was hardly possible. Canning took the two top forms only, and for these Peter was not yet ready – certainly not in mathematics, where he would find himself hopelessly behind.

'Well, my parents say they're getting worried.'

'Don't let them worry you. You're doing all right, and perhaps we can haul your maths up to standard. In fact, of course we can. Is that what's bothering you?'

'Yes,' said Peter, but he was not telling the truth.

Annick had an idea. 'Mr Canning is a man of infinite good nature. If we could get him to coach you for an hour a week – I don't know whether we could, mind.'

'Thank you, sir. But it would be a drag for him. I suppose I could get coaching in the holidays.'

'Let's find out what Mr Canning thinks, anyway.'

Peter brightened a little. 'The way he teaches science is super. He tells you first what it's all about, what the end-product is, as he calls it, and sees you get a bit excited before he makes you weigh all those mucky bits of tin or fix up bits of cotton in front of mirrors.'

'Praise from a pupil, Peter, is praise indeed. May I pass it on?'

The boy said he would rather Annick did not. Mr Canning might construe it as a sort of sucking-up because Peter wanted something, that was, the coaching.

Another silence fell.

Then Peter flushed up to the roots of his hair: it was perceptible even in the emollient light of the lamp. 'Sir, I'd like to tell you something, but—'

'But what?'

'You know we have to go for walks in pairs. I went off on my own. It was Saturday. I was going to buy sweets. Searle was late and I didn't wait for him. If I had, it wouldn't have happened.' He panted a little: the effort to get this out had been a terrible one.

He backed along the sofa as if to escape. Annick, who was experienced, had a faint idea what he was about to be told, and he sighed.

He said, not over-heartily, in case he broke the spell of the moment and frightened the boy into silence, 'Out with it, Petey. Come on.'

'I don't know if I can, sir.'

'Come along, now.'

Peter stood up, tall and forlorn. He could not forbear to glance at the door, as if calculating escape. Then it came out.

'There was a man in a car. He stopped and asked me where the Eastbourne Road was. I told him, and I thought he was going to drive on. But then he swore, as though something had gone wrong with the engine, and jumped out, and I thought he was going to look under the bonnet, but he took a grab at me.'

Annick would have liked to light his pipe, but knew the few seconds spent in doing so would only increase Peter's suspense. The boy was worrying, among other things, as to whether he was to be punished for breaking a school rule. Annick said equably, 'So what did you do?'

'I shoved him as hard as I could and ran for it. He jumped in and drove off.'

'Ever seen him before, hanging around?'

'No, sir.'

'Make of car?'

'I've no idea.'

'Well, listen. There are mad people about, you know that. You had the bad luck to run into one of them. Just put it out of your mind.'

Annick considered this, then shook his head. If he made an issue of it, they would never find the man and it would mean dragging Peter through the whole thing again. A quiet word with the local inspector perhaps, but no more.

'Sir, it was my fault, wasn't it?' A masochistic note, here, plangent.

'You know the law, don't you? So yes, it was partly your fault.'

He could now afford to be brisk, since he had seen the tears of strain gathering on Peter's lower lids.

'You can go now. Go and amuse yourself with your friends and stop wandering about like Hamlet. All right?'

A surreptitious sniff, a nod. 'Thank you, sir.'

'If you do think about the chap, be sorry for him if you can. He's a poor wretch.'

'I'll try,' said Peter, looking anything but sorry. He went away, his back straighter than it had been when he came in.

Annick told the story to Grace when she returned. 'I wonder whether it would be stimulating to a poor schoolmaster occasionally to find a brand-new problem on his plate?'

She protested. 'We've never had a prowler before, have we?'

'No, and probably never shall have again. I had to play the whole thing down, or Peter would have turned it into a large-scale melodrama.'

'I'm glad he felt he could come to you,' she said, putting a finger upon his inner satisfaction, which he had only half-realized. Then she began to speak of next day's match against Rowan Court. She really cared about the school's games successes, and indeed was probably right to do so, since there would be little else to boast about in the school magazine that year.

Next day he found Peter wandering alone again and was irritated. 'Still Hamleting? I do wish you wouldn't, for once. Go and help Mr Canning's crowd.'

Canning had bought up the pieces of a very old car, and was helping some boys to assemble it in the driveway.

'Honestly, sir, it's not that. I'm just finishing a poem.'

'Got it to show me?'

'Not quite yet. I'm almost on the last two lines.'

'You can bring it along when it's done. We could do with something for the magazine, and we may as well publish you early.'

He strolled off, leaving Peter to inspiration. The Massingers saw them part and muttered about Mary's little lamb.

Next day, during morning break, Peter came with unaccustomed shyness to Annick, and showed him the completed work

To Birds: A Sonnet

Musicians to the sun, what noise, what note
Could match what comes from thy orchestral hall?
The sweeter strain that cometh from thy throat
The greater happiness creates withal.
If I could find the secrets of thy song
That lifts so many hearts up from the ground,
Say, then, should I not sing both loud and long
And strengthen sweet love as the world goes round?
The joyful harmony that from this sphere
Gives angels such unmatchable delight
I prithee, sing, so more than I can hear,
Prolong the day until the very night!
O that I could continue the sweet stream
Of my heart's love! Resume, ethereal dream!

Peter Willoughby Quillan, aged 9½ (nearly)

Annick was surprised and delighted. 'Show this to Mr Smith and ask if he'd like it for the magazine.'

He was also delighted to realize that Peter must be feeling much, much better.

'I wrote it up a tree in the Thicket.'

'Did you? Good work.'

Chapter Five

Stephen Smith took back the pirated letters of Fr. Rolfe and gave Rupert *Fanny Hill* instead. 'But you'll find it a bit tame after this lot.'

Rupert hid the book away in what he supposed to be a secret drawer of his desk. What he did not know was that Helen Queen, while typing out his dictation notes one day, had discovered it. She knew all about his special interests and hugged the knowledge fondly to herself. She did not read more than a page or two of the books, because her own tastes did not incline that way; but in a school where she seemed to be of so little importance, it was consoling to have a secret. She was a girl of very few vices beyond that of prying. The more she knew about everyone the more secure she felt. She had no real friends, and being half in love with Stephen seemed to have no future in it. She knew all about Betty Cope, and tended to avoid her: Betty made her feel nervous.

Helen was sadly aware of her own plainness, of the fact that her hair-styles never looked intentional, of her over-long chin and tendency to spots. Her mother had died many years ago, and she had been reared by her father, a dull clergyman with a dull living in Norfolk. It had been a relief to find a job so far away from him.

Her one delight during the past year had been the discovery of Richard Searle's passion for her. Eleven he might he, but passion from one of such green years was better than no passion at all. Tubby, with a romantic fall of butter-coloured hair over a face like a handsome pig's, he followed her around whenever he got the chance, and had once left in her path an inept but imaginative quatrain about 'Helen Queen, Queen Helen'. She was sage enough to know that it was purely the charm of her name that attracted him. But still.

It was a cold, dank day in October. She was alone in the Massingers' house, finishing up some odd jobs from Rupert and making her monthly check of the school books: it was far more comfortable in the cottage than in her rather dark office. She was worried as usual by the growing deficit which seemed, on the surface, anyway, to worry the Annicks so little. Canning's lab equipment was costing too much, despite the fact that he had bought some of it himself, and Mrs Terry's triumphant new contracts with two farmers from whom she now bought the school's essential supplies had jumped up the catering bills to an absurd degree. Several parents were in arrears with fees, and Annick was refusing to press them. The two gardeners were costing too much: one of them would have been enough, since the other was a flagrant skrimshanker. Grace Annick worked in the garden also, but her spare time was limited. Helen wondered whether she should attempt to make a real *démarche*. What good would it do? Any good at all? She could always try.

Her head was beginning to ache. Just to make a change, she fiddled with a wooden boss at the base of the desk, and the secret drawer slid back. What had he got this time? A paperback with lurid cover, *Kisses and Whips*. She opened it idly, and as idly began to read.

His hand was on her shoulder: he must have crossed the room with the silence of a cat. She jumped violently, and was flooded in succession by extreme heat and extreme cold.

'Well, Queen Helen, this is what you get up to, is it?'

'Mr Massinger, it was a pure accident. I must have kicked something and a drawer opened—'

'Even if it did, what business was it of yours to have a good look?'

'I'm sorry, really I am. I wasn't really reading it at all, I—'

'I've suspected you of this before, you little Paula Pry. Well, I

25

read rude books, and I'll go on doing so as long as I like. What's it to you?'

She saw through a sweaty blur that he was not particularly angry.

'It's nothing to me. And it really was an accident. I didn't know—'

He released her, plumped down on the sofa, turned his fiery face towards her own.

'So you didn't expect me back, did you? Well, that was your mistake. What are you going to do about it, eh? And what do you do all the time you're alone in the place? Rout through the bedroom drawers?'

'I don't. I've said I'm sorry. I'm honestly not interested—'

'Shows how much you miss. Now get out of here, pronto.'

Rising, he gripped her round the waist, ran her out of the room and out of the front door. 'Mr Massinger, I've left the ledgers—'

'I'll drop them in at the office. Just for the moment, I don't want to see your face in here any longer.'

To her utter astonishment he kissed her, roughly and wetly, with a great prod of the tongue, in a fashion quite outside her limited experience. 'That's what it's all about, my girl. Now you know.'

She was crying as she walked back to the school and trembling too. With disgust, she thought, but was not quite sure. She need not be afraid of him really: he'd never give her away, because she could give *him* away, couldn't she? Frightened of him, a little, she was.

She passed Blossom Massinger, leading her own P.T. class back from the gym – left, right, left, right! Would he tell her, or were the books a secret from his wife, too? Helen somehow suspected that they were not, and she shivered. But he would not tell about the kiss. Would he ever want to repeat it? She would shudder if he did, she would be sick. Would she be disappointed – was it conceivable that she should be – if he did not?

Leo Canning caught up with her. 'Nearly time for our oats.' He looked at her closely. 'What's up?'

'Nothing.'

'Of course there is.'

'It's a private matter.'

'I see. What are you doing out without a coat on a day like this?'

She had left it in the cottage.

'I'm not cold. I've got a good circulation.'

'You'll be out of circulation altogether if you don't take more care of yourself.'

She tried to hurry past him, but he slowed her down.

'What's it like for you here, Nell?' He was the one of the few persons, who had ever found her a nickname. 'Neither fish, flesh, fowl or—'

She tried to smile. 'I'm as good a herring as Betty Cope.'

'Poor old Bet. Why on earth did she ever want to work in a boys' school?'

She was startled. This, she felt, was knowledge he ought not to have possessed. But Canning knew everything.

She hardly managed to eat any lunch, even though the Massingers were not there. It was intolerable to her to remember the moment when she had been caught spying, yet her thoughts would not leave it. Even the sight of little Searle, peering languorously at her over his slice of Dead Man's Leg, was no comfort today. She did not know how she was to face anyone again. *Anyone*.

Within a fortnight she was Rupert's mistress. She had been forced to return to her routine duties at the cottage, where he had barely spoken to her except to dictate. But one afternoon, when Blossom was away in Eastbourne with a party of boys to see an amateur performance of *The Merchant of Venice*, he had simply marched her upstairs and taken her. Painfully. Just like that. But this time, though she cried a little, she did not tremble. It was only what she had, in her darkest heart, been expecting.

'No need to carry on,' said Rupert. 'Blossom's not enough for me, which is no fault of mine. Nobody's going to know about us, that I do assure you. And I shan't need you all that often.'

She was silly enough to moan that if only he loved her – and he laughed. 'I must like you a bit, mustn't I? So put that in your pipe and smoke it. Now go and get your tea.'

Chapter Six

Parents' Day was always held at the end of October, the idea being that the year was still young enough for hopes to exist that the weather might not be intolerable. There was an excellent cold supper (Mrs Terry was not allowed to cater for this), there were 'speeches' in the form of recitations (an idea borrowed from Eton), there was a brief prize-giving and an address from a notability.

The night before this event was always a sleepless one for Annick, who rolled and sweated between the sheets thinking of everything that might go wrong. Indeed, something had gone wrong this year, for the speech-maker, Bailey's grandfather and a former Lord Mayor of London, had influenza and his substitute was the vicar, whom the boys heard every Sunday in any case. It was a dreadful pity, because Bailey's family represented the highest social point the school had attained. Bailey himself, unhappily, represented nothing, since despite Annick's hope that his substitution of 'ph' for 'f' might indicate a nascent scholar, it was now obvious that it would be a marvel if he could be boosted through Common Entrance.

Grace Annick slept peacefully: such occasions for her were always triumphs. She could, when she tried, make herself look very pretty, and for tomorrow she had an emerald dress and coat, a royal blue hat with emerald scarf surrounding it, which were going to look very striking indeed. So she smoothed her husband's thigh as he fell into one of his uneasy patches of slumber, and by whispering, tried to force into his unconscious mind the idea that all would be well. She did this on the principle that language may be taught by means of a small tape-recorder under the pillow.

She was satisfied about the refreshments, which were being

provided by an ingenious young woman in Chalkwood, who made a speciality of these things: there would be pork pies, veal patties, chicken patties, sliced tongue and ham, new-baked bread and interesting cheeses, bowls of fruit salad spiced with kirsch, and to drink, a choice of cider, *vin rosé* or beer. The gymnasium had been charmingly dressed, under her command and Stephen's, in garlands of green laurel and the surviving chrysanthemums. The school orchestra was more or less in tune. Peter Quillan, though a little young to be chosen to perform, was to recite his own poem about the birds. All boys would have the privilege of going to bed an hour later.

The morning dawned Cambridge blue and looked as if it might be trusted. There was a breathing mist over the sea. It lurked still in the bushes. The grass sparkled vividly, a dew-drop on every blade.

After breakfast, Annick retired to be sick. He always did this on Parents' Day, and no notice was taken of the peculiarity, despite desperate noises from the downstairs lavatory.

That day there were no lessons, so there was a good deal of uproar: but Canning's car still remained to be finally assembled, and Stephen had the brighter boys rehearsing their speeches. Only the Massingers and Mrs Terry were angry: they because there was to be no gym display, and she because, though certainly she was relieved to be spared the extra work, she felt slighted that her own catering had been despised. The little boys had been taken by Betty Cope on an unusually protracted walk.

At six o'clock the first of the cars rolled into the drive, and blossom by blossom the hats began. But no parent looked more effective than Grace. The first thing her eye lit upon was Betty Cope talking to Mrs Quillan and she hoped she was behaving herself. For from Betty's point of view, Mrs Quillan was the most slovenly, and therefore the most detested, of all mothers: vests arrived torn from neck to waist, odd socks arrived unmarked, no handkerchiefs arrived at all. But Betty, in pink, looked amiable and calm. To put no further strain upon her, Grace swept Mrs Quillan and her robust husband, who had just joined them, up to Annick, who was at least able to praise the boy himself.

For Annick, Parents' Day was like some horrible version of a Paul Jones dance. He had barely embarked on a conversation with a mother or father, than he was whizzed round by invisible hands to be confronted with another pair, whom he seldom managed to recognize.

Who was it now? A relief. The parents of the head boy, Denis Fairclough, who would get some minor scholarship comfortably and was so enormously tall (already, at twelve, 5 feet 10½ inches) that he could, and did, assume a rather comfortable position between boys and masters.

'Denis is very steady,' Annick said, 'and we have high hopes. Indeed, I wonder whether we're pitching our hopes – not too low, of course, but perhaps unreasonably so. He'd get into Winchester.'

Mr Fairclough, solicitor, bridled. 'I went to Seaston. So did my father. It will do for Denis.'

But it would not look so splendid on the Honours Board.

'Now do give Alex a decent part in the school play!' Another parent, smart in unseasonable furs. 'I know he's got it in him.'

Annick stiffened. 'Mrs Stern, Alex has great qualities but Mr Smith doesn't find acting one of them.'

'Come, I've been an actress for thirty years! I should *know*. Besides, I'd coach him. You'd see . . .'

'Robert!' Annick greeted, with a cry of relief the volume of which he did not realize, a father whom he liked and admired.

'How are you? And Stephanie? Andrew's doing very well, I'm glad to say.'

'Is it a bit early for him to be so spotty? He was always precocious.' This concealed inordinate parental pride.

'Spots or not' said Annick, at ease, since the father was neither socially nor intellectually grand but a very nice fellow, 'Andy's Greek is coming along like a house afire.'

'And he is an exceedingly *nice* child,' said Grace, joining them. Character estimates were part of her duty, her own province. 'His manners are positively Beau Brummellish and he is so kind to the little ones.'

This pleased the mother: mothers are far more receptive than fathers to admiration of the moral virtues.

Later, they saw Gordon Corso, who was head of a middling-sized electrical firm, deep in conversation with Leo Canning. The two moved off towards the lab.

'Now, everything is going splendidly,' said Grace, 'so you need not twitch, my darling.'

The Massingers were, of course, in the thick of it all, red, roseate, healthy, noisy: whatever the boys might feel about noisy adults, it was valuable on an occasion such as this.

Supper over, everyone went to the gymnasium for what Annick called the 'exercises'. The recitations were brief. Fairclough recited 'Vivamus mea Lesbia, atque amemus,' Maitland some Shakespeare, Quillan, calm and pallid in his unbecoming yellow blazer, made so great a success with his bird sonnet that certain disgruntled parents were heard to whisper that he must have copied it from somewhere, and finally – a surprise – Searle recited *La Cigale et la Fourmi* in very passable French. This had come about because Mrs Murray had complained about him to Annick who, knowing the boy to be something of an exhibitionist, informed him that if he didn't recite in French he wouldn't be reciting at all, and that he had better put on a spurt of energy in Mrs Murray's class to bring himself up, even approximately, to the required standard. In the event Searle, who had a strong histrionic streak, enjoyed himself immensely.

'Pas un seul petit morceau' – squeak –
'De mouche' – here a gesture, indicating the smallness of the fly –
'. . . ou de vermisseau!' The drop of the voice to a sudden baritone. Panic!
'Elle alla crier *famine!* chez la fourmi, sa voisine,
'La priant de lui prêter' – a shrinking of the shoulders now, cowering and beggarly –

'. . . quelque grain pour *subsister*—'

How would the poor grasshopper subsist? Searle milked out every drop of pathos and sat down to surprised applause. Mrs Murray's eyes filled, this time not with frustration but relief.

Then the presentation of prizes by the vicar's wife, the books, and the games cups. Peter Quillan went up to the platform with what seemed to be monotonous regularity. So did Fairclough, one of the few boys privileged, because he was so big, to wear long trousers.

The hall subsided for the vicar's address: the block of yellow-jacketed boys cross-legged in front, the parents in a flowery mass behind.

' "All silent and all damned," ' Stephen Smith whispered to Betty Cope. 'Lord help him if he goes on for more than ten minutes.'

'Well, boys, I expect you have enough of me on Sundays without this infliction this evening. But bear up bravely.'

A sycophantic titter.

The vicar beamed: already he was being a success. He went on to regret the ex-Lord Mayor's absence and apologize once more for his own inadequacy as a substitute. He congratulated staff and boys on the year's work – in fact, saw fit to repeat most of what Annick had said in his own brief report. A soft sigh went through the gym and feet scuffled.

'Now I bet you all think that because this *isn't* Sunday, I shan't mention God this time. Well, you're wrong. I shall mention Him just once because He is in everything.' Some of the smaller boys looked round apprehensively, as if expecting to see a blazing white presence manifesting itself in the ribstalls. 'God is good for you.'

This, recalling so sharply the Guinness advertisement, caused an intake of giggle-repressing breath among the parents.

'Let me tell you a story about a boy I once knew who grew up – as boys do' – the vicar waited for sympathetic response – 'and found himself in the front line trenches during the First World War. His name was Lobworth.' There followed an anecdote of a pointless order about Lobworth, wounded, bringing back to safety one more wounded than he. It might have been less pointless if there had been any further reference to God, but the vicar had taken his self-denying ordinance and was sticking to it. So far as anyone could see, Lobworth had carried off all the prizes at school, and this had given him the moral strength to carry a comrade on his back. 'Yet Lobworth,' the vicar pursued, 'was quite unremarkable when he was a little chap. No one would have guessed what he had in him. For all you boys know, there might be a Lobworth among you this very day.'

There were hypnotized glances, as they looked around for one, in khaki, with halo.

'You'd have liked Lobworth,' said the vicar, with histrionic simplicity, 'yes, all of you would.'

'I do not believe it,' Annick muttered to himself. Stephen, uninhibited, was grinning from ear to ear. The Massingers seemed the only members of the staff who were not perceptibly wriggling. 'I do not believe he can be saying all this.'

'Sh,' said Grace at his side.

But the vicar did not take up more than ten minutes, so the boys, who prized brevity more than content, and were in any case, except for the more sophisticated, a little young to be over-amused by Lobworth, gave him a good round of applause, while parents behind clapped a little more slowly and rhythmically.

Then it was all over, except for the traditional staff party, which the Annicks always enjoyed simply because that particularly trying day was done.

Farewells rang through the clear night: the headlamps of the cars cut lemon swathes through the hedges before swerving on to the main road.

Of the parents, only Gordon Corso remained. Annick asked him to the party, but he refused. 'No, I must get along. But I wanted to say – do you know what a prize you've got in young Canning? You keep him while you can, because it won't be for long.'

The party this year was held at the Massingers', since they had the largest living-room, running the whole breadth of the cottage. Everyone seemed excited, everyone, that is, except Helen Queen, who was silently busying herself with drinks, no smile on her face. Mrs Murray, stimulated by Searle's triumph, called Betty Cope to sit beside her. After a fleeting hesitation the small dark girl, feminine and pretty, did so. Stephen pushed them both further along the sofa and took his seat at Betty's other side. 'All went well? Except for that damned fool vicar. Lobworth, indeed! Never shall I forget Lobworth.'

'Oh come,' said Annick, standing above them, 'he didn't exceed his ten minutes, that's always something.'

'I saw you, Headmaster. You were praying.'

'Bloody Lobworth,' said Canning, joining the group. 'What a speech!'

'Did anyone, but *anyone*, understand it?' Betty was appealing.

Canning insisted that he did. It was all ham-handed symbolism. 'But don't let it worry you. Nobody is going to remember or hold it against you. Only a great brain like mine could really grasp the glories of Lobworth.'

Helen sidled up with a tray of glasses. She seemed to have acquired a habit of looking at nobody, which meant that she was determined never to look at Blossom Massinger.

Mrs Murray touched Betty's hand, then held it. 'You're cold!'

'I'm always cold. It's my rotten circulation.' The hand was withdrawn. Forgetful of Richard Searle, Mrs Murray felt the old sucking loneliness enclosing her.

'Saturday tomorrow. I was wondering whether you'd come and have tea with me?'

'Sorry,' Betty replied, 'but Saturday's not a holiday for all of us. I've got enough name-taping to keep me busy for the entire weekend. Damned parents! And that Quillan woman is the worst. Odd socks! And believe it or not, she sent a pair of underpants back *unwashed*.'

'Petey wouldn't worry whether they were washed or not,' Canning said. 'He's not at the clean stage yet. I'm more concerned with his maths. I think he's strooggling towards the light now, but strooggle it is.' He was coaching the boy for an hour on Saturdays.

'Petey's a pet lamb!' Grace cried. 'And our pride and joy. I only wish he'd play football as if he were on the field at all. I don't think he knows where he is.'

'Damn compulsory games,' said Stephen. 'What good does it do Peter's morale or health to make him pretend to do something that bores him stiff? Far better send him off for a good long walk.'

The Massingers descended and protested. They were great games players, believing in games more than in God. When they talked of 'team-spirit' they managed to sound peculiarly out of date. Rupert was still hoping good reason would be found for beating Peter Quillan, just to show him that he didn't own the earth.

The party finally dribbled away to gossip in corners. Outside the moon was huge, competing with the lamplight. Younger members of the staff, who had lively appetites, were eating leftovers brought from the supper table.

'Bed now, darling,' Grace said fondly. 'It's all over, do you realize that? They've all gone. And you did splendidly.'

Chapter Seven

The Annicks were having a very happy time. In the morning, Stephen began rehearsals of the school play, in which, though they took no part, Cyril and Grace were deeply interested.

In the afternoon they were interviewed by a Japanese who, on behalf of a literary monthly, wished to make a study of the English preparatory school. He arrived with a bulging black bag, like the traditional bag of the doctor who carries a newborn infant: in this one, however, there was a tape-recorder and two superlative cameras. The Annicks were photographed everywhere, beaming outside School House, before the cricket pavilion, by the swimming-pool: for the last shot, they summoned the lower form who trooped out in glory to pose and nudge and giggle.

A halcyon day for Downs Park, in fact. November remained moderately sunny. There was a peppery smell in the air of damp earth, of dying flowers and of flowers to come when winter had passed. Canning's car, fully assembled, stood workmanlike in the drive: he proposed to give some of the older boys driving lessons within the confines of the estate. He continued to be a 'live wire', as the Massingers (who hated him) put it. In the previous week he had given a talk to the senior boys on DNA, pointing out to them the finite dangers: if once we became able to *make life*, what sort of life should we choose to make? He had also, as a side issue, thrown in the information that the three-legged milking stool was an object infinitely more stable than anything which stood on four legs: thus raising the intelligent query as to why any artifact was made with four legs at all.

A halcyon day. After lunch, Cyril and Grace walked down to

the sea and watched it trembling in over the little bay. They dreamed of summer.

But at ten to six, when Annick was in the library supervising the news bulletins, the blow fell.

Blossom Massinger, knowing she would find Grace alone, burst in upon her, weeping.

Now Blossom knew very well all about the episode of Helen and the books, since she always read the books herself and had been told by Rupert about the incident in the light of a funny story. But the discovery that he was sporadically sleeping with Helen (she had actually caught them together that morning) had stunned her. She had been aware for a long time that she was not adequately satisfying her husband's needs, no matter how conscientiously she moaned and bucked and made noises of ecstasy: but it was beyond her comprehension that he should have taken, as it were, a concubine.

'Oh Grace, you've got to get rid of her!'

Grace said feebly, 'Bloss, it can't be serious. And she is such a good secretary.'

'In my house. *On my sofa.*'

'I suppose it would have to be somewhere.'

'Don't laugh at me! Don't dare!'

'But I wasn't laughing! How could I be? Only Helen – well, *Helen.*' She went on to explain that she was sure Rupert would not run away with Helen Queen, or do anything absurd of that order. 'If I were you, I'd try to rise above it.'

It seemed very odd to see Blossom in tears, such a fine games-mistress of a girl, her peach-like cheeks streaked with salt, her curly red hair in a mess.

'Everyone will know, everyone!'

Grace explained reasonably that this was up to Blossom: she herself would never have known, or have guessed, had she not been told. Now if she were to get Helen sacked, this would of course mean telling Cyril: another person in the know. And the mere fact of the sacking would start a ferment of gossip. 'So it is far better, as I said, to rise above it. Rups will soon get very tired of her. It must be,' she added earnestly, 'only a physical thing. Don't you think it would be very much for the better if you and I both kept quiet?'

'I won't have her up at the cottage! It's degrading to Pauline.'

'Pauline?' For a moment Grace was vague. 'Oh, yes, the baby. No, dear, I don't think it can affect Pauline at all. But you might arrange with Rups that he does his dictation in the school office in future. That would be perfectly reasonable.'

'Don't call him Rups.'

'Why ever not?'

'He doesn't deserve it!' Blossom exclaimed, on a kind of scream.

Grace told her to run along, unless she wanted Annick to find her there. The ten minutes' discussion, always held after the news bulletin, must be nearly over. So Blossom went.

Of course, when her husband came in, Grace told him all about it: they told each other everything. Since they had ceased to have intercourse some years ago, they felt in the comfortable position of those who, from the shore, watch the poor swimmers strugglng in the raging waters. 'We can't sack her,' Annick said, 'she's damned good at her job and Rups will soon get tired of her. But use the school office – yes.'

'I think I'd better talk to her all the same,' Grace said thoughtfully: and after supper, when the staff who lived out had dispersed to their homes, she took the car and drove to the next village, where Helen Queen had her lodgings. She did not beat about the bush.

'My dear, I have had a visitation from Mrs Massinger.'

The girl stared at her, but said nothing. There was a little pinkness in her cheeks but it was not a blush: it was something she had quite recently acquired, it seemed in permanency.

'You will see that this can't go on.'

'So you're giving me my notice.' Helen's tone was different from her old, mumbling one. It was almost impudent, though not quite.

'Indeed I am not. The headmaster and I depend on you. But you must not go to the cottage, and you must discourage Mr Massinger. At once.'

The girl got up. She began pacing up and down the carpet, not

Helen on the walls more fair – at least, by contrast with her normal appearance. Her back stiff as a cat's, she held her head high.

'I think that's between Mr Massinger and me.'

'Don't be opaque, dear. Who else should it be between?'

'I don't care if the whole school knows.'

'Well, if that should happen, we *shall* have to give you the sack. So don't let it.'

'I don't want to go back to Norfolk.'

Grace brushed this away. There were many other schools very far from Norfolk, and Helen's references would, naturally, be excellent. 'And now, suppose you sit down? I can't talk to anyone who is on the prowl.'

Sulkily, Helen sat.

'Now do understand, I don't want to make this into what Stephen would call a "production". There are to be no crises. I take it Mr Massinger is not in love with you?'

'I don't really know why you should take it, Mrs Annick, but no, he isn't.'

'Helen, please don't talk to me in a tiresome voice. You are not being scolded. We are simply discussing what can be done. You will have to talk to Rupert, of course, because he must understand why the cottage is out of bounds to you. And he will have to know that his wife has come to me. But there the whole thing can rest.'

'You make it seem easy.'

'That's what I want to do. It won't be, quite, of course.' Grace spoke affectionately now: she was always sorry for people in emotional muddles.

Helen muttered something grudging about making coffee: Grace said that would be very nice. She watched while the girl pottered round the kitchenette.

'Wouldn't you be happier not living alone? There must be some young woman somewhere who would like to share with you.'

'I'm not a sharer, I'm afraid.'

The place did not look as if she were, being of a neatness that was almost dismaying. Everything was dainty, clean and precisely in its place, ornaments arranged with a Poirot-like symmetry along the mantelpiece. Grace could imagine ructions were anything displaced by strange hands.

'You look so lonely. So does Betty Cope. And poor Mrs Murray.'

'Well, I couldn't live with either of them.'

'Would you care to move into School House? The big bed-sitting-room just behind the lower dormitory is going to be free soon, and you could make it look delightful. Save you the trouble of a journey, too.'

'It would suit Mrs Murray better.' Helen smiled faintly, which was at least a reassurance. 'As you see, I'm rather given to putting down roots.'

'It might suit Mrs Murray, at that.' Grace was thoughtful. 'Yes, I could always suggest it.'

The coffee was on the table, coffee excellently made. They drank it for a few minutes in silence.

Then Helen looked up, and this time she did flush, darkly. 'Mrs Annick, I'm afraid I'm being a bit of a pig, when you're so kind. I don't think anyone could be kinder. But I've had a shock – do you understand?'

Grace said she understood very well: and being relieved by the turn things were taking, again permitted herself a little sternness. It certainly must have been a shock to be caught *in flagrante delicto*, especially as this could only have been the outcome of sheer brute carelessness.

'You can't stop Rupert when he gets carried away,' Helen said, simply.

'What I do to keep this school together!' said Grace to her husband, as they lay embraced in the companionable dark.

'If Rupert ever gets it, which God forbid, it will become quite a different place. And, no doubt, a financial success. But he'll do that over my dead body.'

'Oh dear,' said Grace, 'it does seem that once one is over fifty, one thinks a lot about death. Also, it seems far too early to do so.'

'None of us likes to be taken by surprise, so we advance upon a very long period of preparation. Even so, it is by surprise that we shall be taken.'

'I want to go first,' Grace said firmly.

'That would be very selfish of you. In any case you are far too fit.'

They lay silent, smelling the far scent of the sea.

'I want to sleep now,' said Annick, 'I am very, very sleepy.'

Chapter Eight

The school train had gone. The Annicks had seen it off. Leo Canning had travelled up to Victoria with the boys to make sure they didn't fall out of the windows, and the last car fetching a son home to counties not so far away had disappeared from the drive.

The Annicks returned with sighs of relief to School House, instinctively almost on tiptoe, since the silence seemed so profound. The Massingers had gone away for Christmas to relations in the North, Stephen Smith was going off to Grindelwald on Christmas morning so was the only living-in member of the staff still remaining. The last report had been written and was ready for dispatch by Helen.

The business of Helen and Rupert seemed to have settled itself: so far as Grace could tell, they saw little of each other, though what they did furtively she could not. She suspected that the whole affair had cooled off. Blossom no longer went about with reddened eyelids but wore a faintly triumphant, even a Napoleonic, air. Only Helen had changed and was full of a new confidence which the Annicks did not altogether regret. She, too, was going away for the holidays, was off to France with some friend unnamed. Betty Cope had been called for in a car by a square-jawed young woman in canary sweater and corduroy slacks.

Before Helen said goodbye, she presented the accounts with her usual air of disapprobation.

'Come, come, we're not ruined yet.'

'It's none of my business, Mr Annick. But we're still spending far too much, and if Mrs Terry does leave, as she's always threatening she will, we shall have to pay far more for a replacement.'

'But board and lodging and all found—' Grace began.

'The new ones want more than that, if they're going to cook for hordes. They'll probably want extra help.'

'Then we must go on soft-soaping Mrs Terry.'

'Anyway,' Annick said, 'since we became a charity we can pretty well dodge selective employment tax.'

'We could put the fees up,' Helen said sharply.

This, however, he was always reluctant to do. He felt, humbly, that unless he could offer more in the way of academic success (there had been no scholarships that year) he had no right to ask for more money. Next year could be better: Fairclough was safe enough and Davidson might get something. So might Devlin, with a hard push.

When Helen had gone, he said to his wife, 'Peace, perfect peace.'

'For the first few days I always rather miss the row and the rushes and the stompings and all the infant scandals.'

'Talking of infants, Petey will have to move up again next term. It's too easy for him in the Remove and he's getting bored. His mother told me as much, and I couldn't dispute it, much as I should have liked to.'

Stephen came in for a drink on Christmas Eve: this was the sole celebration the Annicks, who were not Christmas-minded, proposed to have. He sat happily on the rug before a fire of logs, nursing his glass. 'I hope I get off all right tomorrow. The idea was that the planes wouldn't be so full.'

One or two holly-berries, shrivelled by the heat, dropped into the hearth, bounced and rolled.

'I wonder what new crazes we'll have next term?' said Annick.

'I'll tell you one coming up, sir. Carpentry. Leo Canning told them quite idly the other day that the most stable of objects for seating purposes was a three-legged milking stool, and that three legs were invariably steadier than four. So Petey Quillan intelligently asked him why all chairs and tables weren't made with three legs and the idea caught on. They think they're going to make a break-through in the furniture line, but God knows where they'll get the wood from.'

Annick said, for him resolutely, that if this was going to be an expensive craze it would have to be stamped on. Spider-collecting had been repulsive but cheap. So had making crystals.

'The play was good,' said Stephen. 'Thank you, I'd like another scotch. Betty looked ravishing when she drew the curtain and you saw the picture.'

'Even Maitland would look ravishing,' said Grace, referring to a conspicuously ugly boy, 'given a build-up like that. Fairclough wasn't too bad and Devlin was really splendid.'

'Quiet, isn't it?'

'That's because you're new to prep schools, Stephen.' Annick smiled at him. 'You notice the sudden hush.'

'Well, don't you?'

'Of course we do,' said Grace. 'It never fails to impress. I can't help but feel that the whole place is full really, but of ghost boys, all hiding away from us. When I go along the corridors I fancy I can hear them breathing.'

Stephen, emboldened by the whisky, by the sudden reality of Christmas and by his own success with the school magazine, in which Quillan's sonnet had been a star item, said to them, 'Will you miss it all awfully one day? When you retire. Though I hope you never will.'

'Who's been talking about our retirement?' Grace spoke sharply, but he did not notice. 'Mr Massinger?'

For a moment Stephen had the delicious belief that he was to be taken into confidence.

'It was only general speculation.'

'Then Mr Massinger,' said Grace, revealing an antipathy Stephen had never suspected to exist, 'may desist from speculation. We're good for some years yet. And we love the school.'

There was a long silence. No confidences were to be forthcoming.

'Mrs Murray will be moving into School House next term,' Annick said at last, 'it ought to be less bleak for her.'

'She has a hell of a time with those brats. Why do French teachers always get it in the neck?'

'It's an ancient tradition. The French are supposed as a nation to he incapable of keeping discipline, and the supposition brushes off on our own nationals who happen to teach the language.'

Stephen asked what about Napoleon, and another silence fell.

To break it Grace said, 'You're pensive, Steve. Penny for them.'

He looked up, his ventriloquist's dummy face bright. 'I've got a new girl-friend. I was wondering about love.'

'What about love?'

'Well, does it really exist—'

'Certainly.'

'Or is it just another word for sex? I can't see myself being tied down for ever, though I have thought about it. That is, it wouldn't be possible yet, but one thinks ahead.'

'You aren't in love, Stephen.'

'Aren't I? Why?'

'Being in love is thinking all the time about the other person. You're only thinking about you.'

'All one sees around one is marriages in ruins.'

'If you only look at the entertainment gossip in the papers, it's true. But you might look at us.'

He did look and, as was common to his age, wondered. They seemed so old to him. Their marriage had lasted, certainly, but did they ever get any excitement out of each other? Listen for each other's key in the door? (Stephen was not so far from love as Grace thought him.) He could not ask.

'The point is,' said Annick shrewdly, 'that we *are* dinosaurs. Fifty-six and fifty respectively. If we were only in our thirties we could hardly hope to settle your doubts, because we might then, for all you know, be heading for the divorce courts. But now we are not.'

'I suppose a shared interest—'

'Right. Your young woman. What interests has she got?'

'Oh, much the same as mine. Reads. Likes music. Not pop, though. She's stuffy about that. Can you take pop, sir?'

'One has to in this school, doesn't one?'

'But can you?' Stephen persisted.

'I think,' said Annick, 'that you want to know too much. Do

you expect me to go in for such self-exposure as to admit that I think nearly all of it is a mere adenoidal noise, thoroughly damaging to the use of the English language? I could never hold up my head again among the boys. Have one for the road.'

Stephen accepted, took the hint and drank quickly. He thanked them for the evening.

'Thank you, Steve,' said Grace. 'We might have had a dull Christmas Eve without you.'

They did not have a dull Christmas, since they had many friends in the county and were welcomed everywhere. The only invitations they had not accepted were for dinner on Christmas Day, for both disliked forced festivity.

One year changed into another, into a new, frosty January with rime on the twigs and a sharp, neutral-coloured sky. Slowly, the staff began to reassemble. Then, in a rush, the boys.

Chapter Nine

And yet another year: spring. The Thicket was in full bud: there were violets under the damp brown leaves. All along the drive primulas bloomed, and the lower field was edged with daffodils. Peter Quillan, aged eleven, was in the top form: there was nowhere else to put him. Fairclough had contributed his mite to the Honours Board and two others were expected to do well in the summer. Whether or not it was because of the early warmth, Annick did not know: but he felt tired.

One day in break, in the densest part of the Thicket, Massinger caught Searle blissfully pleasuring himself to the sound of birdsong. Infuriated, he caught him by the ear and led him into the open, where, of course, a small and interested crowd gathered rapidly. 'I'm taking you to the headmaster.'

His grip on the ear was not hard until Searle, in a tearful panic, tried to pull away. Then the grip increased.

'For God's sake, Rupert,' said Canning, coming up at a run, 'drop him!'

'Mind your own business. You don't know what he's done.'

'I can make a good guess.'

'He's going to the head.'

'He'll go quietly. Drop him.'

This was a delight to the watching boys, and more so as Massinger's temper snapped completely. 'Get out of my way, you interfering lout!'

Canning prised the fingers loose from Searle's ear. The boy stood stock still, rubbing it piteously.

'Stop that! You're not hurt.'

'Don't you touch him again, you bleeder.'

'And I'm reporting you to Annick as well!'

'Report till you're blue in the face. Go on, take the victim into custody, but let him go under his own steam!'

Massinger shouted to the boys – 'What do you think you're doing? Go away, the lot of you.'

Disappointed, they went into slow retreat, though they knew they must have seen most of the fun. It was a shame, though, Mulliner said to Perkins, because the head would have to sack Canning, and they'd be losing a good man. 'Did you hear him on Gagarin? I felt I was *there*!'

Canning, not at all put out, strolled on in the direction of the sea. In his pocket was a letter from Gordon Corso offering him a job at £2,000 a year in his own electrical firm. He had not intended to accept the offer, however handsome by Downs Park standards, because he liked teaching: but it was good to have a bird in the hand if others were to fly out of the bush.

Annick was in his study. 'You wait outside, you dirty little beast,' said Massinger, 'and don't you dare budge an inch.' He knocked and went in.

'What is it, Rupert?' Annick raised his head from a half-cold cup of coffee which he had been stirring but not drinking.

'It's young Searle and he needs beating. I caught him playing with himself in the Thicket. Precocious little ape.'

'It was foolish of him to let himself get caught. But I'm not going to beat for masturbation. I'd have nearly all the upper form waiting in line. You'd better send him in to me. I'll see him by himself.'

'Look here, Headmaster, if I had my way I'd chop that damned Thicket down. Too much goes on there.'

'It's not precisely a zenana. Let me have Searle, will you? I don't want him wetting himself with fright, poor little blighter.'

'Then can I speak to you when you've finished with him? I've got another complaint to make. About Canning.'

'Canning?'

'He tried to interfere with me and abused me in front of the boys. You can't keep him on.'

Annick said, 'Rupert. For the moment, just let me have Searle.'

Massinger flung the door open. 'You can come in.' As the boy sidled into the room, he waited. It was, after all, his capture.

'I'll see you later, Mr Massinger.'

What Annick said to Searle Rupert was never to know, but there was no beating. Searle came out at last, tear-stained but calm, and rushed by as quickly as he could.

'Damned wet week,' Rupert thought. He knocked and re-entered. At that moment the bell rang for classes.

'Look,' said Annick, 'neither of us has time for this now. Come and see me at five.'

'What did you do to Searle?'

'That is not your business. I have punished him. For getting caught.' Hostility, open, blew up between them like a dust-storm.

'Five, then,' Rupert said, pulling himself together with some difficulty. He banged out, and gave the lower form a horrible time for three-quarters of an hour. When an angry man is kept waiting, his anger either cools or burns brighter. Rupert's burned. He could hardly bear to sit through the afternoon, geography with the Remove, maths with Three A. There were boys in the latter class who had witnessed the scene between him and Canning, and on them he came down ferociously. The tendency to snigger within desk lids turned to a tendency to feel the fluttering butterflies in their stomachs. And to make it worse, the bright day suddenly faded and the rain came in a straight, hard patter.

At five he was back in Annick's room. By this time he was almost incoherent with fury.

'If you think it's right that I should be abused in public by a junior master—'

'No, no, I don't think it's right at all.' Annick had heard Rupert's version of the affair, or rather, had managed to piece together an account out of enraged fragments. 'But I shall have to hear Canning's side of it. If you were, in fact, using physical force on Searle—'

'Of course I wasn't! I just took hold of him more or less in play—'

'You didn't sound playful about his offence when you brought him in.'

'And I damned well wasn't feeling playful by that time!'

'Quiet. They can hear you all over the school. Have a cigarette, Rupert, and try to simmer down.'

'I can imagine what Canning's story will be. Putting me in the wrong, if he bloody well thinks he can. The fact remains that he made a row before the boys, and used dirty language.'

By this time, Massinger believed he was a sorely-wronged man. He had genuinely forgotten what words he might have used to Canning, and was unable to understand why Annick didn't send for him and fire him at once.

'You'll have to give him his notice, Headmaster.' That he was so formal showed the depth of his sincerity.

'I won't do it. What do you suggest I do with him? I can't give Canning the slipper, exactly.'

'He's got to apologize to me!'

'Well, well, he's easy-going. I expect he'd agree to that.'

Canning, summoned after the News, had almost total recall. He gave Annick a meticulous and perfectly truthful word by word account of the incident. 'I'm sorry, Headmaster, I oughtn't to have stoock my long nose in it. I don't suppose he was really hurting Searle, but it made me see red. I suppose he wants me to apologize.'

'That's the least Mr Massinger will accept.'

Canning sat bright-eyed and acquiescent. 'And I suppose he'd like it to be in front of somebody? Company parade.'

'Of me, I expect.'

'He'd have it in front of the whole school, if he got the chance.'

'I think the whole school has been sufficiently disturbed already.'

'Honestly, Head, I am sorry so far as you're concerned. I oughtn't to have called him a bleeder.'

'No, you ought not.'

'When does he want the execution? I'll have to find a proper form of words – isn't that what they say?'

'Now look, Leo,' Annick said gravely, 'I'm not sure I oughtn't to have sacked you for this. Mr Massinger was of that opinion. I won't do so because, frankly, you're too valuable to our science side.'

Good, Canning thought: and decided to reject Corso's offer for the time being. In the end, of course, he would raise it and that might be quite another matter.

'But it does seem to me that you are taking this rather flippantly.'

'Well, where did he think he was? Dotheboys Hall?'

'Leo!

'Sorry. Christ, this is my sorry day, isn't it?'

'I think we'd better have this unpleasant business over and done with.' Annick went to the door and called to a small boy passing by. 'Riddell, would you be so kind as to present my compliments to Mr Massinger and ask him whether he would spare me a few minutes of his time? You'll find him in the gym.'

Canning lit a cigarette, immediately stubbed it out. 'Must show proper penitence.' But the diamond eyes were sparkling. 'Holy, holy, holy!'

Annick, trying by this time not to laugh, told him he would prefer him to look more penitent, and the eyes were promptly veiled.

Massinger came in, and stood to a sort of attention.

'Yes, Headmaster.'

'Mr Canning has something to say to you.'

There was a second's pause. Then – 'Oh yes, so I had!' His attention had been distracted by a butterfly stuck hard against the window pane. 'So I had. Mr Massinger, I wish to offer you my apology' – very stately – 'for my behaviour this morning. I realize it wasn't in the best interests of the school.'

'And insulting to me.'

'Agreed. I hope you'll agree to overlook it and we can go on as we were before. *Just* as before.'

Since they had never got on well before, this was ambiguous, and Rupert knew it: but decided to let it go. He knew he was helpless before Annick's determination to keep the oaf at all costs.

'And if that isn't a handsome apology,' Canning went on, before Rupert could get a word in, 'you must put it down to the fact that

I'm not very good at expressing myself, not in this way, anyhow. Let bygones be bygones,' he continued. He was unstoppable. 'Actually, I'm all for bygones. Nothing one ever did the day before yesterday seems all that good, does it? So Mr Massinger's a good boy and I'm a bad one – agreed?'

'Look here, I'm about fed up with—'

'No, no, I'm not being flippant at all. So far as I'm concerned – all over. Party's over. Curtains.'

Annick had been so amused by the whole of Canning's extraordinary speech that for a second, he was afraid he would be unable to keep a straight face. But he said, in the spirit of the occasion, 'Gentlemen, I hope you'll make an end and say nothing more about it, either between ourselves or to others.'

'Your apology is accepted,' Rupert barked out, and went redder than ever. He turned and left the room, Canning, now looking like a bad actor asked to register humility, at his heels.

When they were gone, Annick poured himself a stiff drink which he hoped would not smell by the time he took prayers. He had a small but conscious impression of tension in his stomach these days. For this, scotch was the only palliative.

Rupert went home, angry and dissatisfied. 'Well,' Blossom cried, 'did the beast apologize properly?'

'He did in a loutish way. But he ought to have been fired. Our Cyril gets wetter and wetter as time goes on. What does he think thus is, a school or an old people's home? You wait, if ever I get my hands on it!'

He could only think of one thing to do, to soothe himself.

'But I won't wait till I get my hands on you!'

Following the pattern of their love play, she feigned an attempt to escape, allowed herself to be brought down in something uncomfortably like a rugby tackle, and then let him march her off to the bedroom, where she simulated a pleasure bordering upon the hysterical. She, at least, was at peace these days, now he had so completely dropped that blob of a Helen Queen. She would have to do duty for the two of them.

Annick, that night, did not sleep much. Any disturbance in the school frightened him, making him fear it would suddenly slip beyond his grasp. His commonsense told him that this was silly, that it was as trusted as ever by the parents and as agreeable as any school could manage to be, to the boys: but still he feared. When Grace was lightly snoring, he got up, took his cigarettes and went into the study where he opened his window wide upon the sea-filled night. The rain had ceased, thousands of stars were out. Lights still shone from the Massingers' window on to their lawn. A nightingale began to sing, from somewhere in the direction of the Thicket. He loved it all. He feared for the least threat to it.

Chapter Ten

It was only a fortnight later that a further threat came to his peace of mind, in the shape of a fluttering visit from Mrs Quillan.

'You see, Brian's had this marvellous offer of a semester at Berkeley – he's an academic lawyer, so it would be quite his thing – and he absolutely refuses to go without me. After all, we can't bear to be parted for all that time, it's so dull not having each other to talk to, and naturally we can't leave Peter. So it would mean taking him off your hands for six months, if you wouldn't mind having him back again. California would be the most wonderful experience for him, too.'

She shook her too long hair out of her eyes and smiled radiantly, her cheeks fattening as she did so.

Annick felt the chill down to the soles of his feet. He threw a quick glance at Grace, who was sitting rigidly: she had caught his panic.

'But Mrs Quillan, where will you educate Peter in California? He can't go to one of their state schools, because he'll get no Latin or Greek—'

'Oh, that's all right. I can keep him up to form in that myself.'

'And what about his mathematics? They'll make him work with his age group, no matter how able he is, and at present he's with boys of twelve and thirteen.'

'I'm sure we can cope with that somehow. You see, even if he wasn't thrilled to death already, there's nowhere we can leave him. There are aunts of course, but he really can't bear any of them, and then, it's a question of holidays.' She wrung plump hands and looked piteous.

Annick told her, in a voice as even as he could muster, that he intended to prepare Peter to sit for the Eton scholarship examination in the following year, which would he impossible if he were to lose six months at this time. The Honours Board, light oak, glistening with burnished letters, swam in his mind's eye. He hallucinated Peter's name on it. 'P. Quillan, K.S., Eton.' King's Scholar.

'Oh, I do see your point,' Mrs Quillan said diffidently, 'but you do understand that we've got no alternative? Besides, now Peter's bronchitis has cleared up, that marvellous climate would keep it cleared up, if you know what I mean. There are so many advantages.'

Grace leaned forward. 'Mrs Quillan, let us have Petey.'

'But coming out to us in the holidays, all by himself—'

'No, I meant, let him stay on here. We'd give him as good a time as we could. We'd take him to Greece with us.'

The mother said this was very kind, but that Peter would never – she was given to girlish slang – 'wear it'. Greece might be a temptation, of course – what a wonderful offer! – but there were all the other considerations, and he would break his heart if anything spoiled the trip for him now. 'Brian did suggest something of the sort, I mean, basing himself on the aunts, but—'

The first chink in the armour?

'Will you let me talk to Peter?' Annick said.

The silly look on Mrs Quillan's face was replaced by something different, and sharper. She loosened her hands.

'I couldn't do that without Brian's say-so, and he'd never give it. Besides, I should miss Peter frightfully.'

'If you persuaded your husband that this really would be a blow to his academic chances?'

The idea of the boy slipping away from all his hopes now, had Annick suffering alternate waves of heat and cold.

'I ll tell him what you say, of course. But do bear in mind, Peter's over the moon already.'

'We've seen no signs of it,' Grace said, 'not a word to us or even to Mr Canning. And think how he will miss his science! We really do teach it, you know, unlike most other schools, and Petey's getting up a tremendous interest.'

Mrs Quillan observed that her son was naturally poker-faced and kept his delights, as most of his sorrows, to himself.

'Please talk to your husband,' Grace persisted.

Then tea was brought in – it reminded Annick of Mrs Quillan's first momentous visit – and the parent ate as heartily as any of the boys would have done. She left for half an hour's walk in the playing-fields with her son, but sent him back to his friends before she came to say goodbye to the Annicks. 'Please don't say anything to him before you hear from me.'

A concession, no matter how frail?

Annick was so worried that he was not even perturbed by the news that his daughter's business had failed. Penelope arrived the day after Mrs Quillan had brought the news of California, asking if she could be put up for a while, till she had sorted out her affairs and found something else to do.

'I'll earn my keep, dears. I'll help Helen teach the piano.'

This had recently been added to Helen's duties. She loved it because it brought her more in touch with the boys, whom she believed she 'understood'. She was an amateur psychologist of a potentially dangerous nature.

'I do think, Penny,' Grace said, with a hint of a grumble, 'that you might have warned us that this was likely to happen. We thought everything was going swimmingly.'

'I didn't want to worry you till it was all perfectly obvious.'

'And darling, we can't put you up because Mrs Murray's moved in. They haven't let her old room at Chalkwood, so I suppose—'

'Well, I could drive back and forth. I suppose I couldn't have the Massingers' spare? No,' she answered herself, 'I couldn't. Not with old Ruddy licking his chops at me. It would annoy Blossom.'

'Of course you can't do that. Look, darling, I hate to keep you on the run, but you really ought to dash over to Chalkwood before supper and see if you can get fixed up.'

'If I can't immediately, I suppose I could spend the night on the sofa.'

All at once she began to cry, and they stared at her in amazement. They had no conception of the weeks of strain which had preceded the abandonment of her business, an additional strain on top of the unhappiness she had suffered since her husband died. Grace gingerly put her arms around her and Penelope allowed herself the unusual luxury of weeping on her mother's shoulder.

'Oh, darling! Don't cry.'

'Take no notice of me. It's just that everything has piled up all at once. Give me a drink and I'll go over to Chalkwood right away.'

'There, there, it's going to be all right, it may be all for the best. You're here with us now. What did you do with your own flat?'

'Gave it over to Timmy.' (Her one-time partner.) 'He wanted somewhere to go and I only wanted to get away. We've had an offer for the business, but of course we're going to sell at a howling loss. Oh Lord, how it will howl!'

The smell of stew, a whitish smell, permeated the house.

'Let me dry my eyes and clear off. If I'm late for food, tell Mrs Terry to put a plate in the oven.'

She was just leaving when she met Leo Canning in the hall.

'Hullo, Mrs Saxton! Quite a stranger.'

'I'm to be a fixture. For some time, anyway. I've gone bust.'

He looked at her in his careful, almost diagnostic fashion.

'Bust?'

'I said bust. I'll tell you about it some time. There's no room for me here except on the sofa, so I'm tearing off to fix up something at Mrs Murray's old place.'

'You looked fagged. I'll drive you over.'

Suddenly she felt as if she were indeed exhausted, as if she could barely bring herself to move. 'Would you?'

'Sure. Be a pleasure.'

As she sat beside him in the open car, her black hair blowing, he took a secret glance at her. He had always found her attractive, but never so much as now, when her nerve seemed to have given way. Hitherto, there had always been something rather minatory about Penelope.

She made her arrangements in Chalkwood without difficulty: she would move in next day.

As they drove back to the school he tried to distract her. 'Did you know we've got a crisis on our hands? Your mum and dad don't know that I know. The Quillans are trying to snatch our white hope and bear him off to California for six bloody months. He told me.'

'Oh God! That will about break daddy up. How does the boy feel?'

'Isn't it hard to tell? He simply gave one the facts and implied that I wasn't to leak them. Now I have leaked them. I thought that what you wanted was another worry to take a load off the others. Especially as it's not your own worry.'

The journey was short. They went into the school, where the smell of stew had noticeably thickened and deteriorated.

'If it's what Mrs Terry calls Blanket de Veau,' said Penelope, 'I shall be sick.'

'Then you're sure-fire due to be sick, Mrs Saxton.' Canning's idiom was drawn from many sources. 'Look here, would you care to retreat? I'm sure nobody would care if we excused ourselves and went to the pub for a sandwich. You don't want to have to chatter to everyone tonight. Or would your mum and dad take offence?'

She hesitated. Then she said, 'It sounds attractive. You wait here while I explain us both away.'

Grace was astounded. 'You're going to the pub? With Leo?'

'It was his idea.'

'Mrs Terry won't like it—'

'Damn Mrs Terry. She must learn to endure disappointment. All the more for the top form.'

The top form had the doubtful privilege of staying up to staff supper.

Penelope Saxton had known Canning on and off for a year or so, but had not taken much notice of him. Now, however, in this small but tearful crisis of her life, she felt an intimacy between them. Though she disliked being impressed by anyone or anything, she could not help being so this time. His perception of her distress and her need, and his instant offer to help, even by suggesting something unusual that they might do together, had been peculiarly rapid in action and in timing.

They sat in the small bar-parlour of the Golden Lion before beer and sandwiches, and he listened to the story of her troubles.

'Well, Pen,' he said easily, deciding that the time for formality had passed, 'you have been a bit of a goop, haven't you? You must have seen this coming for months.'

'I suppose I kept on hoping. Even for one splendid solitary sale.'

'You ought to have let me look at the books – no, how could you? You didn't know me well enough.'

She smiled, not brightly, but at least it was a smile.

'Now I do, I suppose. What on earth do you know about the antique business, though?'

He hesitated, as if considering this seriously, his nose pointed, then he said, 'Nothing I couldn't learn in a fortnight's hard work. But I do know about ledgers.'

'Aren't you being a bit conceited? It would have taken you far more than a fortnight's hard work.'

'Not when I look at all the mugs in that particular game. Queers, most of them.'

She told him there was no reason why queers should not be clever.

'Not in the way I am,' he replied cheerfully.

Something of pleasure was creeping into her full consciousness – an emotion she would never have expected to feel when she shut the shop that morning. She thanked him for taking her out.

'Must rescue damsels in distress. And rescue mum and dad if I can: I have to get subtly to work on Petey. No frontal assault. Just words in his ear. He must be a bit disturbed, now I come to think of it, because he jumped Bailey behind the gym this morning and he hasn't done that for ages.'

Penelope slept well that night, even on the sofa.

Next week Annick received a letter from Mrs Quillan.

'Brian says you may talk to Peter if you think it will do any good, but we must warn you that it won't. He's dreaming about the whole thing already, and it would break his heart if he didn't go. Brian and I take the point about interrupting his education, which is the only reason we can see for you saying anything to him at all. I might say that it would break *my* heart if he didn't go. But you and your wife have both been inordinately kind.'

'Petey, have you a games period right now?'

'Yes, sir.'

'If I get Mrs Massinger to let you off, would you like to walk down to the sea?'

'Oh, it's about California.'

They went past the Thicket, down the slope of gorse and on to the path which became increasingly sandy as it tended towards the coarse grasses and fleshy, aqueous seaplants on the edge of the bay. They had spoken little: Annick, taken aback by the boy's immediate response, thought he had better let things run their own course. As they walked slowly along the beach, he noted the deep track of his own limp. It was a beautiful day, the sea almost Mediterranean blue where the shallows did not stripe it with jade and yellow-gold.

He said at last, 'Your parents gave me leave to talk to you.'

'Yes, sir.'

'Of course it would be a wonderful experience for you.'

Peter's poker-face was much in evidence.

'Listen, I can't beat about the bush. Would you consider staying with Grace and me?' It was not by accident that he had used his wife's Christian name, as to an adult. 'We'd do something about holidays. You could come to Greece with us, or Italy, or wherever you chose.'

The gulls billowed overhead, sunlight sweeping their wings.

Peter said nothing.

'I'd like you to stay behind for your own sake – yes, and for mine. You're the only real scholar we've had in years. I think you can do as you please eventually where your career's concerned. But the loss of six months at this particular stage is going to hamper you.'

The boy bent and picked up a chalky yellow shell, which he admired in the palm of his hand.

'Yes, sir.'

'For Pete's sake, Petey,' said Annick, exasperated, 'can't you be a little more communicative?'

'I can see what you mean, sir.'

'Would it be a frightful blow if you didn't go with your parents? It's entirely up to you, of course.'

'Yes, of course it is. Up to me, I mean.' The narrow lips had tightened.

'I wouldn't even try to persuade you if I hadn't had permission to try.'

'Never mind that, sir. Mr Canning's been doing some persuading already.'

'You mean, he knew?'

'Nobody else did. I told him. I do want to see the Golden Gate.'

They came to a cropping of rocks. The boy eyed them longingly.

'All right, Petey, climb on them. And don't get drenched.'

Taking off shoes and socks, Peter made his way painfully over the sharp ridges under the glistening brown seaweed. He poked about in a pool, lifted the weed, cried out in triumph as he retrieved a little green crab. He brought it back on to the sand, and watched it burrow out of sight, its fragile pincers the last things to disappear.

'I don't really know, sir.'

'It would be a sacrifice on your part. For your own future. I know, too, how much it would mean to your parents if you stayed behind. But we'd look after you. And though we're getting on the ancient side, I daresay we could give you quite a pleasant time.'

'Monterey, too. I do want to see that.'

'Why Monterey?'

'I don't know. It sounds nice.'

'Petey, I want to enter you for an Eton scholarship next year.'

'I don't suppose I'd fall much behind. My mother knows Latin and Greek, she's jolly good. Mr Canning thinks my maths would suffer, but I expect I could pick up.'

'Would it be very awful, staying with us? That is, if your parents finally agreed?'

The gulls swung up. The little waves rippled in, a milky line across the demerara sugar of the sand. Peter dug for his crab and failed to find it. 'Excuse me, sir.'

He returned to the rocks, over which he teetered gingerly, stopping to poke and to peer. Against the sun, the tenderness of his years blotted by shadow, he looked uncomfortably like a young man. Annick sat down, cross-legged. It was a peaceful scene: only his heart was beating. Yes, it would be awful for the boy, staying behind with ageing people, missing the Golden Gate by sunset, missing the reality of Monterey. Well, it would have to be faced: this talk they were having was doing not the slightest good.

Peter seemed to have forgotten all else but pleasure in the sea. He had left the rocks now and was paddling in surf, running back on his heels as the waves came in. At last he sat down, just beyond reach of the water, dried his feet with his handkerchief and replaced the shoes and socks which he had been swinging in his hand. He returned to Annick, his shadow long, and after a moment sat down beside him.

'It's very kind of you, sir.'

'I wish I didn't suspect that it was damned selfishness on my part.'

'Actually, I don't mind staying. I didn't want to go to California all that much.'

Annick could hardly believe his ears. His heart rate had accelerated so greatly that it made him feel deaf. 'You didn't?'

'Well, there are various things. I'll miss them. But it was really because the parents wanted it.'

Perversely, Annick began to feel that this boy was a cold fish. Would he really not care whether he were separated from his mother and father for six long months?

'Anyway, I'd like Greece better.'

Annick said slowly, 'Petey, you know you've given me what I want. But I dread telling your mother. They'll suspect undue influence, I'm afraid.'

Peter's eyes flickered with a moth-like passing of amusement. 'Mr Canning's been a bit influential, sir. Not you.'

'Do remember, you can still change your mind. That is, if you're really going to be allowed to change it one way or another.'

Annick knew the holiday intimacy could not but bring about a greater closeness in their relationship: he felt, had been feeling, he now realized, during the whole of this walk together, that it had already begun.

'I'll be allowed. Though *they* won't be pleased. I shall have to write to them lots. Every week.'

'No difficulty to you.'

'Oh, I don't know. Being at school, you see, there's never anything new to say. Sir, it's about time for Mr Massinger's geog. Hadn't I better be getting back?' Now, decision taken, he was on edge to be off.

'Yes, you had. Cut along.'

'Of course, I had to make them think I did.'

'What?'

'Want to go. But I've so many things I ought to be doing. I don't know what they'll say.'

Cold fish and a simulator, as well? What sort of boy was this? A scholar. That was all which mattered for the moment. Yet Annick loved Peter, as he would have loved a son of his own. He sat for a long while looking out to sea, bemused, delighted, guilty. He ought to rush hack and tell Grace, but somehow that could wait. The sea was the texture of the crêpe-de-chine she used to wear so much when she was a girl. Its colours were paling, and the middle distance had taken upon it a silvered violet. A couple of months, and it would be warm enough for swimming. Peter. He'd got Peter. He was going to keep him.

Chapter Eleven

In an unfortunate week in the middle of July, cold, drenching and dithering with rain, the trees thrashing in passion as though they might split and fall, Betty Cope caught a cold which turned to bronchial pneumonia.

She had to be nursed: Mrs Murray, with enthusiasm, agreed to do this. She would administer the necessary antibiotics at four-hourly intervals.

'So I'd better take French,' said Penelope to her parents. 'Mine is passable, and the boys will have less of a frolicsome time with me. Far, far less.' She was a natural teacher; Annick had often been disappointed that she had never wanted to teach professionally. She could control and interest boys, and even if she could never win warmth from them – or made little attempt to win it – he felt it was as well for them to realize now something of the stringency they were likely to meet with as time went on.

Mrs Murray moved into Betty's sitting-room where there was a large and, for this purpose, over-comfortable divan. Her plan was to stay awake, ready for ministrations. It was wonderful to her, this peace, after the cordial anonymity of the school and the pressuring stares of small boys. She listened to Betty's coughing with tenderness, brought her hot drinks and cold, tried with some success to stop her sneaking a cigarette.

'You know you musn't, dear. If the doctor found out—'

'When's he coming?'

'About eleven. How do you feel?'

'Pretty horrible.'

Titania-like as ever, she lay small in her big bed, the short dark hair damp on the pillow. She was very white. Above her head was a wooden crucifix, elaborately carved.

'I wish you'd phone Gwen again. She *ought* to come. She could get off work if she wanted to. I do think she's callous.'

Mrs Murray hated the thought of Gwen and hated to telephone her. But she rang up the office in London.

'Tell Betty I'm sorry,' said the incisive voice, 'and that I'll be down at the week-end. We're right in the thick of things now and I can't be spared. I'll be with her some time on Saturday afternoon.'

'You look such a baby, lying there,' Mrs Murray said to her patient in a mooing tone, 'such a poor baby.'

'Don't be sloppy, Elspeth. And for God's sake find me something to read. Anything. I'll read *Jane Eyre* again – there's a copy on the top shelf.'

'Shall I read to you?'

'Good God, no. It's my bronchial tubes, not my eyes.' But sometimes Betty, too, would sound almost tender, and grateful.

'You're very good to me.'

'Don't you know that I love being with you? You need looking after. I shall stay for a while when you're convalescent.'

Betty said she was not, and would not be, as ill as all that. All the same, the doctor insisted that she had had a bad spell, and was not to think of returning to school for three weeks. So Mrs Murray stayed, sadly absenting herself when Gwen, in her canary sweater, banged in with expensive gifts, chocolates and grapes from Fortnum and Mason's, bottles of *Je Reviens*, scent and toilet water, books in glossy new wrappers. The only comfort she could lay to her unquiet soul was that, despite the lavishness of these offerings, Betty was obviously more attached to Gwen than Gwen to Betty. In fits of unselfishness, she almost hoped that the affection would come to mutuality: for Betty was lonely, wasn't she, and needed someone? Mrs Murray did not flatter herself that she would be indefinitely needed. Such a lovely girl and such a pity! She ought to fall in love with a fine young man and marry, and have children. Mrs Murray would be godmother.

Yet she was not in the least self-deceiving. She knew well enough that beneath her new maternal feeling for the girl was something else: and this something else scared her. It was not right, it could not be right. But she trembled when she was permitted to kiss her goodnight (which Betty did not enjoy) and to wash the narrow back and small breasts with as much modesty as she could achieve. At my time of life, Mrs Murray thought, it is preposterous. She looked at herself in the glass. How could she ever find *you* attractive? You are puffy and getting old.

Meanwhile, Penelope had the French classes, even the Remove, under complete, almost deadly control. Her own accent was not perfect and she did not pretend it was: she made the innovation of getting Norris, now in the top form, to read to each of her classes in turn: his mother was French.

With boys who refused to try, she was sharp. 'I will not have bunkum. The trouble with you is, you're all out of date. It used to be the 'with it' thing in schools to pretend you couldn't speak French. All that's changed. Ellis, the translation you sent up yesterday evening was disgusting. You'll write out *Les Deux Pigeons* for me and show it up before supper.'

'But Mrs Saxton, I won't have time. Mr Canning's got a nature ramble—'

'Mr Canning will release you. Sit up straight, all of you, and don't slack. You look very nasty, the lot of you.'

Annick was not too sure of the value of her discipline. 'Penny, you'll ruin their handwriting.'

'I must have some sort of sanctions. I can't deny them their pudding, because that would only be a relief.'

Sports Day was over, the school was breaking up for the summer holidays. Betty, on her feet again, was moping because Gwen was going to Sweden with somebody else and she herself, she said, felt too limp to make the effort to go far afield.

'Let me take you,' Mrs Murray said, on a burst of nervous energy. They were sitting over supper, which Betty had cooked.

'We'll go to Italy for a fortnight or three weeks. Or France. How would you feel about Paris?'

Betty pushed a slice of Quiche Lorraine about on her plate. You've been terribly kind. But I'm really a loner – you know that.'

Mrs Murray thought she had never heard such nonsense. Would Betty be a 'loner' if Gwen were complaisant? But she went on, trying to keep the tremor from her voice, 'You need a holiday, and you're not strong enough to go alone.'

'No, sorry.' Betty made a decision and ate up her tart at speed. 'Look, you've done enough for me and I must have worn you out. If I go anywhere I'll go alone, but I may not get up enough energy.'

Mrs Murray said in a high voice, 'You wouldn't be a "loner", as you call it, if Gwen were here.' She was saying what she had promised herself she would never say: she had lost control.

Betty touched her newly-done hair. Her eyes were wary. She said nothing.

'You know you wouldn't!'

'Push me over a cigarette.'

'You know you shouldn't—'

'Oh, stop it.' Betty began to smoke, puffing rather defiantly. 'Elspeth, it may be delusional, owing to my weakened state, but it seems to me that you're about to make a scene. And scenes I am not strong enough for. So don't.'

'When have you ever known me "make a scene"?'

'Never. I don't want to now.'

Mrs Murray felt the chill of a cruelty that she knew Betty could not help. She was still weak, still ill. She was to be forgiven.

The girl said, more gently, 'Honestly, Elspeth, you've been wonderful. I shall never be able to thank you. But now I've got to stand on my own feet again – totter on them, if necessary.'

Mrs Murray looked out at the grape-green sky beyond the window. There was a single rosy cloud like a Rorschach blot. In the garden was a silly little pool with goldfish in it, which were always being eaten by cats or each other, or poached by birds. Anyway, something happened to them. She had looked after those fish as well as Betty, sedulously, replacing them as they disappeared, so that when Betty was able to walk outside she would find everything perfect. To leave all this!

She could not prevent herself, though she knew it was futile, from saying hopelessly, 'Why can't we stay together? It's worked so well, hasn't it? I promise I wouldn't get in your way. I'd go right off when Gwen came, or any other of your friends. I'd just be there to help you, that's all.'

Betty suggested that they might have a brandy with their coffee, as a special treat. She said nothing further till they were drinking it. The rosy cloud had turned to violet. The late white roses were starting to glimmer in the descending dusk. ' "And, like a ghost, she glimmers unto me." Is that right? Something like it,' said Mrs Murray.

'Look here, Elspeth. It's no go. It never would be. It's something you can't help and I can't – they call it a "generation gap".'

Mrs Murray flinched. 'Is this how I seem to you? I suppose it's pretty obvious.'

'It's not you personally. It would be anyone. And besides, you're a bit too fond of me. No – wait! I'm not trying to hurt you. But it's no good beating about the bush, is it?'

'As a mother would be fond.' Mrs Murray burst out crying.

'Stop that. I can't bear it now.' She waited till eyes had been dried. 'No, not just as a mother. Do you suppose I don't know? I'm no good at all to you, Elspeth, and I just couldn't endure you being here all the time, being too fond. And you're making scenes right now. What do you suppose it would be like if we went on together?'

Mrs Murray attempted to retreat. Stumbling back upon her dignity, as upon an uneven paving stone, she insisted that Betty was wrong: there was nothing out of the way in her affection, there could never be. She had been married, she had never had any feelings for anyone but a man. She flushed. She had never spoken in this way before. 'Forlorn! The very word is like a bell.' The line came suddenly into her head, shaking her so violently that it was difficult to restrain a fresh outbreak of tears. She knew that she must never cry at Betty, who hated all displays of emotion which were not of her own making.

She said, 'I'll be getting back to the school tomorrow. I'd go tonight but I must give Mrs Annick due warning.'

'Oh, don't be such a coot. If you went stomping back this evening it would look as though we've been quarrelling, which I haven't, at any rate. Believe me, nothing's happened of any importance. You've been superb, and I'm grateful and you're always welcome here. But we're going to go on as we did before all this happened.'

The lofty, rather dark bed-sitter in the school, the orange quilt, the big wardrobe, the reproductions of Redouté roses, the trunk under the blue serge cover containing her most important possessions. All waiting for her to come back to them again, all just a little dusty.

'Another brandy. Go on, Elspeth, be a dog.'

Mrs Murray kept her dignity. 'Thank you, I will, for once. I really don't know what came over me this evening – perhaps I was tired.'

'From nursing me.' Betty's eyes were amused.

'Perhaps. I'm not young.' Mrs Murray could not subdue a huffy tone.

'Get away, you've thirty years at least ahead of you, and you don't look your age.' Betty was kind. 'I think I will go to Italy. There's a pub near Positano where they'd fit me in. I'll come back looking like a Red Indian.'

'When will you go?'

'Early next week.'

'I can pack for you.'

'If I need it, I'll let you know.'

A nightbird burst out singing. It was almost too much, too much the sentimental accident, an overloading of pain.

'I haven't heard her for some time,' said Betty.

They washed up together, Betty doing the drying. Such a pretty cloth, with an abstract design on it in blue and orange. The plates back in the rack, white plates with a small orange pattern around the rims. This has been mine for nearly a month, Mrs Murray thought, and is all to be lost.

'You really are a good old thing,' Betty said, as they parted for the night. She patted her shoulder. 'Truly you are. I shan't forget. Oh God, am I tired! Yes, I do need a change.'

Chapter Twelve

On the Honours Board:

Fairclough, D. M.
Davidson, R. H.
Devlin, J. R. C.

But all dim schools. Devlin could have done far better than Westleigh, but for the obstinacy of his parents. Fairclough did not sit for Westminster since his parents lived in Suffolk, and did not wish him to be far away in London.

Yet so snobbish, Annick thought, we all are. But in this situation how human to long for the best there is, just so long as the best exists! Unlike Grace, he did not believe in the permanency of the world that was his. It might outlast his time – it probably would. But after that? So much more for all, so much less for a relative few? So much intellectual waste? He envied Grace her ability to live in the moment, to make the best of all things, to be so disproportionately pleased when Downs Park beat another school at cricket.

She was a little tired these days, since she had had to take over Betty's work. So much sewing, so much checking of socks, vests, underpants, so much inevitable trouble with the laundry. But the Greek cruise had freshened her greatly, she had enjoyed Peter's sober and interested presence, and when the autumn began she had even nerved herself to tackle Mrs Terry about the food. Not that tackling did much good since Mrs Terry simply could not cook, no matter how hard she tried: but there was a general delusion throughout the staff that 'airing matters' had brought about some improvement.

As for his own fatigue, Annick felt this gaining upon him. He, who had always got briskly out of bed in the morning, now hid his head under the blankets until the last possible moment. The school was rather rowdy, as it generally was at the beginning of the academic year. There were tearful new boys to be soothed (teddy bears were permitted for the first term in the lowest form) and promoted boys to be quelled when the euphoria of their seniority became offensive. The latest craze was for acorn fights in the gym. The boys would collect enormous amounts, set up barricades and from behind them hurl these stinging little bullets at the opposing side. This, an unconscious imitation of trench warfare in the First World War, was a game which could hurt, and Annick seriously considered stopping it. Then, there was the craze for building tree-houses, which seemed only moderately dangerous until Stevenson-Paget fell out of one and broke his leg. Luckily, the onset of wet weather put an end to that. Canning was giving the older boys driving lessons as he had promised, but these were safe enough.

The interviewing of last-minute parents was over, and Annick was feeling guilty. He knew he had turned down a very bright small boy because he had been unnerved by the martial demeanour of the father. Grace was cross with him. But they had a more or less satisfactory new intake, and the last of the homesickness cases had been properly adjusted to school life.

Peter Quillan and Richard Searle were nearly always together. It seemed to Annick that Searle had stopped weaving his fantasies around Helen Queen, and Peter his around Searle. They were taking on the gravitas of clubmen, and it amused him to see them. Both were to sit for scholarships in the summer: Peter for Eton, Searle for Rugby, which had been his father's school. Peter's prospects were very bright and Searle's fairly so. All in all, satisfactory. As Annick had anticipated, the cruise had brought the boy into a closer intimacy with Grace and himself: what he had not anticipated was that Peter, back among his friends, had not been tempted to give the least sign of it.

'Did you know, darling,' said Grace, 'that Helen is carrying on with young Stephen? Seriously.'

'Does that matter?'

'No. But what *can* he see in her?'

'Rups awakened her, as the saying goes. We have to say that for him. Hadn't Steve a young woman of his own? I remember him talking about love. On Christmas Eve.'

'She is rather far away. Poor Helen is providing a stop-gap.'

As for Penelope, she had settled down in the school and seemed in no hurry to strike out again for herself. The sullen look had lifted and she was heard to laugh more often: but after her stern régime the boys were quite relieved to have Mrs Murray for French again.

'Could it be,' said Annick, 'that she rather likes Leo Canning?'

'My dear, he's too young for her!'

'Not all that young. And as bright as a button. I wonder how long we're going to keep him?'

'Not a week, if Rups had his way.'

Between these two there was constant stress: it was one of the very few factors at present troubling the life of the school. The boys, of course, knew, they knew everything. They would know about a potential engagement before the idea had really entered the heads of either of the two persons concerned. They were little seers, all of them, and sometimes nuisances because of this. They took sides with Canning and Massinger, though Massinger's supporters were a mere handful of fanatical games-players. They would have added fuel to the flames had they known how, but they did not. To new boys it was told, hushedly and in delightful awe, how Mr Canning had once called Mr Massinger a bleeder, and before the entire assembled school. Such pinpricks as they could contrive, they did: there were attempts to get out of the classes of one into the other, there was conspicuous, aggressive cheering when Canning took the car out or Massinger hit a dazzling six in a masters and boys match. (Cricket at Downs Park went well on into the autumn.) Both men knew all this. Massinger was angry, Canning did not mind.

But one evening, in the Golden Lion, there was another scene between them: and somehow, possibly through the licensee's son who did a paper round, news of it leaked.

Having no prep to take that evening, Canning had walked down with Penelope for a drink at opening time. It was sweet weather, mild and windless, the air still full of pollen. High up, the chalk of the downs shone like silver-gilt and the smell of the sea was all-pervading. They had barely settled in a corner when Massinger came stamping in and said, at the top of his loud voice, 'Here, you're wanted back at the school. Pronto. Head says you're to cut along.'

'The head put it that way?'

'Never mind how he put it. You stir your stumps. The Corso child's father wants to see you.'

Canning looked thoughtfully at his watch. 'It can wait for five minutes.'

'Look here, when I tell you to cut along, you cut along!'

'Rupert!' said Penelope, 'too many decibels!'

But the attention of the bar had been fully attracted.

'Rupert—' said Canning.

'Don't you damned well call me that. You're only a junior master.'

'Rupert, I don't like your tone. Come to that, I'm not sure I really like you.'

Massinger's face flamed so hotly that it seemed to be surrounded by blue smoke. 'Will you bloody well get back when the head wants you?'

Penelope said sharply, 'Keep your voices down.'

'My voice hasn't been up,' said Canning.

'Well, you keep yours down, Rupert. And don't try to needle Leo because it won't work. Do remember where you are.'

'I'm going to see Mr Corso,' said Canning, 'but I'll be back.'

'What's that, a threat? Come on, Penny, have one with me.'

'I think I'll walk back with Leo.'

'Taking sides, too?'

'I really don't know what's the matter with you tonight. Sit down

73

and stop causing a stir. You're a beak, remember?' Penelope put a firm hand on Massinger's sleeve and he sat.

Canning walked out, unaccompanied.

'Well,' she said angrily, 'and what was all that about? Honestly, Rups, I don't wonder he protested. You can't go around talking to people like that.'

He protested in his turn, speaking at some length. He genuinely wanted Penelope's good opinion and was cursing himself that he should have let all this happen in front of her. But he felt unable to stop, to curb his anger, though he knew he might have to pay for it. He hadn't meant anything, he said, hadn't even pretended to give her father's message literally. It was Canning who had made all the fuss, being so bloody touchy. And in any case, Canning was a drone, fooling around with his science and his nature study and his old cars, a luxury the school could not afford. She shook her head. She was hoping to calm him down before he met Canning again.

'And another thing. He's a rotten disciplinarian.'

'A word my father doesn't use.'

'Oh? Well, I do. He swears like a trooper in front of the brats, and your father never does a thing about it.'

'I don't believe it.'

'He does. I've heard him. The boys love it.' He brooded for a second. 'What does he mean, he'll be back? Thinks I'm going to sit and wait for him? If he does come back I'll kick him!' His voice soared up again, almost with operatic effect. He listened to himself, as if he were an outsider. He had done all he wanted to do, and yet something was driving him on to further silliness.

''E'll kick 'im,' said an awed voice from the bar.

'Outside. Come on.' Penelope jerked Massinger to his feet before he could even finish his beer and took him into the mellowness of the evening. They went slowly up the lane and over the stile to the grounds. These were still dotted with little boys looking like buttercups or wasps, according to the age or grubbiness of their blazers. The girl and man saw Canning coming, like Apollyon, over the field to meet them.

'Now, this is not to be a public performance!' She ran to him, alarmed.

'No. I'll talk to Rupert in the pavilion. Nobody's there.'

'If you think I'm going with you to any damned pavilion—'

'Yes, you are. Come on.'

'You weren't long, Leo. What was it?' She was trying to cause a distraction.

'Corso had a train to catch. He said all there was to say.'

The bell rang for prayers and the boys went running. After a second's pause, Massinger led the way to the small pavilion. Canning followed with Penelope, and pushed the door to behind them.

'Now, look. If you're willing to stop this feuding, I am. I won't tell you to mind your manners, because I don't think you've got any manners to mind, but we must put an end to this, both of us.'

Canning was speaking quietly enough, but his eyes were glittering and his nose seemed very large. He also, like the other man, was looking peculiarly young.

'Of course, Leo, if you're going to be rude in your turn,' Penelope said, 'then it will become more difficult.'

'All right. Sorry. How's that? But I won't be chased into the local and roared at.'

'You young bugger—'

'Not in front of ladies.' Canning was quite sincere in saying this. In many ways he was old-fashioned. 'That I won't stand for.'

'I'll call you something worse than that in a minute!'

Penelope cried, and it seemed to her in a high pipe, 'Will you both shut up? You're like a lot of children!'

Rupert swung, not too heavily, at Canning's jaw. Canning, taken by surprise, as a reflex action swung back very sharply indeed, so much so that he knocked Rupert right through the door, which was not properly latched, and down the three wooden steps on to the grass. Canning stood looking soberly down.

'I didn't mean it to be that hard.'

Rupert got up, with his customary athletic spring. The quicker the better. 'That does it. And you'll find you're finished with the headmaster, too.'

'You hit him first,' said Penelope.

'Get away! I only gave him a light clip—'

'I hope you're not hurt, Roops,' Canning said politely. 'I really do.' He waved his hand in a gesture of eighteenth-century courtesy. 'I couldn't bear it if I thought you were.'

'*No.*' Penelope put herself between them. 'You will not start that silliness again. Rupert, you go back to the cottage. I'll get Leo back to School House.'

Massinger turned and walked away.

'He'll bruise,' said Penelope. 'He'll have bruises to show. You won't.'

'When he went backwards through that door—' Canning gave a whoop of laughter. 'Straight out of *The Magnet*.'

'It was kept from the boys this time, anyway.'

'You wait.'

And indeed, nothing happened for three days. When Rupert appeared at breakfast next morning, Penelope observed that the right side of his jaw was very slightly discoloured, but no more than that. The boys did not seem to notice it and there was no whispering.

Time went by. Mr Canning and Mr Massinger were polite when they met in public. Meanwhile, the paper boy had told what he knew of the story. The wasps of the school buzzed with their yellow stories, and the atmosphere of suppressed excitement was pungent.

On the third day, Annick summoned Canning to his study. He looked grey.

'Leo, what am I going to do about all this? I can't go on and on overlooking things of this kind.'

'I'll understand if you can't. Pity, because I like those little bleeders. Bright too, some of them. Annesley's going to make a first-class scientist and Peter's maths will just about hold up enough to get him through.'

'Leo, I didn't say—'

'I can go to Mr Corso, of course. He's raised the ante, as I thought he would. But I don't fancy it. A bit on the dull side, after all this. Anyway, I don't fancy it yet awhile.'

Annick remarked, it was an odd thing that Canning never attempted to tell his own side of the story.

'Seems too silly, sir. Daft. Grown men calling names and socking each other. So far as I've any excuse, he did bellow at me in the pub, and he did get my dander up a bit. But that's all. Should have remembered he was my senior, shouldn't I, sir?' The diamond gleam.

Annick paced about the room. 'Rupert Massinger's hot-tempered. I know that. And I do know, though I suppose I shouldn't be telling you, that he thinks we can't really afford the science side.'

'Have to have prestige, don't we? But honestly, I love it.' Canning sat patiently, his hands hanging between his knees, his eyes on Annick's face. He did not look like a man fighting to keep his job, though in fact he was.

'I don't know what to do with you.'

'The long, long trail, I suppose.'

'If you gave me your word not to quarrel with Mr Massinger again—'

'Ah, but there I shall have to put my own side of it. Ridiculous ass I've been, I know, but I didn't start it. Guarantee my own good behaviour, yes, but I can't guarantee his.'

'Well, for God's sake, Leo, go and do your best! I don't want an upheaval in the school, and I'm not going to have one.' Annick knew that the more firmly he spoke the weaker he sounded, but he was at his wits' end. He was not going to dismiss Canning. He'd see Massinger go (potential money and all) before that happened. But how he was going to explain himself he could not imagine. He felt, as all but the most resolute headmasters feel at some time in their careers, ground down by the awful Juggernaut of his own staff. He had always been fond of Canning: now, suspecting a growing affection between him and Penelope, he was fonder. But he was in a glum position and was distressingly aware of it.

'Go away now, and try to – what is it the boys say?'

'Play it cool. Yes, I'll try.'

Rupert came to visit him, apparently in a state of near hysteria, his skin seeming to smoke as it had done in the Golden Lion.

'You mean you're still keeping that bastard on?'

Seize on to headmasterly dignity and hold it at all costs.

'I have my reasons for that and you'll have to trust me. I appreciate your point of view, of course, but it seems to me that you were in some part to blame. You know as well as I do that we have to coddle the young masters a little. And you know they're hard to get.'

'We could do away with that fellow lock, stock and barrel! If you must have some science, I know enough to carry on and Blossom's got some chemistry.'

Uncomfortably, at the back of his skull, Annick heard Canning's laughter. 'Got some chemistry!'

'If he doesn't go,' Rupert began, 'then I—' But he did not continue. There were plans germinating in his mind, of which immediate resignation was not one. 'Then I'm damned if I feel I can go on speaking to him,' he substituted, feebly. 'Not in private, anyway.'

Annick began to feel relieved. Fury was surely subsiding, caution taking over. 'In that case, we'll have to separate the two of you. But it's a pity. The corporate life of the school is important to us all.' This sounded, even to his own ears, unbelievably pompous, as bad as the vicar on the subject of Lobworth. 'You know how much Grace and I have always cared about that. Any dissension, and the boys smell it out at once. I often think,' he went on, at last easing himself into a chair and lighting his pipe, 'that boys of that age have extra-sensory perception which they lose at puberty. For which I suppose one must say thank God. Oh, Grace – come in. Rups and I were just going to have a drink.'

'Sorry, I can't stay. Got half an hour's football coaching and it gets dark early.'

'Well!' Grace exclaimed, when he had gone. 'Do you mean you've fixed it?'

'Patched it up, for the time being. Sometimes I think I am a very clever man.'

'I have never doubted it, my love.'

'But perhaps not a strong one.'

In her face was a flicker of alarm. 'What do you mean, not strong?'

'Oh, morally. Shouldn't I have the strength to beat the hell – morally – out of them both?' His mood changed. 'Darling, I must leave you for just a few minutes. I have an execution to carry out.'

This was the gentle slippering of a boy in the second form, who had crawled out of his dormitory window in the night and walked with bravado three times round the parapet of the roof. This was a very serious offence. He could have killed himself: the school as well.

'Oh, is that poor Maxwell? He's weeping half-way up the stairs. He looks so frail, which he isn't really, is he?'

'Then I suppose I'd better hurry and put him out of his misery.'

Annick stared sternly at the little boy, who was making no attempt to conceal his terror. 'Come on, bedroom – execution first, lecture afterwards.'

A watery smile. So long as there was some touch of the facetious, it could not be too terrible.

'Bend over.'

Annick slapped him six times with an old felt slipper, and to do him justice, made an unsuccessful attempt to put a sting into the final stroke. Then, when the child straightened up in relief, he gave him a lecture of some severity.

When told to go, Maxwell hesitated at the door.

'Yes? What is it?'

'Sir.'

'Yes?'

'Is that all a beating means?'

'Not enough for you?'

'Oh yes. But . . . It's always all? No matter what it's for?'

'I'm afraid so.'

'Oh.' Just a touch of disappointment, now the danger was over.

'I agree with you, Maxwell, it is entirely inadequate. But it is only done for something very serious, and I don't want you to forget that. It is what you will learn to call symbolism.'

'Sir, when I get to my public school, will they beat hard?'

'If they beat, it will be hard. But there isn't much of it at most places nowadays and I daresay you will go through your years unscathed. If you don't walk about on roofs.'

Chapter Thirteen

'I love you, Bloss,' said Massinger, and he meant it. She had given him pleasure that night.

Never one to sleep instantly after intercourse, he lay on his strong back and regarded the ceiling.

Though some might have called him an empty man, he was a cunning one. It was true that he had been frightened, that day, by the thought of giving up, on impulse, the cottage, the school. But hadn't he planned to that end? What was it, *reculer pour mieux sauter*? He was pleased by the Gallic recollection. The scene he had provoked with Canning had been crude, but it had left Canning the worse off, since he had not suspected intention. Canning was where he had always been, and he, Massinger, was on a promise of good behaviour. But he was in a position to give Annick a shock, precisely when the moment seemed ripe.

Certain things Rupert really loved, his wife (when he was not put to the necessity of augmenting her) and his games. He was not a good teacher, but games he could teach, and it was entirely due to him that Downs Park had such an excellent athletic record. He believed this was going to be a far more important lure than the poddlings-away of a half-trained scientist at the back of the house. Also, he was potentially an excellent administrator, a gift he proposed to bring into play as soon as possible.

Blossom was sleeping like a lamb, if that was how lambs slept. The light from a passing car swept a fan of yellow over the ceiling. Here, they were near the road.

Yes, cunning: basically, it had all been a trumped-up affair. Had he really been so with rage at the onset of his interview with

Annick? Yes, but ready to quell that rage when he found it would not serve his purpose. He might indeed have got rid of Canning this time: but failing to do so, had been prepared to cut his losses.

'I love you,' said Blossom, out of a dream. He did not answer her. She would not have heard him.

So it might be necessary now to cut the cable, and re-establish that cable (did one?) at a more convenient time.

In his heart he despised Canning, who thought himself so clever, for falling for so silly and contrived a row. Physically tough, he bore him no malice for the farce in the cricket pavilion: that could have gone either way. But to have been such an ass in the pub! Poor Canning, so easily drawn this time. Not all that he cracked himself up to be. He would have lost something of his smart-Alec reputation in the school and in the neighbourhood, which would make it that much easier to get rid of him when the time came.

There was one thing with which nobody would have credited Rupert: he knew it himself: with purity of intention. Yes, he would go to any lengths to get hold of the school: but he believed romantically that such a school he could run to perfection. It would be kept to its present form, though academic success would have to be stiffened: but it would be the kind of place which delighted parents in the beginning and consoled them in the end. It would be a *good school*. There would be far less slackness, far less fraternization (he used this term in his mind) between the senior and junior staff.

In all this he meant well. He generally did mean well except where women were concerned – and so far as that went, could he help himself? It was the way he was made. Blossom understood, or almost. He was glad to be shot of Helen who, despite her pretty body, was ugly. That had been a mistake. As for Penelope, once Canning was out of the way, a fresh start might be made.

For a man of his temperament, though he was lacking in insight, he was not really lacking in honesty. He knew his own limitations, and recognized the lengths to which he would go in plotting. He also recognized in himself that dangerous thing, the violent dislike: which he had for Canning and for that potential catamite of the headmaster's, Peter Quillan. But even as he had the latter thought, he knew that it was nonsense. It was bad to be righteous and nonsensical, something to be resisted. Sighing, he turned over, embracing Blossom where her waist was still slim and sweet. In the next room Pauline, now toddling in her waking hours, slumbered away. To get where he, Rupert, wanted, was going to need hard sense and hard recognition of the truth. Perhaps he was not brilliant at either. But he would have to try.

It was Rupert who at the end of his life, hoped to say that he had fought a good fight, had kept the faith. He had quite serious principles about the upbringing of the very young, and they were not Annick's. He quite liked boys, though they did not much like him. Why not? Because they had all been softened. Astringent, Rupert thought, pleased with the word, I shall be astringent. He saw rows of glowing, healthy, sporting faces beaming up at him as he took morning prayers. Fewer Quillans – though they would need a competence of those: more Faircloughs, more Mulliners. No messing about in the Thicket. That would come down, chop, chop, chop. Sea-bathing from June onwards, whatever the temperature.

Blossom stirred. 'Pet? You're not asleep.'

'No. Nor are you.'

'I was. Darling, if you want—'

'I don't.'

'What were you brooding about?'

'The school. Listen, we may have to quit.'

'Oh no!'

'*Reculer pour mieux sauter.*' His French would not have delighted Mrs Murray. 'Don't worry. Step back a bit to get a better jump.'

'You've been fretting about Canning.'

'About that brute? No, I've not.'

'Then why—'

'Wait till tomorrow.'

'Oh, Rups, Rups' – this with the near-hysteria of sleep which is not noisy but like an indecent confidence – 'they ought to like you more. They ought to *like* you. What have we done?'

'You've done nothing. The Annicks are scared of me.'

'Darling, do we want to scare anybody?'

'Go to sleep.'

'I can't. I—'

'Go to sleep, I tell you.'

And she did, like the beautiful subject of the hypnotist, heavy lids closing, curling up her handsome limbs, knees to breasts, arms crossed, like some stalwart female figure on a Burgundian tomb. Though they didn't curl their knees, Rupert thought dreamily. He had done some travelling.

Dreamy, yes: but unable to sleep. He got up, put on slacks and a sweater, took his torch and crept from the room, not particularly careful on the stairs, since she was sleeping so soundly, and out into the resonant moonlight. Rupert, not given to the feeling of magic, felt it now. He walked over the fields, through the belt of cow-parsley and into the Thicket. In a clearing, the moonlight fell in silver dollars. No rustle from any animal, quiet, quiet, the only noise, his feet on the fallen twigs. God damn it, he said to himself, I must be mad: but it smells good here. He would always remember the night smell of it, even when the Thicket was down.

Too much of a place for secrets altogether, unless they were his own, and his were cut-glass secrets, nothing dark about them. What a day he'd had! It had been a pretty cunning move, to be doggo for so long before storming in upon Annick. Yet the storm had, for the moment, defeated the cunning: very odd, that. Showed you couldn't altogether rely upon yourself. (Yes, he might well have mucked it all up.)

Any more than he could rely upon his sexual self, so much beyond control. It had been rough luck on him, had brought him much trouble. Without the itch, he and Bloss could have been the ideal couple. Now he wanted Penelope Saxton, if only for a night. And if that wasn't possible, whom? That little dike, Betty? He would show her some pleasures that couldn't have come her way. Why not Betty? Was it impossible that she could be flattered by a man?

Normally impervious to beauty, the dapplings of the special night charmed Rupert. So far away, dense in the Thicket, with sleep to come. But not sleep in the Thicket; a dangerous place. The morning would find him bland in his blue-piped pyjamas, cuddled up with Bloss. Dear Bloss. Now, he thought, I lay me down to sleep: and on that idea stepped out into the pouring moonlight and went back to bed.

Even so, he could not quite get to sleep. (What the devil would he be like in the morning?) Peacefully, he reviewed his life. A successful games-playing career, a bit of a struggle academically: he had read geography at Reading. Many girls, many teaching jobs, and then Bloss. Whether her redness, so like his own, had attracted him, he did not know: but he had at once felt like marrying her and within two months had done so. Not so many well-paid jobs: this one at Down Park had been by far the best, with the house attached. In his late twenties, he had come into a sizeable inheritance.

All in all, a satisfactory record. I haven't done much harm. But now, I've got to get on.

Chapter Fourteen

It was a carefully calculated month before Rupert gave in his notice.

'We're O.K. till the end of the term, Cyril,' Rupert said familiarly, feeling that the time for familiarity had come, 'and then Bloss and I both think we should push off.'

Blossom, in green wool, looked quite attractive. She twined her fingers tightly, as she knew how, when wishing to indicate apprehensive dismay.

'But, my dears,' Grace cried, '*why?* It can't be on account of Leo Canning.'

'Of course not,' said Rupert, with a dismissive laugh. 'But Bloss and I have got our way to make and we've both decided that it's time for a change.'

'We'll miss you dreadfully,' whispered Blossom, who was not given to whispering. 'Really dreadfully.'

Annick said, to their surprise and somewhat to their chagrin, 'Well, if you must, you must. I've never tried to keep anyone in my life. So far as I'm concerned, it means finding a new second master, but I suppose such things are possible.'

Grace was proud of him: he always met disasters so.

'We probably shan't make sharp changes at once,' Rupert said, sipping with an air of Trimalchian luxury at his gin. 'We'll need to do some hard thinking. We have our eye on a flat at Eastbourne.'

To Grace, this merely seemed like treachery. To have had their eye on a flat while occupying the cottage! This was a long-term plot, and she knew it.

'And when you're in it, what will you do?'

'Think,' Rupert said amicably.

This was the period free for the staff when the boys were enjoying their last hour of recreation. There was the usual great noise on the stairs and in the corridors. The wasps buzzed between formroom and gym, between the lab and the high play-room where various games, mostly of Canning's invention, had been set up.

'And for how long,' said Grace, with stately grammar, 'will you think?'

'Don't know. Do you, Bloss?'

'The problem,' Annick said steadily, 'or rather, the immediate problem, is games. Grace will do what she can, but rugger is hardly in her line.'

'Oh,' said Rupert, 'you can get some energetic stripling hovering between school and university.'

'You're right, I can do that.' Annick was still unfaltering. 'But it means us ticking over till I can find someone senior. Stephen is under-employed at the moment, so we should be able to carry on.'

Blossom, who had a heart more tender than her husband's, was touched by the headmaster's bravery. She knew it would be no easy matter for him to lose two first-rate games people (she was one herself), so suddenly, from a school in which this activity was bound to matter so much. For a second, and not more, she felt that Rupert was being unkind.

'Well, dears,' said Grace gently, 'all this has to be worked out. In the meantime, we can at least wish you luck.'

'We shall only be in Eastbourne,' Blossom said, on a slightly feverish note, 'so if anything comes unstuck and we can help—'

'Of course we'll help.' Rupert was bluff. 'We'll be around. Lend a hand at any time.'

But of course they would not be around, and Annick would be faced next term, unless he were very lucky, with something like a skeleton staff. He was not fool enough altogether to accept their given motives. What were they both up to? He realized how dependent he had been on their possible financial support – if it had come to the worst – and was ashamed. Should he really have got rid of Leo? He didn't believe this would have mattered one way or the other. Then what could he have done? Anything? Offered a partnership? He was not yet ready for that. But it was probably at the root of the matter. He knew, too, that he was paying less to Rupert than some schools would give him, even with the benefit of the cottage thrown in. He must have somebody as senior: and that somebody would almost certainly want more money: which he couldn't afford.

In the half-hour after supper he had a private classics period with Peter Quillan, who had grown beyond the normal teaching in the top form. When the boy, now very tall for his age, came gravely with his books into the study, Annick had a sudden temptation.

'No work tonight, Petey.'

'No, sir?'

'Too worried.'

'Why, what's going on?'

'I don't know why I should burden your infant mind with this.' Peter grinned appreciatively. 'And there's no reason why I should make you a confidence I don't want spread around the school. Are you ripe enough not to spread it?'

Father and son. The result of a Greek cruise.

'I think so, sir.'

'At the end of this term, Mr and Mrs Massinger will be leaving us.'

Peter was not old enough to forbear to whistle his joy. Then his face fell, as he rapidly reviewed the situation.

'So I shall be without a second master. What do you say?'

'No one to promote, sir?' Peter was developing the cheekiness which sometimes comes from a precocious puberty.

'Would you like a small glass of sherry? Or Coke?'

'Coke, please,' Peter said, but he recognized the solemnity of the hour by the offer made to him.

'Good. Well? Whom would you promote?'

'Mr Canning, sir.'

'Mr Canning may seem venerable to you, but he is twenty-four. No, five.'

'Then I suppose you'll have to try the *Times*, sir, or

Gabbitas-Thring.'

Annick lay back and laughed, feeling happy for the first time since the defection of the Massingers. 'You do know your way around, Petey!'

Peter said it was only what one heard.

'I can get someone young for games.'

'Oh, easy,' Peter remarked, 'if they're no good, they all play games.'

He had recently been permitted to wear long trousers, a treasured privilege at Downs Park. (The objection to their general use was that it was easier to patch broken knees than broken flannels.) He crossed his legs comfortably and admired them. Then he said diffidently, 'Mr Canning could take over second master's duties for the moment.'

'No go, Petey. I must have a grave and reverend signior.'

'Someone who's sixty, sir.'

'I'm not far off that.'

'No, but you're different.'

This phrase gave Annick so much pleasure that he blushed. He said, 'What do you want to do?'

'I told you, sir, law.' Peter was surprised. 'Criminal law, probably, though it's not so paying as company law.'

'No, I mean right now – I can't teach tonight.'

'You mean, I'd better scram.'

'I didn't mean that. But you don't want to listen to me moaning.'

'I'm all right, sir.'

Annick changed the subject. 'You're a wise child. Should I be taking Richard Searle along with you for coaching?'

Briskly – 'Yes, sir.'

'Why?'

'I think Richard does a lot better when he's given a chance.'

'Then he shall join you in future. Tell him, will you?'

'Yes,' said Peter, but looked dubious.

'What's up now?'

'He's pretty mad about pottery.'

Annick said forcefully that in this case, Searle must become less mad. 'He can make his pots on Saturday mornings. I'll let him off P.T. Mrs Annick says he's as clumsy as a new-born colt, anyway.'

'Clumsy as an old horse, sir. A Suffolk Punch, perhaps,' Peter added imaginatively.

Before long, the half hour had drawn to a close.

'When I'm through public school, sir, I'd like to teach here for a term.'

'I'm sure we shall welcome you. But why?'

'I suppose I'd like to have the whip-hand for once. That's what my mother would call ignoble. But I think I'd have ideas.'

Annick watched from the window as the boy set off on the short, solitary walk he always took after coaching. Eleven and a half years, and five feet four of him. Impossible to believe he was so young, or that only two years had passed since he came to the school. Like the plant on the nature film, he had seemed to unfold under one's eyes in the space of minutes. Into a happy boy, so far as Annick's experience went, and self-contained. Whether or not he missed his parents very much, it was impossible to judge. He wrote at length to them weekly, and occasionally in mid-week. But of course, there was never much news, and it would not be like Petey to make much of school gossip. Old beyond his years, he seemed to have aged beyond that. He giggled seldom, and then only with Searle, who sometimes amused him.

And Searle? A beta plus type, still plump, still vaguely romantic in appearance. Annick found him on the dull side and wondered at Peter's attachment to him. Still, you could never imagine what one boy saw in another, at any rate, not until puberty had passed. The green days were full of fantasies, like florid sticky labels, to be attached to the nearest object.

Such small credit we get. The public schools turn them out in their various moulds and get the praise or blame for the results. But we plant and water them, try to nip off the dead shoots as best we may. Nobody mentions us in *Who's Who* at the end of it all.

Grace came in. 'Peter departed? Darling, do turn the lights on. This is most depressing. As if everything wasn't.'

It was so unlike her that he was startled. 'Oh, I don't know. You mean, about Rups?'

'That, of course.'

'Let's not pretend that we ever liked him.'

'It's not our place to like or dislike.'

Annick said they would have to start advertising at once. Did she, he asked her, really mind changes so much? He had hated them for years: now, he was not sure that he did. He stirred restlessly.

The real burden, Grace said rather tartly, did not fall upon him. He had the business of interview and acceptance: it was for her to make the actual installation, to work at the social side of it all, to settle the new man down. 'And if he is a fiend out of hell, dear, I have to settle him just the same.'

In acknowledgment of the justice of this, he put his arm round her. They were very close. Love bound them, and the school: love and common interest. What more could anyone want? It was even hard, after all these years, to see what part the one had played in relation to the other.

'How shabby we are,' Grace said, looking round the room, 'we never renew anything.' She plucked at the cord of an armchair, which had become detached from its piping.

'Is there a point when one simply stops renewing? If so, it is rather sinister.'

'Why? Because we begin to feel life's a bit too short for renewals? We're not so old as that. Look at some of the parents.'

'Why should I? I see enough of them.'

'Renewing,' said Grace, 'always renewing. The energy of some of them terrifies me.'

Indeed they were both a little exhausted and depressed by the day they had lived through. Rumpuses. Upheavals. Renewals enforced.

'Supper.'

'Must we endure Mrs Terry and the staff tonight? Could you manage an omelette?'

'Certainly I could.'

They went into their small private kitchen and ate by themselves: it was rare for them to do this except on occasions of celebration; birthdays, anniversaries. This, if it were a celebration at all, was one of dismay.

Chapter Fifteen

On Sunday they asked Stephen and Mrs Murray to lunch. It was their habit to entertain the staff in rotation, and to an extent they both enjoyed it. They believed it was part of the glue which held the school together.

Mrs Murray arrived, dressed-up and looking mutinous. She was allowing herself to be increasingly cut off from normal life, and even a small social occasion like this was a strain upon her. She did not look pleased to see Stephen, nor he her. Still, Annick thought, they must each make the best of it.

They had been invited because Grace thought both were unhappy. Mrs Murray's unhappiness was, of course, in the order of things and everyone was used to it: which was why she had to be specially kept in mind. But Stephen was uncommonly morose: Grace suspected that his love affair had gone wrong and that Helen was beginning to embarrass him.

'This is very good of you,' Mrs Murray said with full stateliness as she accepted a sherry. 'Most kind.'

'We like to see you all in private whenever we can,' Grace replied. 'For the most part, all we get with you is a word or two when we pass in the corridors.'

'Yes, we are busy.' Mrs Murray's voice was flat.

'You're bringing some of your boys on very well,' said Annick. 'You must be pleased. And one or two of yours are rising into the star-class, Steve. Little Maxwell's poem didn't compare unfavourably with the famous *Birds*.'

'Maxwell's an interesting case,' said Stephen. 'He's a combination of a daredevil and a grizzle. Perhaps that makes for poets.'

The Annicks laughed and Mrs Murray gave a weak smile.

Under the influence of a very good meal, the young man had brightened up a little and was prepared to show off: an encouraging sign, for he was by nature ebullient.

'Do you think we might do a panto this year instead of the usual Shakespeare? There are plenty of people to write it and Mrs Saxton says she'd have a shot at the music.'

'Oh, but surely the parents expect—' Mrs Murray began. There seemed to be no reason for her intervention except for a generalized dislike of jollity.

'And Leo Canning,' Stephen said eagerly, 'says he'll manage a real transformation scene. I bet he could, too.'

'So it's in the air already, is it?' said Annick. 'I suppose I'm the last to hear.'

'We weren't being secretive, sir—'

'Oh, weren't you! But it's a possible idea. What do you think, Grace?'

'Well, Mrs Murray's right. It does need thinking about.'

'*Cinderella*, I thought.' said Stephen, 'with Betty as eponymous heroine and Searle as Prince Charming, that is, if you don't think he's too fat. Quillan might look better, but acting is not his *forte*, and he can't sing.'

Annick protested that they were going too fast. If it were a flop, it would be a sensational one. 'Now with *The Merchant* you can't go wrong.' Yet he was attracted by the idea: he would have been attracted by anything that might lift Stephen from his recent gloom.

'Wouldn't it be fun to risk going wrong for once, sir? To be really ambitious? We've never been too ambitious in the play line, have we? Just ticked over.'

'Rather more than that, surely,' said Annick, a little hurt.

'Very much more!' Mrs Murray was looking huffy about something that was none of her business.

'Mr Canning said he could make a first-rate coach. Plywood and silver paper. All lit up, too.'

'Are you heading a delegation, Steve?'

'No, sir. It was only to put the idea.'

But Annick would give no answer before he had thought things out, and with the dropping of the subject the luncheon party fell into the doldrums again. Mrs Murray took her leave the moment she decently could, and went away with the air of one offended. Stephen made a move to follow her, but Grace said, 'Don't. Not yet. Have some more coffee.'

Annick excused himself, and left the boy alone with his wife.

'I don't see what any of us can do with Mrs Murray,' she said at once.

'Nor do I.' Stephen was pleased to be confided in. 'She is an awful wet blanket, you know. Poor dear. But I oughtn't to say that.'

'It's true enough. And you? Is there anything we can do to help?'

He opened his eyes disingenuously. He did not know what she meant, honestly he didn't.

'You've been sad lately. Love trouble?' Grace was as direct in interrogation as a member of the Bloomsbury sect might once have been.

'More or less. More, in fact.'

'I'm sorry. It will pass. What else can one say?'

'I can't believe it will.'

'I had a dreadful disappointment when I was a girl. I thought I'd never get over it. And then, in the same year, I met my husband.'

'I don't feel I want to meet anybody else, ever again. But thanks, anyway.'

He got up, putting his cup back neatly on the tray. 'I really must be going. It's been fine. Wonderful lunch.' He added, 'Is there any news of a replacement for Mr Massinger?'

She said that they were considering two applicants. Blessedly, she added, replacement was not so difficult as one thought. She did not say that both seemed to be pretty awful, since that was not Stephen's affair and she herself was born to be hopeful.

Next week, Annick engaged Norman Poole, an-ex-army officer in his late fifties. Like Massinger, he would teach some maths, geography and of course, games and P.T. His pretty wife, Delia, looked like being a dead loss: unless she could take art. She had been to an art school and painted a little herself.

Poole was tall, athletic, diffident. It was the diffidence which had, for good or ill, attracted Annick. The other man had been over-brimming with confidence. 'Which is why we should have had him,' said Grace, exasperated.

'Rupert has destroyed my belief in self-confidence for a lifetime. He makes my head ache.' Now that the Massingers were definitely to go, Annick could summon up no pretence of liking him. 'I think you'll find Poole will settle down with us. I want him to come and stay here for a few days before the end of the term and get the feel of the place.'

'And also, let Rups get at him? I really think you must be mad.'

'Then, my dear, I am mad.'

Plans for the pantomime were, of course, proceeding: to a suffering Stephen, they could deny nothing. Peter Quillan was working furiously away at a libretto.

Penelope, fascinated by a new experience, was writing some tunes which Helen, not inventive but more musicianly, had promised to arrange for her. Canning and some of the boys were already building a framework for the coach. Other boys were constructing and painting pumpkins.

Only Betty Cope was in rebellion. 'I'm damned if I'm going on acting with a lot of snotty little boys!' she cried to Mrs Murray, whom she permitted to take tea with her once a fortnight.

'You look so little yourself, you see,' Mrs Murray began softly, before realizing that she was saying the wrong thing in the wrong way. 'But don't do it if you don't want to. Why should you?'

'Why should I, indeed? Good Christ, I've got a love-duet with Searle!' Surreptitiously, her gaze slewed to the crucifix: and surreptitiously, she crossed herself. 'Just imagine it!'

'Then you dig your toes in. What's good enough for other schools is good enough for us.'

'Maxwell can be Cinderella. If he can stop his nose running.'

'Dear, have you quite made up your mind?'

'No, I haven't. But it's making itself up rapidly.'

Yet Betty was still undecided whether the instinct to rebel was going to force itself into action. She knew she was pretty and that she had a pleasant singing voice: she could anticipate the admiration which would come her way. She was not a happy woman, and like most unhappy people, welcomed the exciting event. It took her out of herself, and made the thought of Gwen less poignant. The pantomime would, of course, be her triumph. She might feel she was making a fool of herself, but nobody else would think so. Gwen might even come down for it, and sneer (of course), but be secretly impressed.

'If it weren't for Searle—'

'Then don't act with Searle! You're in a commanding position. You can pick and choose.'

These were wonderful afternoons for Mrs Murray. There was no hope in them, but they held the illusion of hope. For whom could Betty really talk to, but herself? To all others, she was a cold little girl, not really making friends in the school. Mrs Murray lived somehow from one fortnight to the next.

The Pooles came down from London to dine with the Annicks, so that the latter could get a better look at them. It was to be a *partie carrée*, with no intruders even for cocktails. They arrived looking pinched after the long drive.

'How cosy you are here!' Delia Poole exclaimed. 'Yes, please, a very tiny scotch.'

When the glass was brought she hugged it but did not immediately drink. Grace gave her a sharp glance.

Delia was on the small side, blonde, pale-skinned, her eyes large and dark. She had the figure of a schoolgirl and her dress was a little fussy. 'Cosy,' she repeated. 'How lovely to see a coal fire!'

'We're centrally heated,' Grace said, 'the fire's just for show.'

It was as though Mrs Poole was submitting herself to some kind of ordeal. Still she hugged the glass, while the minutes went by. Then, suddenly, she drained it.

She's a nervous type, Annick thought. At the moment she's scared stiff of us. But it won't last.

Norman Poole seemed more at his ease than on his previous

interviews. He was a big, square-shouldered man, with ginger-grey hair of a mouselike softness. His nose turned up above a military moustache.

'Have some more,' Grace said to Delia, 'you're still looking perished. It's like winter outside.'

'I don't know that I should. Well, then, very, very little.'

Delia had curious hands, chalk-white, perfect pink nails. They would have been beautiful had they not been a little claw-like.

'Will you feel like helping us a bit with the art class?' Grace asked her. 'We'd be very grateful, and perhaps your days wouldn't seem so long.'

'I'd love to try: But I've never done any teaching, and I think I'd be scared of the boys.'

'They are nice creatures,' Annick said. 'They would be to you, I think. They love art, so that's half the battle. Would it be impertinent if I told you that they are also appreciative of good looks?'

Grace glanced at her husband with some surprise. This was unlike him. But she thought he might have found out Delia's Achilles heel, since the latter reddened a little, bowed her head and smiled shyly into her lap.

Norman said, 'We're both going to do all we can.'

The talk turned to the pantomime. 'Oh, I wish we were here for that!' Delia said wistfully. 'I did act for a year when I was very young and I loved it. Though I was never quite good enough.'

'I can see you're going to be an asset to us in more ways than one,' Annick said, in the Bluff King Hal tone he could sometimes adopt towards people of whom he was not in the least scared.

Grace said that the Pooles must come down and see it, in any case. She glared at her husband. Just long enough for him to sense her disapproval of what she considered play-acting.

'One thing,' Poole spoke with increasing confidence. 'Have you got a scout troop?'

'No. It doesn't seem to suit the school.'

'What about a little very elementary corps training? Give them a start when they go to their public schools.'

Annick was taken aback. 'Well, I don't know. We're not really geared to it, I don't think.'

'Boys usually like it. It's only a sort of game.'

'Norman,' Delia said in a little girl's voice, 'if Mr Annick doesn't want a corps, he doesn't.'

Grace silently applauded her and gave her another drink before she could protest.

Annick said, 'Well, let's see how things shape up.'

'Well-equipped gym you've got.'

'Not so bad for a school of this size.'

They went into the little dining-room.

'But you're quite self-contained here!' Delia clapped her hands, her eyes upon the table.

'Not so self-contained as you're going to be,' said Grace. 'You don't have to live on the premises. I do hope you'll like the cottage.'

'We simply adored what we saw of it!'

They finished the soup. Then Poole cried, 'Grouse!' as if he had seen no food for a year.

'It's a luxury,' said Grace apologetically, 'but we thought we might indulge for once.'

She was an expert cook, which was why she suffered so much from Mrs Terry. The birds cut pinkly on squares of fried bread spread with their own livers and the pinkness was in delightful contrast with the watercress. White sauce, brown crumbs, game chips. A claret of a good year. What the hell, thought Grace, are we doing this for? Are we touching wood?

Poole tapped his glass. 'Good stuff.' He took a great sniff at the wine, loudly exhaled, then gave a diffident smile.

This, Grace thought, is never going to do. They are not our kind of people.

'I don't know much about wine,' said Delia, 'but this tastes delicious.'

'No, dear, you don't know anything about it, and I've never been able to train you.' He smiled across at her. He was rather a handsome man, Grace decided. Also, he was experienced: perhaps he would get on quite well with the boys? But there must be no nonsense about a cadet corps. Downs Park was not at all militaristic.

Hopeful Grace: as her hopes rose, Annick's sank. He was pretty sure now that he had made the wrong choice, and made it in an asinine manner. It was no good going by references: you must go by your own instincts and he had disregarded his own. Perhaps he had followed his instincts rather too frequently in the selection of boys, since it was the gentle and amiable parents who most appealed to him. What was he going to do with this Prussian now he had got him? He was near to panic.

Chapter Sixteen

It was decided to combine the occasion of the pantomime with a farewell party, given by staff and parents, to the Massingers. The boys would have said their farewells and made their presentation that morning. The choice of gift was left to the top form, which, to Annick's sadistic delight, chose to buy a huge, gilt-framed reproduction of a painting of sunset on snow. At least, he was delighted until it occurred to him that Rups and Bloss might actually like the thing.

Their moving-out, and the Pooles' moving-in, was to be made in the Christmas holidays. For a week already Norman had been staying at the Golden Lion and coming over daily to learn the ropes from Rupert. They seemed to get on well together.

The pantomime was an unqualified and spectacular success. The cardboard pumpkins had been abandoned, and large balloons painted to represent them. As the godmother waved her wand the balloons burst, and on, with a thunderflash, came the silver coach, outlined, even the wheel-spokes, in fairy lights. All without a hitch. Canning grinned in the wings.

A handsome youth called Potter had replaced Searle as Prince Charming, so Betty was appeased. Searle (after initial disappointment) was an unexpectedly lively Ugly Sister. Quillan's libretto was so good that Annick considered having it printed on the school press and sent out as a New Year's card to parents. The music, by Penelope and Helen Queen, was adequate and in a mild way catchy.

'Cheer up,' Peter said to his friend, 'you don't look any uglier than you usually do.'

The combination of pantomime and party had sparked excitement among the parents, even among those who did not in the least care whether the Massingers went or stayed. The Quillans were not present: they would not be back until the end of January, which meant Peter spending yet another holiday at the school.

'So we shall have to make some sort of Christmas this year,' Grace said to her husband, 'or he will be so disappointed.'

'You think so?' Prematurely, Peter had put away a good many childish things.

'There must be a tree, and turkey,' she replied firmly. 'Though perhaps he would settle for pheasant.'

'I should think he damned well would.'

The dining-hall was festive, with elaborate decoration, and a lighting scheme contrived once more by Canning. Ten minutes to eleven: most of them had cars, the few who had not had booked in to various Trust Houses in the district.

Annick went about in his usual state of nervousness, receiving congratulations.

'More ingenuity from your young man,' said Gordon Corso. 'Is there nothing he can't do?'

He will get him away from me yet. Certainly he will, if Leo and Penelope think of getting married, because they will need the money: but there seems to be a lull in that affair.

The boys actually in the pantomime were allowed to hand round drinks and sandwiches, and to retain their costumes. Betty fluttered about bright-eyed, feminine in white tulle with spangles sewn all over it: Mrs Murray's hungry gaze pursued her.

After half an hour of chatter, Annick called for silence.

'You all know that this very happy occasion has its kernel of sadness: we are here to say goodbye to Mr and Mrs Massinger and to thank them for everything they have done for the school over these past years. I need not say how much we shall miss their skill, their energy, the vigour of their personalities.'

For this flatness, prolonged applause. Rupert, relaxed, put his arm round Blossom's broad shoulders.

'You also know that we are here to welcome Mr and Mrs Poole, who are to be their successors. More by chance than anything else, Mr Poole has elected to teach mathematics and geography, an admirable continuity. Those of you whose boys are enthusiastic games-players need not, I am sure, fear for that side of our activities.'

More applause. Poole was looking modest, Delia fidgety, as if she longed for it all to be over.

'The boys made their presentation to Mr Massinger this morning, on their own behalf. On behalf of staff and parents, I will ask our youngest master, Stephen Smith, to present our own token of gratitude.'

What stuff Cyril talks on these occasions, thought Grace. He is naturally quite eloquent, but here we have every cliché in the book.

This time a silver salver, very handsome, inscribed.

Rupert's turn to speak.

Surrounded by sparkling mothers and by the characters of pantomime, he looked, it occurred to Grace, rather like Bottom among the fairies. He was nothing if not benign: it seemed as though there had never been a dangerous side to him, that in this moment of tribute, it had melted quite away. Nick Bottom, or Scrooge reformed.

More clichés.

'I say, I do feel overwhelmed. My wife and I don't know how to thank-you all for this magnificent present. What can we have done to deserve it?'

(Laughter.)

'It's a sad night for us, of course, but you've all made it seem like a happy one. We're going to miss the school, and the boys, and all of you, more than we can say. Well, I don't know what more I can add. Quite overwhelmed, as I remarked. Simply, on behalf of Blossom and myself, thank you very, very much.'

He sat down, wondered what to do with the salver, pushed it on to Blossom's lap.

Annick made a few concluding remarks, and then Canning flooded the room with hi-fi: his own choice: Lehár. Stephen drifted back to Helen, who had been looking out of things.

'And now,' Grace murmured, 'the crumpled napkins, the crumbs, the mess, the awful cleaning-up. Ragged bits of pie, halves of sandwiches, vol-au-vents with a single bite out of them.'

'Night's candles are burned out,' said Annick.

The Christmas holidays went quickly. Grace did go to some lengths for Peter's sake and he seemed pleased: the pheasants were most successful since, as it turned out, he was indifferent to turkey. Stephen and Helen, who had not gone home, were in and out a good deal, and so was Penelope.

'It isn't too dull for you?' Grace asked Peter, a little anxiously.

He smiled at her. 'What Mrs Murray calls *mouvementée*.'

'I don't really know what we're going to do without him when his parents come back,' she said later to Annick, 'he has been so nice.'

He was certainly no trouble. Turning down an invitation from Searle, he seemed content to walk or bicycle in the frosty grounds when he was not working: he went on working steadily, at his own desire. He caught cold, followed by a bad cough, but the doctor said his bronchial tubes were clear. He spent two days in bed, still working a little, when he was not reading books about a boy called Jennings, set in a school much like his own.

Then there was the business of the Pooles' move into the cottage. It was furnished, and they had only to bring familiar augmentations of their own: but Poole asked permission to repaper the sitting-room and paint the kitchen in two shades of blue. Of Delia they saw little.

Panic began to subside. There had been no further mention of a cadet corps, and Poole seemed docile enough. They had feared that he would be out for changes, but it did not look like it. He believed in keeping physically fit, taking half an hour's exercise in the gym every morning before breakfast. When he wasn't papering or painting, he went for long walks. 'Got to know the terrain,' he said.

One morning when he was out, Grace went to call upon Delia to see whether there was anything she could do to help. The time was eleven o'clock. The cottage was so quiet that at first she thought there was no one in, but glancing through the window she saw

Delia moving about a corner cupboard as if rapidly tidying up. Grace hoped she was not going to prove chronically messy.

Delia disappeared from view: Grace thought she had run upstairs. She rang again, and nothing happened. She was just about to turn away when the door opened and Delia appeared, looking flustered, but very pretty in a stagey apron sewn with valentine hearts.

'I'm so sorry I kept you waiting! I do hope you haven't been ringing long. I've just been doing the bedroom and the bell's rather faint up there. I think I'll ask Norman to fix it.'

Yes, she was getting on beautifully: they both were. Everyone had been so helpful, especially Helen Queen. 'What a nice girl she is! She says she used to help Mr Massinger with his letters and would be pleased to help Norman. That is, if he has any letters.'

Grace laughed. If he took over any of the administrative business, letters there would be. 'The second master usually acts as something of a bursar, but I don't know whether your husband—'

'He'd do anything, I know! You've only to ask him.'

Delia glanced at her watch. 'I'm awfully afraid there's no coffee. We've run out. Would it be wildly early for a sherry? Oh, come on, Mrs Annick, let's be terribly debauched because it's still really Christmas, isn't it?'

There is a certain girlishness, Grace thought, endemic among wives in such a school as this. It is necessary because it is comforting. We are needed, yes, and often we do the donkey-work, but we are not as the men are. Neither, of course, are we on sufferance. We are perhaps more like waitresses in a club exclusively for males, who are not on sufferance either.

She felt that, as they sat down to sherry at such an early hour, both of them were gleeful. Sooner or later, if Delia were as silly and as pleasant as she seemed to be, they would fall into an alliance. But against what? Perhaps into an alliance against nobody – was that possible?

'Do you like the new paper?' Delia said timidly. 'It was lovely here before, but Norman and I somehow felt we wanted something our very own. I don't know whether you think that's dreadful.'

'Of course not. Cyril and I always want something of our own and sometimes I think we'd like to make changes: but we never seem to get round to them.'

'We're new brooms,' said Delia, with a sudden glimmering smile, as if confidence had been renewed in her, 'so we feel impelled to fuss around.'

'It all looks very pretty, anyway.'

A tame conversation, but during the course of it, it had changed in atmosphere. Delia looked prettier, stronger, was more in command of herself. Perhaps she would be quite a good teacher. In any case, it was no hardship to watch boys slosh paint about: nobody ever, these days, thought of teaching them to draw.

When she took her leave, Grace was feeling decidedly happier.

But why had Delia been so long in answering the bell? To go to the lavatory, probably, though it seemed odd. Grace dismissed the matter.

Chapter Seventeen

'I have to live with it,' said Poole, 'but for God's sake don't let the others guess.'

She fell into tears, letting herself sink over his knees.

'Pull yourself together.'

Rearing half-up, she said, 'You're exaggerating, you know you are.'

'Listen, I like it here, I don't know when I've liked a place more. I won't have you spoil it.'

'Aren't I doing my best? I take my classes—'

'Yes,' said Poole, 'with all your nerves at full stretch.'

'How can I help my nerves? I do control them—'

'Just.'

'You're unkind. You're so unkind.'

'Don't think I'm not sorry for you. For what you can't help. But you can get more of a grip on yourself, if you really try.'

'You're unkind.'

He said, 'My pretty girl, my pretty girl,' and stroked her hair. He had not meant to provoke a confrontation of this kind, and would not have done so had he not had so pleasant, so harmonious a day. They all liked him! The boys liked him! He wanted to live in the cottage for the rest of his years, doing whatever the Annicks might require of him. The thought of anything spoiling this had thrown him into a kind of frenzy: not a violent one, for he was not a violent man, but it was frenzy by his modest standards. Within a month, he had come to love the school, and everything in it. Everyone in it. The staff was seething with problems, of course, but what conceivable business was that of his? He didn't know about them, he didn't want to know.

Tear-stained, she pulled herself erect and laid her head on his shoulder. 'Am I your pretty girl?'

'You know you are. Always.'

'Then I don't know how you can essagerate – exaggerate so.'

He said weakly, 'Perhaps I do, a bit. But you know how you are: and I don't want the rest of them knowing.'

She replied in a fury, 'But who knows what? What am I supposed to have done? Has anyone complained?'

No, nobody had complained. He just wanted her to be careful.

'I don't believe,' she said, wiping her eyes, recovering her dignity, 'that you've the slightest idea what you're talking about. I admit I get tired at the end of the day—'

'And well before eleven in the morning.'

At this she cried out. It was entirely untrue! She had never heard such rubbish. The tears sprang again, hot and round on her white cheeks. It took him a long time to soothe her.

It was Delia's rough luck that Annick should ask her to take an art class with the older boys in the forty-five minutes before supper. Then, she was not at her best.

She had been trying gallantly to pull her weight. She had volunteered to teach something beyond paint-splashing: in fact, the elementary principles of perspective. So she had been provided with a blackboard and an easel.

The top form watched with interest as she steadily drew, with a sure hand, the diagram of a landscape receding. She talked clearly and to the point. Then, when she reached up to clean the board in readiness for a new example, she skidded backwards over the floor, bringing easel and blackboard down with her. The boys were on their feet. 'It's nothing,' Delia told them from a sitting position, 'really it's not. I think they must have polished under a mat.'

Quillan and Searle came to lift her up. She rested for a second in their arms, then gave both of them separate smiles. 'What an idiot I am!'

The muscles in her cheeks tightened: muscles tightened all over her body. She watched while the easel was set up again, then concluded the lesson, diagrams as neat as ever. But how was she to face staff supper? She must get home as quickly as possible. Yet if she didn't face it, Norman would wonder if anything had happened. She could tell Grace airily enough, 'I had a fall and I'm a bit shaken. I think I'll just have some coffee and a sandwich at home.' But this she could not tell her husband. All the same, she must get home *first*, she could not face the immediate descent into the dining-room.

She must face it. She was steady now, not bruised. But she would not be able to eat, she would be seized by anorexia. The food would stay mashed and staling in her mouth, she would be unable to force it down her gullet. Well, she must try. An hour, and then it would be all right again.

'You all right, Mrs Poole?' Searle inquired.

'Thank you, yes. What a thing to do! I must have looked an ass.'

'Of course not. We were worried about you.'

'That's nice of you, Richard.'

Let it be a soft meal, a mince, something that did not need chewing: for she knew she could not chew.

It was a chicken hash. She managed to swallow a few mouthfuls, and found she could eat her portion of apple pie. Down the length of the table she could see Norman eyeing her. Well, there was nothing to eye. She was all right now, and there was nobody to talk about her. She was pretty sure that the incurious boys would not.

It was his turn to see that the top form got tucked down, so she was blessedly able to return to the cottage alone. There, she pulled herself completely together by her own inevitable method and went to bed. When he came in, she was sitting peaceably against the pillows reading a detective story, or pretending to. I need my glasses changed, she thought.

Every day she grew fonder of Helen Queen. The girl came in regularly at eleven thirty, renewing the routine she had followed with the Massingers. They would have coffee and a little chat, and then Delia would take her twelve o'clock class. Really, everything was fitting in and going splendidly.

Norman was, up to now, a success. Though he used a parade-ground bark on the playing-fields and in the gym, his normal behaviour was gentle: everyone liked him. With the staff he could not outgrow his diffidence. He was deferential to all the older hands, from Annick, even down to Stephen Smith, appearing alarmed only by Canning, whose tongue was too quick for him.

'I admit it,' Grace said to her husband, 'you did make the right choice. But God knows how.'

Domestic worries apart, Poole was happy. By no means a fool, he did not suppose they would want him to stay for ever. He was a bit too old for this kind of thing: it would be his last job. But he was going to hang on to it for as long as he could. There were times when everything seemed better, when he felt carefree, when he believed there was nothing in the world for him to worry about. His pretty girl was steadier, far steadier: perhaps the atmosphere of the place was having its beneficent effect upon her, too.

I only wish I didn't creak when I sprang over that damned horse.

He was a humble man, he always had been. He had made his way in the army largely through the possession of a stentorian voice, and of a capacity for application. Though Delia had her difficult side (he was no longer going to put it more strongly than that) he had never thought himself good enough for her. A pity they had been unable to have children: how pretty their daughter might have been! But they had both visited the doctor, and he knew the fault was his. He had deprived her of that, which was so much. Surely it was up to him to understand her in lesser things?

In fact Norman Poole, certainly no Prussian, was not so far from being a saint, or might have qualified for one had his religious convictions been more secure.

Chapter Eighteen

It was not long after this that a sudden atmosphere of disturbance sprang up in the school. Annick sensed it at once, before any member of his staff except Canning, who had commented that there was something fishy going on. There was whispering in the changing-room, groups formed suddenly and as suddenly scattered. Frank-eyed boys tended to look the other way. There were strange alliances, abrupt meltings from familiarity. It was unpleasant, and there seemed no way of putting a finger on it. Annick would have liked to talk to Peter, but felt this would be unfair. It was already only the boy's coolness and general amiability that prevented him being thought of as a 'teacher's pet': Annick was not going to make him a teacher's sneak. All the same, it was frustrating to have to hold back, for Peter knew.

Annick considered talking to his head boy. Would that be fair? Head boys had never been more than head in name, without special powers, and their selection went on plain seniority. ('No damned merit about it.') The present incumbent was an opaque child of thirteen, who had once failed Common Entrance and must succeed the second time at all costs. Hanford, his name was. Like Peter, he would know what was wrong since obviously there was incessant talk: but he would not have sensed it, innerly. Hanford, privately summoned, promptly took refuge in his own opacity, as if this were a quality of which he had always been aware and had turned to his own use. No, nothing was up so far as he knew. He had heard nothing. He was sorry.

'All this,' Annick said to his wife, 'is damned uncomfortable. Not only is it nasty, but it makes me feel a fool, as if I were the leading figure in blind man's buff. I put my feelers all ways, and I can't touch a thing.'

'Is it sex?' Grace asked.

'I'm pretty sure not. They're too young for anything sexual to go so deep as this. And there isn't any giggling – have you noticed that?'

The break came in a letter from Bailey's mother.

'I hate to bother you about this, and Joel will want to kill me. But in the past two months he has lost the gold watch his grandfather gave him for his birthday—'

'What right has he to have a gold watch at his age?' Grace commented. 'Absurd. He's ten.'

'—quite a nice fountain-pen, and quite a few shillings out of his blazer-pocket. He's awfully careful as a rule, and I've never known him lose things. Of course, he must have had a careless lapse this time, because I'm *sure* it doesn't mean anything else. But if you or Mrs Annick could ask around, it would be very kind of you.'

'So it's theft, Cyril. We have a Fagin somewhere.'

The letter ended, 'I suppose I can't ask you to let me remain anonymous? Joel would be really upset if he thought I had written to you at all.'

Annick said angrily that some parents were intolerable. What was the use of coming to him with a wretched thing like this and expecting him to act with one hand tied behind his back?

'I'll have to talk to one or two of the staff, ask whether they've spotted any boy who had some sort of valuables who isn't displaying them. It's no good bothering Poole, he hasn't been here long enough to have noticed.'

He spoke first to Canning.

'I'll keep an eye out. It's really like that game of remembering objects on a tray, isn't it, Headmaster? Who had what? But I'll flog the old memory.'

Annick flogged his. What possessions had Peter? A pocket-knife, but since he seldom used it there was no reason to believe it had disappeared. A Parker pen: he still had that. Something eluded Annick's memory. Then, one day, during a Greek lesson, he knew what it was. The boys were doing an unseen translation. Peter had finished first and his hands caught in a shaft of sunlight, were idle on the desk. He was not wearing his ring.

It had been his eccentricity to wear, ever since coming to the school and in the face of earlier jeers, a ring of cheap metal shaped like a skull. A piece of fairground junk, probably, but his good luck charm. The sun was not sparkling on the eyes of red glass, which was why Annick had noticed something missing.

As the books were handed up to him he said easily, 'Hullo, Peter, where's your talisman?'

'Sir?'

'Your ring.'

A pause. Then, 'I don't know, sir. It must have slipped off. I reckon my fingers aren't so fat as they were, I don't think. I had a good look round, but no luck.'

'I don't believe I've ever seen you without it. Do you sleep in it?'

The stir in the room was palpable.

'No, sir. It had a bit of a rough edge, and if I rolled on it, it might cut me.'

'Where did you keep it at night?'

'In my locker. But I think it must just have fallen off.'

Annick let this go. He was not yet prepared to make a general inquiry. He was aware when he left the room of a sigh of relief, rather like a small puff of wind.

The next piece of news came from Canning. 'Maxwell's using a biro. When I asked him why, he said he'd lost his fountain-pen. I told him he knew damned well that ball-points weren't allowed, and he'd better have a hunt around for the missing object. He went red as hell and said he'd tried, but he'd ask them to send an Osmeroid from home. Do you suppose they know who the villain is? Are they all protecting somebody?'

'I don't suppose anything. Oh – one of your chaps had a Kennedy dollar, didn't he?'

'Foss did.'

'Ask to see it. Don't make a fuss of any kind if he can't produce it, though.'

But Foss still had his dollar, and another votive object missed by another boy turned up in a Wellington boot.

The atmosphere in the school thickened, and Annick felt more of a fool than ever. Its existence was obvious now to everybody but Mrs Murray, who seemed too sunken in her own griefs to notice. The first boy to complain was a bold newcomer of eight and a half, who spoke to Stephen.

'Sir. I had two bob in my blazer and it's gone.'

'Hole in your pocket?'

'No, sir. Now I shan't have any money till the end of next week.'

(Pocket money was carefully doled out by Betty Cope.)

'Ever lost anything before?'

'Yes sir, sixpence. The week I came.'

'Well, better watch your wealth more carefully in future. I'll give you a bob to tide you over for sweets and that will have to do.'

Annick said that the venues of trouble must be the lockers and the changing-room. 'But I'm damned if I'm going to have some spy lurking around! Anyway, who'd be willing?'

'Helen's got a strong detective instinct,' Stephen said, grinning, 'I've often noticed it. But the changing-room is precisely where she couldn't lurk.'

He was happier nowadays, for her demands upon him had sensibly lessened.

'Have we a kleptomaniac here,' Grace wondered, 'or just a bad boy?'

'We'll know that when we catch him,' Stephen replied. 'But Lord, doesn't it seem revolting for all of us here to go around trying to catch people at all?'

'I agree with you, Steve,' Annick said, 'but I don't see how much longer we're going to live in this welter of suspicion and whispering. It is divorcing us from the boys – do you realize that? It's us against them. They think we're half-wits. They will have to be disabused.'

He sat long in his study, pondering what line he should take. Would it be feasible to ask the vicar to preach on 'Thou shalt not steal', next Sunday, in order to strike terror into the heart of an evil-doer? Or would this simply make the evil-doer rather more careful? He decided against it. The vicar would have to be told the reason for the request, and in consequence his sermon would be appallingly ham-handed.

Meanwhile, he believed he had never had classes so well-behaved, and nor had anyone else. They were all conducted now in a kind of miasmic hush, broken only by unnatural politenesses. Then he made up his mind.

First, he sent round a note asking all members of the staff to attend morning prayers. This was not as a rule obligatory, but he wanted an impressive platform array. Then he waited till there came the first rustle of dispersal, the rising from the benches, and he called out – 'Please sit down again, all of you. I have something to say.'

'Strike a match and we'd all go up with a bang,' Canning murmured to Stephen.

The rustle, subsiding, had been succeeded by a tight silence.

Annick said sharply, 'Hands up, those of you who have lost property of any sort, in money or in kind, during the last two months.'

At first, not a hand raised. The boys stole sidelong looks at one another, as if expecting to see writing appear upon a forehead. Then Joel Bailey, doubtless remembering all he had told his mother and not trusting her, put up a wavering hand.

'One of you. Come on, I want the rest. We haven't all the morning to waste.'

Another hand, then another, till a dozen were in the air. Peter's hand was not raised.

Annick made a count. 'Good. Now I want every one of you who have put a hand up to make a list, when you go to your classrooms, of what you think you have missed.' A relieved shuffle of feet. 'No! I didn't tell you to go yet.'

He looked them slowly over, row by row. If there were a Cain among them, he remained unmarked. One little boy, barely eight, began to cry a little, but this was out of sheer tension.

Annick came to the front of the dais.

'Now, listen. There cannot have been a mass outbreak of pure carelessness. It is beginning to look as though someone is taking things.'

An intake of breath.

'I don't want or intend to make victims. But this can't go on. There has been a beastly feeling in the school ever since it began, which you older boys must have felt as much as I have.

'I want whoever is responsible for these disappearances to come and tell me so. I'm not going to expel him. I won't even punish him. But I must know who he is.

'My method is going to be on the clumsy side. I understand that if a boy suddenly got up and came to speak to me privately, no matter what about, he would fall under suspicion. So, if you remember the method employed in The Forty Thieves – that is, putting a chalk mark on *every* door, I am going to employ something like that. I want to see every member of the school in my study, individually, class by class, tomorrow from ten-thirty onwards. I should think a couple of minutes with each of you will be enough: but there will be time in that two minutes for the responsible person to come clean. Mr Poole will organize this and tell you at prayers tomorrow how it will be worked. Provided this lost property is, so far as possible, given back, I will respect the taker's confidence. Now go back to your classes and don't chatter.'

No one seemed to wish to. Dispersal was quiet.

'I don't see that you can do more,' said Grace. 'Do you think they all understood?'

'I shall interview the top form first and make sure that they do. Then they can clear up any misconceptions in the minds of their juniors.'

He felt some relief that at least action had been taken. But he had no great hopes of the morrow.

It proved to be a dreary day with clouds looped like theatre-curtains on a chalky sky. Annick sat in his study feeling both a brute and a fool.

The head boy first. Then Peter Quillan.

'Petey, why didn't you put your hand up yesterday? You know your ring's gone.'

'Because it could have slipped off, sir, just about. I was scrambling about in the Thicket and it might have happened. So I couldn't take any chances.'

'All right, that will do for now. Send in the next.'

For hours, a parade of boys: bland boys, shifty boys, anxious boys, careful boys: and all of it a total waste of time. When the last had gone Annick felt hopeless.

It was almost a relief to have a gloomy session with Helen and her unbalancing books, with Betty Cope, high-flushed and talkative who had bad news about increased laundry charges and was demanding that the boys should be asked to bring two pairs of pillow-cases instead of one. But she, at least, was cheerful.

'We're sunk, Betty, and no thief caught.'

'What a shame! The trouble is, now it will all cool down and then it will start up again.'

'I'm afraid so. You're looking well.'

'I've had good news. A friend of mine's leaving London for a job in Eastbourne and she's going to share my digs with me. I was feeling a bit solitary.'

'I'm so glad for you.'

'I suppose I oughtn't to have bothered you about that linen, but I can't find Mrs Annick.'

'She's in Seaford for the day. I'm afraid she felt like avoiding the inquisition. Not that I'll have any dramatic news for her when she gets back Betty, all this is making me feel rather sick. We've had a great upheaval and we're back where we started.'

'Do we know whether any of the boys have had recent home troubles?'

'Psychology. I see. No, I haven't heard of any, if they exist. I only hear when parents come to confess of imminent divorces and then I know I'm in for six months of trouble. Yes, why did you come to me about the linen? It could have waited. You know I can't tell one end of a pillow-case from the other.'

Betty smiled brilliantly. 'I simply had to tell somebody my news. Wasn't it idiotic? Sorry, Mr Annick.'

'Never mind. It's nice to see a young face.'

She said she thought he might have seen too many young faces that day, and he laughed.

When she had gone, he thought about Mrs Murray. He knew a good deal about Betty's London friend and wondered how much of a blow this would be to the older woman. Life felt very heavy and very complicated. He was glad when Grace came in.

'No luck. They all claim to be as innocent as angels.'

'And are they?'

'Someone can't be. It's depressing.' He told her about Betty.

'Oh, poor Elspeth!'

'That's what I thought.'

Grace took off her new shoes, which had been pinching her. 'It may be the effect of growing older, but I do sometimes feel that the whole of life is darkening down. Everyone seems to be in some kind of trouble. Elspeth Murray often drives me silly, and I find myself despising her because she's gone mad at her time of life and fallen in love with Betty: it's not only perverse but it's funny. At least, it often seems funny to me. But it isn't to her, and she's going to suffer at least as much as Stephen for his lost girl. I wonder if we can judge by any criterion but individual suffering? People don't feel pain less because they seem to us comic.' She went rapidly on: 'Corporate pain. Revolt against parents, against institutions. Bad housing. Homes crammed with illegitimate children. Have any of them got names? I find I can only think of the individual person, the single sufferer. Does that mean I'm growing old? They laugh at ads about distressed "gentlefolk". Privileged beasts, even to be gentlefolk! But isn't it as bad for them, and in some ways worse? They are so untrained. They are so untrained to suffer, poor old things. And besides, they too are poor, and untrained to be poor. Does this all sound crazy to you?'

He tried to cheer her: all this was so uncharacteristic. 'It's because your feet have been hurting you.'

'Oh, how mundane! I hope that's the reason. But sometimes I

even think about what you and I are doing here, and whether any of it is really worth it.'

'If we didn't exist—'

'If places like this didn't, about six boys in each, like Petey, would suffer. That's all.'

'Six boys like Petey shouldn't have to suffer, so long as it can be avoided.'

'We ought to beat Rowan House on Wednesday,' she said, perceptibly brightening, and he envied her those quick changes of mood for which he had always loved her. Himself, he did not give a damn whether Downs Park did or didn't win a famous victory: but she cared.

'Well, what about our Fagin?' she said at last.

'Nothing. I shall give out a notice that any missing property is to be reported to Mr Poole at once, and then let the whole thing ride. We should have a period of relative peace, and that's all we can hope for.'

Chapter Nineteen

The reason why Penelope was seeing less of Canning was her guiltiness. Twice, since the Massingers had left Downs Park, she had slept with Rupert. She had met him quite by chance one day in Eastbourne, while Blossom was away staying with her sister. They had had a few drinks, and it had happened. There was no love in it: she did not even like him. She had simply yielded to the sexual need which had tormented her so wretchedly since her husband's death. Physically, she had enjoyed every moment of it and it had left her temporarily assuaged: but the relief of assuagement had been followed rapidly by a sickness of self-disgust. On the second occasion they had made a deliberate assignation and Rupert, who knew how to do everything, had taken her to a room in a shady-looking backstreet. Just for the afternoon, cocktails in a nice quiet hotel to follow.

She would have slept with Canning had he asked her, and been happy: but just as he did not approve of bad language in front of ladies, so he did not approve of anticipating marriage. He wanted to marry her.

Naturally constant, she had never in her life played any double game with men, and the playing of this one smeared her imagination. When she met Rupert by a third assignation, this time in a small hotel more or less lost in the Downs, she told him she had come to put an end to it.

'Well, if you must you must,' Rupert said, looking at her with inflamed eyes, 'but we'll celebrate the end in the old way. You can't get me down here and then carry on like the ice-maiden.'

She shrugged.

'Look, I've fixed it with the people here. Told them we must have an hour's peace and quiet. They're not talkers – nobody to talk to. This place will have to pack up within six months.'

'I didn't come to defraud you,' said Penelope, 'so long as you realize that I'm not coming ever again. Let's go and get it over with.'

He stared at her. 'God what a bloody woman you can be!' His lower lip protruded, as if he might cry.

'I'm sorry.'

'If you're feeling guilty about Bloss, you needn't. She's never got on to us. I don't give her the chance.'

'It's not that.'

'What, then, Leo? Are you going to marry your dad's pet oik?'

Penelope said, 'This is a pretty scene, Rupert, isn't it? Both of us being as beastly as we can to the other. For my part I don't want to be. I've reason to be grateful to you.'

'Same to you, fair ladye, spelled with a "y e". Oh, come, cheer up and don't be such a wet blanket! It was fun, wasn't it?'

'In a way.'

It was cold in the upstairs room, under the eaves. Chilly pigeons cooed from their perch on a rainpipe. They both undressed only in part and got as quickly as they could under the blankets. It was a perfunctory business, both of them sexually satisfied, and both restless with discontent.

'I shan't remember that among the great experiences of my life,' Rupert said, surly, as he put on his trousers. 'Go on, straighten up the bed and maybe they'll think we just came up here for a chat.'

Somewhere, a stable clock chimed.

'Come on, opening time. Let's go down and drink.'

She hesitated.

'I said, come on. I'm not going to drive you back to Eastbourne looking like a picture of woe.'

'And you shouldn't drink when you're driving.'

'They aren't going to catch me, my girl, not ever.'

She went down to drink with him. From the terminus, where he would deposit her, there would be a long, cold bus drive. Already there was a slight flurry of snow, just enough to lighten the tones of the grass. The bar parlour was small and warm, the lamps had cherry-coloured shades.

After a pint of beer, she began to feel for him something like affection coupled by compunction. He couldn't help his violent drives, even more than she had recently been unable to help those drives of her own. Big, fattish, in a way handsome, his skin mottled like brawn, he still retained the look of a schoolboy. She put out a hand and touched him. He gazed at her in surprise, hazel eyes baffled.

'That's nice, anyway.'

'I felt we were hostile. I don't want it to be like that.'

'Hostile! That's a word and a half. No, I was only a bit put out because you weren't exactly in an oncoming mood. But we'll part friends, anyway. Have the other half.'

'Is it always like this with you, Rups? You can take women or leave them?'

'All but Bloss. Mind you, if you were feeling different, I mightn't be leaving you so easily. Though it's you who are doing the leaving, isn't it?'

In his clumsy way, he wanted, she believed, to spare her feelings. About his wife, he remained romantic: he would wish to be just a little so about everyone else. How I have changed since Barry died! I can't even be properly grateful to Rupert for what I had to have from him.

'How's Poole shaping up?' he asked her, wishing to change the subject. 'Still O.K.?'

She replied, perfectly: but Delia was so shy that she always seemed a little furtive. Heaven knows what she had to be furtive about.

'I see. And I suppose D.P. is still in the red?'

'It's permanent condition, I suppose. I don't inquire.'

'Can't go on that way for ever.' He paused. Then: 'What about Canning? Is he serious about you? He's a good two years younger than you are.'

'Nearly three. But that doesn't seem all the world. Yes, he's serious enough.'

'And you about him? He'll never change, you know. You'll be a funny couple. Remember how he and I used to get across each other?' He gave a barking laugh, as if it had all been so long ago.

'You mean, that old demon, class,' said Penelope. 'You're out of date, Rups. He's too clever to have any class.'

'If he had an ounce of sense he'd go and work for Corso. Why doesn't he?'

'I think,' she replied, speaking of Canning now as if he were Rupert's friend as well as her own, 'he had such a squalid childhood that he simply loves our shrinking little island of privilege. In fact, he admits it. And when he does decide to go back into the big world, he will work like a beaver till he has made an island of privilege of his own.'

It was easy to talk now, passion spent, things decided. She did not want to leave the warm shelter of the bar. There was a log fire in the grate. Rupert threw halfpennies into it to make blue flames.

'Pretty,' she said. 'Let me throw one, too.'

A child's game. She would remember it.

At last he had to take her back to Eastbourne. He wanted to be home a good half-hour before Blossom got there.

The bus rolled through the phantom snowflakes, overhanging boughs brushing the roof. Is it really so easy as all that? So easy to begin, so easy to end? Yet she knew it would be hard for her, for a long time, to renew her easy relations with Canning, no matter how hurt or puzzled he might be. She felt – she tried to laugh at herself for such atavism – somewhat soiled. If Barry had dreamed for a second that I could have been like this—

She tried to think about him, but already his face was fading in detail from her memory as the faces of the dead so often do. Could she marry Leo? She was half in love with him, yes: but had been wholly in love with Barry. It could never be the same again, not with anyone else.

'Pack up your troubles, dear,' said a woman with a huge basket on her knees, who was crushing her against the windows.

'Such a long face!'

Penelope responded: she found response to strangers easy. 'I was half asleep.'

'I always say, nothing's worth the worrying. Me, I get up in the morning and I sing my head off. Makes a start to the day. My groceries bothering you?'

'Oh no.'

'Shop once a week, get the whole thing over. That's my motto, get everything over.'

Even life, even death. But that's a silly way to think. You know you're more cheerful than you've been for a long time, partly due to Leo and partly – face up to it – due to Rups. God knows what mother would say if she knew.

'Come to the end of the day, you've done it all, see? So you can sleep sound and feel like singing in the morning again. My hubby, he says I make too much noise, but that's better than the silent grave, isn't it? Here, take a look at these grapefruit. Two for a bob. Think they'll ever drop an atom bomb?'

Penelope said that she doubted it. Everyone was as scared as everyone else.

' "We're here because we're here because we're here because we're here," ' the woman sang exuberantly, causing heads to turn. It was now evident that she was a little drunk. 'Me, I take things as they come. So'd you, if you knew what was good for you. Yes, I'm up with the sun, every bloody day, springing out of bed, ready for anything. What's that, thunder?'

Only the long scraping of a heavy bough on the roof of the bus. 'No.'

'Now that I am scared of. God's angry with me, that's what I think. My hub, he says it's scientific, but I tell him we don't know everything and we're not meant to. Well, I get out here. Nice to have had a natter.'

The woman lurched off with her heavy basket and was courteously helped by the conductor. They had reached the middle of Chalkwood. Penelope had another two miles to ride: she was spending the night with her parents while the new paint in her bedroom dried out.

It was with a feeling of comfort to her heart that she came up the drive in sight of the school. Downs Park looked delectable by night, far more so than by day. Of the main structure, two of the contiguous buildings were of 1830: the other was a tactful addition made a hundred years later. None but bedroom curtains were ever closed, and the yellow lights poured out, making the gravel sparkle, catching bushes here and there with Pre-Raphaelite detail and delicacy, every leaf, every twig, distinct. Light fell, as upon massed shields, on the roofs and sides of the staff cars. Despite the cold, the outer door stood open, as it always did until midnight: the inner one kept the warmth in.

All this seemed so beautiful to Penelope that, tired and chilled as she was, she paused to look at it. The aftermath of sexual pleasure was suddenly strong in her, and she glowed. Perhaps the woman on the bus had something to be said for her. Immediate action, immediate clearance, sleep, and raucous morning song. Though I do not see myself raucously singing. It would surprise mother and father if I took to it.

Grace came round the side of the house: she had been seeing that the little ones were all asleep.

'What are you doing, darling? Playing statues?'

'I was just thinking how pretty it all looked.'

'It does, doesn't it? Had a nice time? Have you had any food?' Grace had never said, since Penelope was seventeen, 'Where have you been?'

'No. I'll get myself something.'

Usually, she took her parents much for granted: but tonight it was pleasant to sit over the fire with them, eating the egg and cress sandwiches for which she had a passion. She might have felt guilty but she did not: guilt had left her.

'You'll get fat,' said Grace.

Annick raised his head. 'Did you hear that?' His ears were sharp.

They said no, they had heard nothing.

'It sounded as though somebody screamed, a long way off.'

'A bird,' Grace said.

'I don't think so. I'd better go and look around, if only I knew where to look. Listen!'

This time they did hear it, a faint, shrill noise, not like a bird's.

They ran downstairs, put their coats on and went out into the bitter night.

'It's not the school itself,' Grace said, 'it was too far away.'

'No,' said Canning, feet crunching on the gravel. He wore his top coat over his pyjamas, 'it's from the cottage. I'll dash over and see if anything's up.'

Penelope said she would come with him. She told Annick and Grace to get in out of the cold.

She and Canning ran over the grass to where a single light was burning.

'Someone's up, anyway,' she said.

All the curtains were drawn. The beam was coming through the fanlight over the door.

Canning rang the bell. It was opened almost at once by Poole, who was fully dressed.

'Why, what's up?'

'We all thought we heard someone scream, coming from this direction.'

'Not from here. I was just going to bed.'

'Didn't you hear anything?'

'I didn't, I had the radio on. Delia's asleep, so far as I know.'

Canning hesitated. 'There was something.'

'A bird?'

'That's what we all thought at first, but decided against it. We wondered if something was wrong here.'

Poole did not ask them in.

'It's a mystery to me.'

'Well,' said Canning, 'life is dodgy nowadays. One ought always to investigate screaming, but where does one start?' The woods were dark. No other lights shone anywhere. 'Somebody,' he added with something like relish, 'knifed somebody somewhere. What will we all look like if we heard it but didn't do anything?'

'Look,' said Poole, 'it was almost certainly some damned bird. But the only place I can think of for investigation is the Thicket. Anyone got a torch?'

'Crass of us,' Penelope answered, 'but no. We just tore out to investigate.'

'I've got one. Shall we reconnoitre?'

So they did, the three of them, into the ominous shadows, tripping in rabbit holes, colliding with trees, brambles enlacing their ankles. Dead silence everywhere, except for the noise they made themselves. There appeared to be nothing amiss in the Thicket which, despite the vastness it assumed in the minds of little boys, covered a very small area.

'We must assume it was some bloody owl, then,' Poole said, 'there's nothing more we can do.'

'Silly lot we'll look if they find a body in the grounds tomorrow.' Canning was rueful.

'It seems rather little to ring the police about,' Penelope said tentatively, her eyes asking.

'We can't do that. We'll have to wait. But it's a mare's nest of some sort,' Poole added.

They saw him back to the cottage. Immediately he was inside, he turned the hall light out.

'So now we blunder back, looking fools,' said Canning.

'So now we blunder.'

There was no moon. He took her arm and they made their way cautiously towards the lights of the school. Once he stopped to kiss her. 'O.K., Pen, only taking advantage of the witching hour.'

She returned the kiss and was glad for his warmth near her.

'Drawn blank,' he said cheerfully to the waiting Annicks. 'We must wait for the morning.'

'You both look frozen.' Grace was anxious.

'A little something wouldn't come amiss. None of the boys heard, did they?'

'If they had, they'd certainly put it down to owls. But there's been no sign of it.'

How nice it is, Penelope thought, all of us up late and excited round the fire. An unexpected and comforting end her day.

Morning brought no elucidation.

Chapter Twenty

Stephen inaugurated the school debating society. This, given Annick's blessing, was confined to the top three forms: after all, he said, they would most of them be indulging in this futile activity sooner or later. It began in an atmosphere of gravity. Both the Annicks were there in the library, Canning, Penelope, and Helen Queen. The subject had been forced upon it by Stephen, who did not believe in starting from too low a level. 'This House Believes that it is Good for a Man to Seek a Wife.'

Mauled knees protruded from grey flannel shorts: faces were earnest. Pervading all was the fascinating smell of Boy, compounded of grime, soap, recent sausages, and an inexplicable sweetness, as it were of salad days. All hands had been soaped clean: no one was to be permitted to debate in grubbiness.

Since none of these boys had ever heard a formal debate in his life, it began slowly. Richard Searle was *pro* and a boy called Hewitt, who seemed to have had an unhappy family life, *contra*.

'Of course, I don't know,' said Peter Quillan, seconding the motion, 'but it seems to me that whether a man wants a wife or not, he is going to have a boring old age without one. There are so many things women can do and men can't. Sewing, for example.'

A laugh, here.

'I don't see what's so funny. Sewing's got to be done and most men can't except soldiers. They carry things called hussifs, or they may call them housewives.'

More laughter.

'And then there's cooking,' Peter continued remorselessly.

'I wouldn't want to live on cold open tins and I don't suppose you would, either. Also, it's a matter of having somebody to talk to. I think that's tremendously important.' His voice grew firmer. 'I don't see myself, absolutely decrepit, talking to myself, with all my buttons off and holes in my socks. So, I think it's up to a man to take a wife.'

He sat down, to applause.

Trust Petey,' Annick murmured to Grace, 'he never lets one down.'

A boy called Finlay, who was showing belated promise, seconded the opposition.

'Well, men have clubs. If they wanted women around the whole time, they wouldn't, would they? As for Quillan's buttons and socks, he can learn to look after himself. As he said, soldiers do. As for being lonely or wanting someone to talk to, there are as many men as women in the population—'

'Slightly more,' Canning interjected.

'Slightly more men than women, so there's *always* someone to talk to. One thing nobody's mentioned, not having children. Well, if I had to cope with me, I think I'd rather not have children.'

Applause.

'After all, they cost a lot of money, I bet I do. And then you worry about them all the time. I hate being worried about.'

'A consistent mind,' Annick murmured to Canning. 'Could he be scholarship material?'

'Oh, he could. If only my subject was more use to him. He's a scientist. Give him a try, anyhow, see how he shapes.'

'If you had your way,' said Peter, bursting in upon Finlay, 'the world would come to an end. There'd be no more people.'

'Well,' Finlay retorted, 'I really wouldn't care, would I? Anyway, there would be lots of other men to take wives.'

'But that isn't the point! We're assuming that men do or don't take wives—'

'You can't,' said Finlay, who was increasing Annick's scholarship hopes every time he opened his mouth, 'expect everyone to think the same way as I do. There will always be some saps.'

He sat down, to cordial support.

For the moment, the boys were exhausted. It was time for the masters to take over.

Canning crossed his legs with yoga-like ease. His nose looked preternaturally long.

'I think none of you has mentioned what a man wants of a wife. I know what I do.'

Here, subdued mirth. The school knew that he wanted Penelope.

Ringed with eyes bright as those of Siamese cats in the gloom of a passage, he waited.

'All right, sir,' said Searle. 'What do you want?'

'The old-fashioned virtues. Did any of you think I was "with it"? I'm not. I don't like what "It" is. I don't want any of your working wives, but one who's always there when I come home.'

'To warm your slippers, sir?' Cheek from Finlay.

'No, because I never change my shoes even when I get my feet wet. I want someone I can tell things to at once, not have to wait for her to come in. And I want to smell cooking at once – ah, beautiful! Stewed steak, with carrots and dumplings, and raspberry jam tart.'

Penelope laughed outright.

'I think that sort of wife would be a slave,' said D'Oyley, who wore thick glasses. 'If I ever get married at all, and I haven't made up my mind yet which way to vote, it'll be to someone beautiful and rich, so she won't have to cook.'

'Suppose she's beautiful and poor?' asked Stephen.

'Then I'll ask someone else.'

'Aren't we getting too far from the motion?' Stephen inquired. 'Richard, you have a troubled brow.'

'Me? Oh, I shall get married, I expect, but not till I'm forty. Mr Canning's idea of dinner in the oven made me feel hungry, but man does not live by bread alone. No, I think one needs companionship as one grows old and – and the shadows close in,' Searle added poetically. 'That's why I'm proposing the motion.'

'I shall never get married,' said a boy called Hickling, who had a small, discontented face. 'I don't see the point of it unless you want a lot of children and I don't. My mother says you never stop worrying when you've got them even when they're grown-up. And I don't want to worry ever, if I can help it. Finlay says he doesn't want to be worried about, but I don't think grown-ups really worry as much as one thinks about other people.' (Here a slight stir, as if something not really right had been said.) 'I shall live in a club, which my father seems to do half the time, anyway. The cooking's good in clubs and there are always people to talk to.'

Annick reflected upon this revelation of Hickling's home life. He was learning quite a lot tonight.

'Yes,' Searle came back again, 'and get grey and crabby, and always talk about the same old things, and it will always reek of beer and pipe-smoke. And not have a garden.'

'Bachelors can have gardens if they want,' said Finlay. 'They can live in garden flats or have small houses of their own. Besides, if you get married you're bound to run out of things to talk about sooner or later.'

'We don't,' Grace put in. 'Twenty-four hours seem far too few to gossip about all the things that go on in this place.'

'Do you and Mr Annick gossip about us?' D'Oyley was shy, but very curious.

'Of course. All the time. It is called "taking an interest".'

'But "all our sins remembered—" ' Peter mused, and Annick smiled inwardly. Last term's visit to *Hamlet* had not failed to bear fruit.

'And your virtues too,' he said, 'don't forget that.' He looked at the clock. 'Getting late. I think Searle and Hewitt had better make their concluding speeches.'

When the boys had gone to bed, he congratulated Stephen upon the success of his venture.

'I didn't think it was bad for a first try. They may as well get in some practice before they go off – as some of them will – to be appallingly facetious in student unions.'

'Leo's horrible wife!' said Penelope. 'I am still shuddering. I can see her creeping around on flat feet, not daring to open her mouth, and constantly tottering into the kitchen to watch the stew.'

'She would be allowed to open her mouth,' Canning answered, 'to make intelligent comments on what I'd said to her.'

'Poor Hickling,' said Stephen. 'I always did think there was something wrong there. Have you ever had a chat with his mum? She has all the weight of the world on her shoulders, and his dad keeps letting out huge unnerving barks like a ship's siren. Five siblings, too, hapless little beasts.'

Canning stood up. 'One thing that did get me, was that so many seemed surprised that we talked about them. Humble, aren't they? In a sort of way. I never was.'

'That,' said Penelope, 'doesn't surprise me. Would you much mind running me back? My bike's under repair and I had to walk here this morning.'

He was delighted. He had been fumbling in his mind for some excuse to get her to himself. Also, he was happy that she had asked him for something. She was the kind of girl who seemed to hate asking, and he would so much have loved to be entreated by her.

When they came back to her lodgings she asked him if he would like a cup of tea. 'Coffee at this hour keeps me awake.'

'That would be nectar,' he said.

She turned on the electric fire. 'Soon be warm.'

He watched her as she took off the orange headscarf he much admired, her heavy tweed coat. He thought she was looking fatigued.

'You sit down,' he said, 'and I'll get the tea. I'm domesticated.'

She protested that he did not know where anything was kept.

'In a place this size, the exercise of a bit of common intelligence goes a long way.'

He was back very soon from the small kitchen, with a tray upon which everything was neatly and completely set. 'There, you see.'

'So there doesn't seem much need for that horrible woman who keeps slopping in and out after the stew.'

'Oh, but there is.'

'The boys were instructive, weren't they?'

'Very. I like children.'

'So do I,' said Penelope. 'Did you know that I lost one? It was stillborn.'

'I didn't know. I'm sorry.'

'It all seems very dreamlike now.' She was glad that she had told him. He was one of the few people from whom she found it difficult to keep secrets: only the squalid secret of Massinger burned away at the back of her mind. Well, it would have to burn, until it blackened, and went out.

Later, he put his arms round her and moved his lips up and down her cheek. It was firmly-boned but soft in the hollows, where there was a slight bloom perceptible only to touch. She was content to sit quietly.

'I'd have to accept Corso's offer, of course, as there would have to be a bit more money flying about.' His accent was a little stronger than usual.

'What for?'

'For if we get married, Pen. Won't you have me? I shall go on asking you, you know.'

Now she allowed him to kiss her lips, which he did in a curious, tasting fashion, repeatedly, softly. She felt the spring of excitement: she had never really been roused by him before. But she replied, 'I'm not ready, Leo. Not yet. Not for anyone.'

'Then I'll have to wait until you are, won't I? Only it's hard.'

She said earnestly, 'If you want me to go to bed with you, you know I—'

'I don't like to hear you say that.' He looked at her out of clear, severe eyes. 'I know it's the way girls talk nowadays, but it's not right for you. It's simply not your style, if you know what I mean. I'm going to wait until you're ready to marry me, and then we're going to have a real slap-up wedding with lots of people, and cake and all the rest of it, and then I'm going to take you away with me and put you to bed in my own good time.'

'Oh Leo!' She began to laugh. 'You're a Victorian!'

'Not quite. But you're the type who ought to be a bit of one.'

'Did you mean that about the perfect wife?'

'Of course not, silly. Or not all of it.'

'Wouldn't I go out to work?'

'I'd be a clot if I couldn't keep you properly.'

She said, 'Don't let's talk about it any more tonight.'

When he had gone she lay awake in the dark. He ought, she felt, by his accent, his manner, his ideas, to grate upon her. Would she ever – to be brutal – come to feel and to resent the difference between her genteel education and his? (One had to think of such things.) No, because there was something too remote about him for that. Leo was going a long way and would live his life not by accidents but by choices. He would be precisely as he wished and other people would have to learn to like him that way. There would be no condescending to Leo: she had never seen anybody try.

But she felt becalmed. She was not ready to marry him or anyone else, not yet a while, and she did not mean to be driven into it by her purely physical needs. Her own too-eager response to Massinger frightened her in retrospect; she hated acting out of character, and this time she had done so. It amused her to think that hardly a man in a thousand, loving her, would have refused her as Canning had done: but it was a wry amusement. She believed that he must have had resolute parents of rigid moral standards, and that they had been the last people to whom he had ever seriously given his entire attention. She imagined a little hot parlour, a mahogany table with bobbled green cloth, two stiff arm-chairs, two straight ones, a clock with visible works, two symmetrically-placed vases of pampas grass. In the single bookcase, *The Children's Encyclopaedia*. Then, a school stuck up in the middle of asphalt, where he had been the brightest boy. Head boy, probably, chosen for brightness and rectitude.

She did not doubt that his sexual nature was strong. How, then, did he endure the lonely, enforcedly-companionable life of the school, the bodily deprivation? He was always about the place, never seemed to be away for long.

We should have rather an ugly home, she thought, Leo would want red velvet curtains and fake Jacobean chairs and he wouldn't let me have a say in it.

Oddly enough, this fantasy produced a strengthening sense of resentment. She was used to having her own way: her parents had let her have it, and Barry in his turn. Leo would not be so complaisant. Better by far for him to marry some girl who would say 'Yes, dear, no dear'. Yet she instantly became jealous of the thought of that girl. What I want is another job. I need to strike out again. I'm too much in danger here of doing what people decide I should do.

Next day, she did something which was, for her, quite extraordinary. She had a confidential talk with her mother. Grace attempted to suppress astonishment, to be calm and sensible.

'Yes, dear, I know. I suppose everyone does. Leo is obviously in love with you. Certainly the entire school knows, but then, the boys always do. We live in a goldfish bowl.'

'What I think about it,' Penelope said, 'I don't know at all. Could I make a life with Leo? He would be so very bossy, and in all the ways I didn't like.'

'I think,' Grace said firmly, 'that much of the bossiness is only for show. In some ways he is very unsure of himself.'

'In no ways that I've detected. Leo has a superiority complex.'

'Let's say, where you are concerned.'

'If you were right, it might be tolerable. But if you're wrong—'

' "Curtains" I think Leo would say,' said Grace with a gleam of comedy. 'But don't look on the worst side. Daddy and I would like to see you married again.'

'But to Leo?'

Here Grace was honest. So long as class differences existed in an imperfect world, so they would inevitably be felt. Penelope's generation certainly seemed able to shrug them aside: but how much of the shrugging was genuine? In domestic intimacy, where would the jarring note intrude itself? If there was real love, it might not: but Penelope was not talking like a girl utterly in love.

'I'm not, utterly. But a bit.'

'I think you would get more of your own way than you think, at any rate, in superficial matters. It is Leo's whole character that you have to consider.'

'You and Daddy like him?'

'Enormously. But the boys, inordinately. I think that doesn't go for nothing.'

Penelope had her own touch of fun. 'You don't think I should consult Petey? I know how much store Daddy sets by him.'

'Well, no. I don't think Petey is quite ripe enough to be of use to you in such an important matter.'

The confidential session came to an end.

Chapter Twenty-One

Helen Queen was pleased to have the run of the cottage again. Since the falling-off of Stephen's fleeting affections, life for her had been dull. Not because Stephen had been very good at it: after Rupert, who could possibly seem so?

She was alone, typing and filing, for a full hour, and her work did not fill it. So she went about trying to uncover secrets, not that she meant to profit by any she found, but because they seemed to draw her, as nothing else did, into the common family. She needed to be 'in the thick of things'. And what brought anyone so near to the 'thick' as knowing things others did not?

She liked the Pooles very much, though they puzzled her a little. Norman was devoted to Delia: but on some mornings he seemed distrait, as though she did not exist. As for Delia herself, she was an affectionate little thing, as Helen had cause to know.

Nothing was kept now in the secret drawer; it was unlikely that the Pooles had so much as discovered it. It seemed a sad cavity without the glow of Rupert's books, dusty, an open invitation to death-watch beetle. No diaries were kept, nothing was to be found under the linen upstairs. One thing only: the small oak cupboard in the dining-room was always locked.

But then another thing. Tidying one day in Delia's bedroom, she happened to explore the back of one of the dressing-table drawers, and there she found a sherry-glass, unwashed.

She smelled it delicately, nostrils rounding the rim. Not sherry, whisky. In memory of all the detective stories she had read, she wiped the stem with her handkerchief and put the glass back in place. What an extraordinary place to leave one!

Someone coming in. Delia? She went hastily to the lavatory, flushed it, and came at a normal pace downstairs.

Delia it was.

'You're early, Mrs Poole.'

'Not so very, I don't think.'

'I've just finished clearing up. Mr Poole will find all his letters waiting for him on the desk.'

'Thank you, dear.'

Helen lingered for a second on the porch. Delia had gone into the dining-room. What for? She peered swiftly through the window, as Grace had once done. To the cupboard. She could only see Delia's back, nothing else, and she dared not wait.

She went to take D'Oyley's piano lesson. He was in his second year and coming along rapidly: it looked as though she might have a star pupil.

'No, no, no! This is called *The Evening Star*. When you run up to that top C at the end you don't thump it, you touch it as lightly and sharply as you can, because that *is* the evening star.'

'Oh, is it? I see.'

D'Oyley did as he was told, and very nicely too.

'That's better! Now you might prepare *Sea Mist* for next week. Key of E major, rather more difficult than what you've been doing.'

He said he would try.

'We might send you in for an exam next year. Would you like that?'

'I would, rather.'

She looked curiously into the goggled eyes. 'You like learning, don't you, Jimmy? But do you like listening to music? I don't often see you at Mr Smith's gramophone concerts.'

'I like listening by myself, not with all the rest of them. One knows most of them are bored stiff and that spoils things.'

She sympathized with him. D'Oyley, by no means attractive to everyone, touched her emotions. He was rather a forlorn little boy, a natural solitary with hectic dreams. She remembered him saying, in the debate, that he wanted to marry someone beautiful and rich.

'I go to concerts by myself in the holidays. If my mother goes with me, she always wants to know whether I like things, when I just want to think.'

'What do you like best?'

'Well, Wagner really, and some Bach.'

Grace looked round the door. 'Oh, Helen – am I interrupting? Hullo, Jimmy.'

'Not a bit. We'd just finished. You can run along now.'

As the door shut behind him, Grace said anxiously, 'Could you write off and remind Pearson's father that he's in arrears? Do it tactfully, because I'm sure it's more carelessness than anything else.'

'I don't like their sort of carelessness,' said Helen.

'Oh, don't be too harsh, dear. Cyril would say that even parents were human.'

Helen found to her annoyance that she had left the office keys in the cottage. She wanted to get all her work done before lunch because this was her free afternoon, and she was going to the cinema in Eastbourne. So she hurried back, and in her haste forgot to knock at the front door before going in.

'Sorry,' she began. 'I—'

Delia was at the open cupboard, topping up a whisky bottle with water. The cupboard was crammed with bottles, several having their levels marked with Scotch tape. She spun round with a gasp, banged the door shut, then defiantly opened it again.

'Just having a drink before lunch. Do keep me company!' She brought down glasses from the top shelf.

'I'd love to,' Helen said, recovering herself, 'but I really haven't time.' She explained that she had forgotten her keys and had a pile of work to get through.

Delia, who had flushed brightly, was now white. 'Oh, please do!' she pleaded. 'It's so dreadfully squalid to drink alone, don't you think? I hardly ever do. You'd never believe it,' she chattered on, as she replaced the cap on the topped-up bottle, 'but Norman has the maddest fancy for diluting his whisky *in* the bottle, because he doesn't like adding water afterwards. Did you ever hear anything so dotty?'

Helen had seldom, she thought, heard a dottier lie. She changed her mind suddenly: if she couldn't get to Eastbourne, then she couldn't. 'I'll join you in a very small drink then – gin and tonic, please, or—'

'I'm afraid we're out of tonic. Noilly Prat?'

'Lovely.'

Delia poured Helen quite a large drink, herself a derisorily small one. As if by compulsion, she locked the cupboard.

'It is so nice to take a little time off, isn't it? I mean, give oneself some ridiculous treat now and then.' She sipped her gin like an elderly marquise of great physical delicacy sipping a *tisane*. 'Oh – for pity's sake never tell Norman that I told you about that absurd trick of his – though I know you never would. It's one of his few eccentricities and he simply loathes to feel he's eccentric at all!'

'I wouldn't, anyway.'

'He really is such a dear, you know. I often think how lucky I am to have him. There's some difference of years between us, as I expect you've guessed – nearly fifteen – but it's never made the slightest difference.'

At that moment he came in. Delia jumped up and kissed his cheek. 'Lovely and early, and just in time! Helen and I were giving ourselves just a very small indulgence. Will you join us? Do! It'll be like a party.'

He refused: but returned her kiss. He looked very tired. He was sweating from the gym.

Poor devil, Helen thought, poor devil.

She was glad, now she knew the secret, to get out of the house. What would happen when she had gone? A row, or hopeless resignation?

She wondered how long it would take the Annicks to guess: or, come to that, the school, though little boys, sensitive to amorous overtones, might not be so spry about alcohol. Certainly she would never tell anyone: she never told what she knew, but locked the secrets away, each neatly wrapped, in a drawer of her mind. She had not the slightest desire or instinct to share them.

She managed to get to Eastbourne after all.

Chapter Twenty-Two

'Do come, Gwen, do come!' Betty pleaded. 'The Annicks have specially asked you, and I do want you to see what the school's like.'

'And have Elspeth Murray looking at me like a sick tigress? No, thank you.'

Gwen Morphy was a tall young woman, strong-featured, built like the Winged Victory. She was a partner in a firm of house-agents, and had taken over the Eastbourne branch. Despite her look of permanent aggressiveness she had her softer side: it was a drag driving so far to work every day, but Betty was in love with her, Betty was desolate, and there were worse people than Betty. Certainly there were few prettier. Why she, Gwen, could not entirely respond to this love she didn't know, except that something was missing. *Rapport*, she supposed, whatever that might be.

'Darling, I don't imagine for a moment they'll ask Elspeth. They're far too tactful. And we don't go about in hordes at D.P.'

'That's exactly what you sound as if you're doing. No, I'm not going there to be a poppy-show, as my mother used to call it.'

'Please, please, please. Just for once.' Betty knelt by Gwen's armchair, her grey skirts spreading. 'It's only for drinks. We needn't stay more than an hour.'

'What'll you give me if I do?'

'Anything in the world.' Betty was fervent. 'You know you can always have that.'

So Gwen grudgingly agreed to go. 'Only I hate these damned things that begin at nine.'

It was only a modest after-supper gathering: Penelope and

Canning, Helen and the Pooles. The omission to ask Stephen was another instance of Mrs Annick's tact.

The moment Helen saw Delia she, like Gwen, had reason for fearing parties that began at nine. Setting aside the interval for food, it had given the silly woman the chance for at least four hours' solid drinking. Yet it would not, she thought, be obvious to anyone not 'in the know'. Delia, though pale and puffy about the eyes, sat quite composedly and talked in her usual gentle, prattling voice. She was sipping tomato juice. But Poole, from the other side of the room, where he was talking shop to Canning (he rarely talked anything else) kept stealing glances at her, weary and anxious ones.

Gwen Morphy, stiff at first, soon relaxed with Grace Annick, who treated her, as she did everyone else, as a member of a favoured flock.

'We're so glad Betty isn't still living alone. I know girls like to do it and it may be all right in cities, but I'm sure she must be lonely in the evenings, buried in Chalkwood. I'd go mad myself.'

Annick asked Gwen about her business, and she became amusingly technical about it. She could be amusing if she liked, and having yielded to Betty's plea that she should come to the party at all, was now determined to do her friend credit.

'You can always tell who isn't going to buy a house when you take them round. If they bring out tape-measures and make chalk-marks and cry "Ah, that will be a perfect place for Auntie's bureau," you can bet they'll never buy. They're house-fanciers.'

'Then who does buy?' Annick asked.

'That surly couple who never say a word of appreciation about anything and don't seem to notice the cupboard room but are rather careful about the plumbing. They're terrified to tell you they like the place in case you suddenly beat the price up.'

Betty was looking delighted and shy, like a young girl who has brought her first young man home. 'Darling, do tell them the story about—' and 'Darling, tell Mr Annick about the man who came back and *broke* in—'

'No one can say she tries to pretend,' Penelope murmured to

Canning, 'you'd have thought she wouldn't have worn a corduroy waistcoat tonight.'

'Cat.' His rebuke was old-fashioned. 'Puss, puss.'

'Well,' said Delia, 'I think perhaps another tomato juice, Mrs Annick – how delicious yours is! With vodka? I've never tried it that way. Is it terribly strong? Just a tiny drop, then.' She was sweating all over her upper lip, the beads forming a kind of crystal moustache. Half-rising to take the glass, she failed to grasp it and fell back again on to the sofa.

'Here, let me,' said Helen, putting it firmly into her hand.

'These deep cushions! I'm too short for them, and it makes it so difficult to get up. Aren't I silly?'

Gwen smiled. She would have something to tell her unobservant friend when they got home. 'My legs are long enough,' she said, 'but I always have trouble with sofas.'

Delia put the glass down, wiped her face and rose. 'Excuse me.' Perfectly steadily, though with a touch of over-stateliness, she arose without a stagger and went upstairs.

'It is rather hot in here,' Grace said remorsefully,' but if we open a window tonight we'll be torn to pieces.'

A gale was blowing thrashing the trees about and from time to time roaring like thunder in the chimney.

Annick, who had realized at the beginning of the evening that Delia was drunk, marvelled at his wife's simplicity. But how often did this happen, or was it an isolated event? Anyone could be caught cold sometimes. He hoped he wasn't going to have a fresh nuisance in the school.

'– as an owl,' Gwen muttered.

Betty's brown eyes opened up like field daisies. 'No!' She had been as blind as Grace.

'As two owls. To what place hast brought me, beloved?'

Poole unobtrusively followed his wife, but in a few minutes was down again. Conversation ran fitfully.

'Is Delia all right?' Grace asked him, in a clear carrying tone. 'I'm afraid she was feeling the heat. That sofa's far too near to the fire.'

'Quite all right,' he said. 'Yes, she did feel rather hot. She does sometimes. She's a cold-weather person.'

Helen went quietly upstairs. She met Delia coming out of the bathroom. She had washed her face which, without makeup, was whiter than ever. Only a crust of lipstick still clung to the outer edges of her mouth. 'You O.K.?'

'My dear, of course I am! Why not?' Walking straight past Helen, she returned in good order to the party.

Someone knocked at the door. Elspeth Murray timidly put her head round. 'Oh, Mrs Annick, I'm sorry – I didn't know you had people.'

'Do come in and have a drink.'

'I was bringing back your Galsworthy. I'll come another time.'

'No, no, now. Let me see, you don't know—'

'Miss Morphy and I have met,' said Mrs Murray. 'How do you do, Gwen?'

'Fine. And you?'

Gwen smiled broadly: she could not help it. But then she switched the smile off. It was pathetic really, this clumsy trick. Poor Elspeth! Even with me here, she could not bear not to have been invited.

Penelope said rapidly, 'Come on, Mrs Murray, come and sit by Leo and me. We're having a boring gossip all about infant rioting in the Remove, and Peter's chances, and the increasing hazards of Common Entrance.' She touched her hand. 'Why, you're freezing! Have you been out?'

'Just for a breath of air.'

Mrs Murray's sad gaze was upon Betty's narrow back. The spiky little shoulder blades. The small waist, like the waist of a hospital nurse.

'In a hurricane like this?'

'I don't mind wind.'

'Oh, I hate it!' said Delia chattily, addressing the whole room. 'Cold I adore, but not this – this tornado! I hate lying in bed and listening to it. I always feel it's trying to get at *me*.'

'That's very egocentric of you, dear,' her husband said. 'It would be getting at other people, too.'

'Never mind that! It's what I feel.'

Mrs Murray sat for a while, hearing listlessly the gossip of Penelope and Canning. Then, taking a resolution, she left them abruptly. She went to join the group of Cyril Annick, Helen, Betty and Gwen Morphy, and dropped to the carpet beside Betty as if she were a girl accustomed to sitting on floors.

'No, no, I'm quite comfortable,' she said almost crossly, when Annick tried to give her his chair. 'You know, it is the most extraordinary thing! We're all here together, day after day, and yet some of us hardly seem to see each other! Really, Betty, you might be the invisible woman.'

'You know where to find me. I'm up in the attic counting pillow-slips and sewing on bloody, bloody name-tapes.'

'Did you enjoy the Galsworthy?' Grace asked, joining them. Helen rose and drifted away to talk to Delia.

'Far more after the television serial than I ever did before. But I do hate Irene.'

'I adore Irene,' Gwen said with a gleam.'*Couleur de feuille morte*! Such a grabber, too. I could never have resisted Irene.'

'I think she's a bitch,' said Betty. She looked alarmed, as if suddenly confronted with a living rival. 'I hate her, too.'

'Loathe her!' Mrs Murray cried, falsely feeling solidarity.

'Adorable,' said Gwen. 'Awful, but quite, quite alluring.' She stretched up her arms into the air and her splendid breasts rose.

'So selfish.'

'We all are. Except Mrs Annick. I don't believe you're selfish, are you?'

'Why, dreadfully!' Grace cried. 'I'm always dodging the column.'

Annick put his hand on her arm. He had never been able to resist these public demonstrations of affection, although he knew that to some of the younger staff he looked absurdly uxorious.

Anyway, Helen thought with relief (for she was kind) Delia is all right now. She must have been very sick. I hope to God she's cleared up properly in the bathroom. Better go and see. She sidled upstairs and did so: all was well, but the window was open and the plastic curtains blowing horizontally inwards. She shut it.

Downstairs, the telephone rang. Annick answered it and came smiling to Canning. 'Strangely enough, it's for you. Mr Corso chooses some odd hours to try to rob me of my staff.'

'Sorry, sir. But would you mind telling him you couldn't find me? He can ring again in the morning.'

'Why not take it now?'

'Because,' said Canning, 'it's too much like the bloody knock on the door at midnight.'

'All right.' Annick returned to the telephone and spoke briefly.

'Could have been exciting,' Penelope said to Canning.

'Nope. Only you are exciting.'

The party broke up. 'Elspeth,' Gwen said on the doorstep, 'if you'd like to come back for a nightcap with Betty and me, I'll drive you home again.'

Even in the porch lights, Mrs Murray was seen to flush. 'Thank you but it's far too late. Thank you all the same.'

'What a *nice* person you are, Gwen,' Betty said as they drove away.

'Well, don't moo at me. I only wanted to show the old thing that we could all be chums together, if she wanted it that way. Obviously, she doesn't. Good grief, what an evening! Mrs what's-her-name stoned as hell, Elspeth busting in – you never told me Downs Park was full of these thrills.'

'Do you honestly think Mrs Poole was drunk?'

'Oh, be your age.'

Left alone in the party litter, Grace said sadly, 'Well, that was a funny sort of evening. Nothing went right. I do hope Delia isn't sickening for something.'

Annick told her that she was the most innocent of women. Did she really not know what had been the matter?

'If you mean, was Delia sloshed,' Grace said directly, 'the thought did cross my mind. But it is simply impossible.'

'No, possible, and it was so. Let's hope it doesn't happen often. Poor Norman! He was so embarrassed he didn't know what to do with himself. I like Poole.'

'I think I was too hot and bothered by poor Elspeth Murray to bother much about Delia. Poor dear!'

'I wouldn't much mind,' Annick said, 'if we could find a decent matron, getting rid of Betty. She doesn't mean to be a trouble-maker, but I think she is. I'd like to get a total matron for you, instead of half a one, and release you from some of your chores.'

'I don't do nearly enough,' said Grace.

That evening seemed to be the beginning of a tiresome period. Next morning Mrs Murray took to her bed with, as she expressed it, stomach-trouble. Mrs Terry threatened to leave and had to be cajoled into withdrawing her notice, always a humiliating business for Grace, who knew that the whole thing was play-acting. D'Oyley complained of the loss of half-a-crown. Peter Quillan became temperamental, was succinct on the subject of Caesar and doodled his time away, showing up a blank paper. For which Annick, having no sanctions whatsoever, threatened him.

'Have we all gone mad?' he said to Grace that night. The school doctor came and decreed bed for Mrs Murray for a couple of days, just as a precaution. He could find nothing wrong with her.

One of the new boys reported the loss of a penknife with a malachite handle.

Nothing happened for a week. Then the thefts began again, coming thick and fast.

A slow boy in the Remove, whom Annick had vaguely suspected, had left for Paraguay, where his parents had taken up a diplomatic post: so it was not he. Damn and damn. Especially when the first buds were appearing under the hedges, poppings of chrome yellow through the dark, damp, mossy leaves.

The Massingers met Gwen quite by chance. Dissatisfied with their flat, they went to the nearest house agent's, which happened to be the branch she ran. In the course of conversation they found out that she was Betty Cope's friend, and school gossip was at once open to them.

'My God,' said Rupert. 'Theft and booze! Whatever are we coming to? I knew there was a snag in the Pooles somewhere.'

'But who is the thief?' Blossom asked eagerly. 'I hardly remember the boys now, they seem such an amorphous mass.'

'We don't know,' Gwen replied, 'or rather, Betty doesn't. But the atmosphere seems to me as thick as pea-soup.'

'And the finances?' asked Rupert. 'Know anything of how they're going?'

'Now there, I'd be lost and I think Betty might. She doesn't like that lurking girl Queen, who is the only one except Cyril Annick, really in the know.'

'Well, well, well,' said Rupert.

Chapter Twenty-Three

Annick was coaching Peter alone, since Searle was in bed with influenza. It was a dull, calm day with translucent fog between the trees and a glaze of dew on the grass. His head was aching, and it was a struggle to concentrate.

'Now for the prose. I rather fancy we'll need to do a little spadework here.'

Peter, as usual, had been lost in the recesses of his desk in an effort to sort out the ritual Latin grammar – decayed, and hardly ever used – from a welter of *Plant Life*, divinity, and advanced algebra. The hint of criticism prompted him to look up, with an expression not quite of apprehension, not quite of disdain.

'It's not the actual construction I'm faulting,' Annick pursued. 'All this would make perfectly good sense to Cicero, though parts are rather more like a semi-literate fifth-century scribe. Your subjunctives aren't too happy, either.' He wondered if his anxieties were making him bear too hardly upon the boy, so his tone was more moderate than his words.

The work was still being withheld from Peter; and crane his neck as he might, he could still see nothing more than an indistinct mass of ink on the opposite page. And that might mean anything.

'It's the style that's so worrying,' Annick drilled into his consciousness. 'Examiners love style, the Eton ones especially. For example, it's really high time you got out of the Remove form attitude that every sentence has to end with a verb. Think of Caesar. "*Gallia est omnis divisa in partes tres*". "Into three parts"! That was the point he wanted to make. He didn't want a sentence tailing off – "*Gallia in partes tres divisa est.*" No. "*In partes tres*".'

Peter decided to venture a defence. Sometimes he barely spoke for himself during the coaching periods, yet today he felt instinctively that he had to help things out. 'But Caesar wasn't exactly a *stylist*, sir. It was a – a sort of log-book he was keeping.'

'Log-book or not, he knew how to write good Latin. Anyhow, give your sentences variety and for God's sake keep them concise. You've been using some of your favourite words just a little too much. Nine times out of ten, *volo* is quite as good for "I want" as *ques*, thank you very much. And *ilico* twice over is ludicrous for "immediately", when you can use—'

'*Statim, protinus, continuo, extemplo*,' Peter trotted out, still feeling that in some undefinable way he was being of help.

'That's right,' Annick said drily – he always sounded dry when he was worried – 'A hexameter you might remember, by the way.'

'*Protinus, extemplo*—'

They were interrupted by a deafening rush of feet along the passage outside.

'It's Mr Canning's class, I expect,' said Peter, apologetically.

'Your scientific friends coming out. Lazy devils.' Annick flicked the work over. 'Oh well, all in all, it's very good. You can have a couple of alphas. Let's get back to the unseen book.'

The unseen book was dazzlingly clean from two years of neglect. Peter slapped it open and began authoritatively. 'Most eloquent Marcus Tullius, there are as many descendants of Romulus as—'

The bell rang. They never seemed to get further than this. Perhaps they never would.

'As usual,' Annick said, 'we come to a halt. That's all for now.' Then, abruptly, as the boy was gathering up his books, 'Petey, have you missed anything else recently?'

'Yes, sir. My propelling pencil.' This time there was no hesitation. Peter relinquished the books and sat down again.

'When?'

'Two days ago.'

'Why didn't you go to Mr Poole? You know there's another outbreak of this sort of thing going on.'

'I was meaning to, but somehow – Anyway, I think I would have gone, if you hadn't asked. My mother gave it to me at the beginning of the term. It's silver.'

'You know I said I wanted missing things to be reported.'

The boy looked at him with the pure cobalt gaze that would not lose its clarity for three or four years to come. 'Yes. But it's all so foul. And there was just a vague chance I might have dropped it.'

'As you dropped your ring?'

'Oh, that. Well, yes.'

Annick pushed aside the flap of his coal-black hair. He was more tired than ever and his back ached. He felt hunted down.

'I've no right to ask you this. But have you a shadow of a suspicion who might be responsible?'

Promptly – 'No, sir.'

'If you told me, I promise I wouldn't act upon it. Only perhaps watch out a bit.'

'I don't know, really. It wouldn't be one of the little boys it's far too crafty a job. Besides, some of them weren't here last time it happened. And some of the bigger ones have gone.'

Annick observed that they were still left with a wide field. It couldn't, he said, be allowed to continue: but what were they to do? One couldn't call in the police.

'I could give you a whole list of people it certainly isn't,' Peter said slowly, 'just because I know them. But that wouldn't be fair on the ones I don't know so much about.'

'Aristides the Just. Good for you, I suppose. But God, I wish we had some youthful Sherlock on the premises!'

'All I can say, sir, is that there's an awful lot of Sherlocking going on. Keeping watch, and everything. But most of its footling and no one's got anywhere.'

'Where was that pencil before it disappeared?'

'In my blazer-pocket, in the changing-room. But things have gone from lockers, too.'

'And our lockers don't lock, more's the pity.'

Peter, whose relations with his headmaster were easy enough for him not to wait to be told when he might stand or sit, rose and prowled over to the window. His face lit up. 'Quick, sir, a squirrel!'

It was romping up the trunk of the cedar tree, a wisp of brown smoke on the smoky day.

'Yes, I see him. There he goes!'

'They're not very tame, though, are they? They won't take nuts or crumbs from your hand. Only from Hickling's.'

Hickling was the boy with the unfortunate family background. 'Why from him?'

'I don't know, sir. He's got a sort of mysterious way with them, with birds, too. I shouldn't be surprised if he turned out to be a zoologist or something.'

Annick thought, that the squirrel was a good excuse for changing the subject. I mustn't keep him to it any more. 'How's Richard doing?'

'A bit sorry for himself, Miss Cope says. But it's a terrible bore in the sickroom. Can't I go and see him?'

'Not till the doctor's sure you won't catch his infection. Sorry, Pete. Write him a note, and I'll see it's delivered.'

'May I write it now?'

'Why, what are you due for?'

'Only ballroom dancing.' Peter grinned fleetingly, then composed his features. This was one of Stephen's less successful ideas for preparing them for adulthood. It made them all feel ridiculous, even when Betty came to dance with them.

'I think you might be excused that. All right, get on with your letter.'

Annick had a punctilious word with Stephen, then went to his sitting-room.

'You look all in,' said Grace.

'I am. I wish I could slack off some of my teaching. Could we afford someone quite fresh from school?'

'I don't know. It would be an awful strain. But if we must, we must. I do wish you'd go to the doctor and have a check up.'

He told her he hated doctors. Trollope was right: Doctor Fillgrave was his man. They were all Fillgraves. If Stephen could fit in a little more junior Latin it would help, but he kept himself busy enough already. 'Pity Canning knew no Latin, since his energy seemed infinite.

'Could Penny help there?'

'I doubt it. She's forgotten all she ever knew.'

'Then I really think,' Grace said, 'that she might give herself a refresher course. It would be quite adequate for the needs of the eight-year-olds. I'll have a word with her.'

'I will try if you like,' Penelope agreed. She was dining with them privately that evening. 'I am not quite such an ass as you think I am, and provided I get no more than the two bottom forms thrust upon me, I think I can cope.'

Grace thought how much easier she had been with them both, how much more eager to please, than when she was running her own business. She had always been a kind girl but not a very comfortable one. As a child she had never had a tantrum but many bouts of mulish obstinacy, which might continue for days, with remarkable infant persistence. Her marriage had softened her phenomenally, and her grief at her husband's death had been terrible. Now she seemed not only to be recovering, but becoming a much more agreeable daughter. What would Canning do for her – if it came to that – or do with her? Grace could envisage initial tussles on Katharina-Petruchio lines, and since she thought that kind of thing greatly overrated as a spur to love, was worried. Besides, this Katharina might sometimes win, which would put undesirable ideas into her head.

Annick thought rather differently from Grace, and understood his daughter better. He believed she had suffered a little from being brought up in the school, where so much care, and so much demonstrative affection, had had to be given to others besides herself. Many of Penelope's sulks had originated in her conviction that her parents were by no means her sole possessions – they were owned by so many others. But he did believe that her happy marriage had been happy because it was so brief. Barry had been a very gentle young man, and she had had a year of his utter devotion. She was basically in search of a certain excitement. The honeymoon period over, and no excitement forthcoming, what then? He knew Grace believed that differences in upbringing and education might make an eventual barrier between Canning and her daughter, but Annick did not agree. The stimulation of such an active personality would keep her alert, stop her falling back into the sadness which had sometimes been just perceptible even when she had seemed most happy. And they would have children. As for Grace's Petruchio concept (he was not fool enough to fail to realize that the romantic Canning might well take Petruchio as a good working model), he did not believe Penelope would win a single round. Dwindle into a wife? There would be no dwindling. But, perhaps, a sweetening.

'Desire for a woman's both worship and play.' O'Casey, remembered from many years ago. Annick agreed with that: he was sure Canning would.

Chapter Twenty-Four

The hours between two-thirty and four-thirty were dead ones in School Building. As a rule, only Betty and Helen were occupied: Betty sewing in the attic, Helen locked into the small office, her typewriter clacking. Silence on the polished stairs, in the classrooms, the changing-room. Silence in the dormitories. The boys were freezing on the playing-fields. The Annicks would normally have gone out on local business, seeing farmers, seeing friends. The clock in the hall which had such a quiet tick, acquired a loud one. Mrs Murray sat. in her room, trying to control what seemed to be an intestinal inquietude. She could not sit still. Try as she might, she had to walk up and down, fingers pressed into her stomach. Up and down, up and down. The silence was horrible, intensified only by far-off shouts from the playing-fields.

Today might be the day for the sea, for the quiet, long-planned walk in a mist. But the day had to be chosen. Was this one right? She went to her wardrobe, fumbled in the bottom drawer, which looked like a fake bottom. The box was there, of course it was. There had been no searchers here.

She looked out of the window. The mist was very thin indeed, just enough to make the leafless trees look like Japanese brush-drawings. Colours: khaki-grey, and black. The clotted Thicket seemed, by some delusion of the weather, to have come nearer to the house, like Birnam Wood to Dunsinane.

Then she took out the box and rattled it. She had not seen the contents for a long time, since she always closed her eyes when adding to them, but there did not seem to be very much inside.

She said to herself, half-audibly, 'You must not do this. You know you must not do this. You are *perfectly aware* that you must not.' But the screw in her stomach tightened. Activity was the only thing, activity and danger.

Again she spoke. 'You know what Betty would think of you. She would hate and despise you. Oh yes, you know perfectly well, my dear, you are not a fool.'

Safer to put on coat and headscarf, take the box down to the sea and be rid of it. But would the tide be in? On such a day she could not paddle out into deeper water: and even if she did, the tide might recede further and leave the box high and dry. She might climb up on to the downs, following the coast, and throw it from some safer place. But if she did find deep water, would it sink?

She was outside in the passage, listening. She did not remember leaving the room. The stairs gleamed vertiginously downwards, smelling of lavender polish. Light from a single lamp fell upon the gilded letters of the Honours Board. Not a mouse stirring. Should she go back and get her coat? No. Because, just once more – 'only once more, I promise, Betty, I promise.' Just once more.

She crept into the Remove dormitory and looked along the line of chipped and scratched lockers. No. There was a loose plank that creaked. She dared not risk it again. She crept out, tiptoed down two stairs, then stopped.

'You are like a woman who drinks, you are like Delia Poole. You know how contemptible you are, don't you? And silly. Don't you look silly? Oh God, oh God, I can't stop.'

Down to the hall, on silent feet past the school office, where the typewriter was silent. Through the dining-hall, walking normally: anybody might be on their way through it to any part of the building. The short-cut through the lower form room, stuck about with paintings, magazine covers, miscellaneous scribblings. It smelled of chalk, ink and rubber. The desks themselves were chaotically untidy: they always were till the compulsory clearance at five o'clock. Exercise books, chewed pencils and pens. Something bright caught her eye: an extraordinary object, no doubt another of their good luck charms. This was a cheap thimble, set all over with tiny pieces of coloured glass. She nipped it up and put it in the pocket of her suit.

The tension in her stomach eased for a second, then increased till it became barely endurable. She hurried from the room. No need to tiptoe now, not over the stone flags which could not creak. Into the damp-smelling changing-room, the floor covered in muddy boots, on the hooks grubby towels. The laundry came tomorrow. Then another, double, line of hooks with the wasp-like blazers casting a glow in the murk. Her hand in a pocket. Nothing there. In another and another. Here was something hard: a forbidden thing, a catapult. She stood with it in her hand, looked up and met the eyes of Helen Queen.

Helen was standing in the far doorway which gave on to the yard. No draught, so she hadn't just come in. She must have been lying in wait.

Mrs Murray said in a shrill voice, half on a laugh, half on a gasp, 'So you've had the same idea as me!'

'Have I?'

'I thought I'd look and see what they'd got, so we'd know what sort of things our Fagin was after.'

'Is that what you thought?'

'Don't look at me like that!' Mrs Murray said, 'It's impertinent. You're too young.'

'Look here,' Helen said, 'I've given you a shock and you've given me one. What are we going to do about it?'

'I don't know what you mean "do" about it. About what?' She was half-blind with fear. The yellow blazers melted into each other.

'Have you kept the other stuff? Where is it?'

'Don't dare to talk to me like that, it's an insult! And how do I know that you aren't here sneak-thieving yourself?'

'Better come into the office,' Helen said, sounding like a policewoman, 'it's getting late and anyone can walk in on us here.'

Mrs Murray followed her. In the little hot room she refused a chair. She was trembling.

'I'm not out to persecute you,' Helen said. 'Here, have a cigarette.'

'I don't want one.'

'And I'm not a talker. I never have been. Somehow, I never thought it was one of the boys: I thought it was you.'

'Why should you have thought it was me?'

'People here are so wrapped up in their own concerns,' said Helen, '– for God's sake sit down – that they can't see an inch in front of their noses. You've been as upset and jumpy as a cat. The Annicks ought to have spotted it.'

Mrs Murray sat down and began to cry.

Helen waited patiently till the first paroxysm of tears came to an end. 'I'll tell you what we'll do. If you still have what you've taken – and I want today's loot, too, please – we'll hide it somewhere where it will be quite easily found. Under leaves in the Thicket, probably. Then you're going to promise that you'll never do such a bloody silly thing again, because if you do I shall have to let the cat out of the bag.'

She was kind enough to want to help Mrs Murray, but not kind enough to retain even a minimal tone of respect.

Mrs Murray thought, it is all over. I am here with this terrible girl and I shall never get away again. I know she will tell Betty, she won't be able to help herself. They might as well put me in the pillory and throw filth at me. I can't bear it. I want to die.

'Come on, come on – where have you got your little *cache*? In your room, I suppose. Let's go up.'

The stomach tension had gone. Nothing was left but the hideousness of shame. She could not see beyond the moment: she was trapped in it for ever.

She climbed the stairs behind Helen as if tied to her with rope, like a mountaineer to a guide. Wordless, she opened the wardrobe and took out the box.

'My God,' Helen said, opening it. 'The lot. Quick, what did you take today?'

Pathetically produced, the thimble.

'Where did you get that?'

'The lower formroom.'

'Give it to me, I'll dash down and put it back. It's a risk I'm taking for you. Do you know which desk?'

'No.'

'I'll drop it on the floor where it will be seen. Now don't you move one step!'

Mrs Murray could not have moved. She lay face downwards on the bed and did not weep.

Helen came back. 'Get your things on, and we'll both take this wretched box up to the Thicket. I'm damned if I'm going to do it alone, in case someone spots me and thinks *I'm* Fagin. Come on, will you?' The sub-cockney accent, long-corrected, had returned to Helen's voice. 'Get up! We've got about fifteen minutes' safety before they all come trampling home. With luck, we may not even be seen. If we are, then we're just going for a walk.'

The two women, one young, one middle-aged, went up the fields through the thickening mist, Mrs Murray carrying the box tightly beneath her coat.

A whistle shrilled.

'Buck up,' said Helen, 'bad light's stopped play.'

They entered the sheltering wood, where it was suddenly warmer.

It is a dream, Mrs Murray thought, I shall wake up in my bed. I cannot be out here with Helen, it can't all be over. Dear God, forgive me, forgive me, forgive me.

Under the trees, the autumn's leaves, high-piled, were dropping into mould. 'We can't help what anyone thinks when they do spot it,' Helen muttered, 'they'll just have to wonder. Here, give it over.'

She dug in mould and moist earth, making a cavity a few inches deep. Then she took the box and buried it, piling earth and leaves above it. 'The first crowd to rootle around in here will spot it at once. Watch out for the next fine day.'

They emerged into fog. 'Thank God for that.'

Mrs Murray whispered, 'I ought to thank you. But I know you will tell people.'

'I tell you that I won't. I know a lot of things I don't tell. What made you do it?'

'I don't know. I don't know. It was something I couldn't help. Please don't talk to me any more.'

Alone once again in her bedroom, Mrs Murray abandoned herself to horrible fantasies. Of course it would be known: she would be summoned by Annick and then denounced in front of the school. For of course they would have to clear the boys. She wore a board around her neck with THIEF upon it. Betty was looking at her, wide-eyed and whispering to Gwen Morphy. I am too old, Mrs Murray thought, too old to be treated so, whatever I may have done.

She did not turn on the lights, but lay in the dark, trembling in an ecstasy of mortification.

Chapter Twenty-Five

On the next fine day: Canning took his Nature class out on field-work. It was, in fact, the top form. Though by now he had them working at serious biology, he did not see why they should be allowed to close their eyes to everything available around them. Sissy, they might think it was: he did not. They found red flowers on the elm-trees and he instructed them at length upon the mechanics of the fine wych-elm growing a hundred yards from the school. The hedgerows, to everyone's disappointment, yielded no white sweet violets, but down at the lower end of the playing-fields they found shepherd's purse, lesser celandine and coltsfoot. Downs Park was too far from the nearest farmer using fertilizer to be entirely bereft of its flowers.

'When my father was a boy,' Canning said, 'he only had to look out of the train at the railway cutting to see wild flowers. They came in all shapes and sizes. Look at it now! Filthy bloody muck blowing over, and nothing but dandelions.'

'But sir,' Hanford protested, 'you do have to use the fertilizers, or we wouldn't eat.'

'True, true. But in my heart I'm not scientific so much as romantic – does that surprise you? Willow herb goes a long way, but not enough. Not with me.'

They would now try the Thicket, where there might be cinquefoil – very pretty – and bearsfoot. Hickling came panting up with the discovery of a patch of stinking hellebore, and was commended. But it was D'Oyley who made the find.

'Sir! Sir! Buried treasure!'

'Buried what? What are you babbling about?'

'There's a box here, under all these leaves. Sir, do come and see!'

So Canning came and knelt, long nose pointing. 'There's a box all right.' What do you suppose is in it?'

Doubloons,' said Finlay, 'pieces of eight.'

'Seriously?'

'Not seriously, sir. Probably someone's old socks.'

This raised a laugh. Finlay was becoming known as a wit.

'Anyone,' said Canning, 'see anything against opening it up?'

No one did. There was a shout of approval.

Not too happy himself, he began to prise open the lid, which had stuck with damp. God knew what might be there unsuited to infant eyes. And if it were unsuited, what would he have to explain away? He made his movements deliberately slow, partly because he was anxious, and partly because suspense was fun for the boys. Too small to hide a murdered baby, anyway. His fevered imagination envisaged packed rows of contraceptives. But no, it wasn't light enough for that, and anyway, it rattled.

They were all crowded round him. The lid came up with a squelch.

Then Peter Quillan, who had taken no previous part in the proceedings, since he now despised Nature study, said, 'That's my ring.' He put out a hand to take it.

'No, you don't.' Diamond eyes sparkled. 'This is going back intact to Mr Annick for a check-up.'

Someone cried, 'That's my pen!'

'I'm sure it is. Hold your horses, and you'll be getting it back again soon.'

Annick received the treasure-hoard with incredulous relief. He stared at Canning. 'What child did this?'

'I don't think it was a child, Headmaster. I've got a hunch.'

'For God's sake! Not one of us?'

'I didn't say that. But I do say it isn't a kid's doing. This has been stashed away until recently. What room could the poor little devils find to hoard anything in? They have to spill their belongings all over the place as it is.'

'It's a relief, anyway. Just to have it back. But where it leaves us, I don't know.'

'Very much better off. This looks like a complete haul, doesn't it? If so, Jack shall have Jill – yes, I did a bit of Shakespeare at school, Headmaster – "The man shall have his mare again and all will be well." That's what most of them are going to care about. And I bet you my last fourpence that nothing more is going to disappear.'

Annick was curious. 'Why not?'

'Why hide the lot where it can be found in two twos, if it isn't the grand *finale*? Or, of course, unless somebody else has cottoned on.'

'Somebody else?'

'Just another hunch.'

Annick addressed the school after tea. What was lost had been found. He gave a brief account of where and how. No questions were to be asked. He had a list of the missing property in his room, and if boys came to him, their possessions would be restored.

'Fishy,' Peter muttered to Searle, who was well again. 'Bet he knows who.'

'Bet he doesn't. Bet we never will.'

'This,' said Annick to staff and school, 'has been a pretty miserable incident. But restitution goes a long way to putting things right. I shan't ask you not to talk about it, because of course you will. But I do ask you to let the subject dry up as soon as you feel you've exhausted it.'

He is a very good H.M., Canning thought, he has the gift of saying precisely the right thing. He tunes these children as he might tune a violin, always assuming that he could play one.

Grace cried a little that night.

'Darling! Why so upset?'

'I've *been* so upset.'

'I didn't really know.' Annick was remorseful. 'I should have known.'

'You have enough to put up with, without me being upset all over you.'

'Who did it? I still feel a fool. Canning doesn't think it was a boy.'

'Oh no, no! Then who?'

'If I wanted to look for anyone, which I don't and won't, it would be for the most disturbed person around this place.'

A common idea struck them both: both were silent.

Then Annick said, 'Not Delia Poole.'

'Of course not. I never thought so. One needs a steady hand.'

'And that's our next problem.'

'Oh, dear, you don't mean we'll have to get rid of them? I do like Norman.'

'We can't, at present. But in the end we shall have to.'

For Delia had been getting steadily worse, and all the school knew about her. Twice she had entered her art classes with her normal steady step, then clutched on to a chair or on to the arm of the nearest boy: and within fifteen minutes had been forced to go back to the cottage. Annick had reorganized the timetable for her benefit, so that she took her first class at ten, before – he hoped – she had been able to start drinking: and her second at two-thirty, when equally he hoped that the effects would have worn off with the mid-day meal.

'If she can only get through from ten to ten forty-five, then she can go back and souse unobserved.' But both he and Grace now believed that Delia started drinking the moment she rose in the morning.

Poole was doing his work conscientiously, but was looking increasingly careworn. Even his parade-ground voice had lost its edge.

Then, on a cold morning, in break, Richard Searle, who had been taking one of his solitary walks behind the gym, heard hopeless weeping from the shrubbery, in which Grace had aesthetically placed a wooden bench and a small stone cupid brought back from a holiday in Greece. Kneeling before the bench was Delia Poole, her head on the seat. Searle asked her what was the matter. At first she could not answer him. Then she said, in a voice thickly blurred, 'I'm ill. I can't get up. Help me.'

He tried, but she was like lead.

'Don't get anyone, for God's sake don't get anyone.' She made a frantic effort to rise, staggered, and fell back again, banging her head on an arm of the bench.

'I'll have to,' said Searle.

But knowing what was wrong, he was discreet. He made his way back towards the gymnasium and spoke to the first master he met, who was Canning.

'I need help, sir. Mrs Poole's ill in the shrubbery, I can't get her to walk.'

'Oh God, oh Montreal! It'll take two of us, and we shall be a conspicuous sight. Dick, we must get her back to the cottage after the bell's rung, not before. Who do you go to after break?'

'Mr Smith, for English.'

'I'll make your excuses. I hate dragging you into this, but I must. Lead on, Macduff. Where is she?'

She was where Searle had left her. The blow seemed to have sobered her a little, for she was kneeling upright, rubbing her bruised forehead.

'Whoops-a-daisy,' said Canning disrespectfully, and he hauled her up. 'You sit there. We'll give you a hand in a minute.'

'Fit of giddiness. I don't know why, I felt ill.'

The knees of both her stockings were torn, and one was stained with blood and gravel. She was a pitiful sight, Canning thought, and prayed that they would all be unobserved. Despite Grace's decorative efforts the shrubbery was far too small and dark to be a popular place of retirement. Canning lit a cigarette and offered it to Delia. She waved it away. So he put it in his own mouth. He sat with his arm round her, while Searle stood above them both, teetering from foot to foot.

At last the bell rang, and they heard far-off sounds of running scuffle.

'Give it a few minutes,' said Canning, 'in case of stragglers. Dick, can you sneak out and tell me when the coast's clear?'

Maddeningly, two of the little boys were fighting on the grass. They seemed to be enjoying themselves too much to consider that they would be late for the next period. Searle, technically a prefect but without duties, decided to assume some. 'You two! Get up at once and go into school. Get up, I say!' He collared one of them and lifted him. The other rose. 'Buck up, or you're going to catch it.'

At last, nobody in sight. He went back to the bench. Delia had stopped crying, but lay with her head on Canning's shoulder, half-asleep.

'Come on, Dick, help with our fair burden. You take her left arm.'

They hauled her up. On her feet, she sagged, nearly bringing them both down.

'Stuff that,' Canning said sharply, too desperate to pick his words. 'You can stand if you try. Come on, Searle and I have got you firmly enough. You *must* walk, do you hear? Do you want half the school to spot you?'

She half-opened her eyes, showing blind-looking crescents of light. 'I'm ill.'

'Better stay here then, till we get a doctor.'

'No. Got to go home.'

'That's the general idea. Damn it, stand up! You can.'

They had a better grip on her now, and they got her out into the open. She was trying desperately to co-operate. A step or two, then something like the break into a run, which nearly made them fall. The way back to the cottage was a nightmare.

'Key,' Canning snapped.

She shook her head helplessly. He gave the door a shove and it opened.

'We'll never get her upstairs,' he said to Searle, 'not a hope. If we can lie her down on the sofa it's the best we can do.'

Searle was looking, not pitiful, but disgusted. He had never seen anything like this before. And Delia reeked. They had only just stretched her out on the cushions, when she gave a great sigh and her eyes closed. 'Passed out,' Canning said. 'We can do no more. Sorry about all that, Dick. Store it up with your experience.'

'Look here, sir, hadn't we better get Mr Poole?'

'For crying out loud, no! We can spare her that. Best thing that can happen is that she sleeps it off before he gets in. He's got a straight run of classes till half-past four. You cut along to Mr Smith, tell him I kept you, but that I'll explain. And many thanks. Don't let it prey on your mind, Dick, this world's a hard place for some people.'

When the boy had gone he stood looking thoughtfully down at the drunken woman. Could he do anything else for her, try to bring her round? But he knew it would be practically impossible. If only she would sleep for an hour only, then wake and tidy herself up, so that her state was not too obvious! He found a blanket on the chest in the hall, one of those taken on to the grass on Sports Days, and covered her up. Would Searle talk? Only to Quillan. Poor kid, this had been a rough experience for him. Now, if his own mother drinks half a glass of sherry, he'll write her off as a lush.

Chapter Twenty-Six

Poole came back to find her still sleeping. The room smelled terrible. She must have wakened at some time, for she had been sick on the rug beside the sofa. He took the rug out, threw it on the back lawn and turned the hose on to it. Then he went back to his wife, picked her up and carried her to bed, not bothering to undress her. He was crying. What had happened? How had they come to such ruin? They had been so happy. A sad, pale man with wet cheeks, the tears trickling past his snub nose on to the ends of his military moustache, he sat at her feet and sometimes he patted her.

At six, she awoke. 'Oh, Norman, I'm so glad you're back! What's the time?'

He told her.

'I was so frightened! I was just out for a walk when I had this awful dizzy fit. I hope it's not my heart! I don't know how I managed to get back again.' This was true. She had no recollection of the dreadful procession from the shrubbery. She sat up, threw off the bedclothes and tried to straighten her crumpled dress. She saw the condition of her stockings. 'Oh, dear, I must have had a fall. Hold me, do, just for a minute. I feel so giddy still.'

He held her in silence.

'Better,' said Delia. 'I'll be down in a minute. Do you mind bringing me a drink?'

Hopelessly, he obeyed. He watched her as she sipped at it, slowly and genteelly, saw her colour return.

'My poor, pretty girl,' he said at last. 'We shall have to talk.'

'To talk? What about? I still feel too queer for talking.'

'Not now, later.'

'I do hope it's not my heart.'

'No, it's not your heart.'

'You know I hate doctors.'

'Drink that up and then change,' he said abruptly. 'You've got to come to School Building for supper. I don't want people talking.'

'You were talking about talking.' Her tone was sullen.

'Other people, I mean.'

'I won't go over there. I'm not well enough. How can you be so callous!'

'Oh, you'll come. You must. I'm sick of making excuses for you.' His voice was hardening.

'Is it so much to make an excuse after I've been taken ill? I've had an awful shock, and you don't seem able to realize it!'

'Get changed,' said Poole.

But she refused to leave the cottage. She was too frightened to meet knowing eyes. Someone must have brought her home, since her last recollection was kneeling alone by the shrubbery bench. Who? One person, perhaps two, would have the secret. 'No, you go. I'll scramble an egg for myself. Tell them I wasn't well. You needn't make a great thing of it.'

While she slowly dressed, waiting for him to go out, she looked out of the window, and saw the drawing-room rug, sodden, in the middle of the lawn. A sparrow on it, picking at something nameless. She shivered, shut her eyes. Listened. Was that the door? She looked out of the landing window. Yes, there he was, walking slowly across the field. She ran down quite nimbly. What she needed was a drink. She had to have a drink, or she would be frightened.

Delia was indeed frightened lest her drinking, as she put it to herself, 'got out of hand'. Two funny things had happened, the one in the art room, now today. She had heard that when people really got too bad, they saw horrible things – enormous spiders, snakes. Sometimes she felt hopelessly trapped. Norman had been so good. It was a trouble they had only once mentioned between them, and she would not forget that in a hurry. She was afraid he might send her for a 'cure', a terrible ordeal where despising people made you even wash your teeth in your favourite drink after giving you things to make you sick. She could not bear that, to go off with suitcase packed with pretty things to ineffable humiliation.

She scrubbed the rug, brought it in and hung it in the airing cupboard. Then, after making up her face becomingly, and having just two more drinks (only two) she sat daintily down to await him. She looked cool and serene; she did not think he would badger her. Not tonight.

He came in at nine.

'My darling, pretty girl, this has got to stop.' He looked unlike himself. He had never been a very 'sure' man, at least in his relations with her: but now sureness sat on him, no matter what a strain it might be to keep it there.

She opened her eyes wide. 'Stop? What has got to stop?'

He told her. She flushed brilliantly. 'Don't talk to me like that! It's all nonsense.'

'I must. It is ruining us here and I was so happy.'

'But you must know it's nonsense. I was ill today – that's all. Anyone can feel ill.'

'You weren't ill,' he said, 'You were dead drunk.'

She answered him very quietly. 'If you dare to talk to me like that, I will scream. As I screamed before. You remember.'

'If you do, I will put my hand over your mouth and hold it there.'

'You wouldn't dare to do that! I'll—'

He did as he said he would. She champed her jaws, trying to catch his flesh, but it was too hard for penetration. Then, he moved his palm so that her mouth was wide open and she could not snap at all. She was wild with terror. That Norman could do this to her! She put up her hands and tried to force his own down, but it was like iron.

'You won't scream. You won't rouse half the school as you did last time. If you promise to sit quiet and listen to me, I'll let you go. But if you start anything, I'll gag you again. I mean it.'

Her eyes promised. He released her and she fell back on the sofa. Curiously, she was aware of her appearance: of how frail she must look, how shaken, how abused.

'You hurt my mouth.' She had to hold fast to something, to an affront, offered by him.

'I'm sorry.'

'I said, you hurt my mouth.'

'Delia, this can't go on. You're not a fool. I know. The Annicks know. Damn it, half the boys know! What are we going to do?'

Now she clung to him. 'It's all a mad exaggeration. I swear it is. I was ill today.'

'No. I won't have that. What time do you start in the morning? The moment I leave the house?'

'I'm not well, I'm not well.'

'Of course you're not, but not in the way you mean it. Do you remember who brought you home?'

She shook her head, stupidly repeating, 'I was ill, I was ill.'

'Delia, do you realize what this is costing me? Even in terms of money? It's ruinous.'

'But don't I often pay myself?'

He nearly said 'with what?' but he knew. He had noticed how, over a period of time, the jewellery he had been able to give her, an inheritance from his mother, had disappeared.

He put his head in his hands. He said at last, 'Do you want a drink now?'

She hesitated, and the struggle went on within her. She said, with a vicarage garden party air, 'Thank you, a very small one.'

So they were together again on the awful roundabout. If he refused to give her drink, she would become incapable of thinking. If he did not refuse her, she would slowly become drunk again. He was fumbling to catch the lucid interval.

'Delia. What's gone wrong? Is it anything to do with sex?' He would have liked to put this better: he was of the generation which avoided circumlocution. This too, was a circumlocution, he supposed, but it would have to do. 'I know it's not often I—'

Meanly, she seized the false excuse. 'Often? It's not at all.'

'Is it that, then?'

He sat before her, in a humiliation darkly grey as her own.

'I don't know what it is. I only know I have to keep up. It isn't easy for me to keep up!'

'Delia, listen to me. Could you confine yourself to social drinking only? I mean, when people were here?'

'Of course I could. It wouldn't be difficult at all. I can take it or leave it really, only I haven't been too fit lately, and I needed to pull myself together. I'm perfectly in control, thank you.' She poured scorn at him for doubting her.

'Darling. I love you so much. You know that. Will you try?'

She was silent and rebellious.

'If you don't stop you will lose your looks. Do you realize that you are beginning to lose your looks?'

It was the only appeal to her that could have had the least chance of success. In panic she put a hand to smooth her hair, smooth the line of her jaw, finger the fine skin under her eyes. 'I'm not! I'm not!'

'It's beginning,' Poole said relentlessly, 'But you can stop it. You must.'

Frantically she groped for her bag, for a mirror, studied herself. 'There's nothing wrong with me!'

'I can see a change. My pretty girl, you *are* so pretty. Can't you help yourself?'

'I'll scream,' she said feebly.

'No. That's all over now. Try to rest. I want to help you.'

She reached out her hand to her glass.

'Take it slowly,' he said, 'because you'll get no more tonight. Sleep is what you need.'

'Yes, I do, don't I? Oh, Norman, I do need sleep!'

She fell into his arms, her head on his shoulder, for the first time in many dreadful months of internal dialogue feeling comforted. For once – if only for a few retractable moments – not to have to pretend, not to lie! The sense of a great consolation swept over her, warming her, as if she had been wrapped in a soft blanket on a cold night. She had known much suffering, and it had been lonely and in silence, a suffering only assuaged by the very shame that caused it. She had married him out of inexplicable impulse – for she had known successful men – and out of love: he had given her his whole love in return, in a fashion that had astonished her by its wholeness. What had she done to him? And to herself? Raising her head, she could just see herself in the glass on the wall behind him. I am still pretty. If I ceased to be, could he go on loving me? It was the first time she had been afraid of losing that love. Tonight he had seemed, despite his injustice, his exaggeration, his mistrust, more of a man and more desirable to her.

'It will only be with other people, socially,' she said. 'I promise. I do promise!'

That night she slept in a sweetness of exhaustion: it seemed to her that she had never slept so well since childhood. Surely she was saved? The beautiful, evangelical word rang in her ears at the moment of awakening.

She took her first class smoothly, putting from her mind the thought that someone in it *might know*. But by lunchtime she was planning for herself a social life.

'Mrs Annick! Won't you and the headmaster drop in for a drink with Norman and me tonight? We seem to see so little of each other out of school and we should love it!' (Though she did not consciously formulate the thought, she would be able to slip herself an extra drink for every one of theirs.) 'And Leo, you too!'

She felt a stir of unease. His gaze was too steady on her face.

He himself was thinking that it was all too 'pretty please' in the soppy American phrase. What was she up to now? Why all this sudden hospitality?

'I'm afraid I can't,' he said, 'I've got some carpentering to do, and it won't wait, because the kids want to paint it tomorrow. Another time.'

The Annicks accepted, and sat through a curiously decorous evening. Certainly, Annick thought, she was drinking less than usual, but did not fail to notice how she would top up her own glass when her husband was looking the other way. There's been a row of some sort. Can he get her under control? If he can't they will have to go, and God knows what I will do then.

On subsequent evenings she invited Helen, Betty Cope, Stephen, Mrs Murray. She was like the fluttering wife of an ambassador devotedly about the husband's business. Only Mrs Murray refused, and she was so remote, these days, so furtive, that nobody could expect her to accept. In fact, Delia, whose heart was gentle, worried a great deal about Mrs Murray, when she was not worrying about herself. She hated to see the unhappiness, which wreathed the poor woman like smoke. Delia, at times, was not unhappy at all. There were even moments when the sun shone for her, when she believed that on a *very little stimulus* she was making a conquest of herself. No, certainly she did not like other people to be sad.

The slowly-opening spring delighted her. Bushes that had made a black fog, now made a fog faintly tinged with green. Canning, meeting her one day on the playing-field, took her into the hedgerows and pointed out plants to her. He was kind and considerate, and she found herself suspecting him. Could it have been he who had brought her home on that day sickening to remember? But she liked the colour of the small flowers poking out through a mesh of grass and leaves. They made her feel small and new and bright herself. After all, she *was* triumphing. Norman left the cottage at nine-thirty. By keeping a firm grip, busying herself about the kitchen, she could stave off the desire to drink till nearly eleven o'clock. In consequence, her cooking became quite elaborate. Then, at half-past eleven, she was strengthened enough to take a class. She even went to the lengths of asking Betty whether she might help with junior dancing from two-thirty to three-fifteen: it would keep her away from home, and oh, she wanted to be kept!

She was sure that Norman was becoming increasingly pleased with her.

One day, as she was leaving School Building, she was accosted in a hurried manner by Mrs Murray.

'You've been so kind, always asking me over, but I haven't felt too well, and I haven't accepted. I wondered if, though, this evening, just for half an hour—'

'That would be lovely, but you won't see Norman, I'm afraid. It's his Masonic night.'

'I should enjoy a chat with you, of course, a little chat. Nine o'clock?'

Chapter Twenty-Seven

Mrs Murray could bear it no longer. Everyone knew about her, she was sure of that, though not a word had been spoken. She hardly dared look anyone in the face, certainly not Helen, whom she avoided as she might have avoided a policeman. Her French lessons were a torment to her: they were all cruel, all of them, and she hated them all. But worse than all this, just as Delia Poole needed to drink, she needed to steal.

Not daring to start again, she felt the withdrawal symptoms similar to those of a drunkard. Hour by hour she sat in her room, her hands tightly gripped. Oh, to creep down the stairs, to take the risks, the glorious releasing risks! But all that was over. Sometimes she opened her Bible at random, hoping for help from that source: but was always confronted by a page of genealogies, or some incomprehensible matter from the letters of St Paul. She prayed, but nobody listened, and no voice said to her, 'Peace, be still.'

The symptoms began with a stirring in the pit of her stomach, as though she wanted to relieve herself, but when she tried, she could not. This was succeeded by a clenching sensation, as of a squeezing fist just below the midriff. This would get worse and worse, until she felt she could hardly breathe. She got up and walked about, which was easing: any sort of activity was easing. Yet what she needed was violent activity, to creep, to run low-stooping, to take the hazard of the silent passages, just to dare! She could not dare. Somewhere she would find the watchful Helen, and this time Helen would tell.

The early afternoons were the worst times, for she had no occupation. She tried knitting, but her fingers were numb. She could not read. She tried remembering, but she had no longer anything to do with the studious girl in Paris who had eaten such wonderful meals whenever money arrived from home. Somehow, she had to exist till four-thirty, when she could go to the staff-room for tea, and other people would be there. She could not talk to them very much, but she felt the protection of their presence. Sometimes she could sleep for an hour, but sleeping did not refresh her and she arose to indigestion and general, indefinable wretchedness. But oh, the comfort of the sleep itself! For she always dreamed, and all her dreams were beautiful. Some had names. One was called 'Blue Horizon and Correspondence'. Through another resounded a word potent as sesame, though she did not know what it meant. *Pontchartrain.* She had only to evoke it just before she slept to be transported into a quiet coloured paradise, where nothing could worry her because nothing had, or was meant to have, meaning.

From waking life there must be a way of escape, and she thought perhaps (if she dared) she might have discovered it. She had plotted very carefully. Immediately before leaving for the cottage, she took four sleeping tablets. One was the usual dose. Would four be too little? She dared not risk more. They were slow in action, anyway. The important thing was to stay there no more than an hour.

She walked quickly along the sanded path, past the swimming pool, on which dead leaves and insects were floating, and a boy's little boat with cotton sail, down the slope towards the lighted window. Delia opened the door. She was wearing a dress covered with tiny coloured flowers on a black ground, and a string of amber beads. She looked very hostess-like.

'Now this is really lovely! I'm so glad you've come.'

She smelled of drink, but not strongly.

'Make yourself really comfortable, and we'll have a wonderful gossip all about school shop. There isn't anything else, really, is there? What would you like to drink?'

Mrs Murray said she would like whisky, and watched closely as Delia poured out two large ones.

'Do tell me,' Delia cried, companionably settling herself on the sofa at Mrs Murray's side, 'do you think Mr Annick is setting too much store on that Quillan boy? It would be awful if things went wrong for him, and I adore the Annicks, don't you?'

'I suppose Peter could sit for Westminster next year.'

'But then he wouldn't be so young, and isn't that all part of the charm?'

Pleasant to sit in this artily-cluttered room, Mrs Murray thought, just listening. There was a lamp painted with houses from Amsterdam, the windows cut out so that the glow could stream through. Though she supposed it was not in good taste, yet it attracted her. She did not feel at all drowsy yet, and she must not. 'We must keep our fingers crossed,' she said.

'And is Penelope going to marry Leo Canning? I can't feel he's right for her, but they are around together an awful lot. It seems such a difference in *background*.'

'I don't think people care about that much nowadays,' said Mrs Murray.

'Or do they just pretend they don't. I don't believe some of them would have the moral courage . . . Of course, Penny might change Leo a lot. She's very strong-minded.' They talked for a while about class distinctions, which Delia affected to scorn. 'We do need a new romance here, don't we? I adore to watch them flower, as they say. I did think Stephen was keen on Betty Cope, but that seems to be over.'

'Yes, that's over. I don't think it ever began.'

Delia leaned forward, excited and quite innocent. 'Do you remember that perfectly weird young woman Betty brought to the Annicks? The one with the waistcoat? I couldn't take my eyes off her!'

Mrs Murray emptied her glass. Delia refilled it, and her own.

'You'll never believe it, but Norman and I have always lived rather a sheltered life in a way, that is, always with boys. I've never seen a real lesbian before. I suppose she is one?'

'I don't know.' The first warning of sleepiness: that she did not care what was being said. Nothing was hurting her. 'I haven't much experience myself.'

'I thought she was quite fun, despite it all. But it did make me think. Surely Betty can't be one?'

'Oh no,' said Mrs Murray.

'Anything more marvellously feminine than Betty – she's sweet to look at, isn't she?'

'Very.'

'I was sure I must be wrong. But in that case, how can she stand being with that girl? People must talk, don't you think so?'

'I don't believe Betty cares.'

They talked for half an hour longer, and Mrs Murray's eyelids were dangerously heavy.

'I'm so sorry, but I've suddenly come over so tired. I think I'd better get back to bed. It has been so nice.'

'One for the road! Please! A very little one!'

Mrs Murray accepted a large one and drank it. She must not, as stage people said, 'rush her exit'. Somehow she must take her leave with dignity and get well away, to where she intended to go. She saw Delia's disappointment that she was leaving so early, but she could not care. Also, she saw that she was looking a little surprised. 'The old soak,' she is thinking. If only she knew.

She was safely out of the house and on her way up the path in the full moonlight. She was very dazed now and her steps were unsteady. I must not fall, not yet. Twenty steps more, that is all it needs. The shadows were sharp-edged on the steel-blue grass. The lights from the school were shining out. She skirted it somehow, holding on to the wall as she went, but behind the gymnasium fell on her knees. I must go on, even if I have to crawl.

So she crawled, the stout, elderly woman, on all fours, trying to prop open her closing eyes. To the edge of the swimming pool. With an immense effort she stood, and took one more step. Her last thought – she was almost asleep – 'Not so cold.' But her winter clothes were protecting her, for a moment or so bearing her up. 'Blue Horizon and Correspondence', then *'Pontchartrain'*. She did not even know she drowned.

Chapter Twenty-Eight

'Poor old dear,' Canning said, 'now we'll have to reconsecrate the swimming pool.'

'Oh, don't.'

'I bet my last bob she was at the bottom of those thefts.'

'I know she was,' Penelope replied, 'but you're never to let it go any further.'

'What do you think I am?' He stared at her.

'Helen caught her at it. She kept it to herself, but after Elspeth died it got on her nerves and she told daddy. She said it was between him and her, and she certainly wasn't going to give evidence at the inquest. Anyway, who would want her to?'

'Let poor Elspeth depart in peace.'

'Leo, you're grating on me today.'

'Sorry. But don't go imagining you're the only person that feels it.' It was true. He did feel it: but could take refuge only in facetiousness. Also, he was tired after a struggle to console the Annicks, to make them see that this would not irreparably damage the school, despite the considerable press publicity. 'What a way to choose! Lucky we never use the pool till next term. Give everyone time to forget. Not nice, swimming there now.'

'You're still grating,' said Penelope, and walked away.

He was not too perturbed by this, feeling ultimately sure of her: but it made him thoughtful. Had he, in fact, been wrong in his refusal to sleep with her? He had not, of course, 'kept himself pure for the girl he married', as his mother had ridiculously advised him: he had had a good many women. But he had preserved a dream – also fostered, in all probability, by his mother – of a 'proper' wedding night, a triumphant consummation. So he wanted it to be with Penelope. Nevertheless, he realized that he could be depriving her of the sexual life that she needed, that he was, in fact, behaving selfishly. She was becoming increasingly edgy with him. He would have been seriously worried had he thought she liked him less. He knew she was only 'a little' in love with him, yet he did not believe that 'little' was diminishing. They were still together in all the time available to them both.

Despite his surface romanticism, he was basically realistic and determined. It would be painful to throw away the dream of a formal wedding, fully choral (though as a widow she might jib at that), a honeymoon trip abroad, timeless moments looking out to a moonlit sea in a world smelling like Mozambique of orange-flowers, the ecstatic undressing and bedding. It was the dream of a boy who had known back streets, grime, the hard rub to live with, the few modest domestic comforts so dear to his parents. How many ideas from the women's magazines that his mother had read so fervently, had she succeeded in passing on to him? He was only now beginning to wonder and to question. In what they called the 'permissive society' he knew he would seem a ridiculous misfit, that is, if people realized what was going through his mind.

It might be high time that he accepted Corso's offer. It would double his salary, and give him quite enough to offer Penelope. It might, indeed, enable him to take a firmer line with her. And he was clever enough to realize that his career prospects would be high. He loved the school, though, loved its enclosed atmosphere; it was all he had missed for so many years. It had been dreary at the technical college, living in digs. This was like being the jam in the middle of a nice warm doughnut. But it could not go on for ever, not this schoolmastering, however much he might enjoy it. He knew he was gifted and that he was not being stretched. The moment must come when he would begin to fret.

When he came to School Building he met Annick and a young man – who might be no more than eighteen – coming out of it. Annick was smiling. 'Oh, Leo! This is Giles Pettifer, who is coming to teach French next term. We're in luck.' Pettifer was somewhat like a bison. He had a very low forehead and a thatch of thick, curling dark hair. He did not look like a piece of luck to Canning, but one could always hope for the best.

'Mr Canning takes our science side,' Annick said, a little grandiosely. 'He's developed it in a remarkable fashion. Well,' he added to the boy, 'if you really won't stay and lunch with us, you must be thinking about your train. The bus will be along in a few minutes – the stop's opposite the end of the drive.'

'I'll run you to the station in the car,' Canning said, 'the bus isn't too reliable, and it crawls.'

'That's awfully kind of you.' The boy looked grateful.

When they were alone he said, 'I must say I've got cold feet. I never did any teaching before. I'm filling in time before Cambridge. Modern languages.'

'You'll settle down to it.'

'I'm not sure I can control a class.' A flash of a smile: he had very white teeth. 'They say French masters are natural prey.'

'If you need to stamp on 'em, do. At once. Let them take the slightest advantage, even for once, and they've got you.'

'Did you have any trouble – at first?'

'Not really. But then, my job's all gimmicks. I'm always showing them something, or making them do something, so they never have time to play up. You'll like it all right here. Mr and Mrs Annick are nice people and the staff aren't a bad lot. Come on, be of good heart!'

'I'll be glad when I'm through the first week, though.'

Eighteen? Canning thought, as he watched Pettifer walk away through the station yard. Perhaps not so much. He still seemed to be growing, since his trousers were a little too short and his wrists protruded a couple of inches from his jacket. But he can't be worse than poor old Elspeth Murray. Nobody could be.

When he got back, he congratulated Annick on such a quick replacement. Then he said – 'Anything up?'

'No. I just had a twinge. I'm having a lot of indigestion these days. I suppose I can hardly blame Mrs Terry. Yes, we have been lucky. The boy's got a very fine school record, and furthermore, he was brought up in France till he was ten. His father was some kind of embassy official at one time.'

'How did you get him? Gabbitas-Thring? Well, it will be a very youthful addition to our little family.'

'You're not exactly a nonagenarian yourself,' said Annick.

After lunch, Canning sought out Penelope. 'Don't row with me. Come and snog in the Thicket.'

She burst out laughing. 'Leo, you're incorrigible!'

'Were you rowing?'

'Not really. Only I can't feel flippant about poor Mrs Murray.'

'I can't feel it, either, but I can be it. It's my way of letting off steam, did you but know it.'

The Thicket was warm, sun-spotted through the high branches. Here it was really spring, even to a silver burst of blackthorn, luminous as a galaxy of stars. There were primroses and winter aconite. Penelope found a single snowdrop.

'Boys' place really,' said Canning, 'used for pure meditation, infant wickedness and romantic love in the seedling state. But just now, ours.' He laid his hands on her breasts and fondled her. 'I love you, Pen.'

She stared into his brilliant eyes as if she loved him, too, but said nothing.

'Doing anything this evening? Good works? A date? I hope not.'

She shook her head.

'I'm coming back with you and I think I'll be staying.'

'Leo!' She was not sure whether or not to laugh. 'It would violate all your principles.'

The warmth was lovely about them, and the earth smelled sweet.

'The whole point of having principles,' he said, 'is that they can be changed. A man who never learns enough to change a principle is a silly clot. Do you want me to come?'

'I don't know. Yes, I do. But let's see.' Penelope frowned. 'You realize the dangers? If I said I'd marry you, it would spoil that image of a wedding-night, wouldn't it?'

'Not now. That's what I mean by changing principles. I think you're a bit lonely, Pen.'

Delicately put.'

'Well, aren't you?'

She answered honestly, 'Sometimes yes, sometimes no. But I don't want to use you in that way.'

'And you accuse me of "grating"!'

'Did I grate?'

'Like a nutmeg-grater. Yes.'

'Sorry.'

'Not that you are. It's almost always you who do the accusing. And let me tell you something, my girl: when you do, you sound like the lady of the manor. Don't imagine I'm going to stand for that, indefinitely. The classless society, see?'

'You are talking awful nonsense.'

'Kiss me. No, I don't mean that I kiss you. I mean that you kiss me.'

'Leo!'

'There you go again. Come on, do as I tell you. It will be an experience.'

Moving away from him, she broke a sprig of blackthorn. 'Pretty.'

'Pen.'

She kissed him on the mouth. Instantly, he seized on her like a drunken man seizing a lamp-post. Both of them staggered and nearly fell.

'Leo!'

'Quiet. It's nice here, and we've only got five more minutes. Will you cook me supper?'

'What do you want?'

'I like eating as people do who have never had much money. Frozen beef rissoles – very nice, and no trouble to you.'

'Seriously?'

'Oh, quite. After Mrs Terry's cuisine, it will be something to look forward to. Tasty.'

'Chips or mashed?'

'Mashed, and no lumps. Have you got the proper kitchen equipment? And onion rings.'

'This is very unromantic,' said Penelope.

'Real love is.'

Chapter Twenty-Nine

Annick was interviewing two ferocious parents. 'David is very bright,' said the mother, black eyes snapping, a fur hat set well back on her whisky-coloured hair. 'Oh, entirely,' said her husband, who was a property speculator. 'You can't go wrong with him. Top of his form every time.'

'I'm sure he is, Mr Hale-Cowan, but we've a waiting-list—'

'You know and I know,' said the mother, 'that one can get over that sort of thing for the right boy.'

They produced samples of David's work, shooting them at Annick like paper darts, and he looked over them despondently. No exaggeration here. But could he really endure the parents?

'Now look,' said Hale-Cowan earnestly, 'we want David to come here, because it's only a stone's throw away, and we can see him often. But judging by that board of yours, you haven't much of an academic record. He'd help out there, if I know him.'

Annick got up. 'I'm sorry, I can't fit him in. We're booked up for two terms.'

'Look,' Hale-Cowan began again, 'I'm only being realistic. If I've hurt your feelings, I'm sorry. But you're offering the right kind of place and I believe we're offering the right kind of boy.'

'Harry,' his wife murmured.

Annick felt that he had never met so dreadful a pair, and longed only to get rid of them. The agony of meeting them again on Sports Days! He said feebly, 'I'll let you know. If a vacancy comes up—'

Grace came in, and introduced herself. She listened to the saga of David, then said positively, 'I'm sure we shall be able to find a place for him.' To her husband – 'I'm sure we shall, aren't you, darling?'

They could have it out later. He said, weakly, 'We can only try.'

When the terrible parents had left, Annick said, 'For God's sake, what have you let me in for?'

'Cyril, we need boys like that. It is just no *good* you fussing about their fathers and mothers. You can't live off Petey Quillan for ever. In any case, you'll only have him for another term.'

'Do you realize that you've pretty well let me in for those monsters? Oh, why can't you mind your own business!'

'Cyril!'

'No, I mean it. I don't want those people. I don't want their son.'

'Listen, on their showing he's a brilliant child and we need a few.' She was shaken by even so slight a rebuke from him as she had received.

'You will talk to the Hale-Cowans on Sports Days. I swear I won't. You've brought it on your own head.'

She was pleased to see that he was recovering his good humour.

Next week, the Massingers came to the special staff-supper, which always marked the breaking-up of school. It was special because on these occasions Grace insisted on 'helping' Mrs Terry, which meant, to make pies or cook roasts while confining the latter to the vegetables. This was much resented, but Grace was firm.

They were all there, even Delia, subdued in a dress elaborately flounced.

'Sorry you had all that business about poor old Murray,' Rupert said to Annick.

'It made my blood run cold,' said Blossom. 'I just couldn't get it out of my mind.'

'Still,' Rupert went on, 'a nine days' wonder – people's memories are short.'

'I suppose they are,' Poole said, 'but there's always whispers of "that school where ..."'

Delia gave a little scream. 'Norman! Don't be so depressing! This is a gala night. Mrs Annick, this is a quite wonderful pie. I do congratulate you.'

'Wonderful it is,' said Canning. 'I feel like a good gorge.' He smiled at her. He had come to believe that she was making a very great effort, and efforts were things he respected.

'Poor kids,' said Stephen, 'if they only knew what they were missing!'

Even the top form was excluded from this treat, being fed – though a little more excitingly than usual – an hour earlier. They had had hamburgers, chips and onion rings, which were unfailingly popular.

Annick looked along the table. A comforting sight, soothing even his accustomed fatigue. Though his digestion still troubled him, he made an effort to eat. The nearest we can get to Trimalchio's feast, he thought. But it does seem that the worst of our disasters is getting forgotten, or accepted. His daughter seemed to him beautiful that night: sometimes she did, and sometimes she didn't. Handsome, yes, but there had been months in which she had had no light in her.

'Well, Helen!' cried Massinger bluffly, and she jumped. 'Still keeping us solvent? You look blooming.'

That, Grace felt, was not too kind.

Two of his mistresses here, Penelope thought, his harem. But I am not embarrassed any more than Helen is. He had told her about Helen Queen: he was not a reticent man. She was relieved that he was not arch with her, not bantering. The sporting instinct? Perhaps. He would know about Canning and herself.

'Helen's simply taking on more and more,' Betty Cope said earnestly, 'she's a treasure.' She turned to the other girl, who smiled back at her. 'All that work in the office, and piano too, and now she's helping with the dancing!'

'They hate dancing,' Rupert said accurately. 'They'd rather have an extra period's P.T.'

Stephen said, 'I don't care what they hate. I'm determined to see that they get a bit of spit and polish and learn to use their great clumsy feet in a manner more becoming. Their feet are always too big for them.'

One of the doors opened. Two boys peered in, oo-ered at the candlelit scene, giggled and ran away. 'They're drinking wine!' one of them was heard to say.

'Now they will go back to their dormitory,' said Annick, 'and report on us in terms of wild exaggeration. The Arabian Nights will be nothing to it. Delia, you aren't eating. Have some pudding – it's Grace's own.'

She protested that she had an appetite like a sparrow. 'But so have you, Mr Annick. So you can't talk.'

She was beginning, Canning observed, to look fidgety, as if she wished the whole meal were at an end.

She said suddenly, in a loud voice that fell into a random silence, 'Oh, I do wish Elspeth were here! How one misses her!'

Nobody really missed her at all: she had been for too long too remote from the life of the school.

'That goes without saying,' Grace replied, in a tone implying that it should not have been said. 'Will you have some fruit?'

Delia had flushed a brilliant geranium pink. 'Well, I don't care, but somehow it seems awful, all of us having a marvellous time here, as though she'd never existed!'

'What are our scholarship chances for next year?' Poole said. He was terrified, knowing the frightful impatience eating at her like a crab. 'Peter and Dicky Searle this time. Who's coming along?'

'Hickling just possibly,' Annick answered. 'D'Oyley conceivably, though his Greek's a bit feeble. I'll try to bring him on.'

Delia accepted coffee and began to gulp at it. Her colour remained high.

'You're like Quilp, Mrs Poole,' Stephen said, meaning to cause a diversion, 'you can drink things steaming. Can you eat eggs with the shells on, too?'

All at once she gagged violently, covering her mouth with her hands. She gasped, 'Sorry—' fumbled for a handkerchief and gagged into it again. Her throat moved upwards. Pushing back her chair, she ran from the room.

'Oh dear,' said Grace, 'I'd better go after her.'

Poole said, 'No, please don't. She had a bit of a stomach upset today. She'll be back in a minute.'

But it was fifteen minutes before she returned, time to run to the cottage and back again. She came back to her seat, very white, but composed. Canning, sitting next to her, smelled brandy. Oh my God, he said to himself, this is the end.

Rupert Massinger was watching the incident bright-eyed. He was solicitous. 'Are you sure you feel all right now, Mrs Poole? Let me give you some water.'

'No, no, everything's perfectly O.K. How silly of me! I don't know what you must think.'

Everybody knew what to think. Poole looked wretched. He went on talking about potential scholars.

When supper came to an end, they all dispersed but the Massingers, who had been asked by the Annicks for a drink.

Rupert lit his pipe and drew upon it deeply. He was waiting for his moment, and they knew it.

'Well, it was a lovely supper, Grace,' Blossom said, 'I did enjoy it so much. I must say I felt rather nostalgic, listening to the good old school gossip, while Rupert and I are eating the bread of idleness. We simply can't make up our minds yet what we want to do. We've got a very nice new flat, though – you must come and see it.' Her face was round and girlish under her bright red hair, a shade or two lighter than her husband's.

Grace asked after their daughter, and they talked for a little while about children.

Rupert said at last, 'Well, that was something of a scene tonight, wasn't it? Is poor Mrs Poole past all control? No good pretending one doesn't notice. She must have rushed back home and had a good treble. You can't keep them, can you, Cyril?'

Annick said that he simply didn't know. Everyone was worried, and only to Poole did anyone pretend there was a secret.

'Surely tonight,' Grace said, 'it could have been taken for what she said it was?'

'It's not a matter of a single night.' Rupert knocked his pipe out, and lit a cigarette. 'It's what she is going to do one Sports Day or on the play night. You'll have her weaving around like mad Ophelia throwing flowers at the parents, with a bottle tucked underneath her arm.' He seemed pleased by this fancy.

'It's Poole I'm so sorry for,' said Annick. 'He's a good chap and he's been useful here, but he's just about at the end of his tether.'

'You look at the end of yours, if I may say so.'

'Do I?' Annick glanced sideways into a wall mirror. His eyes were anxious. 'I suppose I'm finding all this as trying as anyone else.'

Grace exclaimed – 'Rupert, you are being very depressing! If only he can keep Delia in some sort of order, I believe we can go on for a long time.'

He shook his head.

'I'm sure we can. If we make up our minds to.'

'And close the ranks,' said Annick.

Rupert said formally, 'I'd welcome a business chat with you some time, H.M. Shall I ring you?'

'Why yes, do.'

'How's Canning doing?' This with the good-natured smile of one who bore no malice.

'Brightest and best,' Grace replied. 'He's got the boys on to boat-building now. He swears at them, but they love him.'

'Leo has his points,' Rupert said easily.

At last the Massingers left.

'That damned woman!'

'Which, Cyril?'

'Delia, of course. What a wreck of an evening!'

She tried to persuade him that he was making too much of it all. The incident had been brief enough, and everyone had been concerned to shrug it off.

He put his arm round her waist, his head on her shoulder. He closed his eyes.

'What is it?'

'Dear,' he said, 'I can't cope. I don't know how I can go on coping. First Elspeth Murray and then this. And I am so tired, so tired. Every new day seems such a drag.'

She was alarmed. 'You really must see a doctor. All you need is a tonic, I know it is.'

'No doctors. Have we got any of those green and black pills left? We had them for Penny. I might try one of those from time to time.'

Grace said she would look and see. Scared as she was for her husband, some childish whimper inside her mind complained that all her efforts had been spoiled. The struggle with Mrs Terry. Then the splendid pie, and the lemon mousse. The candlelight. Spoiled by Delia Poole.

Penelope came in.

'Haven't you gone home yet?' said Grace.

'No. I went down to the pub for a drink with Leo. I'm going now. I only dropped in to say that I hoped you weren't worrying too much. Delia was a nuisance, but it honestly wasn't all that conspicuous.'

Annick had not raised his head from Grace's shoulder. Penelope looked at them with the mixed emotions of the child who is glad its parents love each other, but a little embarrassed, a little jealous, that they should so openly show it. 'Daddy?'

He sat up. 'Oh, I'm all right. Just fagged and a bit weighed down.'

'Are you thinking of sacking the Pooles?'

'With a term's notice, yes.'

'Don't.' Penelope was decisive. 'We can't yet tell how it's all going to work out, and we've got to take chances. Besides, you'll break poor Norman's heart. He's a sad man.'

'What does Leo think?'

'The same as I do. Go on covering up. We all can, if we try.'

Chapter Thirty

It was a sweet spring day with a week to go until Easter. Scores of little boys, butter-coloured, piled into the school train, scrummed for seats, took out comics and sweets in preparation for the journey. This time, the Pooles were travelling to London with them. The Annicks stood on the platform, ready to wave their farewells. A blessed respite, a whole month of it. And the Pooles would be in Devonshire.

The whistle blew. Heads protruded from windows, cheering, yelling goodbye. A vast number of hands struggled for waving space. The train drew out of the station, a yellow serpent, the colour slowly fading away as heads were withdrawn and distance supervened.

They were to be alone. Canning and Penelope had already gone to France.

'Do you suppose they're sleeping together?' asked Grace, with the slight nervousness of her generation.

'Oh, I expect so.'

Annick was right.

They went down to the beach. The tide was out, exposing the brown and green satin of the weedy rocks. It was such a small cove, so hidden away, that they tended to regard it as their own, and were not pleased to see a party of early picnickers.

'Kick them,' Annick said cheerfully. The release from school pressures had made him feel better and he was even moderately hungry, would have liked one of the meat pies the strangers were unpacking from a professional-looking hamper.

Grace pressed his arm. They moved along the water's edge. The sea glittered outwards to a rim of silver and the sand sparkled in all its multiplicity of coloured components, the tiny wet stones, the translucent fragments of shell, the green ovals of bottle-glass. Annick remembered his conversation with Peter, on the day he had been so anxious that the boy should not go to California. He remembered the little green crab which had burrowed into the wet sand and had been lost for ever.

'What have we got for lunch?'

'How nice, to hear that from you! Nothing exciting, I'm afraid. Eggs. Some cold sausages. Or I can open a tin of something.'

Sausages seemed in tune with Annick's picnic mood, and he said so.

They went slowly back to the school.

Their felicity was not long undisturbed, however, for in the following week Rupert Massinger came for his formal talk, and without saying anything, made it clear that he wished to see Annick alone.

He was renewing his offer of a partnership, and had raised it. At present it would be a sleeping partnership: later, he hoped to come back into the school. It was obvious to him that it would not be possible to keep the Pooles, and that their place would be vacant again. He would put all his cards on the table: eventually, when Annick considered retirement, he wished to buy Downs Park. He knew he wasn't a good teacher, and he intended to do little of that. The admin would be his business, and some part in games. He would make an effort to step up scholastic success – 'We're losing out to other schools there, Cyril, and there's no need for that. It's a matter of picking boys for brain and just relying on their brawn for a bit. Not that I like saying so.'

'I never picked for brawn,' Annick mused. He did not know why he was not more affronted by the sudden bleakness of this offer and the criticism implied in it.

For a second master, Rupert went on, he would look for a good classic, and trust to the student stream, wanting work before university or immediately afterwards, to supply assistance. He and Blossom had had a rest and were longing to get back into harness.

They had always been happy at Downs Park, it had been like home to them. Both of them would be very careful to retain the family atmosphere. 'Well,' he said at last, 'what do you think?'

'I don't know what to think. I haven't talked of retiring, that I know of. You seem to be pressuring me somewhat, Rupert.'

Rupert replied easily that of course his thinking was pretty long-term, that is, so far as taking over went. Naturally, it couldn't be anything else, could it? But he would be a fool if he hadn't known that the school was having its financial troubles and that some money might be welcome. 'A good bit of it would be Bloss's,' he confessed, 'Her father left her quite a packet last winter.'

'I see. And what would you do about the science side?'

Rupert gave a genuine laugh. 'I'd rather cross that bridge when we come to it, if ever we do! Of course I'd keep on with science teaching, but on the scale Canning does it I can't help feeling it's a bit time-wasting. It's precious little use in the scholarship exams, or Common Entrance.'

'You'd sack Canning, I suppose? You two didn't hit it off particularly well.'

Again the genial laugh. Sack Canning? There would be no need. He was bound to up and go soon in the course of things: he was an ambitious chap, he would be considering his career.

'I see. You don't expect an immediate answer to all this, I take it?'

Lord no, said Rupert, he was only flying a kite or two.

'Expensive kites.'

'I know you've got your worries.'

'Yes. It's no good telling you I haven't.'

Annick suddenly felt the whole weight of them. For a minute or so he was silent.

Then Rupert said, 'I'll tell you what, Cyril. I like to be frank, as you know, and there ought to be absolute frankness between you and me. As dominies, we're poles apart – that's what you think, isn't it? But perhaps we only seem so. I've got the good of Downs Park at heart, you know that. Together we could shore it up again, and after that—'

'You mean, after my retirement, or decease.'

'What decease? Oh rot! You'll live to be a hundred like old Potter.' It was true that the first headmaster had lived till ninety-two and had meddled interferingly with his successor until the day he died. 'No. I really am thinking long-term. That's how I always think – Bloss will tell you.'

Annick did not need to be told anything by Blossom. He had always disliked the Massingers, he had not wanted them in this place. But was he indulging his own natural animosities at the expense of the school?

When Rupert had gone, he described the interview to Grace.

'Yes, and he almost turned me out of my own sitting-room! I felt as enraged as Mrs Proudie. What was his general tone like?'

'One of jolly, comradely insolence. But I don't know whether I oughtn't to take that: he's just being Rupert – his essential nature.'

'Oh, darling, you won't do this!'

'I don't think so. But I won't pretend to you that I'm sure.'

The visit had rubbed some of the gloss off their holiday. Fits of energy – Where should they go for the day? To Brighton? To London? – tended to tail away and they spent most of their time reading or listening to music. One morning Annick said, 'I think I will let that damned doctor take a look at me. My bowels are all over the shop and I don't seem able to digest a thing.'

So he went, and returned half-encouraged, half-despondent. 'He can't find anything wrong, though he says we might have a few X-rays. He thinks it's pure nerves and he's given me pills. You'd better pray that the pills do some good.'

Grace pretended delight, but she was deeply afraid. What would those X-rays show? She went around in a state of smiling terror. On the day he was due to attend the hospital, she secretly telephoned their doctor.

'Ralph. Do something for me.'

'Anything for you.'

'Get those X-ray photographs as soon as you can. I can't bear the suspense.'

'My dear girl, he's picking me up at the house and I'm running him along. I'll stick around till I get results. But if you want my sober judgment, I don't believe there's anything in the least out of the way with Cyril. He's as jumpy as a cat, but I can steady him down. Try not to worry. I'll stick to him closer than a brother. I promise you.'

She told him how kind he was.

All that day she roamed about the empty school, unable to settle to anything. She played the piano in the music-room for a few minutes, jumped up and went to the gym where she did a tentative exercise or two on the wall-bars: she was getting stiff. She wouldn't be able to keep this up much longer. She made herself a sandwich, poured a drink, then put it back into the bottle. No false stimulants. The skies greyed over and all the shine had gone from the sea. She began to prepare supper, something that would keep in the oven. From the Thicket, a maddening bird cried out again and again before sleep. How long would it be before she could expect him? At least an hour. Yet she found herself listening for the sound of the car.

When the telephone rang into the silence she started up in fright. Buzz, buzz, buzz, a call-box. Then a clank of money, and his voice.

'Darling? I'm just on my way home. All the photographs are O.K. I thought I wouldn't keep you waiting.'

'Oh, bless you for that! Where are you?'

'A mile or so out of Eastbourne. I was driving along when I spotted a box and thought I might as well give you a call. I should be back in about forty-five minutes, if the traffic's not heavy.'

'I wish I had a pheasant for you! And champagne!'

'No pheasants at this time of the year. Darling, I must ring off now. Be seeing you.'

She ran round the school turning up all the lights, even in the empty dormitories. She was still trembling a little and crying with relief. The maddening bird was silent now, and she wished he would cry again, to add to the celebration. Only beef stew. Would there be time to make a cheese soufflé? He loved that. She believed he would return home without indigestion.

The telephone rang again, this time the doctor. 'I thought I'd give you the good news.'

'Oh, Ralph, Cyril's done so! He stopped on the way. I'm so happy!'

Now the soufflé in the oven: they would have it before or after the beef, according to what time he got in. When she heard the car, she ran out to him.

'And you pretended you weren't worrying,' he said to her, almost reproachfully after a while. He belched, and grinned. 'As you see, I haven't quite been cured overnight!'

Next morning brought a letter from Peter, from Paris.

Dear Mr and Mrs Annick,

I hope you're enjoying the holidays. It must be wonderful to have a bit of peace from all of us.

Paris is wonderful, and I am eating like mad. Did you ever eat snails? I love them.

It's really warm here and all the chestnut-trees are out. Yesterday we sat in the Luxembourg Gardens and my mother gave me an hour's coaching, so that my Greek shouldn't start slipping. I don't really think it will, but I don't mind. It's a nice place to be coached in, if you have to. My mother was rather nervous in case you might mind, or that her methods would be different from yours, but actually they're much the same.

There's a gorgeous drink here called Vermouth Cassis, tasting of blackcurrants. Do you know it?

('He's boasting,' Grace put in.)

My father says it's stronger than I think, but they indulge me. When in Paris do as the Parisians do, I expect! I think I'd like a year at the Sorbonne, one of these days, that is, if my French stands up to it.

Well, I haven't much more to say, except that we're going on a *bateau-mouche* this afternoon.

('Swanking too,' said Grace.)

I do hope you're both well, and enjoying yourselves and having a good rest.

Love,

Peter.

When Penelope returned, she said, 'One always runs into people! Leo and I ran slap into Peter Quillan and his mama just outside the Opera.'

'When was that?' Grace asked.

Penelope told her.

'And he never mentioned it in his letter. What a tactful little boy he is!'

'They are all tactful. You might call it cagey.'

Canning had not returned with her: he was staying on for another week.

'You look blooming,' Grace said.

'I feel it.'

So the felicity of the holiday was restored.

Chapter Thirty-One

The new term began auspiciously. Giles Pettifer, just over eighteen years of age, might have slunk to his first supper as though wishing to be unobserved, now and for all time, but when he took his first French class, the picture altered. For he was a natural disciplinarian, and near enough to his pupils in age that he could anticipate their thoughts. Boys accustomed to Mrs Murray sat in awe. How were they to deal with this low-foreheaded animal except by doing some work? They could see no way out.

He resembled Mrs Murray only in his devotion to the proper use of the lips.

'I will not stand for such disgusting noises. Your lips are flexible, remember that. It's no use mumbling at me out of the side of your mouths, and imagining that you're speaking French.'

A boy who put a frog in his desk was asked to return the frog to the pool, and then given an hour's extra prep. Another boy who fancied himself a master of comedy was requested to go outside and run round the cricket-field, well within Giles's eye-range until the impulse had burned itself out. None of the boys liked him, but French got taught. They did, however respect him: of the French teachers they had known, he was the only one, not including Penelope, who never so much as threatened to send them to the headmaster. He did not need to.

'He's a born schoolmaster,' Annick said to Canning. 'I only wish to God we had a hope of keeping him.'

At staff gatherings, Giles behaved with a kind of sullen deference. In his own classroom, he was a power.

Penelope and Canning appeared to be happily allied, but neither spoke of being married. Betty Cope was silent and miserable, for Gwen Morphy had gone off to live in Eastbourne, claiming that the double journey every day was driving her mad. In fact, she had a new lover. Helen Queen had met a young man in the holidays and was hopeful: she was always dropping his name. Nothing out of the way had happened to Stephen Smith.

But this was the great term of scholarship elections, and Annick could think of little else. Searle seemed to be on a perfectly even keel, but it was Peter he watched. Since the holidays, the boy had seemed abnormally high-spirited and carefree, far more sociable, even given to some atavistic bursts of horse-play: and any semblance of the unusual tended to worry Annick. Nevertheless, Peter's work showed no deterioration.

One morning, Giles Pettifer came to see Annick to ask if he might be excused Sunday lunch. His father was coming down, and wanted to take him out.

'Of course you can. But we'd also rather like to meet him ourselves. Would he care to come back here for an early evening drink, do you suppose?'

'I'm sure he would, sir.'

'And for supper, if he likes, but it's not an attraction on Sundays, I'm afraid.'

Giles's father, who was a baronet, proved to be something of a surprise. Quite unlike a bison himself, he was a man of little over forty, tall, fair, thin. He had a short but high-bridged nose, which gave him a bird-like appearance. His wife had divorced him two years ago.

'It's good of you to come, Sir James,' Annick said, always made uneasy by comparative grandeur. 'Giles has made a splendid start, and we only wish we had him for good.'

'I know he's happy with you all,' said Pettifer.

Giles glowered again: he really could not help it. In fact, he got on excellently with his father, while disapproving of him.

Penelope came in and was introduced. How pretty she looks! Grace thought. She saw Pettifer stare at her daughter for a flick of a moment before shaking hands.

Then a cricket ball came smashing through the window, just missing Grace's head, and rolled underneath the piano.

Annick threw up the sash. Glass tinkled. 'Who did that?'

Peter Quillan detached himself from a knot of boys. 'Sorry, sir,' he called gaily upwards, 'I was trying to lodge it in the drainpipe.'

'Damned silly thing to do! You might have hurt someone. I'll see you after supper.'

Annick returned apologetically to his guest. 'That's the first time I've ever known that happen. You'll think we make a habit of it.'

'Oh dear,' said Grace, now we shall have to put up with an awful draught until we can get the glaziers in. Was that *Petey*?'

'It was.'

'He must have gone mad.'

'I did that to a ball once,' Pettifer said, 'accidental-on-purpose. But I got beaten for it.'

Very fair: finely-lined white skin, blue eyes, pale grey suit, grey tie. He had elegance: and perhaps a touch, Grace thought, of the *louche*.

'I'd beat young Quillan,' Annick said – he was still upset – 'if I ever beat anyone. He's too old for a slipper.'

Penelope put her head back and laughed, colour rising up her long throat. 'You know you wouldn't! Not that sacred hide!'

Grace was busy with brown paper and Scotch tape, repairing the pane.

'Not so sacred now I've got Hale-Cowan. He'll probably make rings round Peter one of these days.'

'You know I was right, getting you to take him,' said Grace placidly.

'I'm sorry,' Penelope said to Pettifer, 'we can't stop talking shop.'

'Don't stop for my sake, I love it. Why is Quillan's – is that his name? – hide sacred?'

They told him.

'What will you do?' he asked Annick. 'Take him to Eton yourself and stay over with him? You know people there, I expect.'

Annick said, with a touch of chagrin, that he didn't. They would stay at the hotel by the bridge.

'College was beyond my wildest dreams: I was an indifferent scholar.' Pettifer added that he had a friend there now, one of the younger masters. Would Annick like him to write? They could have a drink together to break the monotony on both sides – and 'I'm sure he'd made a point of getting the results to you the moment they came through. Saves suspense. His name's Broughton.'

Annick was pleased, and thanked him. He asked him if he would stay for supper and meet the staff.

He was sorry. He had an engagement. 'I'll tell you what, though: I'd like a look at the school if it isn't a bad time for you.'

Annick glanced at his watch. He said that he would have to take evening prayers in a few minutes, but that Grace and Penelope would be glad to show him round. 'Not,' he added, and Grace could have slapped him, 'that it's much to look at.'

'You should have seen my prep school. There wasn't a whole piece of furniture in the place.'

'They scribble on everything,' Giles put in, 'and hack about with penknives. I jump on them when I catch them.'

When Annick returned from prayers, he found Pettifer gone and Penelope laughing about him.

'He's very nice – certainly he means to be – but he made Leo mad. He told me afterwards that he'd been treated like a lab assistant.'

'Had he?'

'Oh no! It's simply that he'd got an experiment set up and Sir J without waiting to be introduced, said "What on earth's that? Do let me have a look." '

'Sounds harmless,' said Annick.

'It was. But Leo can be touchy, you know. And he doesn't like titles. I think Sir J is rather sweet. But who *can* Giles resemble? His mother? I imagine some black-avised woman with hair down to the beginning of her nose.'

After supper, there was Peter to be interviewed. He came unsummoned to the study and gave Annick his cobalt smile.

'Petey. What am I to do with you?'

'Well, sir, I'd actually rather have the slipper than do lines, if it's all the same to you. I've got masses of work to get through.'

Annick ignored this cheek.

'Don't play the fool. Sit down. I want to talk to you.'

Peter sat, bright and attentive.

'What's up with you? By your modest standards, you're on the verge of Riot and Misrule. Is anything the matter?'

'I don't think so, sir. Just letting off steam.'

Annick suspected that he had been trying to release a good deal of tension. 'You'll pay for the broken glass. And you will not send home for replenishment of funds.'

'That's all right, sir.'

'You're not worrying about the election, are you?'

'Perhaps a bit. Three days of exams sounds a bit grim.'

Annick said earnestly, and quite untruthfully, 'Well, I'm not setting too much store by it, believe me. You're young, you've all the time in the world. Suppose things do come unstuck – which I don't for a moment believe they will – there's always next year.' He paused. 'You're not under pressure from your parents, are you?' He hated to pry, but felt this was now necessary.

Peter thought for a while. 'Not exactly – in fact, I wouldn't say so at all. But my mother just assumes that nothing *can* come unstuck, and that's a bit off-putting, isn't it, sir?'

And I, too, have made the same mistake. Annick tried to sound bracing. 'I can see that it might be. But I hope you don't feel that here. In fact, Mrs Annick and I were only anxious that you should have a trial run, as it were. More to get you into the swing of these things, than anything else. Of course, if you should strike it lucky, we'd be immensely pleased. But that's all.'

Peter lowered his eyes. A corner of his mouth twitched.

He is not believing a word I say, and why should he? 'Just take it in your stride.'

An absurd remark. Peter twitched again. He said, however, 'Oh, I'll try. But next year's a long time. By the way, sir, Mr Canning says he can put a piece of glass in. There's nothing much he can't do, is there?'

'Well, if he does, you'll still pay the bill I should have had to pay the glazier.'

'Certainly, sir.'

They were standing side by side, looking out across the playing-fields of May. It was not quite dark, and above the distant woods there was a belt of green. The birds were flying home. Annick felt the sentimental ache, wishing he had had a son. It was hardly fair that that clever, silly-looking woman should have borne Peter. He tried to comfort himself by thinking of David Hale-Cowan, a disagreeable little boy who was distinctly bright. Perhaps he would become less disagreeable, less cocky, as the years went on: but he doubted it.

'Can I go now, sir?'

It seemed like a betrayal.

'Yes, you can go,' said Annick.

Chapter Thirty-Two

Delia had not only abandoned her art classes but had completely withdrawn from the life of the school. She ate at home, when she did eat: the only time anyone caught sight of her was when she scuttled out in a furtive manner to the general shop. Poole was kind and gentle with her, but she knew his misery and it tormented her. Hadn't she done her best to please him, simply by keeping out of the way? Didn't he realize how lonely it was for her, eating alone, sitting for hours alone? Yet for all this, she was grateful for her loneliness, since she could continue unchecked what she believed was her 'controlled' drinking. She lived for the most part on hastily-made sandwiches, occasionally opening a tin of beans, or spaghetti. 'If you stayed in sometimes,' she complained to Poole, 'I'd cook for you properly. I don't know why you have to eat that horrible stuff over at the school.'

He told her it was one way he could save money. 'Because we're spending all we have, and more.'

She knew he was in debt: she had seen bills lying around unpaid. She wanted to cry out that it should not be like this any more, that she would stop drinking altogether, would do anything to please him: but she knew it would be impossible. So she remained silent, ashamed, frustrated, and hot with anger at herself and her husband.

'You must know I love you,' she said one evening, despairingly.

'Pretty girl. Yes, I know you do. There are things you can't help.'

'Oh, why do you say I can't? I have helped?'

'Not enough. Not enough to make a difference.'

Grace called at the cottage once or twice, but a cold, genteel reception made her aware that visits were not welcome. She went sadly away.

'I can do nothing more,' she said to Annick.

'Don't try. We've got to forget it.'

'Anyway' – her face brightened – 'we have our compensations. Everything else is going well. By the way, do you mind if I let Joe Finlay take P.T. now and then under supervision? He does love it and there are times when it makes me feel dizzy.'

'Not if his parents won't think we're exploiting him. Pupil-teacher, unpaid.'

'They're very nice parents, and they won't dispute anything that gives Joe pleasure.'

She went off, revived, to acquaint Finlay with his new position of authority. Grace could never let good news wait.

Annick lay back on the sagging sofa and thought about her. He had been very lucky: if she were entirely enchanting only to him, she was everyone's idea of a nice woman. Grace, he felt, could have lived in any age – as a Roman wife, placidly running the household and being considerate to the slaves, as the wife of a Crusader administering with equal placidity the affairs of the castle during her lord's absences. Never thinking whether his enterprises were, or were not, ridiculous. Simply getting on with the job. Growing age sat sweetly upon Grace, lightly and becomingly salting her hair, but not bringing ferociously to bear upon the muscles of her neck and jaw. Still neat-waisted, still pretty: and on Open Days, she could astonish by an appearance of glamour. What a beastly word, he thought, debased by the newspapers. Definition: the deluding influence of charm upon the eyes. Origin: *gramary*. Merlyn's isle of Gramary, where you and I may fare? You and I: no more delightful conjunction than that when things had gone well. And they had gone well. He remembered the days when they had known sexual delights, and had not infrequently quarrelled: as if these two things were linked. Martial: 'It is not possible to live with you, nor without you.' *Nec tecum possum vivere nec sine te.* Now it would be impossible to live without her. Any advantage to the sexual failure? It could be so. Now, he would have hated to quarrel with Grace had such a thing been conceivable. For to quarrelling in marriage, there could be no more than one proper ending. So there was no strife between them, only a valuable peace. At night they lay peacefully in each other's arms, for ten minutes before sleeping back to back. They talked. The best moments in the twenty-four hours.

He changed his position on the damaged springs, and his thoughts returned to himself. With or without X-rays, he could not believe that he was wholly well. His digestion was still poor, his bowels loose in the mornings. He belched, broke wind. What did all these people know? Bed was getting far too comfortable, and the desire for it too luxurious. He fretted. He would have to get well – or to feel it – for Grace's sake. What would she do without him? Or I, he thought, without her?

Cries of boys and birds arose from the playing-fields, a confusion and a shrilling. How he would miss it all. To give it over to Rupert! He loved the boys, loved their beardlessness, the tenderness of their flesh, and had no illusions. They would grow beards on those cheeks of chamois-leather, would meet with problems with which he had nothing to do. They would forget him in the importance of their public schools. Sometimes a freak boy, thirty years of age, but rooted in adolescence, would return on state occasions. That was all. Some boys returned as fathers: but that was different. How many hours to bed? He was tired. Shall I get there by candlelight? Answer: Yes and back again. The worst of it: *back again*.

He jumped, with a creaking of joints. For God's sake, what am I playing at? I'm not ill. None of them thinks that I am ill. How many hours to bed? One, two, three, four, five. Then, the delinquescence of the bone into the soft mattress, the gentle pillows, the enveloping warmth, the sense of a beneficent reality. You are perfectly all right now, aren't you? Then why shouldn't you be during the day? I don't know. I only want to go to sleep. We ought to buy a kitten, I should like to tuck down with a kitten. We should purr together.

Penelope came in, smiling as broadly as her narrow face would permit. 'I've been asked out!'

'That can't be too unusual an event,' Annick said, with an effort.

'Lunch in London, at the Caprice! Don't tell me that happens often.'

'Who by?'

'Guess.'

Annick shook his head.

'Giles's papa!'

'I see. When?'

'The day after tomorrow. I haven't,' Penelope said, in a cliché rare by her standards, 'a thing to wear.'

'What does Leo think?'

She almost struck an attitude. 'Why should he think anything? For God's sake—'

'Your business, not mine. But he'll think, all right.'

She looked as if she was about to slam out of the room: she had reached the door. Then she came back again and sat down. 'Are you one hundred per cent pro Leo, as mummy is?'

'My dear girl, it is your affair and I'd rather it was.'

'Yes, but are you?'

'I'm very fond of Leo. I shouldn't like to see him hurt.'

'Who's hurting him? Just to go out to lunch—'

'Then don't tell him? There's no need.'

'That would be sneaky!' Penelope said indignantly.

Annick sometimes felt she was young for her age. 'If you young people realized how often a little sneakiness – white sneakiness, a little white lying – saves a lot of pain, you wouldn't be such prigs.'

She smiled. 'Am I a prig?'

'The young are awful prigs.'

'Perhaps I should have said, am I young? I don't feel it.'

'If you aren't young, then I am old. And I don't want to believe that.'

'Well, still believing in honesty, I'm going along to tell Leo.'

She found him alone in his classroom, marking exercise-books. She told him. 'You don't mind?'

She had expected him to say, 'Of course not.' But he was slow in replying, and when he did so, looked straight into her eyes as if exploring them. 'I've no rights over you.'

'Darling!' She was, and she sounded, fond. 'Of course you have rights, now.' Moving beside him, she put her arms round his neck and crossed them on his breast.

He shook his head. 'Do as you please.'

'You don't mind, though?'

He unlaced her from him and stood up. He had gone pale, and his eyes were bright.

'Of course I mind! Rushing off to meet a bloody baronet you've only seen once in your life. I can't stop you going, and wouldn't if I could, but yes, I mind.'

She kissed him. He did not respond.

'Leo! What a storm in teacup! I'm curious, that's all, and I confess I shouldn't mind a lovely expensive meal after Mrs Terry's cooking. Don't start quarrelling.'

'Listen, I'm as jealous as hell of you and you'd better get it into your head that I always will be. If we get married it will be the same.'

She said she was not quite sure she liked the sound of that.

'What sort of a man is it who wouldn't be? Just a bleeding ponce.'

'I shall be angry with you in a minute. You're making an idiotic fuss about nothing. If I'd anything to hide, why should I have told you at all? I could have been going to London just for shopping and my hair.'

'You told me because you wanted me to be prepared.'

She tried to talk to him sensibly. How could she refuse, indefinitely, an invitation so kindly given, and by Giles's father? He might have thought she had a thin time, stuck at Downs Park, and had wanted to give her a treat. She was not going to an assignation. She was going to a good meal. 'And I'll tell you all about it.'

'Listen. I know I may be making a damned fool of myself, but then again, I may not be. Go and do what you like. Because we're sleeping together' – he preferred circumlocution – 'it doesn't mean that I have any rights over you at all. Go on! You're as free as a bird so far as I'm concerned.'

'All right, I won't go. I'll telephone him and tell him something's cropped up. He won't know that I've got a medieval lover.'

Surprisingly, this made him smile, and the knotted muscles in his cheeks relaxed. 'You'll be there all right, gasping for food. I don't really suppose you're gasping for the bart.'

She walked away from him, her face puzzled. She was happy with him: he had sexual skill and had given her comfort and release. She liked and admired him. Probably she loved him. But she could not conceal from herself that in small ways he did grate upon her, and would go on doing so. Though of course I may grate on him. Secretly, he thinks I am rather a snob – potentially, anyway, and he would like to break me down. It had been so much better in Paris, as it were on neutral ground. She felt irritation and tenderness.

He came to her, pulled up her sweater and began to fondle her breasts.

She said, 'Stop that. Not now.'

'Why not?'

'You make me feel *used*.'

'What are you talking about?'

'I don't quite know. But Leo, not now. Tonight.'

'What do you mean, make you feel used? Do I always do that?'

'Of course not. It was only for a second. I didn't really think.'

'Then try to think. It was the hell of a thing to say.'

She explained patiently: they had been fighting and he had touched her just a little time before the end of hostilities. It was only mis-timing, no more than that. She apologized, as she thought, handsomely: and was irritated again when Canning took this for a signal for the large-scale scene of reconciliation for which she was not yet ready. However, she played it according to his rules (aware of the shame of 'playing') and two days later met Pettifer in London as she had planned.

First meetings, so Penelope discovered, are deceptive. It is the second meeting which counts. At the school, she had thought him pleasant, but a little airy-fairy, or 'flah-flah' as Canning would scornfully have put it. In the restaurant, she was met by a thoughtful not too talkative man who seemed rather anxious.

'It was nice of you to come, Mrs Saxton.' He inquired after her parents, after his son.

'Giles is very clever,' she replied, trying not to be too obviously attracted by a bountiful menu-card: but her eyes kept straying to it. She added honestly, 'He may not give of his best to everyone, but he's a Napoleon to his form.'

'Shall we order drinks and then think about food, before we really start to talk? I'm afraid I get very hungry, and that distracts me. Let's push the main business out of the way.'

Red crinkled velvet, golden lamps, not much light. Penelope's mouth watered. Having dealt with the menu, she now found it hard to keep her eyes wandering in search of what television people called 'celebrities'. Two of them were just within range. She thought, I have become a simple rustic. I peer, and I stare.

'No,' said Pettifer freshly, as if a statement of his had been disrupted, 'I try not to worry about Giles, but I do. It seems to me that you are all very good to him. And he is not really very responsive.'

'The boys are making a transition,' Penelope said, 'between terror and positive liking. I like him immensely myself. I know my parents do.'

'I was more taken by your parents than I can say.'

'Thank you.'

'They made me feel so much at ease,' he said, 'and so often I'm not.'

She could scarcely hold back a rustic exclamation of surprise at this.

'I'm not good at meeting new people,' he said. 'I'm always thinking what they may be thinking of me. Normally, Giles is the same.'

She saw a beautiful woman in the darkened mirror on a far wall, and realized that it was herself.

She addressed him formally.

'Jim,' he said.

'I promise you that Giles has settled down perfectly. You need never worry about him.'

'He and I were always close. He was never on good terms with his mother.'

Penelope would have liked to know more about this mother, but Pettifer did not go on. Instead, he asked her about herself, probing with delicacy till he had the story of her marriage, her widowhood, the antique-shop venture and its collapse.

'I see. Isn't life rather dull for you now?'

'I have plenty to do.'

'I suppose you'll marry again,' he said directly.

She said she did not know. His gaze remained upon her, unblinking. 'I dropped a crashing brick the other day.'

'I didn't notice.'

'I think you did. I upset that very intelligent young science master.'

'Leo can be huffy.'

'I'm sorry, all the same.' He urged her to brandy.

'I don't think I will. I shall be so sleepy, and I have overeaten already.'

When he saw her to a taxi, he did not mention seeing her again. She did not know whether she was disappointed or relieved.

To Canning, she gave a light-hearted account of the luncheon. It had been very agreeable, but perfectly ordinary.

'Good. I wanted it to be ordinary.'

'So it was all a great rumpus about nothing, wasn't it?'

He did not reply.

Chapter Thirty-Three

'Another invitation to staff supper,' Rupert said to Blossom, as they sat in their ornate flat. The taste was hers. He had always dreamed of himself as living in something like a ship's cabin, bare, shining, shipshape. 'Significant, don't you think? It's a sacrifice to make, but worth it.'

She refilled his glass without being asked.

'If all goes well, I shall be starting more or less from scratch. A challenge.'

'Who will you throw out?'

'Not Canning, if he behaves himself, though his powers will have to be cut down. But I think he will leave of his own accord. That little sneak Helen will get the boot, I assure you. I shall read dirty books if I like – a harmless pursuit—'

She giggled, and her skin mottled more redly, though this was not unbecoming.

'—and I won't have her creeping around me. Betty Cope will leave anyway if her sorrows become too much for her. Stephen's safe; he's an unambitious man. I'd hang on to that Pettifer boy with my eyeteeth, but I think his mind's made up.'

'Like a strewn battlefield,' said Blossom.

'I will unstrew. Baroness Orczy, remember? "I will repay." '

'I don't think that was Baroness Orczy.'

'I do.'

'You always do,' she praised him. They had been very comfortable together lately. She was entirely used by now to his random women: she knew she was a permanency.

'And the Thicket. That goes. It blocks the view of the sea, and besides, a school like that oughtn't to have a hiding-place where you never know what the kids are up to. Not that one can't guess. We'll up staff salaries,' he went on. 'Annick can't afford to do that, but we can. That will make replacements easier.' He told her that already he had not let the grass grow under his feet: he believed he could lure old Anderson from Rowan House – 'a bit long in the tooth, but knows his job' – and two young men from an Eastbourne school. 'So it won't look like a shambles for long.'

She admired him, patted his arm.

It would have surprised him, had he the least idea how brutally bored she had been during these months of enforced idleness. She was an energetic woman, physically active beyond the norm: but all her other interests were bound up in his ambitions, and nothing else. She was longing for him to get back into what she called 'harness' for it would be a harness for herself. Solitary for long hours, while he was about his mysterious business enterprises, she had not known how to fill the time. She was no great reader. She was, even, no great shopper: not for her the taking-off and the trying-on in overheated rooms set aside for that purpose. She would have welcomed more children: but after Pauline, nothing had happened. She had never heard the phrase, 'an inner life': had she done so, she would not have known what it meant. For Blossom, life was action and action was all the poetry she knew. She would look out from their bedroom at the sea and wonder why it always seemed so inactive, when people were being sick on it.

The night of the staff supper was very warm for May, so much so that Annick suggested they should take coffee out on to the lawn. There was a golden sky, and the gorse in a stream of gold melted down to the sands. The hedges were white with blossom. The air smelled of sea and flowers.

Grace, who had made up a four at tennis before the meal with Stephen, Blossom and Poole, looked tired. Also, she had been spurring Mrs Terry to special efforts. They had eaten a chicken mince with poached eggs, and cherry tart.

'You know,' she said to Canning. 'I'm very much afraid my tennis days are over. I get puffed.'

He consoled her: everyone got puffed. He was subdued that night, in so far as he could be, and though he had talked away about space travel, sonic booms, the Common Market, it had not been with his usual intensity. Penelope was not there; she had theatre tickets, she said, obtained after great difficulty, and she saw enough of the staff in any case. She would spend the night in London with a girl she knew.

'Blossom doesn't,' said Grace, 'and you don't either, do you, Norman?'

His sad snub face lit up for her. 'Of course I do, but I'm ashamed to let people see it. What a beautiful night!'

They were all standing together in a group.

Canning spilled his coffee. 'Whoops! Sorry. But it won't hurt the lawn.'

'You could fancy Puck in the Thicket and Bottom and Quince, couldn't you?' Helen cried romantically. She was in love, and aching a little because, on this magnificent evening, he was not with her. She had bloomed again, Grace noticed, as she had done after the affair (Had there really been one?) with Rupert Massinger. Her eyes looked brighter, her chin, a prematurely elderly one, more firm. But she still had the best figure of all of them, even prettier than Betty's, who, below her tiny waist, was a little too large round the hips.

Grace knew a passionate eagerness that tonight, at least, they should all *feel* together. We were a family here once: it must not change. Things have gone wrong, but they must be put right again. Somehow, she and Annick would achieve the miracle. Strenuously, with their hearts and minds, they would do it. She moved closer to him and put her arm through his.

She became aware that she had had a tune running in her head all day, from the moment she awakened. Surely that was bad? It was an attempt to hitch a troubled mind to the reality of music: only, the music took over, grinding, insistent, unstoppable. Now she knew what the tune was.

Praise, my soul, the King of Heaven,

> To His feet thy tribute bring,
> Ransomed, healed, restored, forgiven—

But why that particular hymn? She thought she knew. Ransomed, healed, restored. She wished the sound of it in her head would cease.

> Praise, my soul, the King of Heaven ...

Stop it. Concentrate on the flowers, the singing and the gold. No, preferably not the singing.

'Anything the matter?' Annick whispered.

'No. Oh, my God!'

Their faces had been turned towards the cottage, and he saw what she had seen.

'Oh, no,' murmured Annick.

Giles Pettifer, who had been taking no active part in the evening, disappeared at once. He detested trouble.

Delia Poole was weaving her way uphill towards them. She looked like a sheet of paper blown by the wind, but there was no wind. She had on her grey dress, with scallops of white.

She cried out, 'Hi, everyone!' Everyone turned.

Poole muttered something and started down in her direction.

'Christ, let's all go in before it happens,' said Canning, 'Giles has.' Nobody stirred. They were held there, waiting to see what might happen next.

Her husband had reached her, had put his arm around her shoulders, but she wrenched free of him and came on at a staggering trot.

'I said, "Hi, everyone!" What is this, a wake?'

'Hullo, Delia,' Annick said with ghastly cordiality. 'How nice!'

'Nice for me, isn't it, you junketing up here and me shut in that bloody cottage, hour after hour – I'm joining the party. Anyone mind?'

Her face was flushed almost to blackness, and her cheeks had swollen.

'Go away, Norman, I'm not a cripple. I said "Hi" and nobody answered, and now I say "Anyone mind?" '

'Of course we don't mind,' Stephen said quickly, 'you're far too much of a stranger as it is.'

She took four tottering steps, established herself in their midst. She had tried to make herself nice for the party, but had left a single curler at the back of her head. Betty Cope quickly unpinned it and Delia did not notice.

'Come on, old girl,' said Poole, 'you're not well. Come on home.' Stephen stationed himself, as a willing escort.

'I am well! Anyone think I'm not well? If you think I'm drunk, anyone would be, stuck in that place, never a soul to speak to! Hour after hour after hour after hour.'

She flapped her arms about, more than ever like a sheet of paper, or a desolate goose lost on the edge of a marsh.

'Delia,' Annick began, 'it's getting chilly and we were all going in. If you'll come with me—'

'Bugger you! Who are you?'

'Oh no, you don't,' said Grace. 'Delia, behave yourself. You've got to.'

'I'll take her.' Poole gripped his wife about the waist. 'Yes, Stephen, lend me a hand.'

'You leave me alone! I've come to the party. When did I last go to any bloody party?'

'Stagey,' Canning said to Helen. 'She could stop it perfectly well if she wanted to.'

The curler, fallen from Betty's hand, rested lightly, in strawberry pink plastic, on a tuft of grass.

He took it up and pitched it into a flower-bed.

Delia fell into a flood of sweaty tears. They were so heavy that in a moment her face seemed obliterated by them, like windscreen glass under rain. 'Just let me know if I'm not welcome. I shall understand. I know when I'm not welcome. Somebody say something. For Christ's sake, say something.'

Her knees sagged. Slung between Stephen and her husband, she was copiously sick. Stephen leaped aside to avoid the flow over his shoes. Poole endured it.

Grace said firmly, 'Everyone go inside. I'll stay with Norman.'

Rupert, who up to now had been an interested, and by no means disinterested, spectator, pushed her gently aside. 'You go in yourself. She doesn't want the help of a good woman. She needs carrying.'

He told Poole to hold her steady for a moment, while he mopped up her face and the front of her dress with his handkerchief. This he tossed away. Then, taking her up in his arms, he walked with her easily down the hill, the two other men trailing behind.

'I'm so sorry,' Annick said to nobody in particular. 'It's no good pretending any more.'

'Since when have we been pretending?' Canning muttered.

They watched the small procession move through the last belt of amber-coloured light, and into the shadows.

'Poor dear,' Helen said passionately and meaning it, 'she did feel alone. Can't anyone see that?'

'Some people are a damn sight better off alone,' said Canning, 'and should realize it.'

The party, in embarrassment, broke up. 'I'll look in at the cottage and pick Rups up on my way,' said Blossom. 'There may be something I can do, and it really is no place for poor little Stephen.'

Grace said she would come too.

'No, don't. If she needs another woman around, I'm it, and Rups can deal with anything.'

'He may have to deal with anything and everything,' Annick said wearily. 'This is the last straw.'

'Darling, it isn't!' Grace threw the whole force of her energy into this. Backbone was not everything, and she had admired her husband for other things more important. But the effort to provide backbone, as it had been to provide a manufactured article, was hers. 'We can ride this out, we can ride anything out if we try. We are *not* going to give up!'

'I didn't say we were. But I am feeling very tired.'

'Thus provided, pardoned, guided,' Grace sang inwardly, 'Nothing can our peace destroy.'

Next morning, before school, Poole came to him.

'Headmaster, I must give in my notice. As from the end of this term.'

Annick said he was more than sorry. Could nothing be done? 'We've liked having you. I think we could carry on.'

Poole shook his head. 'No. It's about time I retired in any case, and I shall have to look after Delia now.'

He was wearing jeans and his green games sweater. He looked very old.

'I shall have to be with her all the time. I can't tell you how much she's suffering. She remembers everything this morning, and she just lies in bed and won't speak.' His hands hung down between his knees, almost touching the carpet. 'It has been going on for years, getting worse and worse. At all schools up to now, I've somehow managed. Not any more.'

He said he had twice urged her to take a cure, but that the idea had terrified her and she had burst into fits of screaming. Of course, he himself had failed her in some way: that was obvious. So he must be with her always now.

'If it's only last night,' Annick said uneasily, 'can't you and she forget it? Grace always likes to think that we're all very close-knit here and that things which might trouble another community need not worry us.'

Despairing eyes, heavily-ringed, the whites tainted with yellow, looked into his. 'It won't be one night. You know it's happened before, and it will go on. I was so happy here.'

Annick felt sick with pity. To see another man so exposed before him was a torment. A thin, ageing man with nothing to look forward to, near to tears. How, he wondered, when he was out of work, would he manage for money? Already, Delia was drinking most of what he had.

'You'll replace me easily enough, won't you?'

'Not easily, no.'

Annick thought of the Massingers crouched like cheerful red wolves at the door. He did not think he could bear the thought of their return.

'Look here, stick it out for another term.'

'I can't do it. I'm sorry.' Poole got up. 'You're very kind, Headmaster, but you don't understand how it is. I've got a class to take now, and I can't bear being away from Delia even for an hour.' He paused. 'Do you know what I have to do? I have to give her drinks just to get her through the day. I'm going to give her one now. She enjoys it so much more if I *give* it, if I permit it, it calms her so much. She can make it last longer, I know she can. Sometimes she tries so hard. It's awful to see her try.'

He thanked Annick again for his kindness, for all that he had done, and he went away.

Just before lunch, there was another visitor.

Delia.

She was neatly dressed, heavily made-up. She was very stately.

'Mr Annick, can you spare me five minutes? I've come to apologize, of course, and I hope, to explain.'

At his invitation she sat erect on the sofa, legs daintily crossed at the ankles.

'I wish you'd forget it,' he said.

'But I'm afraid I made a frightful fool of myself and I really do feel remorseful!' She managed a little laugh. 'Do, do, do let me tell you what happened.'

He had no option but to hear her out.

It was all most mysterious, she said. She had been sleeping during the afternoon and had woken so dazed! The feeling simply wouldn't wear off, so just before dinner she had poured herself a drink – only one, because she really drank so little, but she had hoped it would pull her together. Then, to her dismay, it had gone straight to her head. Wasn't it freakish, how these things happened? First she had felt giddy, then frightened. Her only idea was to find people, not to be alone. She had fallen into a sort of dream, she had not known what she was saying or doing. 'I knew you were all there, that's all, and I wanted to tell you I was feeling ill, but the words wouldn't come right!' This time, she gave a frantic titter.

No, he thought, they had certainly not come right.

'I believe I was rather rude, but it was fright. That's why I do drink so little, because of the extraordinary effect it has on me sometimes. I suppose we don't know much about it even now, do we? What it has to do with metabolism, and all that.'

She was not sober now: she had fortified herself to deliver this stream of ridiculous invention.

He could not feel compassion for her, only disgust. When he could get her out of the room, he would open a window.

Histrionically, she shot out both her hands. 'Dear Mr Annick, do say you forgive me. I should feel miles better if you did.'

He nodded. He could not speak. The white hands, palms upward, white as sugar icing, seemed to float on the air: then were stealthily withdrawn into her lap.

'Metabolism,' she said earnestly, 'is such a weird thing. I'm sure something's wrong with mine.' Then, sharply – 'Did Norman come to see you this morning?'

'Yes. He gave me his resignation. Didn't he tell you he was going to?'

'But I didn't know he meant it! I thought he was only punishing me. He was so angry with me because he thinks I let him down. He adores the school – it's a positive cult with him – and to feel that there should be a *spoiling* element, me I mean, well, it was just too much. You didn't accept it, did you?'

'I had no choice.'

She said simply, 'I don't know what we are going to do,' and she wept.

He could bear no more of it. He went into the bedroom, where Grace was tidying up.

'For God's sake, go and cope with Delia Poole and take her home. She's told me a string of nightmarish lies and now she's in floods of tears. I'm at my wits' end with her.'

'All right. You go on down.'

Grace marched into the sitting-room. 'Delia, you must go home. Stop crying, please. I'll come with you.'

Holding her arm tightly, she propelled the woman downstairs and out of the building, not caring who saw either of them.

Buttercups and daisies were thick on the lawn.

'Oh, the pretty flowers!' Grace found herself humming at the back of her mind. 'Coming in the springtime, tell of sunny hours.' Now that would be with her all day.

'Metabolism,' Delia was saying, 'it's such a funny thing. I was telling Mr Annick that I'm sure mine is disturbed. Perhaps I ought to see a doctor.'

'Perhaps you ought. Will you be all right now, or shall I come in with you?'

'No, don't. Don't! I'm not tidy. I've had no time to clear up. I'd hate you to see the place like that, such a pretty place and we love it so.'

Grace could guess. Unwashed dishes in the sink, if they had even got so far as the sink, dust everywhere glittering in the strong sun, smeary glasses with lipstick at the rim. For once in her optimistic life she felt entirely incapable of giving help.

'All right,' she said.

Chapter Thirty-Four

'You know you spent the night with bloody Pettifer,' Canning said as they walked together through the nursery innocence of buttercups and daisies.

Penelope was furious. 'I did not!' (In fact, she had merely had a drink with him before the theatre, which she had dutifully attended with a woman friend – as she had said.)

'You're seeing him, though.'

'Even if that was true, do you suppose I sleep with everyone I see? Really, Leo, this can't go on! You're treating me like a criminal. You cross-examine me.'

'Not that way, let's go down to the sands. Am I? I could be, I suppose. But he's a menace to me, that man is, and you know it. For God's sake marry me, Pen, or we shall go on like this.'

'That's precisely what we shan't do, go on. Not if you don't behave yourself better.'

'My blood's not chilled, if that's what you think.'

'Then it ought to be.'

They walked in silence, the gorse about the path smelling like fresh butter. Penelope walked stiffly with her head high, as if to prove that she had nothing to be guilty about. She had.

The truth was that she had been attracted by the gentle smoothness of Jim Pettifer, and perhaps by more than that. (Any element of snobbery she disclaimed.) Whenever the telephone rang she had hoped every time against all reason, that it was he, but he had asked her out only twice. In the honest part of her mind, she knew that he had made Canning seem oafish: just as she knew that Canning was a man immeasurably more clever. In bed at night,

223

she could not resist a fantasy in which Pettifer fell in love with her and they were married. A new life. She was not sure that she would enjoy being Giles's stepmother, but that was of no great account. A glowing world of restaurants and smart shops filled her imagination: her mind swam with golden lamps. Yet she was not in the least in love with him, and would not be unless he pursued her more vigorously. In which case, she couldn't be sure what she might do.

She shook herself angrily. This was girl's dreaming and it was not for her. They came through the gorse screen on to the sands and walked together. She stopped. She had made up her mind. Everything seemed to her crystal clear.

'Leo. I didn't sleep with Jim, of course, but I did have a quick drink with him. It must have been for less than an hour.'

He said nothing.

'But there's something else I must tell you, though it's old history now. I did have an affair with Rupert.'

He swung round on her. His face was white as chalk, his jaw hung as if by hinges, and his eyes were flaring.

'*Why did you tell me that?*'

'Too late, she remembered her father's recommendation of 'white sneakiness'. 'I wanted things to be quite straight between us. That is if we—'

'If we what?'

'It meant nothing. Only I was feeling so damned deprived. You don't know what it was like for me.'

He left her, walking rapidly away through the bushes. She was overcome with panic: she felt the hot flush spreading all over her throat, over her head like a wet hood. She called after him, but he did not turn back. So she began to run.

'Leo, please! I only wanted to be honest. I couldn't bear for us not to be.' The awful coaxing note, that would do her no good.

'Get away from me.'

She dared not follow further. She did not know what harm she had done by yielding to a violent impulse to confess to him. In some vague way, she had believed that by doing so she would rid herself of the Pettifer fantasy, and so make things better between Canning and herself.

What's done cannot be undone.

Where was he going? He was racing up the slope, up the field, cutting across the pitch where cricket was in progress, towards the school. She tried to feel anger rather than fright. Did he think they were living in the nineteenth century? He had a nineteenth-century mind, he always would have. People were frank these days. They didn't make enormous fusses about what was natural. It dawned upon her, horribly, that she had entirely forgotten how much, in any case, he detested Rupert.

She went on slowly, and on the way met her mother.

'Darling! What's the matter?' Grace was always quick to see the change in a familiar face.

'I've had a row with Leo.'

'It's patchable, I hope?' Grace believed that almost everything was, including international disputes.

'I don't think it is. Anyway, I must go and see.'

'May I know what it's about?'

'One day I'll tell you.'

Penelope found Canning on the telephone in the school office, oblivious to Helen's presence.

'Mr Corso, please. No, I want to speak to him personally. Tell him it's Leo Canning.'

Penelope stood helpless. Helen glanced inquiringly at her.

Leo turned. 'Go away. Can't you see I'm on the phone?'

Helen jumped and left. Penelope stayed.

'Mr Corso? I don't know if your offer's still open. Yes. Well, O.K. Thank you. I'll have to do another term after this one, but then – Yes, I'll come and see you next week. Thanks.' He hung up, pushed past Penelope and went upstairs. She heard a door bang. He was in his own bedroom.

She stood desolately on the landing, looking from the window on to the field where the boys were now racing back to tea. Peter Quillan was giving a pick-a-back ride to one of the little boys, who was screaming with pleasure. The grass, the trees, the flowering hedges ran together, as in a too-wet water colour.

Penelope, feeling that to be by herself was unendurable, went in search of her mother. Annick was at tea with the boys, so she found Grace alone. She told her quite starkly what had happened.

'You dreadful fool!' Grace cried involuntarily. 'How could you?'

'I don't know how I could. But I did, and everything's terrible.'

'My poor Penny. You'll have to wait till Leo's calmed down.'

'Oh yes, and I've lost him for you.'

'What do you mean?'

'He's taken Corso's offer.'

Grace was silent. The whole thing was so bad that she had to let it sink fully into her consciousness. She said with an effort, 'We knew we couldn't keep him for ever, anyway.'

'Don't tell daddy about Rupert. Just tell him there was somebody, and I told Leo that. Promise you won't tell him.'

Grace did, but it was a promise she would break. She had no secrets from her husband, except for a few half-forgotten minor secrets of the heart. He would be shocked, yes: but only because it *was* Rupert. Penelope was not a girl, she had known marriage. Of course she could not have borne life alone.

Grace saw the young woman's helpless misery and ached for her. Few things were more terrible to Grace than those which called for no action: here there was no action to be taken.

She said cautiously, wanting to break the silence, 'Why do you think he's leaving us now? To get away from you?'

'What else? I suppose the end of the world hasn't really come, but this is like a nightmare.'

To such nightmares could indulgence in fantasy lead. All those waking dreams, in bed, about the glittering life, the planet-like dance of the golden globes, had come to this.

'No, it hasn't really,' said Grace. 'It is something bad that has happened today. Then tomorrow it will seem a little better – anyway, a little more straight – and then it will all have happened the day before yesterday, which always seems like a long time.'

'I don't know what to do.'

'Darling, there is nothing to be done.'

'Leo's giving us another term, anyway,' Penelope said, forcing her voice. 'That's something.'

'So if you want him,' Grace said, putting an arm round her, 'at least he'll be here. Yes, it is something.' After a moment or so she asked, 'Are you in love with him?'

'I don't know. I think so. I go to bed with him, of course. Did you know that?'

'I thought it was like that.'

'It was wonderful,' Penelope said, 'that part of it. I suppose you're shocked. First Rupert and now this. You must think I'm a tart.'

'The word shocks me, because you're trying to make me angry with you by using it. The rest, I understand. With,' Grace added, a faint gleam of humour in her eyes, 'reservations in the case of your earlier choice.'

'Don't. Don't make jokes. I'm not ready for them.' She moved restlessly. 'I must go to Leo.'

'You can't, now. He'll be taking extra maths. Even if you could go, you shouldn't.'

'Perhaps if you were a bit less understanding, I could bear it better!'

'I will call you a "tart" or anything else unpleasant you like to name, if it will help things. But I'd rather not. Come, let's think about tomorrow. You can talk to Leo then.'

'I don't believe he'll listen.'

'Then the next day.'

Penelope shook her head.

She saw Canning at supper, but he did not speak to her. This was so unusual that people glanced sideways at them: he did not seem to care. After the meal he ostentatiously collected several of the older boys. 'Come on, we can get in half an hour on the boat before it gets dark.'

He was still the same savage white, his nose protruding in a darker colour. Why, she thought, he is really quite ugly. She longed for him.

Active as her mother, she could not bear doing nothing at all.

She went to the patch of gravel behind the gymnasium where the boat lay. Canning knelt by it, loudly instructing the boys who had crowded about him. Though Penelope's shadow fell long across the blue canvas, he did not even look up. She might have been a ghost. Humiliated, she went away.

During the next two days, all her attempts to speak to him failed. But on the night of the third day, after she was in bed, he drove over to Chalkwood and came to her lodgings. He followed her into the bedroom and undressed. 'Move over. I'll take Massinger's leavings.'

She obeyed, and he did take them: all too quickly, afterwards falling asleep at once. Sick with disappointment, she lay long awake. She awoke to find a pallid dawn in the room and his pressure on her shoulders. 'Roll over, I want you again.'

This time he gave her so much pleasure that she could have wept with gratitude.

He looked curiously into her face, ran his fingers down her nose and over her mouth. 'So what's it to be?'

'I don't know what you mean.'

'I can forget it all in time, I suppose. No matter how sickening. But I shall never trust you. Can you put up with that?'

She begged him to trust her. She thought (she told him) that she must have gone mad.

'I never shall. You did go mad, I think. I've got to be getting back.'

If he had asked her to marry him then, she would have said, yes, but he did not. He clambered into his clothes with an appearance of difficulty, as if they had suddenly become too small for him. When he had gone, she fell back into her former condition of doubt. Neither live with him nor live without him: her father would have understood, had she but known it. Bodily appeased, she was able to consider her mental state and know she was resentful. It was possible that she had been punished, and, whether she deserved it or not, that was a thought she could not endure.

She found a moment to speak to him during the day. 'Will you still be going to Corso?'

He stared. 'Why on earth not?'

'Is there any need, when you and I—'

'I want more money. I've got to have it.' That morning he handed in his resignation to Annick, who was profoundly relieved that he was prepared to stay for another term. 'We shall miss you, Leo, though we knew it wasn't for ever.'

On the following day Penelope, whose resentment had stiffened, accepted an invitation to lunch in London with Jim Pettifer. This time, however, she was not going to talk about it. In any case, it meant nothing.

Chapter Thirty-Five

The school was not destined to lose Betty Cope who, at the end of May, had a stroke of luck. She was accustomed to visit the draper's at Chalkwood to replace such linen as parents were themselves dilatory in replacing. One day, behind the counter, she found a new assistant, a big, close-cropped, muscular girl with leaf-shaped green eyes of unnatural steadiness, and they recognized each other at once.

Of course, it was going to need skill and slow-going. This was a local girl of small education, professionally deferential. Betty had been to a good London school where she had done poorly, except in needlework. It would need a good many visits, with much unspoken, and just a little spoken, too. She took to making more and more trips to Chalkwood in the school car, sometimes merely on the pretext that she had run out of cotton or tape.

The girl's name turned out to Tricia, or so she said it was. She was twenty. She had been a shop assistant in Eastbourne for five years, but had returned home to look after a sickly mother.

'Of course, living by myself, I do get lonely sometimes,' Betty said chattily.

'Oh, I would, I'm sure. I'm not sure I could stick it.'

'I'm busy all day, and then in the evenings, when I want to relax – Well, it's not much fun even going to a cinema, all by yourself.'

'You need someone to talk it over with, don't you?' said Tricia. 'That's half the fun, I always say.'

So the ground work was laid.

Sports Day was bright but unseasonably cold. However, it was graced by the presence of a bishop and Helen Queen's young man.

The latter was rather short and his glasses were thick but he wore the more subdued clothes of Carnaby Street, upon which he had obviously spent a good deal of money. Dicky Searle looked at glowing Helen and remembered his early dreams.

Parents wrapped in car rugs sat round the edges of the field, making a coloured litter. Grace, who had bought a pink suit far too light for the weather, rejected a top coat, which would have spoiled the effect, but was wearing a thick woollen vest. Finlay had just won the high jump. 'It's not fair,' Searle said to Peter, 'all he's got to go is raise a leg and put it over.'

'And I've got to make a fool of myself in the obstacle race, because I'm no good at anything else.'

'Bet you'll come last.'

'Bet I will.'

Annick, as usual, was wandering about in a state of nervous tension. 'Yes, Mrs D'Oyley, we have great hopes of Joe,' or, to another, 'You must be feeling happy about Sebastian.' Pettifer came smiling up to him, introducing a pleasant-faced little man of about thirty-five. 'This is Thorold Broughton. If he can give you any help when you're at Eton, he will.'

'I'd be delighted. You'll find the time hanging heavily while your boy's scribbling away. It's a trying business.'

Annick thanked him.

'I suppose at the end of the day, you'll do the usual thing and grill him about his papers. It shouldn't be done, but it always is.'

'I don't know that I'll be able to resist it.'

'A terrible sight,' Broughton said cheerfully. 'Nerve-racked heads and nerve-racked boys, mulling the stuff over in the lounges. Put him to bed early, and we can have a drink.'

Pettifer greeted Penelope as she went by, but no more than that.

Clapping broke out all round the field as a new record was announced. Finlay again, the long jump. Giles Pettifer was referee: he had a megaphone and a whistle and his father looked at him fondly.

'All this,' he remarked to Grace. 'Nothing is more English in England. Which I expect has been said before.'

'Privilege,' she answered. 'At times it makes me ashamed. But so long as we still have the independent schools, places like this are needed to feed them. They all look happy, don't you think?'

Pettifer nodded.

'Any happiness seems better than none, in this day and age.'

'We don't really know they're happy, do we?' said Stephen, who had been standing by. 'They must bellyache to their parents sometimes, or we shouldn't have some of their mums sweetly bellyaching at us. Which does happen. God knows what they put in their letters when they have their malcontent fits.'

'You don't censor letters at all?' Pettifer asked Grace.

'Only for the first fortnight after they come here, in case they terrify their mamas with their homesickness and tales of horror. One of them even wrote that he believed Mrs Terry was putting something in his soup to make him ill.'

'Perhaps she does that to all of us,' Stephen said, 'and we've been too obtuse to notice it.'

'But surely his mother didn't believe that?' Pettifer inquired.

'To be fair, she didn't. But she did mention it with a light laugh, when she saw Cyril again.' Grace's laugh was not so light.

'I thought you said those letters were censored?'

'Oh, we let that one go through. There's reason in all things.'

'Well,' he said, 'I'm keeping avid parents away from you, Mrs Annick, so I'll stroll around.'

He strolled purposefully in the direction of Penelope, saw that she was standing with Canning, hesitated, then came up to her.

'Great fun, isn't it? But cold.'

'Bitter. I don't know how to wait till tea-time.'

Canning merely nodded his head.

'I was monopolizing your mother, and there's a queue waiting for her.'

'There always is. She's very game.'

Canning looked at his watch. 'Parent's race. I've got to organize that.' He went away.

'Pen, will you have dinner with me next week?'

She coloured, and did not at once reply.

'Lunch, if it suits you better, but it's such a bleak meal, don't you think?'

'I don't think I can.' It was a struggle to say this.

'Why not? Canning? Is it so serious?' He bent down and looked under the brim of her broad Sports Day hat. It was an intimate gesture and look: she was afraid someone would see them.

'It has been, yes.'

'And still is?'

No reply.

'But suppose I'm not? I like going out with you, talking to you. Is there much harm in that?'

'I don't like hurting Leo for the non-serious.' Again she coloured, frightened in case she seemed to be pressing him.

'Then if it were serious, you wouldn't mind hurting him so much?'

She realized that there was a little cruelty in him, and it gave her a shock.

'Of course I should mind.'

'I'll telephone you.'

'No,' she said in a burst of courage, 'don't. I know you've no feeling for me – no real feeling – and I can't give Leo more pain than I have done just because I like to go up to London with you and have fun. It isn't fair!' This she said on a childish note, and recognized it as such.

'I don't think you know very much about my feelings.'

Canning was marshalling the more athletic mothers and fathers to race three-legged in pairs. Some ambitious mothers were taking their shoes off.

'If I'm coming last in the obstacle race,' Peter said to Searle, 'it's dead sure my parents are going to come last in this one. I wish they could just be next to last, for once.'

Pettifer said to Penelope, 'I will telephone, just on the off-chance. I'd better circle now, before I make myself conspicuous.'

She stood alone, her heart beating too strongly. She had tried to put an end to it, hadn't she? She would still put an end. Yet she had done it so badly. She was sure he must have thought she was angling for an acceleration of their relations, even hoping for marriage.

The wind was biting. Shouts of laughter rose from the field. Mrs Quillan had fallen, bringing her husband down with her. She had lost her horticultural hat, and several of the fathers were chasing it as it trundled away over the grass. Penelope went indoors, to where the tea-urns were steaming, and the tables were set with sandwiches, chicken and prawn *bouchées*, and small iced cakes in pink, lemon, chocolate and white. 'Nelly,' she said, to one of the girls who came in to help on these occasions, 'give me a cup right now. I'm frozen to the marrow.'

'You do look pretty, Mrs Saxton.'

'Pretty cold.'

A feeble joke. But she saw her image as she fancied she must have looked to him, in the green hat, the white dress sprinkled with green leaves under a coat of darker green. She could have fallen in love with herself. For a second she was afraid that she was going to cry. What for? A sacrifice? She had made none. Nevertheless, she had an overpowering sense of loss.

The first wave of frozen parents streamed in, and she had to turn her attention to them.

'Isn't it absurd how we all dress up,' said Mrs Quillan. 'We do it so the boys should be proud of us, but of course they never notice unless they think we've made ourselves look ridiculous, and then they're the reverse of proud. Peter gave me a very nasty look when I lost my hat.'

'But the staff dress up, too.' Penelope was trying to pin her attention to the silly-faced woman who was so clever. 'We do it to impress the parents. I wonder if they are impressed?'

'That's different. You do it as a compliment to them. But I often wonder why I go to these lengths for Peter's sake. He just looks me up and down, and nods or frowns as the case may be. You know,' she added inconsequentially, 'One of the marvellous things about these schools is that you never hear the horrors till they're over. Miss Queen writes to say that Peter had chicken-pox or measles, or whatever, but that he's quite fit again. You can't imagine the awful worry it saves.'

Canning joined them, and spoke to her easily. 'I'm feeling quite confident about Peter's maths. He's really put his back into them.'

'Poor dear! They were nearly my undoing. Of course, we had to do the most absurd problems in those days – you know, "if ten men are employed to put up a greenhouse in eleven days and one-half is done in eight days, how many more men must be employed by the contractor to finish the work on time?" The answer always seemed to be about fifty, but I couldn't work it out for wondering why the contractor was such an excessively stupid man, and what he looked like. Fat and blank, I used to think, with a cast in one eye.'

Canning laughed at this. 'I know what you mean. But I've got Peter hot and strong on the new maths, and it doesn't involve dopey contractors at all.'

Annick came up and out of nervousness said, in a manner unlike him, 'The great day approaches.'

'Peter will be all right,' said his mother, without emphasis.

'I'm pretty sure he will, but with examiners you never know—'

'They would have to be abnormally dense,' said Mrs Quillan.

They were joined by her barking husband, whose voice made Annick jump. 'Everything ticking over O.K.?'

'I think so.'

'Peter will be all right, we never worry about him.'

But you should, Penelope thought, in a fit of compassion: it must be dreadful to be relied upon quite so much. This clever pair, to whom everything has come so easily, may do him harm.

Peter did not look as though harm were being done to him. In his senior capacity, he was going the rounds with sandwiches and cakes. He was very courteous, very mature: almost, Penelope decided, he was 'making a leg'. 'We all love him,' she said to Mrs Quillan.

Grace, who had come up, heard this. 'We all do. He is a very nice boy.'

'But you have so many to love. Isn't it an emotional drain on you?'

'Perhaps we get used to loving.'

'Some more than others, surely.'

'Yes, we're human. We do our best, though. And it is always hard when they leave us.'

'Not when all of them do, surely.'

'There have been difficult cases,' Grace said, with her embracing smile. 'But I've never met a boy I actually didn't like.'

I have, Annick thought, overhearing: he had been talking to the Hale-Cowans.

'There,' Mrs Hale-Cowan cried, 'isn't he all I said? I never boast without cause.'

'David is a very bright child. I could wish him a shade more considerate in his behaviour to his teachers.'

To have said this, Annick must have been seriously stung.

'You mean,' his mother asked, 'that he's rude? But he always was. One talks and talks, but what can one do about it? He's so brimming over with confidence.'

'I'll talk to him again,' said David's father, smiling with a show of teeth, 'but it won't do much good. Still, one can always hope.'

'This is a generation,' Mrs Hale-Cowan put in, 'so different from ours. Don't you think one has to make the wildest allowances?'

'I think David is a bit too young for allowances to be made,' said Annick. 'If he were fourteen, I should perhaps make them. Incidentally, you might ask him to address the staff formally, as "sir", or "Mr So-and-So". It's customary.'

'I suppose David would feel it was a little slavish,' said his mother, 'but naturally I do, I *do* see your point.'

'What does he call them?' Hale-Cowan inquired detachedly, as if this were a matter in the public interest.

'He calls them "you".'

The bishop spoke gracefully, and briefly, at the prize-giving. Here comes Petey for the last time, Annick thought. He had a twinge of misery.

When it was all over and the last car had gone, Penelope went to Canning.

He opened his mouth.

'No! This is not the occasion for a row. Jim did ask me to dinner and I said no. And I asked him not to telephone.'

He hugged her. 'You really did? Did he get the message?'

'I think so.'

'He better had. Pen, are you going to marry me?'

'Why are you leaving the school?'

'Don't be silly, to get more money for you. I can afford things now. What about it?'

She asked him still to wait a little. The rags and tatters of the day were too much about her yet, and she was very tired. It was not a time for decision.

Chapter Thirty-Six

When they had unpacked, Peter and Annick went for a stroll through Eton. It was a little after six o'clock and a fair evening. Penguin boys in black tails and white ties were hurrying back from class through the pastel High Street, young ankle bones protruding from trousers too short, faces burnished by the rose of the sun. The chestnut trees were in flower, pink and white on red brick. 'It's the uniforms that make it really,' said Peter, 'it would be a pity to change. My mother says a picture's made effective by its use of blacks and whites. She says Boudin shows how. My aunt's got a Boudin, a real one.'

Annick, sick with nervousness, longed to get back to the hotel for a drink, but Peter was pleasantly lingering. They went into School Yard, and stood before the green statue of Henry VI. 'The Founder,' Annick said.

'He looks a nice little man.'

'I'd better show you where you have to go tomorrow.'

'In another minute, sir.'

They went into the cloisters, where the square of grass was moistly brilliant in surrounding gloom, and Peter studied the names of the innumerable dead. 'I say, there were a lot of them!'

'Comes of privilege,' Annick said. 'They were privileged to become officers at once in the First World War, and then they led their men over the top and got shot down like rabbits. I believe their life expectancy was between a fortnight and three weeks.'

He ran his band along a name. 'You had to pay high for your privilege in the days of trench warfare.'

' "Oh, What a Lovely War",' said Peter. He had seen the film.

The quarter chimed from Lupton's tower and a scurry of older boys went by them, humping books under their arms. 'They do look old,' Peter said, a little apprehensively. He cleared his throat, twice.

'You'll be as old as they are before you know where you are. Come on, you may not be thirsty but I assure you I am.'

Windsor Castle rose splendid and golden above the town, wholly visible in a gap between the houses. It was a greyish gold, as if age had settled like smoke in the interstices of the stones. Above it the sky too was golden, paling into harebell blue. 'It looks quite enormous,' Peter remarked, 'as if it could swallow you up.'

On the way back to the hotel he said, 'This is a very long street, isn't it?'

Annick looked at him in surprise. 'It doesn't seem like it to me. Are you tired?'

'A bit.'

'Then it's high time for a Coke.'

The lounge overlooking the river was full of troubled-looking headmasters in charge of young boys, the latter smart in new sports jackets and grey flannels, hair newly-cut, nails nice and clean. Annick ordered a large whisky for himself, and found a table by the window. Boats skimmed the water, delicate as toys. Peter drank his Coca-Cola quickly and again cleared his throat. 'Perhaps I'd better go upstairs and do a bit of revising before dinner.'

'No, you don't. That's over for now. Take your rest while you can get it.'

Broughton came in, looking for them. No, he hadn't come to stay, only to see that all was well. He would look in for a drink after dinner – 'because you may not want to leave your charge on the first night.'

'I don't mind being left, really,' said Peter, 'I don't mind a bit.'

'Well, you may be left tomorrow,' Annick told him.

Later – 'Hungry yet?' They went into the dining-room.

'You'd better indulge yourself tonight and get your strength up. What do you feel like eating?'

Peter studied the menu card for a long time. He chose melon, followed by duckling: but when the food came he ate only a few mouthfuls.

'What's the matter? Isn't it all right?'

'It's fine, sir, but somehow I just can't manage much.'

Stage-fright, Annick thought. He glanced about him at other boys eating stolidly and copiously. His nervousness, which the whisky had lulled, began to return to him. 'Coffee, or will it keep you awake? Pudding?'

Peter said he would have nothing more.

They went back early to the lounge, and talked in a desultory fashion. Beyond the panes, the sky was turning to violet and the reflected lamps hung in it, amber, three by three.

Annick said, 'Petey, you keep clearing your throat. Anything wrong?'

The boy pondered, coughed experimentally. 'It's a little dry, I think. Nothing much.'

Annick's hand flashed out and caught at his wrist.

'Sir?'

'Taking your pulse.'

Fast? Perhaps a little. But the pulse of a child was quicker than that of an adult. He touched the boy's forehead. Was it at all hot? Not for a crowded room, surely, and considering all the excitement.

'Would you like an early night?'

'Soon, not quite now,' Peter said, and so for a while soothed him. If he wanted to stay up, this must mean that he was well.

An inward voice addressed Annick. But you ought to find out. He repressed it. He was getting too neurotic about the whole thing, letting his imagination have rein.

At half-past nine, Broughton came in. Peter almost at once excused himself: now he thought he would like to go to bed. 'Will you call me at eight, sir? You know I never can wake up of my own accord.'

'I will,' Annick promised, watching him as he made his way between the crowded tables, out of the lounge. He made up his mind to look into Peter's room later, to be certain that all was well with him.

'Nice boy,' said Broughton, 'I wish him luck. What are you

having?'

'No, what are you?'

They argued for a moment, which was, to Annick, an easing one. The mere disappearance of Peter had reduced his fear and he felt almost festive, as he always did when spending an evening in an unfamiliar place. Broughton proved to be an amiable and gossipy companion, not minding much what he said. He talked school scandal, he made happy fun of other masters.

'God knows what it's like to be a boy here, certainly I never was.'

Annick for the first time noticed the residue of a regional accent, not unlike Canning's.

'Jim Pettifer's a nice chap,' Broughton said airily, 'bit of a ram, but nice.'

Annick was startled. 'Ram?'

'Rows of women. Always the same with him. I envy him, I tell you. Did you ever know Norah?'

'Norah who?'

'Norah Pettifer.'

'I don't know her at all. I only met him recently, when his son came to us to do some teaching.'

'My foot straight in it,' said Broughton, 'but I wasn't being pejorative. Jim was immensely like her, so I'm told. Not a flier, but amiable.'

Annick was thinking furiously of Penelope. She had, he knew, been attracted and flattered by the man. Had it cut deep with her? He prayed to God that it hadn't, for something in Broughton's quite unmalevolent tone had been convincing. He said carefully, 'There was a divorce, wasn't there?'

Two,' said Broughton. 'Jim married at twenty, and had Giles at twenty-two. That was Esmée. A few years ago – Four, five? I forget – Esmée divorced him and he married Norah. That was even less of a go of course. He couldn't leave the shop-girls alone, even when he was here, but it was an improvement on the Grecian mode. We have quite enough of that to cope with.'

'He couldn't leave the shop-girls alone.' Annick wondered whether he sounded as upset as he felt. 'I expect it's the kind of problem which comes in too late to be a worry to my kind of school. The Grecian mode, as you put it.'

'Oh, if you worry, you're sunk,' said Broughton, 'one just has to consider the norm, and try to find out what the norm is. It's usually a pretty dismal one.'

'Do you like being here?' Yet Annick's thoughts had flown from Penelope (who could take care of herself) to the bedroom upstairs.

'Like it? Yes. So many don't. I do. I like the place, I like the boys, I like teaching. And I have ambition. Look, I must be going, and I daresay you want an early night. Give us a ring tomorrow.' Broughton scribbled down a number. 'I warn you, I live in squalor. I have three cats.'

When he had gone, Annick went upstairs and listened at Peter's door. Not a sound. He peered in. The curtains had not been drawn and the boy lay sleeping in full moonlight, heavily, it seemed. A relief. Nervous symptoms, nothing more. Walking delicately, he drew the curtains across. Then Peter coughed, and struggled over on to his other side. Annick gingerly placed a hand half an inch away from the boy's cheek. Did he seem hot? No more so than he might be, under too many blankets on a mild night.

Peter coughed again, twisted round and lay on his back.

Annick slept poorly.

Chapter Thirty-Seven

He woke Peter at eight next morning, and was relieved to hear a normal-sounding response. 'I'm almost dressed sir. I'll be down in ten minutes.'

When he did come Annick thought: he has a good colour, anyway. Flushed? Excitement again.

But Peter ate only toast for breakfast.

'This won't do! You must stoke up. You're going to need it.'

'Sorry, sir. I can't.'

A radiant morning. 'You've got a wonderful day for it. Not that you'll see much of the sun, I'm afraid.'

Then, again, the cough: but harder this time.

'Peter, are you feeling all right?'

'Yes, sir, I think so. I'll be fine when I get down to work, I should think.'

'But look here, how *do* you feel, exactly?'

'Well, it is a bit stuffy in here. I could do with some air.'

'I ought to get a thermometer.'

The boy looked alarmed. 'No, sir, please! There's nothing wrong with me, honestly. Besides, I haven't much time left, either.' He looked at his watch.

'Is it going all right? Have you wound it? You'll need to keep track.'

The morning might have been radiant, but it had turned at least ten degrees colder. 'You'd better fetch your macintosh.'

'Oh no! Nobody else is wearing one.'

'Put a sweater on, then. Go on, rush upstairs and get it.'

'Sir, I'll be late! I must go, really.'

Annick walked along with him to the School Hall, on which a steady stream of boys, some with their headmasters, was converging. 'You're shivering,' he said, 'you really should have had that sweater.'

'Nerves, sir,' said Peter, and grinned.

'Good luck.'

'Thanks.'

He may be quite different at lunch-time, Annick thought, when the first newness of the experience has worn off. But if he isn't, he's got to see a doctor. He dreaded calling one in. What if the man said Peter must go to bed? All would have been in vain, all the years, the hopes. He tried to read the papers, do the crossword puzzle in the *Times*: he could think of nothing but Peter. The morning seemed interminable.

The boy came back, however, looking more normal, and the high flush had subsided. But he was thoughtful.

'How did it go?'

'Passable, sir, I think. Anyway, I hope so. The Unseen was a beast.'

'Let's look at the papers.'

They had fifteen minutes to spare before they need go in to lunch. 'What would you like to drink?'

Peter said he would rather have something long and cold – no, not coke; perhaps lemon squash. Annick, who rarely drank during the day, made an exception for himself this time. He did not know yet whether he dared to feel relief. He studied the paper. 'What did you do with this one? It's sticky?'

But Peter shook his head. 'If you don't mind, sir, I can't go through it now. Tonight, perhaps. I think I will go up and get my sweater.'

Had he been well enough to sit for examination, that first morning? I have got to put him first, not myself. *I have got to put him first.*

Peter ate a little soup and half an omelette. That was something, perhaps.

'Feeling fit for the second round?' The hideous, head-masterly, bluff note.

244

'I think so.'

'What's on this afternoon?'

'Latin verse and prose.'

'That should be O.K. for you.'

Peter did not reply.

The afternoon, like the morning, crawled. Unable to endure inactivity, Annick went for a walk, through the playing-fields to Fellow's Eyot, where some boys were fishing. An idyllic scene. He was racked with anxiety.

He waited outside the School Hall for Peter to emerge. Ought I to be waiting? I must look like a damned nanny. At last the doors opened and the flood of boys streamed out, Peter belatedly, and walking slow. Not seeing Annick at first he stooped, took out his handkerchief and coughed violently, as if he had been repressing this for hours. He looked white and tired.

'Oh, hullo, sir, all over for today.' He spoke almost jauntily. 'As a matter of fact, I finished half an hour ago.'

'So easy, then?'

'I wouldn't say that. I just dried up suddenly. I think I got down everything needed, though.'

'Feel like a glance through those papers after tea, or would you rather forget the whole thing?'

'Yes, if you don't mind.'

'If I don't mind what?'

'Not bothering with them. "The moving finger writes," ' Peter added – he had recently read the *Rubaiyat* – 'You know how it goes on. And all my tears aren't going to wash out a word of it.'

Examination papers were spread out among the glasses and potato chips, pored over by earnest boys and tense schoolmasters. Peter looked at them all with something like scorn, and perhaps a little like regret.

I am worrying myself sick for no reason. He's in high old form. 'No, you're right. We'll forget all about it. By the way, I ran into Mr Broughton when I went out. He wants us to come to his house for a drink before dinner.'

Peter hesitated. 'All right. Only I did rather want to look up a few things.'

'Is that wise? I rather doubt it.'

'I would like to. You go, sir.'

Annick went, heavy-hearted. He did not tell Broughton his fears.

At dinner, for the second time, Peter picked at his food.

'You aren't well, are you?' Annick said, with an effort of will. This possibility he did not wish to face.

'Oh, I'm fine. Really.'

'You're starving yourself.'

'I've had plenty. As much as I want, anyway. I do wish you wouldn't worry so much, sir, because then I start worrying too. There's *nothing* the matter with me.'

'I'd still like a thermometer.'

'Please, sir, it is quite all right! All I've got is a bit of a cough, and I'm afraid I'll disturb the others if I let it go. There's nothing more than that.'

For the rest of the evening, Peter was placid. He did not attempt to do any more work, but read *Prester John*, which he had brought with him.

The next day passed much like the first, and Annick went hot and cold by turns. The trouble with me is that I've set too much on this boy, and now I'm imagining disasters. He has a bit of a cough and he's nervous. It disturbed him that Peter would not be taken inch by inch through his papers. It was only after dinner that terror struck him.

This time Peter made no attempt whatsoever to eat. He pushed the food around his plate, sitting tense, as if about to spring, while Annick made what showing he could. The cough did not seem so persistent, but the flush had returned, giving to his eyes the brilliance of a cat's. After the meal, when he and Annick were back in the lounge, he spoke purposefully. 'Sir, I'm doing what I can, but I have a feeling that it's not my best. Somehow, I'm finding it hard to concentrate. I may let you down.'

Annick did not answer at once. He was in a crisis of conscience. He knew he ought to get a doctor to Peter, and knew also that if he did, the chances were that the boy would not be allowed to sit the final day. The question of right and wrong was not complicated, and he was aware that he was longing to do wrong, to take the risk.

'I'm sorry,' Peter said again. He pretended to return to *Prester John*.

Am I such a brute that I'm prepared to take risks with this boy for my own self-aggrandizement?

'If you did feel like glancing through the papers,' he began tentatively, 'I'm sure we should soon see—'

A man's eyes looked out at him from the boy's face. 'I can't. Honestly I can't.'

Annick half-rose, sat down again. He said courageously, though his voice sounded strangulated as if he had suddenly desired a woman, 'Peter, I'm going to let a doctor have a look at you. They'll tell me whom to ring at the desk.'

Peter's tears sprang up, obliterating the manliness, and they nearly fell. He all but shouted – 'No!'

'I must.'

'Oh please, don't! I've only got a day to go. I'll be better tomorrow, and perhaps I'll make up for today. Please don't call a doctor, it's pointless. I've started, and I've got to go on.'

Annick said, weakly. 'If you're not better tomorrow morning—'
By then it would be too late. Peter would have risen, and gone off. to his early start. 'No, that won't do. I tell you what, I'll call Mr Broughton. He'll put me on to someone.'

'I won't see a doctor. I don't need one. Sir, I *don't*.' He paused. 'I've got so far—'

'Then you have been feeling rotten?'

Peter replied desperately that he had been a little under the weather, but that it was nothing, nothing at all.

The thermometer, then. They would have one in the hotel? Surely. And if the mercury rose, standing implacable at the point beyond ignoring? Then it must not, Annick said to himself, be ignored. If he did so, he would never forgive himself. Nevertheless, he clung passionately to the minutes in which he could only guess, not possibly know.

Again – the antiphon. Boys, even boys as young as Peter, often exhibited anxiety symptoms over examinations. They ran temperatures which meant nothing. That was well-known. He hadn't coughed for quite half an hour, had he?

Dear God, he had to do right. He said, again weakly, 'I do think we must have your temperature taken.'

Peter said, 'I'd spit it out.' His eyes blazed. 'Sir, I would. I don't need fussing over, I'm all right. Only I had to tell you that I wasn't exactly shining today, so that if I had no luck you wouldn't be surprised – Please, just let me go upstairs. I'll be O.K. in the morning.'

'If you need me in the night—' This was not merely weak, but feeble.

'I shall sleep like a log.'

Long after Peter was in bed, Annick went to his room and stood over him in a torment of irresolution. The boy was sleeping so densely that he was able to touch his forehead and cheek without waking him. They were hot and dry. What now? It was too late to fetch a doctor out. The thermometer? It would mean disturbing Peter. So the resolution had really been taken, hadn't it? In his own favour. Because he had been so greedy for the gilded name, and because he had loved Peter. He had wanted all things for him, at any price. At the price, perhaps, of Peter's health. God, what am I doing? What have I already done?

He realized what the boy must have been fighting, in the solitude of his sturdy mind.

Oh, shut up, go to bed, bad luck it may be, but it's only the start of a common cold. You are dramatizing the whole thing. Tomorrow—

Annick came to Peter's room four or five times during the night. Sometimes the cough re-asserted itself: he slid another pillow under the boy's head, to raise him up. Sometimes he seemed much cooler. Surely he was sweating? By morning he might have sweated it out.

Morning came in a grey drizzle and there was no light upon the river which had a solid look, as if it might be grey macadam. The willows hung despondently. Wet boys in tails quickened pace up the High Street. A few umbrellas jolted by.

Peter now had a running nose and was anxious about his supply of handkerchiefs. Annick gave him a large one.

'Think it's just an ordinary snuffle?'

'I expect so, I'm aching a bit though. My back.'

Annick made up his mind. When breakfast was finished, he burst out – 'You're not going to sit today!'

'Sir!'

'You're not well enough. We've just got to cut our losses. I'll ring up your mother and tell her we'll be in London this morning instead of tonight.'

This time Peter was strained to the point of falling tears. 'I've gone so far, I must finish. I swear I'll be all right. I *must* go on.'

'I daren't let you.'

'Sir, I'll be late. Nearly everyone's gone already.' Not quite, but they were going.

Peter wiped furiously at his eyes and took a step towards the door. Annick caught his sleeve.

'No,' the boy said furiously, 'no, I won't be stopped. I can't be. Not now.'

He pulled himself free and ran. Before Annick could catch up with him he was out of the hotel and lost in the sodden crowds. He had been on the verge of hysteria. What could I have done with him more than I have done?

At lunchtime Peter came in, wet, quiet, subdued, perhaps a little apprehensive. 'Sorry, sir. But I just had to go on. I've only got the general paper to come, and that should be all right.' His nose and eyes were red and swollen and his mouth looked shrivelled. He ate, very slowly, some soup and a fruit jelly.

Neither of them spoke much. Annick was too loaded with guilt to try. Even in that last, half-hearted attempt at discipline he had failed, his daemon driving him to failure. Of course no good could come of it and this sick boy had made his monumental effort in vain. All the tenderness of guilt was Annick's too, the wretched warmth of loving betrayed. Nothing left now but the interview.

How would the boy cope with that? Somehow, it seemed, he had coped, but Annick asked no questions.

When it was all over he made Peter drink a cup of tea. He had packed the bags of both of them, and had brought them down into the hall. They were to meet Mrs Quillan at Waterloo, where she would take her son home for a few days.

'We'll go first class and pay the excess,' he heard himself say in a jollying voice, 'you've deserved a bit of luxury.'

The castle was invisible now behind great loops of rain. They had the carriage to themselves.

'I mucked it up,' Peter said, 'my essay was rotten.'

Annick looked at the paper, put so slackly into his hand. 'Which subject did you choose?' He was told. 'Not a bad choice. I don't believe you could go far wrong with that.'

'It's no good hoping, sir. Please don't hope. It was just bloody awful luck, me being like this.'

'How are you feeling now?'

'My head aches a bit. My back does, too, but that's because of all the sitting.'

Alone in his corner seat, the child looked so wretched, so forlorn, so dragged down by tiredness, that Annick could not forbear to give him comfort. He sat next to him, trying to warm him with the proximity of his own body heat. 'Could you get half an hour's sleep if you tried? Put your head on my shoulder, if it's more comfortable.'

'I'm all right, sir. No, I couldn't sleep. Not for just that short time.' He stared stonily out of the windows, at the blossoming hedges, greyed and awry with the rain.

'You're not worrying, are you? I told you it was really only to be a trial run.'

'I'm glad it's over.'

'God, so am I.'

'It's not been much fun for you.'

'What does it matter about me?' Annick cried, almost angrily. 'You've been a hero. Nothing can alter that.'

Mrs Quillan, in her Sports Day hat, was waiting at the barrier.

Peter went and clung to her. She looked slightly surprised. 'Well, darling, how did it go? Mr Annick, you have been so kind, we're so grateful. How was it, Petey?'

'Mummy, I've made a muck-up, a complete and utter muck-up. I wasn't well.'

'I'm quite sure you haven't, pet,' she replied placidly. 'Not well? What's the matter?'

'I'm afraid Peter's had a very bad cold,' said Annick. 'It's been rough luck on him.'

She held her son at arm's length. 'Why, yes, so you have! Didn't you have any aspirin with you?'

'I was worried stiff,' Annick went on steadfastly, 'about whether I ought to have got a doctor or not. I didn't know what to do.'

'I didn't want a doctor!' said Peter. 'He'd have sent me to bed, or something awful. But it would have been all the same if he had. I've spoiled everything.'

'You'll have a doctor now, anyway,' Mrs Quillan told him. She did not seem much disturbed. 'Come on, the car's waiting.'

As they walked to it she said to Annick, her noise pointing sharply, 'Have you been through his papers with him?'

'No. He was too fagged out by the end of the day.'

'Well, then, I will, as soon as he's himself again.' He caught the flash of anxiety which she was trying so hard to conceal, behind her eyes. But he believed it was only Peter's health that troubled her.

'Mr Annick, do come back with us for a drink. I know Bryan will want to thank you too.'

He excused himself. His homeward train left in twenty minutes.

She put Peter quickly into the car, a carriage rug round him. On his face for the first time in those agonizing days, was a look of peace. She lingered for a moment outside.

'I hope to God I did right,' said Annick.

'I'm sure you took every care of him. And short of actual death' – she laughed, but flinched at her own words – 'you could never have stopped him sitting. By the way, how do you suppose he actually has done?' Peter was out of earshot.

'In the circumstances,' Annick said shortly, 'I can't believe he was at his best. It's a pity, but there's always another time.'

'I do thank you, anyway. But I'm sure you underestimate him. I'll take him back now and get him to bed with hot milk. Did you know that he adores hot milk, with the skin on it? I think it's an obscene taste.'

She got into the driving seat. Peter waved wanly through the window. He had cocooned himself in the rug, up to his chin.

Annick went towards his train, feeling the immediate weight off his shoulders. But he was still guilty, still hopelessly miserable. He dreaded what he was bound to confess to Grace.

Chapter Thirty-Eight

He had barely arrived home when the telephone rang. 'For you, Cyril,' said Grace. 'It's Mrs Quillan.'

In dread he lifted the receiver: but her voice held its usual note of ebullient meaninglessness.

'Mr Annick? I did think you'd want to know. Well, the doctor has been and Peter has 'flu. His lungs are clear, thank heaven. We'll have to keep him in bed for a week, even though you've seen him through the worst of it. He's quite happy now, sitting up in bed and drinking his horrible milk.'

'Thank you so much for telling me. I've been worried stiff.'

'My dear, you must have been! Anyway, he's quite cheerful and he sends you and Mrs Annick his love. Don't bother about his election results – he'll have coped. And if he hasn't, don't worry either.'

This, from Mrs Quillan, was brave.

'I don't. But I'm relieved about Peter.'

'He says he "fancies" a boiled egg. Where does he get these dreadful terms from?'

'Not from my school,' said Annick, for the moment euphoric.

When he had put the receiver back into its bed, he sat beside Grace and held her. 'So Petey will be all right,' she said. 'I mean, physically. You must have had a dreadful time.'

'I did. I shall never forget it – Because, my darling, I did wrong.'

She tried to comfort him further: at least, he had had some comfort already from Mrs Quillan's telephone call. Yet his conscience was unquiet. He had taken a grave risk, had done so out of ambition: it was proper punishment that the risk should have been in vain.

'You don't think,' said Grace, 'that Petey may have done better than you suppose?'

'No. You should have seen him, as I did.' He cleared his vision and peered into her face. 'You look tired.'

'I am, rather. But not so much as you are.'

'Promise me?'

'What?'

'You're feeling all right?'

'Of course I am.' Doubt was in her face. She repeated, 'Of course I am. Are you coming to bed? A good long night may do us both good.'

There was another telephone call that evening, from Richard Searle's mother. She sounded jubilant. Dicky was – if not confident – she wasn't tempting fate – feeling that he had been lucky in his papers.

'So we shall have one name,' Grace said. She lifted Annick's still boyish flap of hair, let it fall back into place.

'Touch wood,' he said.

'Touch wood, indeed, but I have great faith in Dicky's judgment. Even when he was a little boy, it was always sound.'

Lying with her that night, he felt that to be in bed was very heaven. She smelled like peace. After the frightful nights with Peter in the hotel, this was lovely beyond believing. He wished not to fall asleep, so that he need not lose the savour of it. Even if his more jealous hopes had deserted him, he had still the hope of being always with his wife. She stirred out of his one-armed embrace and came against his breast.

'We have been happy, haven't we?' Her voice came out of blackness.

'Why so valedictory?'

'But we have been.'

'Remarkably,' said Annick. 'We have had all the luck. We shall have more. I'll ring the Quillans in the morning.'

'Yes, darling, do. Sleep now.'

The rain was rushing down outside, steady, hushing, reassuring.

Annick felt her weight. She had fallen asleep. Delicately, he disengaged her arms, laid her on her left side, the one she favoured most. She seemed so light that it was like handling a girl. Soon he, too, slept.

By morning the rain had gone away and the sky dazzled. 'Oh, lovely,' she said as, up before her, he parted the curtains.

Now the waiting for examination results, perhaps for three or four days. Though there was only Searle's to wait for.

After breakfast Penelope came to her mother.

'You remember Timmy?' Her partner in the antique shop. 'He's opening up a shop in Deal, and he wants me to come in with him. Would you mind very much if I went?'

'It's your life,' said Grace. 'But are you sure it's what you really want?'

'I only know that I've got to get away.' The girl's face was troubled and dark. She sat with unnatural quietness, her hands in her lap. 'I've been in such a state of worry for quite a long time. I don't feel I'll be able to think clearly unless I put a distance between this place and myself.'

'Something has happened.'

'Yes.'

Penelope told the story. During Annick's absence in Eton, she had dined in London with Pettifer. This time, Canning had not suspected her, which made it worse. He had said that he would never trust her again, but his real nature was essentially trustful. It had been an unhappy meal spoiled by her conscience: she had felt she was enclosed in glass, Pettifer remote. Yet throughout, the atmosphere had been tense: it was as if they were both waiting for the curtain to rise upon a lighted stage.

'I'd better tell you,' Grace interrupted. 'Your father learned while he was away that Pettifer has a hectic reputation for womanizing. I'm sorry to be sordid, but it's as well that you should know.'

Penelope smiled. She said she had been told that too, by Pettifer himself.

'So the curtain did rise,' said Grace.

It had been past eleven o'clock when he began to speak to her of what had been on his mind. Philandering he admitted: for years it had been a sort of compulsion and had, he knew, done a lot of people a good deal of harm. But he believed, blessedly, that he was getting beyond all that. He wanted her to know that she might blame his two divorces entirely upon himself. 'I am not altogether an estimable character,' he had said.

'Which was disarming,' said Penelope.

Then he had asked her to marry him, and almost without thinking she had said no. 'It was a shock. "No" seemed the only thing to say.'

'The bright lights had seemed so fascinating before,' she admitted frankly, 'enormous menu-cards, finger-bowls, *friandises* – although I never eat them, they are nice to look at – and oh yes, I suppose the title. I've seen myself in swansdown at the London Clinic with photographers around having given birth to the heir.'

'He wouldn't have been,' Grace said practically. 'Giles is.'

'No. Still, another heir would have been impressive.' She repeated, 'Anyway, I did say no. He looked so startled. But it had dawned on me that I wasn't in the least in love with him, and wouldn't be. The trouble is, that I can't say yes to Leo, and if I don't everything is going to be dreadful. Nothing comes right for me.'

Fond as she was of Canning, Grace could not resist a twinge of disappointment. Like most mothers, she found it hard to resist the ignoble dream of a fairytale marriage.

'Are you going to tell Leo?'

'No. Not this time. Once bitten, twice shy.'

'What is he going to think if you leave here?'

'I don't know. That's something I haven't yet faced.'

'Well, I think you'd be an ass to go running off to Deal,' Grace said, 'it will solve nothing at all.'

When Penelope had gone, she felt suddenly exhausted. Too many worries altogether, crowding in. I wouldn't mind having a good vomit if I felt I could, but I never can. It occurred to her with a pang that her daughter, unlike Cyril and herself, was singularly shallow-natured. She could really settle to nothing, she had never been able to. If her husband had not died, she would soon have become indecisive about her relations with him. For Penelope, there was always something unattainable at the end of the rainbow, but nothing so easily visualized, so practical as a crock of gold. No, just a something, a disturbing something, constantly dancing, like a yo-yo on a string, just out of sight of her conscious desires.

She said to Annick after tea, 'Do you know, I feel so sleepy? I'm going to lie down for half an hour.'

This was so surprising that he stared at her. 'Are you sure you're all right?' He forgot about his own ill-health, as he imagined it, when contemplating the possibility of ill-health for her.

'Of course I am! I'm just self indulgent.' She said nothing to him about Penelope. She did not feel like it, not just then. The stairs seemed to her like a steep-pitched ladder and she was grateful to throw herself upon the bed. In her mind another tune was running – *The First Cuckoo in Spring*, incessantly repeated. She rose to draw the curtains against the pouring sunshine, then lay back again. Softness received her: her bones seemed to melt into it. To lie down was always a comfort because it was the *last* thing one could do: there was never anything beyond that. I shall have to get some sort of tonic, she thought, for some reason I am very run-down. Damn the First Cuckoo, and damn this yawning. For she could stop neither. It was some time before she slept.

After prayers, Annick, a little perturbed, came in search of her. She was lying on her back, her eyes open and in the dim light she seemed to be munching.

She managed to say, her words hardly comprehensible, 'Help me. I'm scared.'

He pulled back the curtains and at once saw that something – a slight but terrifying something – had happened to her face.

'Darling, what is it?'

'Help me move my left leg. It's gone dead. I had a nightmare.' She tried to smile. 'A daymare.'

He raised her on the pillows, his pulses pounding. 'Can you get both legs over on to the floor?'

'I'll try.' Her voice was a little clearer. He saw her struggle, then fall back. 'Only pins and needles.'

'I'm getting Ralph.'

He ran to the stairhead, calling to the nearest boy, 'Find Mrs Saxton and bring here here.' Penelope came running up. She looked at her mother and blanched.

'Telephone Ralph Keats and tell him to come as quickly as possible. If he's not in, get someone else. Anyone.'

'Only pins and needles,' Grace munched at them. He could see that she was making an enormous effort to move.

'No, don't, stay there.'

She was now fully awake, still scared, her face still twisted, but in command of herself.

'Pins and needles down my left leg and arm, that's all it is. It will go away soon.'

He held her tightly, kissed her cheek again and again.

The doctor was in, and was with them within twenty minutes. He took one look at Grace, said a few words of reassurance, made an examination.

'Look!' she cried, 'I can move my leg a bit now!'

'You'd better rest. For a few days, anyhow.'

'I'll get you undressed, darling,' said Penelope.

Ralph Keats spoke to Annick outside the room. 'I'm afraid she's had a slight stroke. It isn't too bad, but we shall have to take precautions for a while. A fortnight in bed – perhaps not so long. We'll see how she gets on.'

Annick could not speak. He had always been expecting something like this to happen to himself, but not to her.

'Try not to worry. I'll look in later tonight.' He gave instructions, to be conveyed to Penelope.

Grace said slyly to her daughter, 'Does my face look funny?'

'No more so than usual, darling.'

'I'm not speaking quite as I ought. I know that. I've had a stroke, haven't I, Penny?'

Penelope pooh-poohed this, wondered whether she was right to do so, and whether she would be believed. 'Don't be silly. I'm sure it's only fatigue. You'll be all right in no time. I'm an excellent nurse. And I shan't be going to Deal.'

The effort to say so much had exhausted Grace. She lay back, now and then lifting her arm to see if she could hold it steady, but she could not.

'Do stop experimenting, mother. After a good night's sleep it will be as right as rain, I promise you.'

The staff had to be told. 'I'll take turn and turn about with Penelope,' said Betty Cope, who always believed it better to be practical than overtly sympathetic.

Keats looked in again after supper, and said he felt rather relieved. 'We have got away with something, thank God. It could have been far worse.'

When he had left, and Annick had gone to bed to sleep wretchedly at the side of a peaceful wife, Penelope wrote a letter. She was staying at the school for the next few nights.

Dear Timmy,

I really have thought your offer over, and was attracted by it. But my mother has had a stroke – not too serious, we all hope – so I shall be nursing her for some time to come.

In any case, I should have to say no. It would mean that I was running away from all my personal problems and leaving them to remain in the same chaos. I've done that before, and I won't do it again.

Yes, we'd have had fun – we always did: we could have lost a lot more money together, couldn't we?

I don't know what I'm going to do next – I can't see anything beyond my mother's illness, which, of course, has shaken us all dreadfully. And of the two of them – my parents – I really think my father looks worse.

This apart, I don't think you'd find me very happy to be with. I may marry, and that might pull me together: I simply don't know. You always listened to the tale of my woes so patiently, and I miss you now. But I'm dull, I'm not lively, I'm short of ideas and enthusiasm, and I'd be a poor partner.

Thank you all the same, very, very, very much. Love to Leslie – I hope he's having fewer of his headaches. And, as always, love and gratitude to you.

Pen.

With a depressed feeling of duty done she went to bed on the sitting-room sofa, where she could be near to Grace if she were needed.

Next day Grace seemed a good deal better. It was possible to imagine, at least, that the distortion of her facial muscles was fading. She had more power in arm and leg: it was all Penelope could do, at one point, to keep her in bed. The munching look had gone, and though her speech was not perfect, it was much improved.

Her illness had shadowed the school. Even the boys, knowing something was wrong, were playing in a subdued fashion.

'It seems very quiet all of a sudden,' Grace said. 'Oh dear, breakfast in bed! A long-forgotten luxury.' (She said 'lussury'.) 'I don't know that I can eat all that, though.'

Annick said, 'Eat what you can.' He was aching with love and fear for her. He did not know how he was going to get through the day, how he would manage to take his classes: but he had no substitute.

That evening the news came through that Searle had won a scholarship to Rugby, low on the list, perhaps, but he had done it. Annick on his way downstairs, barely gave the Honours Board a glance. No news of Peter.

On the following morning Grace seemed remarkably better, and Ralph Keats was pleased with her: but Annick had lost hope. He could not carry on without her. He believed that she would never again be able to work as she had done. He had been through the books with Helen: they were showing a redder deficit. And Poole was going, eventually Canning was going.

Yielding to a violent impulse of the kind which had directed or misdirected his whole life, he telephoned Massinger and found him in.

'If you're still prepared to make an offer, Rupert, I'm going to accept it.'

A short silence then. 'You mean it, old man? To buy right out?'

Caricaturing himself already, Annick thought. 'Yes, Grace has been ill, and that's about the last straw.'

'I am sorry! What is it?'

He was told.

'Do give her the very best from Bloss and me. Look here – I don't want to seem crude, but you're not going to backpedal on this?'

'No. Write to me, will you?'

'Want it on paper?'

'I haven't had it at all, yet.'

'You won't be disappointed. If all goes well, I can promise you I won't let Downs Park get on the slippery slope.'

Annick hung up. He knew he had sold the school.

In the late afternoon, the offer arrived by special messenger, and it was a handsome one. He wrote an instant acceptance and went to the post with it himself. Now he must keep it all from Grace, till she was herself again. As he came back to the drive, he was oppressed by the finality of what he had done. Never had the school seemed so desirable. The fields were vivid with little boys in their wasp-coloured, buttercup-coloured, blazers and the air resounded with their voices. This had been his life and it was to be so no more. There was nothing left for him but retirement, and looking after Grace. There would be one precious term in which transfer was made – but did he want to be there a moment afterwards? He could not endure the thought of the blows of the axe at the roots of the Thicket. They must be out before that happened.

But we can't run, like rabbits. There will be so much to do, parents to be informed, smoothness achieved somehow. The legal formalities – which would not take much time, if he knew anything about Massinger.

Grace was sitting up in bed, awaiting him. She looked almost normal, and her arms and legs were functioning. 'Darling, do tell Ralph that I am not going to lark around in the sheets a second more than he thinks necessary! I am really very bored, and I know Penny is.'

'I'm not bored,' Penelope said, smiling, looking up from her mending. She had been helping Betty, in return for Betty's help. 'I'm far too occupied.'

'I have given you all an awful time,' Grace said apologetically. 'And really, all for nothing. Was that the telephone again? It seems to have been ringing all day.'

Annick went to answer it.

Over the wire, Broughton's voice, heightened by the excitement of bringing news, sounded as strongly accented as Canning's.

'Sorry not to have roong before, the results were late. Well, he's doone pretty well all he could do. He's coom first.'

Chapter Thirty-Nine

'Oh, wonderful, Petey!' Grace cried. A flush, like the last mingling of strawberries and cream in the saucer, made her look pretty again. 'I thought he'd do it!'

'I said he would,' said Betty, darning socks, though she had said nothing of the kind.

'You must send him a wire at once!'

Annick sent a greetings telegram.

A telegram came in response.

THANKS SO MUCH AM VERY PLEASED BUT
ASTONISHED LOVE PETER

Mrs Quillan telephoned, expressing her gratitude. She was not surprised.

'I knew he'd do it,' Grace repeated.

'You'd have known nothing of the sort, if you'd been through what I did.' Now that she was better, he felt he could resume his old comfortable attitude towards her, even his random touch of irritability.

'If he'd let you go through the papers, you'd have known—'

'Only a brute would have made him,' said Annick. The names would be on the Honours Board: and it was no more, in reality, his school. Massinger would reign over them. He dreaded the moment when he must tell Grace, tell Penelope. He knew the first would be broken-hearted and the second censorious. On impulse – he seemed unable to resist this – he sought out Canning.

'Leo, come down to the Lion for a beer. I want to talk to you.

It will only take half an hour. If I don't talk to somebody, I shall go off my head.'

A very young man to take into confidence, but one day, perhaps, Penelope's husband.

Canning listened to the story in silence, his nose looming. 'I've heard less sensible things in my time, Headmaster. Though I'm sorry about it.' He paused. 'Sorry if I'm behaving like an egomaniac, but I'll be gone before Massinger takes over, won't I?'

'On present showing, yes.'

'One good thing. Otherwise, I couldn't have stuck it out.'

'He's a good administrator.'

'Bastard,' said Canning simply, afterwards making only a perfunctory apology.

Annick's rebuke was equally perfunctory.

'They'll be moving back into the cottage, I suppose. You won't be staying on in School Building, of course?'

'No. I'm wondering whether Rupert would let us have the remaining lease of his flat. I daresay Grace and I would like Eastbourne all right.'

To leave the roses, now in full bloom, the fields full of boys, the doomed Thicket, and the glimpse of the sea.

'You're young to retire completely, though, aren't you?'

'Othello's occupation's gone.'

A grin. 'Even I can guess where that comes from.'

'I might think of another job of some sort later, I suppose. But not now. What about you? If I know anything of Corso, he has big things in mind.'

'They'll take some time to get big. I'm not keen on the idea: I've liked it here. But I won't, not with you going.'

'Somehow,' Annick said, 'I have got to break all this to Grace.'

They walked slowly back together between the pungent hedges, the ditches full of cow-parsley.

Canning said, 'You know I want to marry Pen, don't you?'

'Yes.'

'Would you mind?'

'No. I'd like it.'

'Thanks. I can't get her to make her mind up, though. Oh, I know what it is. We were educated differently and though she can say what she likes, that counts with her.'

'Then it shouldn't.'

' "Oh, you nasty common boy—" Sometimes I feel it's almost like that.' For a moment Canning looked much older than he was, and careworn.

'I'm perfectly sure it's not like that,' Annick replied with some energy. 'It's just not Penelope.'

'Certainly she thinks it's not. Perhaps I've got a chip on my shoulder. Well, if she still won't give me an answer, I shall wait seven years for her, like the chap in the Bible. Or, come to that, as long as I have to.'

Annick wished him luck.

He went to Grace next day. She was sitting up in a chair by the window, fretful because the doctor would not let her go downstairs just yet. Only a slight slurring of speech, an almost imperceptible downward list at the corner of an eye and one side of the mouth, betrayed what had happened to her.

Quietly, he told her what he had done.

She was aghast. 'Oh no! Not just like that!'

'Dear, you knew it had to come.'

She started to cry. 'I don't think I can bear it.'

'Oh, darling!' He smoothed her curling hair.

He could see the effort she made at once to pull herself together. 'Sorry about that. Of course I shall bear it, if I have to. But what are we going to do?'

He discussed his plans with her. She listened without comment.

'If it hadn't been for me breaking down in this idiotic way—' she began.

'No. It would have had to happen sooner or later.'

'When will you tell the staff?'

'At supper, on the last night.'

'Celebration night,' she said bitterly. 'And the boys?'

'They'll learn in the holiday.'

He went downstairs and sent Penelope up to her. Then he

telephoned the signwriter: he had two more names for the board and he wanted them put there as soon as possible, the last things he would have for his own. For over these, Rupert would never reign. They were his, would always be: his names, not Rupert's.

Dicky Searle, who was back at school, passed by him as he came out of the office. Annick called to him.

'I've just been arranging to put you up there in letters of pure gold.'

Searle expressed pleasure.

'You know how pleased we all are with you.'

'It's nothing to what Peter did,' said Searle, with a good-natured grin. He had fined down over the last year, and the romantic look imagined upon him was approaching reality. Also, he was half-a-head taller. 'Quite fantastic, what with him being ill!'

'We're proud of you both.'

Searle gave an appreciative wriggle.

'I'm asking you and your parents, and Peter and his, to staff supper. I hope they'll be able to come.'

They were. Everyone was present, with the exception of Delia Poole. Peter, very grown up in civilian clothes, gravely received congratulations.

'Of course,' said Mrs Quillan, 'the moment he was able to sit up and take notice, we went through the papers with him. I had no worries after that.'

'We're going for a Greek cruise in the holidays,' Peter said, 'almost the same one as you took me on.'

Annick smiled at him. 'I suppose you've left school already, and have put the ocean between us.'

'No, sir, I won't have left till after supper.'

He was driving back to London with his parents.

'His maths were surprisingly competent,' Quillan barked. 'I must thank Mr Canning for that, mustn't I?'

'Don't thank me,' said Canning, who had just come up. 'It was Peter slogging away.'

Searle's father laughed. 'I once met an American who said we talked about our children as if they were horse-flesh.'

'Yes, I agree,' Annick said, 'it is all wrong. But none of us can resist it. It adds a sporting touch to life.'

Now that he was leaving, he was suddenly no longer afraid of parents. Since he had one term to go, it was he would interview the new applicants. Not Rupert. But he could see what sort of legacy he might leave him.

At the end of the meal, Annick rose to his feet and tapped on the table for silence. This was so unusual a procedure that all the staff stared at him, and even the more experienced parents were puzzled.

'I have something to tell you. At the end of next half, Grace and I are giving over the school to Mr and Mrs Massinger, whom you all know.'

The *frisson* was unmistakable. Nobody was pleased, which laid some comfort to his soul.

'For various personal reasons, my wife and I are anxious for an early retirement.'

There were sidelong glances at Grace's face, still vestigially awry, but pretty.

'You will remember how active and enthusiastic Rupert and Blossom Massinger were in all our affairs. I know they will bring a new life and energy to the school.'

'Thank God you're leaving,' Mrs Quillan murmured to her son.

'To be honest with you,' Annick went on, 'I don't feel so energetic as I once did. Perhaps I am selfish to mind it so much: but perhaps I should be more selfish if I hung on when I shouldn't do so.

'I can't tell the staff how grateful I am for their loyalty—'

'Guff,' said Canning to Penelope. 'They liked him. If they hadn't there would have been no damned loyalty. What the hell does it mean?'

'—how much they have all meant to me,' Annick was continuing. He was launched on that easy, platitudinous speech which had hitherto come to him with such difficulty. 'They know it without the telling. Personally, Grace and I are unhappy about leaving here. But we feel we are doing the best thing for Downs Park.'

'Which he knows he is bloody well not,' said Canning, 'though he hadn't much option.'

'Will you be quiet?' Penelope cruelly gripped his knee and dug her nails in. This did not hurt him very much.

'Mr and Mrs Massinger aren't with us tonight. It was of their own choosing. They felt it was simply a goodbye from Grace and me, and that they could say hullo in their own good time.' He paid warm tribute to the Pooles, and said, sincerely, how deeply sorry the school would be to lose them. He was not, of course, referring to Delia, he simply left her to be counted in. Poole sat stiffly erect, trying to smile. Everyone felt his unhappiness. 'Well, I think that's all. I hope you'll join us for drinks in the sitting-room. We shall need to toast Peter Quillan and Dicky Searle.'

Grace got up abruptly. She had not been asked to speak: she was going to do so.

'I want to join in all that. But I also want to say that Cyril and I still have one term with you, and that's something. We shall treasure every moment of it, and we shall make the most of every moment.' She sat down.

Applause broke out, from people uncertain what they were applauding.

The parents tactfully left early. Peter and Dicky made their rounds of farewells to the staff. Annick and Grace came to the door with them.

'You'll write to us and let us know how you're getting on?'

They said they would. 'And thank you for everything, sir,' said Peter. Searle echoed him.

The Searles were the first to drive away. Peter, waiting for his mother to find a lost scarf, moved uneasily from foot to foot. Then Grace took him in her arms and kissed him, to which he responded as spontaneously as he had done when, as a new boy to the school, he had particularly needed her comfort. 'Come down and see us sometimes, will you, Petey?'

'Of course he will,' said Mrs Quillan, 'but you and Grace are often up in London, aren't you? So you must also come and see us.'

'Not so often these days, but we'll let you know.'

'We'll be writing soon,' she told him. 'I want to thank you properly for all you've done for Peter, and speech is such a poor medium of expression, don't you think?'

They were gone at last. Annick put his arm round Grace's shoulders.

'I think I need to cry,' she said.

'You can't. That's what the staff will want to do, and you mustn't give them any competition.'

He was right. The staff were standing around in the sitting-room, drinking glumly and apart, as if they were strangers to one another. Even Giles Pettifer, who had nothing to lose since he would soon be going up to Cambridge, looked disturbed.

Stephen was the first to speak. 'Well, sir, this is a facer.'

'I would have told you all before, but it was decided so quickly. You know, I'm sure things are going to perk up under Mr Massinger.' He shuddered at the word even as he used it.

'One term with you, anyway,' Betty said, brightening. At least she was now happy in her own life. If Gwen Morphy had fallen over Beachy Head she would not have cared.

'My God, "perk",' Canning muttered.

Helen Queen, who also had the promise of happiness – she was, she believed, bringing her young man nearer and nearer to the point of proposing – began to calm down. The announcement had upset her: she hated changes, and did not like the idea of working again for Massinger. She wondered if he would sack her, but felt she was far too useful for that. Then again, if working for him did become intolerable there might be something better for her. The young man held ideas about perfect love and trust being far better than the artificial tie of marriage, but she thought he was growing out of that. Not for Helen the snatched life, the inevitable pill, the fear either that it might not work or would make her fat, or give her a coronary thrombosis. She wanted a little house of her own with a garden – but not too large a garden, because it meant so much work. In her mind she bordered it with scylla and primroses.

It occurred to Penelope, too late, that if she had married Canning they might have taken over the school themselves. How would he have reacted to that? Of course, he would have been no good with the parents, but perhaps she could have helped out there. The idea melted as soon as she had held it for a second, like a snowflake on the palm of a warm hand. No, he wasn't cut out for a headmaster. Or, more precisely perhaps, wasn't cut out for looking like one. Her heart stirred, she did not know why. She smiled at him and touched his hand.

'I'm sorry to break up the party,' Poole said, 'but I must be getting back to Delia.' He had long given up making excuses for her absence.

'I'll walk back with you,' Annick said.

There was no moon, and they had to pick their way cautiously. 'I should have told you first.'

'Why me? I'm going, anyhow.'

'I wish you weren't. How is Delia?'

'Much the same. Sometimes I think she is getting a grip on herself – she does try so hard. But really, I know things will never change. The best I can do is to keep them as they are.'

'Would she see me, do you suppose? I don't mean tonight.'

'I think so. She's fond of Grace too. I thought Grace was looking fine tonight. She's over it, isn't she?'

'Thank God, so it seems,' said Annick.

They stood together on the doorstep of the dark house. 'She's gone to bed. Will you come in and have a nightcap with me?'

Annick refused, adding that he must be getting back to Grace. 'School train, tomorrow. The wavings and goodbyes, and the whistle blowing. Then reports to write. I've almost finished my part of that. I'll let you have the whole batch the day after tomorrow.' He paused. 'You've been splendid. I mean that. I wish we could have gone on working together for years.'

'So do I,' said Poole. His hunched shadow showed for a moment in the glass panel of the door as he turned the light on.

Chapter Forty

Annick successfully negotiated the taking-over of the Massingers' flat. Blossom and Rupert would be back in the cottage just before the end of the holidays, after which Rupert would resume his former work for a term before taking over completely. Meanwhile, he got the Annicks an excellent sub-let until Christmas.

They were not taking a summer holiday. To be quiet in the school would be enough for them. And there seemed so much to be done.

Annick sat wearily down to write innumerable explanatory letters to the parents.

'We're in a curious lull of life, aren't we?' Penelope said to her mother. 'I feel as if we'd gone already, yet we're still here for nearly five months longer. It seems so odd.'

'I wish you'd go away, darling, now that I'm all right again.'

'You're all right again, but you can't do quite so much.'

'What is there to do?' Grace lifted her fine eyes. 'It's silly to bother about me. Leo was talking about Istanbul: it sounded wonderful.'

'If Leo and I go anywhere, it will be to Brighton for a couple of days.'

All things must come to an end: but when they do so, they do so suddenly, not in their actuality but in their foreshadowing. One moment, all is mobile and serene: in the next, the halting shadow is there, and it is at the sight of it that we first stop, not when the foot stubs the barrier itself. The fine summer held its course: the trees were heavy under a load of sunlight. Annick and Grace walked down to the sea every day, unable to believe that there must be a last time they would take this walk together. Yet it was for the end that they were preparing, as slowly as a Victorian girl, engaged, prepared linen for her married life. Their shadows crept longer as the sun went down on the last flare, and so did they. In the evenings, Canning joined them for a meal, almost the son of the house but not quite.

The Annicks, by invitation, went down one evening to say goodbye to Delia Poole. They had chosen the hour of five, when she might only just have begun her evening's drinking.

She seemed steady and subdued. She had abandoned all idea of making up her face, and her hair needed tinting, showing a dark line along the parting. How thin she is, Grace thought. Annick thought, how old she is.

'It's lovely to see you,' said Delia. 'Do come in. I'm afraid I've been under the weather. Only nerves, really, but nerves can hurt, can't they? Do forgive the mess. No, please don't even look at it. We're almost packed, but everything makes dust. Goodness, it's early! But we could have an early drink without a sense of sin, just on this one occasion, couldn't we?'

The sitting-room, so fresh under the Massingers (as it would be again), had a look of decay, as if there was not a piece of furniture without broken springs. Books had been piled into packing-cases.

'It's only our books and clothes to go,' she said vaguely, 'and a few oddments; of course, all the rest is yours.'

Her sugar hands shook as she picked up a crystal decanter.

Poole came in. 'Let me do the honours, darling.' She gave him an open look of shame and gratitude, and thrust her nose into the glass like a drinking stork.

Chattily, she drew the Annicks' attention to a necklace of coral-coloured plastic, like a miniature lei. 'Norman gave it to me for my birthday. Wasn't it sweet of him? I'm really all for forgetting birthdays now I'm getting on, but he always remembers!'

She looked and spoke as if she were showing off a lover, or a young bridegroom.

'We're going to miss you all so dreadfully, you know. You've been so nice to us.'

They murmured platitudes, gossiped rapidly, while her eyes roved towards the cupboard. She glanced sidelong at Annick's and Grace's glasses. She was longing for them to drink up so that she might refresh her own.

'What a business moving is, isn't it? There's so much to think about. I try to make lists and things, but they always get lost. I still can't get over Peter. What a triumph it was for him, and being ill as well!'

Rising abruptly she went straight-backed to a table on which was a vase of flowers and pretended to rearrange them. Then, as if drawn by an invisible wire, she marched to the cupboard and defiantly poured herself another gin, half a tumbler-full. Poole watched her, his face unchanging.

'Yes, and Searle too. It's been quite a term, hasn't it?'

'I'm very pleased about Dicky,' said Annick. 'He has nothing like Peter's *flair*, but he's a very determined child.'

'You'll enter D'Oyley next year, won't you?' asked Poole. 'I should say he had a decent chance.'

'He's able enough. But that will be Massinger's business by that time. I should be leaving him a good many new boys, too. I start interviewing tomorrow, and how I dread it!'

'It's all my fault,' Delia said loudly. 'You think I don't know it, but I do.'

Poole stirred. 'Don't start that again, darling. It does no good. And anyway, I'm due for retirement.'

'Why,' she flung at him, 'couldn't you have married some nice stodgy girl who'd have been a help to you instead of a hindrance?'

Grace sighed, and tried to laugh. 'Really, Delia, how can you expect a husband to answer that? You are preposterous sometimes, you know.' She could sense that the woman's rage was rising, wanted to stem it.

'Yes, that's what I am, aren't I? Preposterous? Of course, all nervy people are. It's hell to live with them, it's hell to live with me. But let's stop pretending that I'm not preposterous, shall we?'

The Annicks realized that she must have been drinking for at least an hour before they came.

'Did you hear that, Norman? I'm preposterous. Well, it's dead true, isn't it?'

'Now, don't be silly, Delia,' Grace said firmly, 'I only meant it in fun. We've all been very fond of you, and sorry you weren't well enough to carry on with the art classes. You were bringing them along quite wonderfully. Hodgkins is going to turn out an excellent potter, and all due to you.'

'Preposterous, I know. Norman, give me a drink.'

'You haven't finished that one.'

'If you won't, I'll have to help myself.' She half-rose.

He said, 'I'd rather you didn't. A bit later, darling. You've got to keep clear-headed with all the work there still is to do. You mustn't get too tired.'

'Now who's being preposterous?' She had been toying with a few books placed on the top of an uncovered crate, picking up first one and then another. 'Of course I'm not tired. I only need a bit of bucking up—'

'We must go, I'm afraid,' Annick said, 'we seem to have an awful lot to do, too.'

'No, no. You must have one for the road. No, no, don't go yet. I don't get much in the way of company, do I? It's because I'm preposterous, isn't it? But it's a treat having you here, even if I am a drag. I say you're not to go.' Delia got up and was halted by Poole.

'Sit down.'

She did. She picked up a book and threw it full at him, catching him on the cheekbone. He fielded it as it fell from him and tossed it back into the crate.

'*Naughty* temper!' Delia cried, on a whoop of relish. 'Naughty Delia! Smack her hand.' She smacked her own.

The sharp edge had grazed his flesh.

'I think you'd better go,' he said to the Annicks, 'I am helpless, you see.'

He rose.

'Preposterous,' she roared from the sofa, from which she had not budged, 'that's what you are, aren't you?'

'Goodbye, Delia,' Grace said.

'Oh, goodbye, goodbye. Norman, don't you know you're preposterous?'

He rubbed his cheek.

'Now pretend you're hurt! Go on, play the old soldier!'

He said to the Annicks, 'I'll see you out.' They stood on the step, the air was sweet after the fug in the sitting-room. 'I'm sorry about that. I can't say more. She'll quieten down soon, she always does – quite suddenly.' He too, said goodbye and went without a backward glance into the house.

Delia screamed, three times.

'The night bird,' Grace said sadly. 'Poor devils both of them, I suppose. I shall be so glad now when they're gone. He will take that awful broken life of his away somewhere, and I daresay we shall never hear of either of them again. Worse, I daresay we shan't think about them, either. Any more than we think much of poor Mrs Murray,' she added.

Annick's tone was dry. 'Oh, they'll provide school gossip for ever and ever, you may be sure of that. This is such a tiny world, that an ounce of gossip has to be spread a long way.'

Grace picked some roses as they went, and buried her face in them. In the chillier stratum of the upper air, the moon was rising before the sun had set.

Next day, parents to see: titled parents, sent by Pettifer.

Annick felt no awe of them and no need to lick his lips. Whatever he might have said to Poole, the dread was gone.

'I can assure you of one thing,' said the father, 'Rodney's going to be a damned fine games player. I wasn't bad in my time – I was a rugger blue – and he's following in my footsteps.'

'He's not exactly wonderful in class,' said the mother, 'but we're sure that's simply because they've never taught him *how* to work properly. It makes him seem lazy, though I swear he isn't. He can *swot* away like a mad thing at anything that really interests him.' She was given to over-emphasizing words more or less at random.

I do not want this dullard, Annick thought. 'Well, could you bring him down to see me? I could judge better for myself. I suppose his reading and writing are quite fluent?'

'Oh, reading, yes,' the mother said anxiously, 'for anyone who likes being outdoors so much, he manages to spend hours with his head in a book.'

'His writing's fair,' said the father, 'though his spelling leaves a good deal to be desired. But I daresay you need all sorts in a school like this. I hope – I may say I even expect – to see Roddy in the Eton and Harrow match one of these days. His cricket's miles above average.'

Just the boy for Rupert. So does it matter to me? Nevertheless Annick temporized. He made an arrangement to visit them in London and see what he thought of Rodney.

Next day, another pair, very confident. The father was something or other in the diplomatic service. The mother was meek and pretty and did not say much, but confidence was evident in her silence.

'Oliver has come top of his form for the last five terms. I won't go so far as to credit him with precocity, but he's something of a flier. He writes plays in verse.'

At eight? Another Peter?

'He's no great games player; adequate, but no more. Still, you may be able to encourage him. You've got fine playing-fields here. He may like that far better than having to go to Barnes in the school bus.'

'It takes all sorts to make a place like this,' Annick said, remembering the father of the day before. He said he could not, at this moment, be quite sure of a vacancy: yet he was determined to take Oliver. It was true, for once, that vacancies were scarce: applications for this kind of school ebbed and flowed in a mysterious way. He made an appointment to see the boy in London, on the same day as he had agreed to see Rodney.

'You are getting masterful, darling,' Grace said, when all this had been reported to her. 'Perhaps you'd better take them both, to counter each other. I wouldn't mind myself seeing one of our children playing for Eton. Certainly Petey never will.'

'It would be Harrow in this case. The father's school.'

In two days' time, another pair, to plead for an offspring who appeared to have no gifts at all.

'Not too brilliant at games,' the mother said eagerly, 'but when we took him on a cruise, he was an absolute tiger at deck-tennis, which must mean something, don't you think?'

'William,' the father said, 'is quite good at English. And French.'

'Has he done any Latin yet?'

'Well, yes, but I don't think he's quite got the hang of it. That's why we so much want him to come to you.'

'He's a very nice boy,' said his mother, 'even if he is my own son. I've never had a day's trouble with him, and he makes friends so easily. I'm sure you'd like him.'

'One might say he'd got the social virtues,' said the father. 'We think he's one of these rather late developers who are going to make a sudden leap, before long.'

I do not want William, Annick said firmly to himself, and I will not have him. He asked for a headmaster's report, but held out little hope.

'We've let it go so late, I'm afraid,' the mother mourned.

So it went on.

Chapter Forty-One

The Massingers were re-installed in the cottage, seeming to spread their own healthy ruddiness around it. The autumn term began, the school train steamed in upon a day of mist and burning leaves, the boys poured back.

Grace said anxiously to Blossom, 'When you take over, you will make a fuss of the little ones, won't you? They've never left home before, and of course its a terrible wrench for them. Cuddle them, and see they get kissed good-night.'

'You bet I will,' Blossom said gaily. 'I've watched your technique and I'll make them all snug as bugs in rugs.'

Only I never thought of them as bugs, in rugs or elsewhere.

'You can slacken the apron-strings when they're nine – which will be quite a wrench for you, I expect,' (she did not expect it) 'but they do need mothering until then.'

'Cross my heart and hope to die,' Blossom replied, 'I'll do just what you want. I'll swear it. Homesickness and all, I'll cope.'

A new top form: no Petey, no Searle, no Finlay, no half-dozen cherished others. Promoted faces.

As it happened, Grace found herself with a serious homesickness problem at once: little Rodney Wayland, the games player, who had been taken at her inclination, and against Annick's. When she came to tuck him down on his first night, he clung around her neck and would not let her go. She saw that the other boys were more or less calm, waited for a while and then went back to him. He was lying on his back, his face full of terror and loss. Again he clutched her.

'I want to go back to mummy. Please, I want to go back. I can't bear it.'

'Darling, in the morning, everything will look quite different.'

They were whispering to each other, for in that dormitory all the other boys were now asleep, including the clever Oliver Stroud, who had displayed more stoicism than most.

'It won't, it won't, I know it won't.' His cheek against her own was sticky with tears.

What brutes Americans think we are, Grace mused, sending our children away so young! We rationalize it: we say it is better they should get used to leaving us now than at the onset of adolescence, which will only present a parting with additional troubles. Anyone who has a school like this, with such young children, knows that even the most heart-torn will be screaming and racing round within a fortnight. We ask the parents not to take them out for the first three weeks, so as not to unsettle them, but could that be because we are afraid they may unsettle us? Are we brutes? I don't think so, but there are times when I just don't know.

'Listen, Rodney,' she said persuasively, 'will you see how tomorrow goes, and then come and tell me? I'm always there when you want me. I know the first day is an awful muddle – everything seems so big, doesn't it? In fact, you're worrying whether you'll ever find your classroom. Darling, this is quite a small school, and after breakfast tomorrow, D'Oyley will find it for you. Just ask him whatever you like. He's a gentle sort of boy.'

Surreptitiously, she felt his pillow. It was sodden with tears. She lifted him up and turned it over.

'You shall write to your parents tomorrow, I promise.'

'I don't write very well.'

'They won't care about that, will they? So long as it's you who writes. And you'll soon learn to write beautifully. Is anything else worrying you?'

His owl's eyes shimmered in the gloom. Dormitory curtains were never drawn.

'Mrs Annick – if I do something dreadful, what happens?'

She understood. 'Why, darling? Were you thinking that we cane people, or something old-fashioned like that? You won't do anything dreadful, and if you did, you would probably only be stopped games for an afternoon.'

He gave a great, unchildlike sigh, but seemed to be assuaged. 'I'm not the only one who cried,' he said.

'Of course not. I never thought you were. Won't you stop now, though?'

A freshet of tears sprang in their bountiful silver. 'All the others did.'

Grace dried his face. 'Now listen, I'm going to sit with you till you fall asleep. I won't go away.'

'Some of the boys look so big.'

'They're not really. And you'll be big soon. Sooner than you think.'

'I want mummy!'

'Yes, and she wants you. But for tonight, you must put up with me.'

It was an hour before he slept, and in that time Grace did not move from his bedside.

'Where on earth have you been?' Annick asked her, when she returned wearily to the sitting-room.

'On the usual first-night errands of comfort. Poor little Rodney Wayland was by far the worst.'

'And Oliver?'

'By far the best. But I think he was tired out. Isn't it strange, that this small school should look like a vast mansion to them all?'

'A week here disposes of that idea.'

'But what a week! It must all be such a terrible daze to them.'

'I know. And you were wondering, as you always do, what sort of monsters we are.'

'As I always do.'

The roses had gone, but dahlias, Michaelmas daisies, French marigolds and pink geraniums sufficiently like roses, were massed against the green borders. The copper beech burned hot purple in the sun. Little boys were at the immemorial task of bringing down conkers with sticks. The sunflowers echoed with yellow blazers, some of them touchingly new. They would not look new for long. Rupert was throwing a tennis ball around and Rodney Wayland, now more or less acclimatized after a week, was catching it with scornful ease, every time it came his way. Canning, keeping his distance, had a senior group working on an ambitious project, to build an annexe on to the little pavilion. The light fell on his fair lank hair and reddened the fine skin along the bone of his nose. 'No, you clot, you've got the damned plank upside down!'

'Tush,' said Penelope, who was watching, 'you'll get them into bad habits with your shocking language.'

'Oh, Mr Canning doesn't mean it, Mrs Saxton,' said D'Oyley, looking up at her, hammer in hand, 'he knows we take no notice.'

'I wasn't speaking to you, Joe,' she said. 'Mind your own business.'

'That boy will say something really appallingly impudent one of these days,' she remarked later as she and Canning walked back to the school, 'such as "Why don't you two get married?" '

'Well, why don't we?'

She did not reply to this. 'Though I must say he's come on recently. I used to think he was something of a mouse.'

'Some of them are emerging from the mouse stage now they're free of Peter's shadow. I always thought he awed them, a bit.'

Just as Pettifer's image was growing blessedly faint, Penelope had a letter from him. She replied to it at once, then showed it without comment to Grace.

Pen, dear,

I'm afraid I'm not strong on anything but persistence. I asked you to marry me once, and you said no. I'm asking you once more, and here it is on paper.

You're not in love with me, I know, but don't you think you could be? We have always enjoyed being together (at least, I hope you've enjoyed it) and I think we could be happy. I'm not going to deny that there have been several women since my divorce, but you are the only one I have wanted to marry and I want that very much indeed.

Like Johnny Eames – do you love Trollope? I do – I tend

to pester. I won't do so again if your answer is a resounding No. But don't let it be. If you even tell me you'll think it over again it will be enough.

Does the thought of Giles as a stepson dismay you too much? I know he likes you, anyhow. And he'll be going his own way. As for us, we should be doing a lot of travelling, I hope. Do you like being on the move? I do. I keep on collecting places, as I collected stamps when I was a boy.

Please think again. That's all I'm asking. How would you fancy Chichén-Itzá? Is it a lure? For God's sake, tell me what would be a lure, and I'll try it.

Do answer quickly. I am very much in love with you, and I keep seeing you in a glass darkly, as I did in a mirror at the Caprice.

Jim.

'So I am sought, at least,' Penelope said, looking troubled. 'I've written an answer and I'm going to the post with it.'

'What is the answer?' Grace asked fearfully.

'A resounding No. Only a kind one, I hope. I tried to make it so.' Her eyes filled. This was so rare a thing that her mother was startled. 'At least no one can accuse me of hankering after the fleshpots.'

They sat in silence for a while. Penelope took the letter back and put it in her bag.

'Darling, tell me why. Why you said No.'

'Because I'm going to marry Leo.'

'I'm glad!' Grace held out her arms, but Penelope evaded them.

'Don't be too glad. Perhaps you'd better be sorry for Leo – who doesn't know yet by the way – because I shall be doing it for all the wrong reasons.'

Grace asked what those wrong reasons were. She wanted to rejoice, but she was perturbed.

Penelope began to talk, slowly, painstakingly. The truth was that she could not now contemplate any sort of new life. She had felt for some time past that she was becoming almost pathologically set in her ways – 'like people who have agoraphobia and can't bear to go outside the house'. With Canning, whom she only half-loved, she felt safe. It would not mean a real break of any kind. She was locked, she said, in what she knew, of what was about her. Try as she might, she believed she might not always be good to Canning: yet she relied upon the inner strength which might make him keep a control upon her worst impulses. 'He knows me, all along the line. That I am selfish. That I have frozen into some pattern of my own that I can't break.' Perhaps she should have broken it forcibly, and gone to Timmy at Deal: she would never be sure whether that would have been the way out. 'But, Mummy, I'm afraid to take a step outside the door of the cell I've made for myself. It's a very nice cell, and most of the time I'm happy in it.'

'You do realize,' Grace said, with a touch of acerbity, 'that a new life is just what Leo will eventually bring you? He won't remain static, he's too clever. And Corso has plans for him. He's going straight up whatever ladder presents itself and you will have to go too.'

'I have thought of that. But it seems so remote.'

'It is not at all remote. Don't be so silly. Penny, I'd be glad about this if I thought you were going to give Leo anything. Are you?'

'My beautiful self,' Penelope answered, rather bitterly, 'and he's used to that. I shall tell him tonight. I have made a quiet, inward sort of mess of my life up to now, of which he is perfectly well aware. If he can take it, I can.'

Grace said energetically, 'I hate this! I hate it for you and for Leo. You have no right to get married, just for the sake of it.'

'I have no right to keep him hanging on without reason.'

'You won't go on harping back to Jim Pettifer?'

'I shall harp back to nothing. Jim might have been right for me, but I wasn't for him.'

'So you're prepared to be wrong for Leo? Do you despise him that much?' Grace was angry.

Penelope flared. 'Who said I despised him? I don't. I respect him enormously, and I know he's too good for me.'

'That sounds very much like cant.'

'We're quarrelling,' said Penelope, 'and that's horrible.'

'It's life, anyway. What you've been telling me isn't life at all.'

When Canning came to Penelope that night she told him, in her selfish honesty, almost precisely what she had told her mother.

He sat very quietly on the edge of the bed, probing his fingers through his hair. 'So you've turned down the bart. Taken a bit of time about it, haven't you? Did you sleep with him?'

'No. That I wouldn't lie about.'

'Well,' he said slowly, 'I suppose I've won. I'd take you at any price, because I love you. But don't imagine it will be a stick-in-the-mud existence for me for your sake, because it won't. I must get on, I must go up. Corso's not offering me the moon, but a rung on the way to it. Poetic, aren't I?' He added, more gently, 'Pen, there's a bit of class-war between you and me.'

This she disclaimed.

'But I warn you, I shall win it. You can't pose to me, as you did to your mother, as someone who's a bit round the bend, a case for the head-shrinkers. You're not. You're simply the kind of woman who dithers instinctively, and I think I'm the one to stop you dithering. I shall try. Let's have no more hovering, though, but get it over and done with. I can only offer you a registry office—' (This was cunning, on his part.)

'Register,' she said. 'The other kind's for servants.'

'Can't resist it even now, can you? Because I no longer believe in any old White Whiskers above the bright blue sky. Will that be all right?'

'I wasn't expecting St Margaret's, Westminster, with eighteen bridesmaids. I thought you were the one for that.'

He shook his head.

'When, then?'

'When you like,' she said, exhausted.

He made love to her that night quite differently, very gently, as if afraid she might break. Afterwards she lay in his arms (he did not, for once, immediately fall asleep) and felt a great (if egoistic) contentment.

'If you don't believe in old White Whiskers,' she said, 'what could it possibly matter to you if you just said you did?'

'So you do want a vicar?'

'This will astonish you, but I am a sort of believer.'

'O.K. I will appear in a frock coat—'

'Morning coat.'

'Whatever it is – goddam it! – if that's what you want.'

'No,' said Penelope. 'We'll do it your way.'

At once he turned on the lamp and looked into her face. 'My way?'

'Your way.'

'Kiss me, Kate' Annick would have murmured, had he known it all, not realizing the sourness and danger that lay behind. His daughter, more realistic, contemplated both. What sort of woman am I? What am I offering? Yet she trusted Canning. She would have no second thoughts on the night before her wedding.

Of course the school, informed in celebrating fashion at tea, screamed with joy. Annick believed in telling the school things, as a farmer might have behaved in telling the bees. Boys deprived of home and parents, of the mystic, scarcely-comprehended, backing of married life, were excited by the thought of a wedding. These ageing people, as it seemed to them, could fall in love then, as people did in the cinema? (Canning was twenty-six.) They saw some mysterious continuity in life, something like a rope which they might grip in a rough sea. Penelope became miraculously beautiful in their clear, ignorant eyes.

She and Canning were married discreetly three weeks later, in the local church. She was played in by the Minuet from *Le Tombeau de Couperin* (her choice) and out by *Lohengrin* (Canning's). The vicar gave an idiotic address, implying that the two were about to embark on a journey together as perilous as Scott's to the South Pole. Penelope had, after all, had her way, and did not know that, in reality, it was her husband's way, also.

Chapter Forty-Two

The generous autumn sharpened into early winter, and the flowers began to brown and shrivel.

To the Annicks, everything seemed so normal that it was dreamlike. Stephen was hard at work on the play, an audacious choice, since it was *Henry IV, Part I:* but he was inspired by Hodgkins, who had developed so much as an actor that he might just – not too excessively padded – make an acceptable Falstaff. The Cannings, who would move to London at term's end, were taking an active part: Penelope contriving new costumes at the lowest possible expense. Canning building a permanent set modelled on one he had seen at Stratford-on-Avon. Sounds of sawing and hammering filled the air.

All this time, Annick felt himself drawing nearer to Grace, as if some invisible magnetism was holding her to his side. They rarely spoke of the real end, though one night she wept in his arms and gave no explanation.

The Massingers could not have been more agreeable, more eager to please, and invitations flowed from them. Even to Canning Rupert was polite. Penelope and Helen he treated as if he had never been to bed with either of them: and both were relieved. Like huge, glossy red bumble-bees, Rupert and Blossom hummed and buzzed about the school, both taking care, however, not in the slightest degree to encroach upon the Annicks' now temporary prerogatives.

'Do you think he could have actually improved, Cyril?' Grace had recovered some of her customary hopefulness. 'The boys seem to like him far better than they did. Perhaps he really is going to make a go of it. What do you think?'

'Watch and pray,' he said. 'Though next year it will be better if we pray and don't watch. He will give me a deferential welcome whenever I want to come here, but in his heart he won't find me *persona grata*.'

It was morning break, and they were walking in the garden. Oliver Stroud came shyly up to them, a smeary piece of paper in his hand. He was a good-looking child with very dark eyes, blue-black, and as Peter had been, was tall for his age. 'Sir, I've written a poem.'

'Good,' said Annick. 'May I see?'

Silently, Oliver held it out.

It was an eight-line verse about Hereward the Wake, imaginative, precociously neat in form.

'This is very good.'

'Is it, sir? Thank you, sir.'

'Mr Smith might like it for the magazine. Peter Quillan wrote a poem for him once, but he was a bit older than you are. Will you give it him or shall I?'

Oliver could not decide. 'All right, then I will.'

Grace looked fondly after him as he went away. 'He will be Rupert's Petey,' said Annick. 'Curious, isn't it, the way some things repeat themselves? I wish he was going to be mine. But old Stevenson will look after him: he's a very good classic.'

This was the man Rupert had successfully seduced from Rowan House to come as second master. He was quietly, but by no means surreptitiously, building up his staff. He had come several times to Annick for advice.

'I hope Blossom will be able to cope with only one gardener,' said Grace. 'It's lucky that we're going in a way, because I couldn't have struggled on with that and we could never have afforded a second man.'

'Oh, the whole place is going to spring into riotous and luxuriant growth. Damn it, I ought to be pleased, but I'm not. What sort of growth will it be?'

'You can't really fault anything he's done yet, can you?'

'Far from it.'

'The character of the school will change, of course, that's inevitable and we mustn't repine.'

'I do repine,' said Annick.

Rupert loudly praised Canning for the work he was doing on the pavilion, adding how sorry he was that he would not be staying on. He could afford this, now.

'Thanks. Pen and I will be moving to London, of course.'

'There were times—' Rupert began. 'It was just a load of old rubbish, of course and I shouldn't like there to be any hard feelings.'

'There aren't.' Canning's eyes rayed like diamonds. 'But I would like to know what you're going to do with my scientists.'

'Oh, I've found a chap who will teach them the fundamentals quite adequately. He'll do that and senior maths, as you do now.'

'They've been used to rather more than the fundamentals.'

'Well, we were just lucky to have you, weren't we? Science teachers at this level don't grow on every bush.'

'What about my lab?'

'My dear Leo, that's for the new man to decide. He may not want to do quite so much as you do. And you can't deny that we're short of space.'

'I bought a good bit of that equipment out of my own pocket. I shall be glad to give it to the school.'

'How very decent of you!' Rupert said gaily. He patted Canning's shoulder and walked quickly away, before a new rumpus could develop.

The night of the play was to mark the formal introduction of the Massingers to the parents. For that reason, Annick arranged that *Henry IV* should start an hour earlier than usual, and that there should be a party afterwards.

They had had so many parties, so many great events, special days, gatherings part professional, part social.

On the morning of that day, Annick went down to the gymnasium where Canning had surpassed himself. He had built a simple set of wooden uprights, stairs and traverses, to be used for a royal court, an inn, a battlefield. All this had been studied from Stratford designs and reduced to their modest needs by the boys themselves. The throne was in place now, hung with scarlet crepe-paper and painted gold. Heraldic banners, conceived by Penelope and created in the art class, were being put into place. There was to be a dress rehearsal that afternoon. After congratulating Canning and his helpers he went to the dining-room, which Betty and Helen were decorating with Chinese lanterns and chrysanthemum sheaves. This, too, was impressive.

'We shall go out with a bang rather than a whimper,' he observed to the young women. Betty looked puzzled, but Helen said, 'This isn't the world ending, though. Not really.'

'For me it is.'

He watched the rehearsal. Hodgkins was a lively Falstaff, even though, in white whiskers and padding, he looked a little absurd. 'One always has surprises doing these things,' murmured Stephen. 'I'd have put my money on Hodgkins, but Henderson's Hotspur is the star of the show.'

'A fairly easy part. Good and flashy.'

'Yes, but I'll be surprised if that boy doesn't become a professional actor one of these days. I think we shall see you off in style, sir.'

'You're staying on, aren't you, Stephen?'

'I think so. I've always hit it off quite well with Mr Massinger.'

'To bring a slovenly unhandsome corpse
Betwixt the wind and his nobility,'

Henderson was reciting, wingedly poised, a splendid sheen on his twelve-year-old face.

Annick waited a while to watch D'Oyley's appearance as Lady Hotspur. The child looked unpleasantly pretty, as boys do when they are dressed as girls. 'Even so young, a bad principle,' he said. 'If I were staying I'd try to get some real girls in.'

'The boys would only act them off their heads.'

Chapter Forty-Three

To Annick's strained imagination, all the parents seemed euphoric. Could it be that they did not in the least care whether he stayed or went? He was only for five years, or less, a part of their lives. The Hale-Cowans and Strouds, parents of triumphant children – at least, they seemed set to be triumphant – appeared to him more euphoric than most, sickeningly so. He was tempted to give them all the bad news he could muster. That David Hale-Cowan had all the makings of a first-class tyrant, and that Oliver's maths were pitiable. He did neither of these things.

The Quillans were there and so was Peter, trying not to look superior. The sight of him stirred Grace almost to the tears that, had she been a weaker woman, she would have been on the point of shedding all day. She remembered the first night he had come to them, a little boy all at sea, returning her kiss as if she were not a stranger but the only hope to which he had now to cling. Here he was, overgrown, nearly as tall as Cyril in sharp brown trousers and a herring-bone jacket: vestigially a young man. All of what – twelve? Almost thirteen. Give him four years and he really would be a young man.

'I'm glad you've come, Petey,' she said.

'I wouldn't miss this for anything, Mrs Annick.'

The play proved the greatest success Downs Park had known. The audience, for ever mistaking the substance for the shadow, gave its greatest appreciation to Falstaff. Only Betty Cope was a little sullen: was it because she was ageing that she had not been offered a female part? Stephen had flattered her into believing that she would not have *seemed* old enough for Mistress Quickly.

'So I go out on a magnesium flare, as it were,' Annick said to Canning. 'None of this being any responsibility of mine. Stephen is the hero. And you are, too.'

'A magnesium flare. I like that, Cyril.' For Canning was now addressing his father-in-law. 'Shows you've learned something from the stinks side.'

'Come, I am not a total ignoramus.'

'There won't be much of a stinks side under Rupert. But I suppose it doesn't matter now.'

'What do we sing tonight? Auld Lang Syne?'

'Don't be crude, Leo,' said Penelope, who had heard him. She had not as yet a married look. 'All of us who are being left behind are feeling like hell. It may be illogical, but it is a fact.'

'You're forgetting that this was a sort of heaven for me, too.'

'One you can't possibly afford indefinitely,' said Annick.

'Perhaps not. But I like to loiter. I have a bloody big nose to put to any grindstone.'

The party had now begun, and the ash and pastry crumbs were accumulating on the floor. Blue smoke wreathed itself round the Chinese lanterns. One of them caught fire, and Betty Cope smartly put it out. Corso, a fat, apelike man with sly, sharp eyes came up to Annick, ostensibly to express pleasure at the apotheosis of his quite undistinguished son to the top form. Then he said, 'I feel I have broken the commandment about not coveting my neighbour's property.'

'If you mean Leo, there's really nothing here for him now. I mean, Rupert Massinger will almost certainly reduce the science teaching. Perhaps we were doing rather a lot of it for a school of this kind.'

'Good thing if every school of this kind could do the same. But that's asking for the moon.' Feeling, perhaps, that honour had been satisfied, Corso went away.

Grace and Annick went on the familiar rounds, trying to have a word with everybody. They were professional in this and some of the parents, who were not so expert as party givers, wondered how they did it. It was also Stephen's night for being conspicuous:

ventriloquist's dummy face beaming, he received congratulations. So did Canning, for his permanent set.

'The last party,' Annick murmured to Grace, when they came together for a moment as in an intricate figure of an ancient dance.

'Not the last of the parents, quite. There's always breaking up.'

'No. This is our end.'

It was Rupert's time to speak. Annick introduced him briefly. As he did so he noticed, with amazement and apprehension, that a door had opened and Delia Poole had slipped into the room. She did it very quietly, sat down on a chair by the far wall.

Rupert shot up like a jack-in-a-box. It was one of his tricks, this sudden rearing to his feet: it was meant to connote youth and energy. Everyone of his red hairs had taken a point of gold from the lantern-light. Blossom, audaciously wearing shocking pink, smiled up at him and touched his arm in the encouragement he did not need.

'Ladies and gentlemen – parents, I would rather say, as we all feel knit pretty closely together through the boys, I think. Eh? First of all, I want to say something about Mr and Mrs Annick. What they've done for Downs Park can't be easily assessed. They've worked like dogs—'

Not elegant, Annick thought.

'They've given this school its entire personality, which is a pretty unique one, I must say. I know how rotten some of you must be feeling, if I may put it like that – no, perhaps how rotten all of you must be feeling, to see them go. But all good things come to an end, and it's up to me and my wife to carry on where they left off. I want us to go on being a sort of special family—'

Grace saw a maturely sick look on Peter's face.

—'because that's what we all are, aren't we?'

Applause. From the less sensitive, it was hearty. 'Bravo!' shouted Hale-Cowan, who knew nothing about it, as yet.

'I mean to keep up that very special atmosphere, so you can feel, as you always have done with Mr and Mrs Annick, our ever-welcome guests. Come down when you like, come to see your boys and don't forget to come and see us too.'

More applause.

'I won't pretend that Blossom and I – we've never been very formal at Downs Park, have we? That's one of the things I like about it. Where was I? Oh. Mustn't pretend that Blossom and I aren't all steamed up with new ideas. We really mean to put this school on the map—'

'A nice compliment to your father, I don't think,' Canning murmured to Penelope.

'—athletically and academically—'

'You see which he's put first.'

'Hold your tongue,' she said under her breath.

'—make it as famous as some other institutions of the same kind that I won't name, except that there's one in Oxfordshire and another – but no names, no packdrill. We've always kept ourselves deliberately small, and I think we've been right to do so. But I won't promise that in future we shan't contemplate a bit of expansion.'

Here there was a slight stir, which could have been one of uneasiness.

'Mind you, if that should happen, it's a long-term idea, anyway. Blossom and I wouldn't let it change the character of Downs Park. Not by a jot or tittle.

'Next term we shall be having some staff changes. Leo Canning, as you all know, will be leaving us. This is a cause for our sincere regret, especially as he will be taking his lovely wife with him.'

Delia Poole arose, having put in her gallant if unremarked appearance and slipped away. They never saw her again.

Poole sighed deeply with relief, his sad dog's face for a moment brightening.

'Perhaps we could take this opportunity to offer the newly-weds – awful phrase, eh? our warmest congratulations and best wishes.'

Canning and Penelope were applauded with enthusiasm.

'What an extraordinary person,' Mrs Quillan murmured to her husband.

'No, quite the reverse. That's the pity of it.'

Rupert went on: 'Next term, I hope you'll give a hearty welcome to Mr Anderson, who has come to us from Rowan House—' a glint of triumph here – 'to teach classics. He is a first-class man, and I am lucky to have his services. We shall also welcome Mr Dean and Mr Fairlight, both just down from university and both full of the kind of go this school needs. Mr Dean will be teaching history and geography, Mr Fairlight French and – if anyone wants it – Russian! That's one innovation. I don't think, if you'll all pardon me, that I'm going to let you in for any more of them for the moment because I've still got a great deal of thinking to do: but I give you my word that whatever rabbits Blossom and I may pull out of our hats, they'll be pleasant ones. Pleasant surprises, is what I mean to say.'

'Christ,' said Canning, 'he does spell it out! And he's going to be long-winded too. Poor bloody parents. Do you remember when I knocked him through the pavilion door?' He was convulsed with laughter, and one or two parents, noting this, took it as a clue to laugh at Rupert's joke.

'Well, I'm not going to keep you by chuntering on. I never was much of a speaker, not like Mr Annick. My aim is to get results in work and play. Now we're offering French and Russian, perhaps to get bilingual boys—'

There were glances of surprise, secretly interchanged, at this extraordinary change of subject: but Rupert had an object in mind.

'—which, by the way, reminds me of a story I heard recently. There was once a little mouse, who could never get out of its hole because of a big cat watching outside. Whenever he put out even half a whisker, he'd hear a great MIAOUW—'

Rupert was rather good at cat noises.

'—and back he'd go again. Well, this went on for a long time—'

'Like you,' Canning murmured.

'—till one night, when he was just risking another whisker, he heard this: WOOF, WOOF! MIAOUW! Woof, woof, woof' – protracted animal impersonations here. 'Then, at last, he heard only Woof, woof, woof. So he sprang out of his hole, to have the cat catch him by the back of the neck. "There, my lad," said the cat, "now you see the advantages of being bilingual!"'

This was received with appreciation. Having told his funny story, he now seemed at a loss and wound up quickly.

'That's all I've got to say. Wish me luck, all of you, because I'm going to need it. Now let's get on with the party.'

The Cannings slipped out for a breath of fresh air. Penelope kissed her husband. 'That was a speech and a half!'

'Looking back, at an interval of five minutes,' he replied, 'I must say I'd be sorry to have missed it. Poor bleeding Downs Park! Poor Cyril! Poor Grace.'

She told him not to underestimate Rupert. Demosthenes he might not be, but he was clever. The school would expand as he said, it would prosper, it would make money.

'And be quite a different place.'

'Oh yes. But he will play it cool at first, very cool. He won't rush at anything till everyone is lulled into a sense of false security, and then he'll go all out. We shall not be there to see it.'

'No,' said Canning. 'I shall be in a bigger and better lab.'

They returned to the party, which had not yet reached staling-point. There was no doubt that some of the parents, far from being alarmed by Rupert, had been pleased by his energy and bounce.

'Damned funny story about the cat,' said Hale-Cowan. 'I'd never heard that one.'

Peter and his parents, the Annicks noted, had gone, and they were glad not to have had to bear a second farewell. 'I think the Quillans balanced tact against an appearance of rudeness,' said Grace, 'and decided that for once, rudeness was tact.'

'I shall have to congratulate Rupert on his speech. It will be my final really arduous duty.'

When the parents had at last gone home, with the familiar swerve of headlamps along the drive, the Massingers were radiant.

'Well, I think they all enjoyed that, didn't they?'

'I'm sure they did,' said Annick.

'Feel I didn't quite give you or Grace your due. But,' Rupert added gracefully, 'nobody could ever do that, could they, Bloss?'

Blossom, who was really quite a nice woman, gave Grace a kiss on the cheek. 'Nobody could.'

'And the play was a smash hit. If young Stephen gets too big for his boots, I shall be the last to blame him.'

Annick and Grace excused themselves, said good night and went slowly downstairs to bed, pausing for a second to look up at the Honours Board. 'His, from now,' he said. 'But that name will always be mine.'

They looked out of a window. It was a frosty night and the moon was full. There was a slight sprinkling of snow. 'Early, this year.'

'Yes.'

Chapter Forty-Four

They were to move into the flat at Eastbourne in the week after Christmas, though certainly the Massingers had made no attempt to hurry them. Grace threw herself into the practical and administrative business of moving house, and Annick was a little anxious on her account: but she would not rest. Papers, years old, to be sorted through, the inessential ones to be destroyed. But which were really inessential? She could not leave behind a single letter of appreciation from a parent, though she knew she would never look at it again. The dusting and packing of books, the packing of clothing.

The arrangement had at first been that they should leave their furniture for the next occupant, Anderson, and take over the far smarter furniture of the flat: but this Grace hotly resisted. She did not mind shabbiness or broken springs, she needed to have her own things around her. So it was agreed that there should be the laborious business of transferring Blossom's elegancies to the school private quarters, at the same time as the Annicks' inelegancies were transferred to Eastbourne.

'Darling, I do wish you'd stop for an hour. Stop now, and have a drink.'

She arose from dusty knees. 'All right.'

It seemed to him that the distortion of her face, which had been so slight for some time that it would have been unnoticeable save to anyone who knew her intimately, was now a little more perceptible.

'Cyril, I am ashamed of myself. I have let our rooms get into a dreadful mess. But there was so much to do everywhere else.'

'Don't worry. Do you think that I should even notice?'

During those days, they both tried to suspend all but their immediate thoughts. Annick noticed that she went about the house and grounds without sidelong glances, her gaze fixed steadily before her.

'How ghastly our bits and pieces are going to look against their posh curtains,' Grace said. Curtains and carpets were to be left *in situ* on both sides.

'How ghastly their stuff will look against our dingy ones, come to that.'

The Massingers were bright and helpful. 'Surely there's something I can do for you, Grace?' Blossom asked.

'I don't think so, thank you. I think everything's just about done. There were some men who seemed to be inspecting the Thicket this morning.'

Blossom was apologetic. 'It was only a preliminary look. But you know Rup has never liked it. I tell him, I think you're ridiculous, the boys have always adored it and it does no harm. He says, though, that he wants everything nice and open. He feels boys often go there to be up to no good, if you know what I mean.'

'They will be up to no good anywhere,' Grace said, in a tired voice, 'if that's their intention. The Thicket's so pretty, and it's full of flowers in spring. Besides,' she added, 'most of them are such very little boys.'

'Rup is going to grow fruit trees up there, he says. They'll look pretty, too.'

The destruction of those secret places so necessary to human life.

'I suppose it will be no affair of ours.'

'We want you to think the school is always your affair,' Blossom said fervently. 'Rups is going to want your advice over such a lot of things.'

'Of course, it will be there if he does want it. But I think he is pretty self-sufficient.'

Grace was glad when Blossom went back to the cottage. She was troubled again by tunes running through her head: for the last two days it had been the *Eriskay Love Lilt*. Maddening. She tried to change it for another tune, but it was with her on waking, and left her only when she fell asleep. It was with her throughout the moving day, when the weather was wild and wet, and all the furniture was soaked as it came out of the van, with her during the frantic unpacking and straightening of the following day. Then the music fell silent.

'We can see the sea,' she said to Annick, 'just. If we crane a little we can see the Fish Tower.'

Holy Eastbourne, heavy, elderly, portentous, hallowed by the pleasure-makers and the sick who had visited her for generations: Eastbourne of the great grey stone hotels, the swept lawns, the regimented flower beds, and the huge suicide cliff above.

'We can see *more* sea,' she went on, with a hopeful look upon her face, 'than we could before. I love water.'

There was fitful sunlight, lemon-coloured through the clouds and upon the ocean. The storms of the last days, though they had now subsided, had their aftermath on the weighty rollers coming into the beach, and the pyrotechnic bursting of foam over the groynes.

'Can we be happy here?' he asked her.

Her eyes clear as a child's, she smiled at him. 'We have to be, so of course we shall be. I'd rather be in the worst place with you than in the best with anyone else, and you have to admit that this isn't at all bad. Really, it is quite handsome.'

It was an Edwardian mansion flat, high-ceilinged, painted white throughout at Blossom's desire. At the drawing-room windows hung curtains of prussian blue, white and parrot green. 'Of course, our things do look as awful as I thought they would. But we could have the sofa re-covered, couldn't we?'

'Certainly we could. We shall be saving money from now on.'

The first time they took a walk along the front, they both felt the same thing, though neither confessed it. They felt old. Old, set, bowed of back, perhaps looking even a little ridiculous. Yet they were not old at all: it was age that they were dreaming upon themselves. What sort of fantasy is this? Grace wondered. It is a bad one, and we must shake it off. The important thing is to find something to occupy ourselves.

'You know you said you might think of doing a little teaching?' she said.

'Did I?'

'You did. Would it lower your dignity?'

'If I went as a junior master to one of the Eastbourne schools, along with all the undergraduates or graduates filling in time before they do something else, yes, my dear, it would lower my dignity all right. I should feel like some tragic, destroyed figure out of an old German film.'

'*The Blue Angel*.'

'People would find it necessary to break eggs over my head. Are you cold? Would you like to go back or shall we have tea somewhere?'

'Somewhere with Palm Court music, if there is any left. I can see you mean to be thoroughly masochistic, and you may as well do that in style.'

There was a Palm Court orchestra, three-piece, but it was playing *Eleanor Rigby*. Not Novello, not Léhar.

'What I might do,' said Annick, as the tea revived his spirits, 'is to look for a bit of coaching. That could be done in dignity and silence, don't you think?'

A very old woman was staring at them intently.

'Are we doing something to attract attention,' Grace said, 'Or is that somebody you know?'

'Not that I'm aware of.'

In a few minutes a waiter brought them a note, written in an old but strong hand. 'Mr Annick, perhaps you would come and sit with me for a few minutes. I can't come to you until my companion gets back, because I don't walk very easily without help. Madeline Potter.'

'Good God!' Annick exclaimed. He smiled across at her, rose at once and pulled Grace to her feet.

'You don't remember me – please sit down – but I remember

you.' The old woman had a voice as strong, for her age, as her handwriting. 'My husband had Downs Park before you came.'

'And he's never been forgotten there,' Annick said easily. 'Legends about Mr Potter have been carried down among us.'

'Bet you couldn't tell me what legends if I were to ask you, so I won't. We had some happy days there. How's it all going now? Modernized, eh?'

He explained that he had himself just retired.

'What for? You're still a young man.'

Was this the abruptness of her generation, Grace asked herself, or did it come with age? Shall I be like that? I don't think I'd mind.

'Not so young that I don't think it's time to pass on the torch.'

'*Vitae lampada*. "Play up, play up, and play the game." But you don't teach that now. You teach them that man, what's his name, James Joyce.'

Annick laughed. 'Well, not quite.'

'Silly poem, anyway. My husband was a great cricketer. He said that in cricketing terms the first verse was nonsense. Why was there a blinding light at that hour in the evening, eh? And why should the fellow get a ribboned coat for being last man in? Mind you, the *Lays of Ancient Rome* were another matter. Gave the children a feeling for verse. The swing of it, my husband used to say. But don't let me chatter on. Tell me all about the school, and who is succeeding you.'

He gave a rosy account of the Massingers, assuring her mechanically that none of the tradition would be lost under the new régime.

'Wait till they've settled in, and I might get myself driven out there. Be strange, seeing it again. Do you think they'd mind if I did?'

He told her this would certainly be treated as a state visit.

She turned to Grace.

'Do you like boys, Mrs Annick? I always did. Not girls, though. Such ugly little things till they grow up, their elastics break and their hair-ribbons are always dirty. But those are things of the past, I daresay.'

'My general impression is,' Grace remarked, rallying to Mrs Potter's own tone of converse, 'that the younger generation, with all its faults, is cleaner.'

'There was a pretty little wood up the hill behind the school. I forget what they called it. There were a lot of violets there in the spring-time, very sweet-smelling.'

Annick was sorry that, should she ever pay her projected – perhaps fantasied – visit, she would not find the little wood again.

'But tell me,' she pressed, 'I try to keep up with the times, I don't want to become too much of an old fogey. Aren't places like Downs Park going to be squeezed right out?'

He said he did not know. He doubted it.

'There are people who would tell you that they should be squeezed out.'

'Indeed there are.'

'Perhaps they're right. But I enjoy sunsets: the sunset is often so much the best part of the day. Bet you've got out purposely before the sunset comes.'

'It wasn't that,' he said.

Her companion came, a strong-looking, indeed quite a happy-looking woman, contrary altogether to Grace's ideas of oppressed companions. She was courteously introduced, with a few words of praise.

'And now,' said Mrs Potter, 'I'm going up to my rest. Always do before dinner. I wake up with an appetite to enjoy my food. Food is one of the best things left to me, but it's not all. No, not by any means. Not all. I like keeping up with the times.'

They left her, not wanting to watch as she was raised from, her chair and taken very gently, as if she were as breakable as a gingerbread biscuit, from the room.

'She is rather splendid,' Grace said, 'I can't believe that life wasn't fun under the Potters.'

As they walked home the clouds slid back and a roaring scarlet sunset spread over the sea.

'Perhaps they are the best of it,' said Annick.

'What, sunsets? No, they're not. It's all right as a thought for her, but not for us.'

Back in the flat, she gave herself to feverish activity. There was not a piece of china which wasn't filthy, such silver as they had was looking like junk. He could not stop her working and did not try, since her face was full of colour and she seemed absorbed in the effort to make everything for them both as shining as possible.

'Don't do too much,' he said, but without conviction.

'I'm not doing too much. I'm simply footling, but to some purpose.'

When they were in bed, she said she was too tired to sleep at once. 'I asked for that, didn't I? Do you mind if I sit up a little and keep the light on?'

The bedside lamp, in this still unfamiliar room, was mellow: it soothed her. She told him, on impulse, of the tunes that would not go away. They did change about, which was one thing: but *In Haven* was dominant, and she was sick and tired of it.

He asked her whether she remembered Mark Twain's story on the same theme. There was a man haunted by a jingle which ran,

Punch, brothers, punch with care,
Punch in the presence of the passenjare.

It tormented him till he had the idea of singing it to someone else, who immediately found his days and nights bedevilled by it, while the original sufferer went away healed. 'Try singing your tune to me, and see what that will do.'

'I will, but I have to sing most of the accompaniment too. It sounds most peculiar.'

He listened to her. 'There. Now perhaps it will get a grip on me, and then you'll be all right.'

She said she thought she could now sleep, and held out her arms to him.

'You've forgotten your hair-net,' he said surprised. 'Did you know that?' She always wore one at night, to subdue the hair that was a little too wiry.

'So I have! How silly of me! Anyway, I'm too tired to put it on now. I'll have to be in a mess for once.'

The lamp was switched off. He slept.

He was awakened by a voice so hoarse that he did not recognize it. Hoarse: and slurred. In a panic, he jumped out of bed and put the top light on.

'Cyril. Cyril.'

Her mouth gaped square, her eyes, unfocused, tried to meet his own.

'All right, all right, darling, I'm here. Wait a minute. I'll get the doctor.'

'You – stay – here.'

Then she could speak no more. Only the whites of her eyes showed. She lay still.

Frantically he fumbled for her pulse, but could feel no beat. Of course there is a beat, only I can't find it.

He must fetch a doctor. He froze. What doctor? They had not even thought about registering with one in Eastbourne, and though they had passed many brass plates on their walks, he could not remember a name. He went to the telephone. They must find him a doctor at once. It was an emergency, he said, trying to keep his voice steady. His wife was desperately ill.

While he waited by her dead body for the interminable half-hour before help came, the tune she had sung to him repeated itself over and over in the back of his mind. It was not a new one to him: if it had been, it might not have taken root: but together they had once heard it at a concert. He wanted to take her into his arms, to fondle and comfort her, but dared not disturb her. People could be revived, sometimes, he had heard that. He was scared even to risk the 'kiss of life' that he had heard about but never learned to administer. He began to pray, trying to fix his mind upon the cross formed by the panels of the bedroom door. He was almost mad with grief, fear, yes and even with the lingering hope.

Chapter Forty-Five

He could not bear anyone to speak to him about her. He had inserted in the newspapers, 'Funeral private. No letters, please.' He asked the telephone exchange to put through no calls for him. Penelope and Canning, who had come at once, were asked to go away again.

'Listen,' said Penelope, 'she was your wife, but she was my mother, and I loved her.'

Only the three of them were present when she was buried by the church near to the school, which the boys had used as their chapel. The Massingers he rebuffed: he was sorry, but he had to be alone. As he limped along the sanded path behind the bearers, he was crying without concealment. Penelope gave up any attempt to take his arm.

It was the kind of day Grace had liked, sharp but very blue, with the deceptive scent in the air of the spring that would not be coming yet.

'My God,' Canning whispered, at the graveside, 'I suppose he is going to get over this, but I don't know how.'

There were flowers, of course: from the Massingers personally, and from the school. Penelope's close, round bunch of pink roses, incongruously suggestive of nineteenth-century ballrooms, was laid upon the coffin.

They walked back to the car, taking the short cut through the upper field, shifting in its usual kaleidoscope of yellow blazers, but Annick looked neither to left nor to right.

The Cannings stayed with him, against his will, in the spare room and were there for three nights.

On the last, Penelope spoke to him alone.

'Father, there's a time when one has to start doing something normal, and it can't come too early. I want you to have a drink.'

He made a gesture of rejection.

'I'm going to give you one. Think of it as a sedative. Please.'

He sipped at the glass she gave him, then, as if taken by a violent thirst, drained it. But he would not have it refilled. He gazed at her, his eyes flaring.

'She would loathe you to grieve for her like this, and you know it.'

'What business is it of hers what I do now? It is mine only.' He spoke as if Grace had been his enemy.

'And you can't stay here by yourself in this horrible flat. Leo and I will find you something near us in London.'

She expected him to refuse, to say that nothing would move him from where he was: but he said, 'No, I suppose I can't. You must do as you please.'

'Darling.' Endearments between Penelope and her father were rare. 'I'm glad about that, anyway. I don't like you being alone now. Would you like me to stay on here for a little while? I know Leo would spare me.'

'Well, I should think he would, if that's what I wanted, but I don't. I'm better alone, just for the moment.'

Every day he went for a long walk along the sea-front, past the Fish Tower, to where the road climbed sharply upwards towards Beachy Head. One bright afternoon, unseasonably warm, he was hailed by a strong old voice. He stopped. Mrs Potter, in a wheel-chair propelled half by herself and half by her companion, caught up with him.

'Well, and how are you? And how's that nice wife of yours? I've been meaning to ask you to take pity on me and come to tea.'

'My wife's dead.'

The blood rose under her transparent flesh, fine as the skin on hot milk. The companion flushed with shock, and for her sake.

'Forgive me,' Annick said, quite gently – he had not sounded gentle for a long while – 'I'd forgotten that people didn't know.'

Still she was speechless. At last she said, 'That nice, nice gal! No use saying I'm sorry. Some things are too bad to be sorry about. Like to walk along with me, or feel you can't talk?'

He did walk with her, and told her as briefly as he could what had happened.

'So it was quick. They say that's a blessing and of course they're right, but it's not for you. When a thing like this happens whatever one says is wrong. I think we wish we were poets, so that we could put things as Tennyson did. My dear boy' – she spoke as if he were indeed one – 'what are you going to do?'

He replied that he would go to London and probably look for some tutoring.

'Couldn't do better. And now it's colder, and I'm turning back.' She gave him her papery hand, covered with tiny violet spots, like hundreds and thousands. 'No more words, I'm not Tennyson. You know how I feel.'

He walked on and up the cliff-side. Grace, he said to his wife, I didn't mean that about it not being your business.

That night he had his telephone reconnected.

It was a relief to move from Eastbourne, last scene of her indomitable hopes, and settle in London. He soon found two boys to coach, both of whom had failed their 'A' levels and hoped to be luckier next time. One seemed to him impenetrably stupid, the other, who had eyes as small and darting as a sparrow's, almost pathologically lazy. But between them they took up several hours of his week.

It was two months after Grace's death that he heard from Peter. He was coming to the end of the first devastating stage of grief, in which he hated to receive a letter; now, he was beginning perversely to feel that people were callous if they did not write to him, though he knew he had frightened many of them away.

Peter's letter was awkward, lacking in his usual sophisticated flow.

Dear Mr Annick,

I didn't write before. It seemed too awful and I didn't know whether you would want it. I am sure you know how I feel.

All is well here. I am working hard. I have won the term prize for Latin.

By the way, I had to translate a poem yesterday, which of course you must know but I didn't. I enclose the translation. It is not very good.

Love, Peter.

A sheet of paper was folded inside, written in the familiar neat hand. Annick looked at it. Yes, he knew it, an epitaph of the second century BC. And he knew why Peter's letter had been so brief.

Stranger, what I have to say is little; stand forward and read thoroughly.

This is the ugly tomb of a beautiful woman. Her parents called her Claudia. She loved her husband with all her heart. She bore him two sons; of these, one she left on earth, the other she placed under the earth. She spoke with charming speech and also moved with graceful gait.

She served her house; she spun wool. I have spoken; go.

Lightning Source UK Ltd.
Milton Keynes UK
UKHW040612080223
416593UK00002B/4

9 781447 216155